MW00638710

SULLA'S FIST

A NOVEL OF THE ROMAN LEGION

THE SERTORIUS SCROLLS
BOOK FIVE

VINCENT B. DAVIS II

THIRTEENTH PRESS

For permission requests, write to the publisher, addressed

"Attention: Permissions Coordinator," at the address below.

Thirteenth Press

www.vincentbdavisii.com

Ordering Information:

Quantity sales. Special discounts are available on quantity purchases by corporations, associations, and others. For details, contact the publisher at the address above.

Printed in the United States of America

For my beautiful bride, Ashley. I loved you before I was born and I'll love you long after I'm gone. You are my partner, my best friend, the flag I fight for, and the home where I find my rest. Every book I've ever written and ever will write are dedicated to you.

I love you "my heart all".

THE SERTORIUS SCROLLS
READING ORDER

Although this book can be read and enjoyed on its own, The Sertorius Scrolls series is intended to be read in chronological order:

DRAMATIS PERSONAE

Albinus—*medicus* serving in the legions of Quintus Sertorius

Apollonius—freed *servus* of Quintus Sertorius, close friend, and confidant. Serving in Sertorius's legion during the Social War

Arrea—wife of Quintus Sertorius, freed slave

Caepio, Gnaeus Servilius—former patron of Quintus Sertorius, grandfather of Marcus Caepio

Caepio, Marcus Servilius—Praetor during the Social Wars, grandson of Gnaeus and son of Quintus

Caepio, Quintus Servilius—former patron of Quintus Sertorius, father of Marcus Caepio

Caesar, Gaius Julius—a child at the time of the Social War, nephew by marriage of Gaius Marius. Nephew of 91 BC consul Sextus Julius Caesar. Son of man by same name. Future dictator

Caesar, Lucius Julius—one of two consuls for 90 BC, one of the commanders in the northern theater of the Social War

Caesar, Sextus Julius—previous year's consul. Served as proconsul during the Social War

Cicero, Marcus Tullius—serving as a junior tribune under Lucius Cornelius Sulla during the Social War. A friend of Gavius Sertorius. Later becomes famous as an orator, writer, and statesman

Cluentius, Lucius—a former friend of Lucius Cornelius Sulla. A leading statesman of the Italian city of Pompeii

Didius, Titus—former consul. Quintus Sertorius served under Didius and is returning from this campaign at the beginning of the Social War

Hirtuleius, Aius—younger brother of Lucius Hirtuleius

Hirtuleius, Lucius—childhood friend of Quintus Sertorius. Served alongside Quintus in the war against the Cimbri and Teutones, and in Greece

Insteius, Aulus—childhood friend of Quintus Sertorius. Served in Greece alongside Quintus. Twin brother of Spurius

Insteius, Spurius—childhood friend of Quintus Sertorius. Served in Greece alongside Quintus. Twin brother of Aulus

Leptis—*primus pilus* (first spear) centurion under Quintus Sertorius. Previously served in Greece

Livianus—proconsul at the time of the Social War. Technically, Sertorius served under him at this time, but as Livianus was on the far side of the Alps, Sertorius commanded with relative autonomy

Lucullus, Lucius Licinius—*tribunus laticlavius* (senior tribune) under the command of Lucius Cornelius Sulla during the time of the Social War. Friend of Gavius Sertorius

Lupus, Publius Rutilius—consul during the Social War. A distant relative of Gaius Marius, who served under Lupus at this time

Marius, Gaius—former consul (six times previously) who was considered the "Third Founder of Rome" for his success in defeating the Cimbri and Teutones. Serving as a legatus under Lupus at the time of the Social War. Uncle of Gaius Julius Caesar. Bitter rival of Lucius Cornelius Sulla

Mutilus, Gaius Papius—a Samnite noble who was elected "consul" by the rebelling Italic League during the Social War. He leads the main Samnite army in southern Italy

Pollux—dog of Quintus Sertorius, brought back with him from Greece. Named after the twin gods Castor and Pollux as a reference to a friend, Castor, who served with Sertorius in Greece.

Rhea—mother of Quintus Sertorius, grandmother of Gavius Sertorius.

Scaurus, Marcus Aemilius—former consul of the Roman Republic. Serving as the father of the senate (*princeps senatus*) at the beginning of the Social War

Sertorius, Gavius—a son of Titus Sertorius by birth. After his father's death in battle and his mother's suicide, he was adopted by his uncle Quintus Sertorius. Raised by Arrea, wife of Quintus Sertorius, while his adoptive father was away at war

Sertorius, Proculus—deceased father of Quintus and Titus Sertorius, husband of Rhea. An influential local magistrate in the village of Nursia

Sertorius, Quintus—protagonist of The Sertorius Scrolls. Son of Proculus Sertorius and Rhea, brother of Titus Sertorius. Husband of Arrea and adoptive father of Gavius Sertorius. Former officer of the legions with over a dozen years of military service

Sertorius, Titus—deceased brother of Quintus Sertorius. Son of Proculus Sertorius and Rhea. Birth father of Gavius Sertorius

Silo, Quintus Poppaedius—leader of the rebelling Italian tribe of the Marsi. Elected as consul by the Italic League, he led the Marsi and many other tribes hostile to Rome in northern Italy. He was called the "heart and soul" of the rebellion

Strabo, Gnaeus Pompeius—a prominent member from a noble family in Picenum. Despite being a "new man," he levied a large army from those local to Picenum and fought against rebel tribes there throughout the Social War

Sulla, Lucius Cornelius—a rising politician and military commander in the Roman Republic. Born to a tarnished but patrician family. A legatus under the command of Lucius Caesar at the time of the Social War. A bitter rival of Gaius Marius

Tranquillus—a wealthy man native to Mutina. He hosts Arrea during the Social War. Husband of Tullia

Tullia—wife of Tranquillus, host of Arrea during the Social War

TRIBES OF THE SOCIAL WAR

TRIBES LOYAL TO ROME OR NEUTRAL

Campanians—Comprised the area and peoples around the important city of Capua. Comprised the most fertile soil in Italy, this was an area Rome was determined to protect at all costs. In addition, Campania was considered to rear the best horses and cavalrymen in Italy. Many cities within Campania, including Pompeii, which did not have citizenship, quickly joined the rebellion.

Etruscans—The Italian tribe of Etruria, which was delimited by two rivers: the Arno and the Tiber. Etruscans, the dominant civilization of Italy previously, had fought many wars against Rome but had altogether assimilated with Roman culture. Whether or not they would join other tribes in rebellion wasn't settled until the end of the war and was a matter of great importance to the Romans who relied on their support.

Latins—An Italic tribe in central Italy and along the western coast, including the city of Rome and the surrounding territories.

Umbrians—an Italic tribe in central Italy, situated close to Rome. They did not support either side during the Punic Wars. Unlike the Etruscans, most of their people lived in small villages rather than cities. They were heavily integrated with Rome in the third century BC. Whether they would remain loyal to Rome was not a foregone conclusion, and Rome would continue to be concerned about their possible defection throughout the war.

ITALIC LEAGUE TRIBES

Apulians—An Italic tribe in the southeastern peninsular section of Italy. Although they were reluctant to join the rebels, they were surrounded by many tribes who opposed Rome and therefore would be a target if they stayed loyal. They were one of the last tribes to join the rebellion. The Roman colony of Venusia within Apulia was one of the only Roman colonies that joined the rebels, primarily out of fear of being destroyed by those already supporting the rebellion.

Frentani—An Italic tribe on Italy's southeastern coast. Closely connected with the Samnites. They were particularly important because they controlled the Adriatic seaboard of Italy.

Hirpini—A Samnite tribe in southern Italy, sometimes lumped in with other Samnites and considered a distinct and independent tribe. Their name in Oscan, the language which they still spoke during the Social War, means "wolf." Their land surrounded the important Roman colony of Beneventum.

Lucanians—A tribe in southern Italy that was closely connected with the Samnites. They spoke Oscan, the same tongue as the Samnites and other rebelling tribes. They supported Pyrrhus and Hannibal Barca during their wars against Rome. In the Second Punic War, they were ravaged by both Rome and the mercenaries of Carthage and never fully recovered from these disasters.

Marrucini—a small tribe very close with the Vestini who were one of the earliest to join in the war. They fought alongside the Marsi in many battles.

Marsi—The first tribe to take up arms against Rome in the Social War. Along with the Samnites, they were the most active leading tribes during the conflict. They were situated very close to Rome by the Via Valeria, less than sixty-five miles from Rome itself. Their primary leader during the Social War was Quintus Poppaedius Silo.

Paeligni—a mountain-occupying tribe near modern Abruzzo. They were close in proximity and affinity to the Marsi and quickly joined them in rebellion. One of their cities, Corfinium, was named the capital of the Italic League and thus renamed "Italica."

Picentes—fought Rome several times previously and instigated the Social War by killing all Romans within the city of Asculum, including a relative of Caepio's. The city of Asculum would be a main objective for both sides throughout the war. Pompeius Strabo (and his son, who became known as Pompey the Great) were native to Picenum and raised locals to fight back against their tribesmen.

Samnites—Rome's oldest enemies, they had fought many wars against Rome before. Most recently, they joined Hannibal during the Second Punic War, and Pyrrhus of Epirus during the Pyrrhic War before that. Rome held hatred for the Samnites for battles they lost to them in the past. It was a foregone conclusion that they would join the rebellion once they began, and they led the rebel efforts throughout. Their primary leader during the war was Gaius Mutilus Papius.

Vestini—a Sabine tribe forced by the Romans into an alliance in 302 BC. They were one of the first tribes to join the war effort against Rome after the rebellion at Asculum.

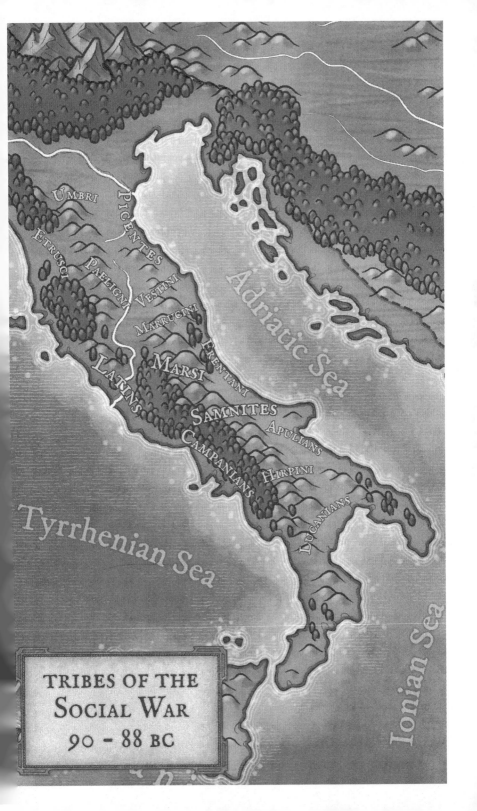

Umbri

Etrusci

Picentes

Paeligni

Vestini

Marrucini

Frentani

Marsi

Latins

Samnites

Apulians

Campanians

Hirpini

Lucanians

Adriatic Sea

Tyrrhenian Sea

Ionian Sea

TRIBES OF THE
SOCIAL WAR
90 - 88 BC

MUTINA

FIRMUM

ASCULUM

Adriatic Sea

NURSIA

CORFINIUM

ROME   ALBA   AESERNIA

CAPUA

ACERRAE   NOLA   VENUSIA

POMPEII   BRUNDISIUM

Tyrrhenian Sea   STABIAE   GRUMENTUM

SALERNUM

Ionian Sea

CITIES OF THE
SOCIAL WAR
90 – 88 BC

Join the Legion to receive Vincent's spinoff series "The Marius Scrolls" for FREE! Just scan the QR code below.

SCROLL I

Quintus Sertorius—Three Days after the Kalends of March, 664 Ab Urbe Condita

The earth trembled beneath the relentless stomp of ten thousand Roman legionaries. They bashed their swords against their shields and chanted an ancient prayer to Mars.

A song of triumph and victory rang out from trumpets and buccinae as we passed under the crenellated stone archway of the Porta Triumphalis. Beyond them, the cries of thousands waited to overwhelm us.

Scarlet covered the stone path, and scarlet rained down from above.

Rose petals, thrown by the rapturous mob. But I thought of blood. Of the battlefield.

My horse must have been thinking the same thing, and she jerked her head against the reins. I ran my fingers through her mane, and whispered they meant us no harm, even though she couldn't hear it.

I lifted a hand to shade my eye from the sun and scanned the crowd. My gaze darted about in search of my wife and child. It was impossible to find anything within those roaring, pulsating thousands, but I had to try.

Roman citizens leaned out of windows and crowded the rooftops of nearby buildings. The trumpets' brazen roar was little more than a distant bleating of sheep amid the peoples' cry.

Guards struggled to keep the mob out of our path as mothers extended small children for a kiss and young women reached out to touch our hands. We were forced to thin out and extend our ranks just to make it through the narrow path of the Via Triumphalis.

Soon the rose petals gave way to horse dung, shattered piss pots, and rotten vegetables. The applause faded to jeering and curses as the crowds pelted our captive Greek rebels with whatever they had available to them.

The shackled prisoners before us hung their heads, refusing to give the mob the satisfaction of crying out, and not brave or foolish enough to look at them. The jagged chains linking all their ankles clattered against the stone road as they staggered onward to their fate.

At the front of our procession rode our triumphant general, Titus Didius, conqueror of the Greek rebellion. Atop his four-horsed chariot he stood with one hand raised to greet his adoring citizens. He depicted himself as the most ancient of gods, Saturn, with dried red clay painting his face. It was Roman tradition for triumphant generals to dress as their patron god for the day, but I still found it frivolous. There was nothing divine about what we did in Greece.

My fellow officers raised their hands to salute the crowd as well. I had to remind myself to do so. I cared nothing for their applause. They knew nothing of what we lost in Greece.

They didn't know Castor, or the countless scores of men who died in my arms during the Greek revolt.

They knew nothing of what we gained either. By putting down a burgeoning rebellion, we saved countless Roman lives, maintained their freedom, kept them safe and far away from war. But they thought only of the plunder-laden wagons trailing our procession. Of the marble statues, ornate vases, and jewels collected from Greek temples.

I could think of nothing but finding Arrea and Gavius. They were out there, somewhere among these drunken Romans. My wife—I found her as a Gallic slave, but she followed me and endured everything beside me as a free woman. My son—born as my nephew, adopted as my own after his father's death in battle. I loved them both with a fierceness that superseded even my devotion to the Republic. But so much time had passed since last I saw them.

Were they smiling? Waving? Cheering with the rest of them? Did they watch for me as well? And, most importantly, did they care to see me at all?

After a slow, half-hour march from the Field of Mars, we reached the Via Sacra. As we passed Vesta's temple, thousands within the forum erupted in applause. From the rooftops of the Temple of Castor and Pollux and the Argiletum, clinging to ancient marble columns on the Regium, Romans were every-where. It made the crowds of the Circus Maximus look like a simple social gathering by comparison. We fought for all these citizens in Greece, but I didn't recognize a single one of them.

As he ordered us to a halt, Proconsul Didius swung from his chariot gracefully and strode the steps to the temple of Jupiter Capitolinus. The city sang our praise, but I could hear nothing but a cacophony of echoes in my helmet. Just like the den of arms.

He flicked his wrists, and the guards led the prisoners off to the Tullianum for their execution. The city was howling for their blood, but few wished to witness several hundred men being strangled to death before them.

I shook my head at the thought of all the rations and clean water we wasted to sustain these prisoners for the entire journey back to Rome, just to have them slaughtered in silence. Perhaps the people wouldn't cheer for brutality so if they could only see its fruition.

Priestly servants led a laureled bull up the temple steps and to the center of two marble columns. With the help of the chief haruspex and a ceremonial knife, Didius sliced through the thick neck of the beast. Its collapse thundered throughout the forum until the rapturous applause of the crowd swallowed it up.

The haruspex split the bull from neck to navel. Searching hands ran over the entrails and extracted organs for observation. As predicted, the results were favorable. Our victory pleased the gods.

The ceremony lasted another hour or so. Despite the spectacle of the occasion, I was barely paying attention. Without drawing too much attention to myself, I continued to scan the crowds in search of a familiar face. I could only hope my family was nearby in the blind spot created by the absence of my left eye. It'd been nearly sixteen years since a slinger's rock cost me my eye, but at least I escaped with my life. Few others at the Battle of Arausio were so fortunate.

At one point, Didius took a moment to name a few officers who displayed exemplary service and valor in battle. My name was called along with my good friends Lucius Hirtuleius and the Insteius twins, Spurius and Aulus. We unsheathed our swords and extended them high into the air as the crowds applauded just for us in that moment. I appreciated their praise for the sake of my men, who sacrificed so much, but only the admiration of Arrea and Gavius meant something to me.

Didius concluded the triumph with the announcement of free bread and wine for all citizens. I released the legions to partake in banquets, gladiator games, and chariot races sponsored by our triumphant general.

My dear friends were swift to pass off their steeds and join in the revelry. I declined the invitation to join. I delayed only to recover the dog I'd brought back from Greece, who'd been waiting for me on the Field of Mars. With him by my side, I turned toward the Aventine hill. My home was nearby, and I'd waited long enough to return.

When the door to my home opened, the guard opened his mouth to announce my entry, but I raised a finger to my lips.

It was silly, I knew. We'd been waiting on the Field of Mars outside the city walls for two months to prepare for Didius's triumph. Via my letters, I made it clear I wanted us all to meet in our family domus as soon as the triumph was concluded.

Arrea and Gavius knew I was coming.

But there was a part of me that hoped, foolishly hoped, I could catch them by surprise. I wanted to see them in their element. As they were while I was away and fighting for so long.

I pushed past the guard but gave him a pat on the shoulder for his compliance.

I might as well have been walking into a stranger's home. There were busts along the walls of men I did not recognize. Lily pads danced in the impluvium. The mosaics on the floor told stories of the early Sabines. I'd commissioned those designs myself. Even so, I could remember none of it.

I slipped off my muddy sandals and set them by the door. No sense in marring my return with a stained floor.

But my dog, Pollux, tugged on his leash, and I could contain his excitement no longer. I released my grip, and he bolted to the closest bedroom to inspect everything he could find.

I considered going to find him but couldn't contain my own excitement any more than Pollux. I passed by the impluvium, and made straight for the peristylum, keeping to the shadows.

Years passed since I'd last been home, but I knew Arrea would be in the gardens if she'd returned quickly enough. I was right.

She was bent gracefully near a fishpond. It hadn't been there when I left.

Arrea was humming something sweet and dropping a few bread flakes into the pond from a burlap sack on her hip.

My Arrea. Standing not too far from where I'd asked her to be my wife. She was facing away from me, but I'd laid awake imagining that soft hum for years in Greece. I could recognize it anywhere.

I stepped out from the shadows and straightened my shoulders, straightened my sword belt. My heart beat quicker than it did even during the triumph, as I imagined all the things she might say to me.

I tried to recall everything I'd planned to say, but all the words were tangled up in my mind, and I could think of nothing before I blurted out, "Arrea."

She whipped around.

"Quintus," she said. There were more words threatening to spill from her lips but nothing else came.

I froze for a moment, rooted as if Medusa's gaze ensnared me.

She'd changed. The darkness of her hair had faded, I think. Eight years had touched her, but she was still beautiful. More beautiful, actually. There was nothing so divine in all the sacred temples of Greece.

I shuddered to imagine what I looked like. I was thirty-six years old. After years in slavery, Arrea couldn't remember the precise day of her birth, but we always believed she was just a few years younger than me.

I'd been twenty-eight when I left. She'd married a strapping young senator. One could describe me as many things, but 'strapping young senator' was no longer one of them.

"This isn't what I wore over there," I said, rather stupidly. "They had us dress up for the triumph."

She said nothing else but ran into my arms.

I closed my eye and drank deeply from the rose scent of her

hair. The same as it'd ever been. I kissed her head and thanked the gods.

"Rome welcomes her conquering hero!" a voice said somewhere before me.

My eye shot open. It was a voice I knew well, and not one that belonged to a member of my family.

I clenched my jaw and scanned the garden until I spotted Lucius Sulla.

Unlike Arrea and me, he hadn't aged a day. His hair still as blond, his blue eyes still as striking as the last time I'd seen him.

Regardless of the time passed, I resented him just as much. The last time I'd seen Sulla, he was marching a band of armed senators to illegally slaughter three of my former political associates. Of course, he had the backing of the senate, and they celebrated Sulla for these murders rather than punishing him.

And this was after years of serving in the legions beside him, enduring his veiled threats and attempts at bribery each day. Sulla was the last man in Rome I wanted to see beside my wife.

"Lucius Sulla, a pleasure." In Arrea's presence, I attempted to speak to him with respect. "I did not expect you here today."

He stretched out his arms until I released Arrea and embraced him. "Nor did I expect to be here," he said. "But with my good friend Quintus returning after so long? I couldn't imagine not greeting you."

He grabbed me by my arms and sized me up. "What a fine specimen you are, greater even than I remembered," he said.

I freed myself from him as peacefully as I could manage, my mind focusing on the singular task of putting myself in between Sulla and my bride. "If you'll forgive me," I said, "I've had enough undue praise for the day."

I'd laid awake night after night for years, imagining this moment, and Sulla's presence soiled it.

All the while, Sulla's white-toothed smile was wide and beaming. "Sertorius the humble. You may never accept how valuable you are to the Republic, but the rest of Rome . . . we salute you." He gave a legionary's salute.

Why did Arrea allow him into our home? And on a day like this?

"Where is my son?" I clapped my hands together in feigned good cheer.

"Gavius?" Sulla asked.

The only son I have, I thought. "That's the one."

Sulla nodded. "I know you have the desire to see him again. . . . Arrea, would you like to tell him?"

I turned to find her smiling too. The same smile that had made me fall in love now angered me. She bore herself nearer to me, but I felt myself stepping back.

"Where is my son?" I asked.

"He has followed in your footsteps, Quintus." Arrea placed a delicate hand on my shoulder. "He's joined the legion as a junior military tribune."

I hadn't realized I'd been clutching onto my shield so tightly, but I thrust it down to the ground now.

"Without my permission?"

Arrea cocked her head. "You were not here, Quintus," she said. "We thought you'd be proud."

I looked down and took a few breaths to collect myself, but my fists trembled. I tried to remind myself she wasn't a legionary under my command, but it did nothing to stay my frustration.

"Who is 'we'?" I asked.

She looked rather confused. "Well, Sulla thought so and Gavius and I agreed."

"You're right." Sulla frowned. "You should have been consulted. I sent a letter or two myself, but I'm sure they never arrived."

"They did not." I stared through him.

"I did not mean to upset you, Quintus." He ran his fingers through his blond mane.

He was no friend of mine to be using my first name, but I chose not to mention it. Arrea was already looking to him as if she was apologizing on my behalf.

My tone deepened. "Where is my son?"

"He is with my army in southern Italy, not far from Nola," Sulla said.

My chest ached like I'd been struck with a hammer. Swords and spears and sinew and blood. My son would see it all, and Sulla was the man now responsible for his protection.

"With *your* army?" I said, my breath coming short and quick against my will.

"Yes, gathering as a show of force to keep those rowdy Italians in line." Sulla shrugged, cool and collected. "And he makes for a fine young legionary if I've ever seen one."

I caught Arrea smiling again out of the corner of my eye.

"Tell me then," I said. "If you could take leave to come see me here, why couldn't my son?"

Sulla held up his hands in protest, wounded by the perceived accusation. "He has been *dying* to see you, Quintus. He thought, rather, you might want to see him there. In camp. All grown up." Sulla looked up, imagining him. "I offered him leave. He made it clear he wanted to receive you in camp."

The more he smiled, the more upset I became. Arrea stared at us blankly, as if she didn't know we were enemies. As if she had no memories of all the times I spoke of his deceptions. She couldn't see it, but there was venom in his eyes. He knew exactly what he was doing.

After a deep breath, I said, "I'll see you out now, Sulla. I've been away a very long time and I should like some time alone with my wife."

Again, he held his hands up in protest, as if afraid the returning legate had become a dangerous beast after so long at war.

"Of course, of course." He bowed his head. "First, only let me congratulate you on your upcoming quaestorship. I had no notion you had intention of running for office, but you'll make a fine magistrate."

"What?" I said.

His eyes delighted in my surprise. "Now, now, don't play coy, magistrate." He squinted and tilted his head as if he just couldn't believe what he was hearing.

"You're mistaken. I've offered myself for no such position."

Arrea now placed a hand on her chest. She acted just as surprised as Sulla, but unlike him I could tell her reaction was genuine.

"That is odious to hear." He tapped his lip. "You must have wealthy benefactors supporting you."

"Let me see you to the door." I summoned a smile.

I ushered him to the exit but stopped to whisper in his ear. "Never try to come between me and my family again."

"I protected your family while you were gone, gave your son position and opportunity, and yet still you treat me with suspicion and contempt." He shook his head. "I assumed you to be too principled to support me but had not expected animosity."

"Sulla, I know you too well to mistake your actions for friendship. There is always a motive."

His eyes twitched with poorly concealed amusement. "Indeed." He kissed both my cheeks before whispering, "Still, perhaps you should speak to me more kindly. I hold Gavius here." He gestured to his palm. "He is in my camp. I can make him live forever, or . . ." He tightened his palm into a white-knuckled fist, then raised his voice for all our *servi* to hear. "I look forward to your arrival at our camp!"

He departed. Sulla made his point, and he was glad to do it.

He knew I'd just returned to my wife after years apart, and he hoped arguments would soil our reunion.

There was more to be said, but I refused to let him win. Not this time.

SCROLL II

QUINTUS SERTORIUS—THREE Days after the Kalends of March, 664 Ab Urbe Condita

"What was that about, Quintus?" Arrea raised her voice when I returned to the garden. "A guest in our house, and you treat him that way?"

My breath was deep and labored. I tried to respond but there was too much to say to make sense of it all.

"Well?" she said. "Are you not happy to see me?" Her eyes glistened. I could feel her wound.

I repressed the stream of accusations flooding my mind. "What should we do to celebrate our reunion?"

"You're avoiding the question." Arrea crossed her arms. "I do not know whether you are disappointed in me or Gavius or Sulla . . ."

I swallowed. "Why do you assume me disappointed? I am relieved to be home." The words felt foreign, like someone else spoke them.

"Because I've been with you for sixteen years, Quintus," she said. "Perhaps you've been gone for eight of them, but I know you better than myself."

"Why was he in my home?"

"Excuse me?"

"Our home, Arrea," I said. "Why was Sulla in our home?"

She crossed her arms. "He said he wanted to see you."

"How many times have I complained to you about him? How many times have I told you of his veiled threats and empty flattery?"

She shook her head. "That was years ago. Sulla told me . . . he said there were misunderstandings, but you two had reconciled. He considers you one of his closest friends."

I turned away. "Of course he said that, Arrea. He was using you to get to me."

Her eyes narrowed to slits. "He has never done . . ."

I unbuckled my sword belt and my breast plate and tossed them at the foot of a water basin. "And now my son is in his camp. Under his guidance," I said. "I'm grieved, Arrea. Deeply grieved."

I turned to find her sorrow replaced by the famous temper of a Gallic woman.

"While you were gone—out there fighting only *Dis* knows what—he was here to protect us." She pointed a finger at my chest like a dagger. "Last year, when the city was burning with revolts and looters ran rampant, it was Lucius Sulla who sent men to protect us."

I tried to form a protest. I came up with nothing.

"He looked after us. He spoke kindly to your son when he missed you."

I said through clenched teeth, "Did you lie with him?"

"What?" she said.

"Did you lie with him?"

Her mouth hung open in utter disbelief. She would have thrown something at me if there was anything but leaves and birdseed nearby.

"I'm sorry." I shook my head. "I should not have said that."

Her lips trembled, but from rage or sorrow—I did not know which.

I heard the patter of dog paws behind me as Pollux rushed into the room, knocking over a stucco water jug near the flowerbed.

He ran right past both of us and made it to one of the garden shrubs, hiked up his leg, and marked his territory.

"Who is this?" she said.

"Pollux," I said. "A dog I've brought back from Greece."

"I see that."

"Clearly he thinks he's outside," I said.

She covered her mouth as if afraid of what words might fall out otherwise.

"Arrea." I stepped toward her, my anger cooled by guilt.

"And after all these years of waiting . . . waiting and listening to the city criers reporting horrific battles in Greece . . ." Tears pooled up in her eyes now.

"Arrea." I reached out but she stepped away.

Her voice was weak, the breath trapped in her lungs. "And all this time I've thought of nothing but returning to your arms," she said. "And this is how you return to me? With rudeness and accusations."

"My wife," I said, and finally she allowed me to touch her arm. "I have longed for your touch . . . I dreamt of you every night. I've counted down to this moment since the day I set foot aboard that ship."

She quickly wiped away a tear, never one to reveal weakness when she could avoid it. When the next tear fell, I brushed it away for her.

"It grieves me I've hurt you." I pulled her into my arms. She did not embrace me in return, but placed her head against my chest and no longer contained her tears. "Forgive me," I said.

At length I felt her delicate hands stretching out over my back.

Pollux, intrigued by the display of affection, rushed to us with a wagging tail.

To my relief, Arrea sniffled and laughed.

"And what are we to do with this silly mutt?" she said.

I gave Pollux a pat on the head. "Like always, Arrea," I said, "together, we will figure it out."

And I meant it too. But my stomach still churned.

According to Sulla, I'd been elected quaestor, a position I never sought and knew nothing about.

There were whispers of a civil war, or at least that's what I called it, threatening to engulf Italy.

And now Gavius was in the legion. My boy—entrusted to my care with the dying breath of his father—was now in Sulla's hands.

"Fourth hour, fourth hour," the timekeeper sounded off from outside the room, ringing his little bell.

My eye peeled open, and I to my feet.

I said, "Gods below, I've overslept." I turned and strapped on my leather eyepatch, attempting to spare Arrea the sight of the marred flesh beneath.

She groaned and rolled over. "There are no legionaries to drill today, Quintus. Why not sleep in a little longer?"

The blush of her warm cheeks nearly lured me back into bed.

"The senate is meeting." I sighed. "They're formally welcoming us back from the campaign."

"You aren't required to go, are you?" she said.

I rubbed the sleep from my eye. "No, but it would be seen as a slight to general Didius if I don't make an appearance. He was a troublesome man to win over," I said. "I'd rather not lose his support now that I've earned it."

In truth, today was the day the senate would determine our

response to the threat of rebellion. They'd been waiting on our entry to ensure Didius could voice his opinion. All our futures—mine, my family's, the Republic's—would be decided in this meeting.

But I wasn't quite ready to share that with Arrea so soon after my return.

She didn't reply, but her eyes were open now as she ran her fingers over the frayed edges of her cotton pillow.

I sighed. Already leaving her again. "Help me put on my toga?" I asked.

Arrea stood and opened the shutters above our bed. Sunlight, birdsong, and friendly chatter flooded in. She made her way to an oak chest at the foot of our bed and unlatched the brass locks. Within was an old but familiar long piece of white cloth. I lifted my arms as she spun it around me.

"I think you've improved," I said. Growing up in Gaul, she never learned how to don a man in a toga. I'd always asked her to help me, but she usually struggled until we'd have to ask one of the *servi* for help. It was no simple task, and the folds needed to be perfect or the whole senate house would make a fuss over it.

Her voice was soft as the feathers of our maroon quilt. "I had plenty of practice. Gavius required assistance every morning after he donned the toga virilis."

I centered myself before a bronze mirror and squinted to make out my image. I disliked what I saw.

"*Cac*, I barely fit them now," I said. "I've put on weight."

She chuckled and reached up to feel my arm and shoulder. "You've certainly grown. Your limbs are the size of Gallic tree trunks. I don't ever recall you being so . . . substantial," she said with some humor.

"Just keep focusing on my limbs then and not my midsection," I said. "I'll have to buy a few new togae in the marketplace when I return." Then I added, "Need anything?"

My old friend Apollonius appeared in the doorway. It was

remarkable how much I'd missed him the one night we'd been apart. After spending nearly every day together for the past decade, it was hard to remember I once purchased him from a slave auction in Gaul. Perhaps the best decision of my life was returning his freedom to him. He was my dearest friend.

"*Amice*, you look like a shade of Hades," I said.

His white hair was in tufts and his typically neat beard was going in every direction. I'd known him for years and never seen him like this.

He smiled and rubbed at his eyes. "Perhaps I am."

"What time did you return last night?" Arrea hurried to embrace him. "I must have been fast asleep."

"All respectable people were fast asleep, my dear Arrea," he said. Apollonius looked to me and shook his head. "Your friends Lucius and the Insteius twins were determined to get the old man drunk last night. They plied me with wine until I could barely see straight."

I let back my head and belly-laughed at the thought. The most reserved and virtuous man in Rome, drunk out of his wits. If only I'd seen it, for I knew it was unlikely to happen again in the future.

"Well, I'll sacrifice to whatever god saw you home safely," I said.

"Oh, you can thank your companions for that," he said with a grin. "They brought me home before continuing their night of debauchery."

"I'm so happy to have you home." Arrea took his hand.

Arrea's father hadn't been worth much, but in Apollonius she found a fine substitute. I knew she'd likely missed him as much as me while we were in Greece.

"It's been too long, my lady," he said. "I'm overjoyed to be home."

I was pleased and relieved to hear him say that. After finding and liberating his niece from slavery, he'd made the difficult decision to leave her in Greece with a loving family. Still, I knew the decision was hard for him, and I'd worried he'd never be the same.

I said, "I must be going." I tucked the final fold of my toga.

"Be careful on your way out," Apollonius said with a grimace. "Pollux has . . . made himself at home in the atrium. The smell was particularly foul this morning."

Arrea hung her head.

"We'll have it cleaned," I reassured her. "I'll train him in due time." I hoped that was true.

I made for the exit but Apollonius followed me. "Quintus, there is one thing you should know before you leave."

"What is it, my friend?" I needed to leave, but refused to slight him.

"There were some . . . heated discussions in the forum last night."

I said, "Even on a night of festivities, this sounds routine enough to me." A *servus* helped slip on my red senator's slippers.

"Yes, well . . . it was your old general Gaius Marius at the forefront."

I exhaled and said a silent prayer I wouldn't get caught up in whatever this was about.

Apollonius continued, "It appears he and Sulla are having some dispute over the display of certain statues in the city."

I shook my head. "Of course. The important matters. Whispers of war on our doorstep, of course we must discuss the placement of our statues."

He pursed his lips, and I could tell he, at least, considered it serious. "The statues depict Sulla winning the war over the Numidians. Marius feels slighted."

As in most things, Apollonius was right. The feud between Marius and his former pupil, Sulla, had threatened violence on the Republic before. The situation could only escalate so much further before blood would be spilt.

Welcome back to Rome, Quintus Sertorius. "I must be going. I'm sure to learn more about it shortly."

Mars's month was only beginning, but already the mornings were warm. The sun was bright and full in the east, and heat clung to the air like a wet blanket. Perfect for war season, others might say. Others who, no doubt, had never fought in sweltering heat, I'm sure.

I passed by the familiar sights and smells of Roman city life on my way to the Forum. Women hung wet clothes from lines between insulae, bakers kneaded bread as soft as an earlobe. *Servi* swept up rose petals and animal dung from the previous day's triumph. Dogs with tangled hair gnawed greedily on the discarded bones of roasted hen. Drovers ushered livestock through the narrow streets to the cattle market, little bells jingling around the animals' necks.

Eight years change people, at least Arrea and I. But Rome was very much the same. I took a small measure of comfort in that.

I greeted citizens along the way to the Curia Hostilia, where the senate was convening. Many of them followed behind me but were careful to stop short of the sacred boundaries of those tall bronze doors, remaining only to peer inside.

Already the senate house was buzzing with anticipatory whispers, the same as it usually did before a hotly contested debate. I'd felt at home giving speeches before the senate the last time I'd been in Rome. It'd been too long now. I could scarcely remember how to introduce myself properly.

"Returning legatus of the fourth legion, Quintus Sertorius!" someone said upon my entry.

My eye was still adjusting to the dark as the senate house

unanimously rose and applauded me. I'd hoped to sulk into the back rows and sit down quietly, but I should've known better.

"Thank you, conscript fathers," I said, "Thank you."

The mosaic floors were uneven and worn down from so many hundreds of years of strutting senators. The air within was as dusty and old as Rome itself. Sunlight poured in through open rafters, where pigeons chirped in total ignorance of who we were or what we stood for.

"Sertorius," I heard my name called. Titus Didius waved for me to join him.

"Quintus Sertorius, my lad, I'm glad you've returned!" Marius's booming voice rose above the rest from the other side of the senate floor. He, too, lifted his arms to welcome me.

I recalled the same feeling when determining which of my childhood playmates to sit with when our tutor allowed us to eat lunch. But this was much more important than that. Who I sat behind symbolized many things. Who I supported. Who I would follow. I would honor one man with so simple a gesture and offend the other.

It was impossible not to notice the striking figure of Sulla, juxtaposed with so many rotund and old men beside him. He smiled at my predicament.

I made my way to sit behind Didius. We'd just returned from war together, after all. How could I not join him?

I'd spent years fighting for Rome and caught up in battles between other men's egos. I simply wished to make it through that meeting without a new assignment.

Some of the senators gasped and others snickered. I caught sight of Marius sitting and crossing his arms. I no longer adored Marius as I once had, but I didn't wish to provoke his ire. I could only pray his dispute with Sulla would distract him from the slight.

The father of the senate, Marcus Scaurus, rose to his feet and strode to the middle of the senate house. He had a walking stick now, and his back was hunched. It surprised me to find him still alive, as callous as that might sound.

"First, we must begin today's proceedings with praise for the conquering heroes who've returned to us," Scaurus said. "Victors, we salute you!"

Didius stood and tugged at my toga until I did the same. They cheered for us again, some more than others. Half the senate floor poured on the praise so heavily one might have believed they meant it. The other side clapped slowly and did not rise, making it clear they thought little of our victory.

When at last the sycophants allowed the applause to die down, Marius immediately stood.

Several senators groaned and shook their heads. This must have been a common occurrence of late.

Marius straightened himself. He contained much of the youthful energy that had made him one of Rome's greatest warriors, but age was catching up with him as well. If my midsection had grown, his had doubled. But when he raised his mallet-like fist, it reminded me why senators across Italy would always fear him.

"I wish to once again bring up the issue of the statues."

Many senators jeered, while those around him stomped their feet to show their approval.

He continued, "They are an insult to my *dignitas*, and that of every man who served alongside me in the war against Jugurtha."

Sulla leapt to his feet with the grace of a Numidian cheetah. "I was one of those men, Gaius Marius," he said, his voice softer but no less resolute. "If you still recall. If the Numidian King Bocchus wishes to show his gratitude for my role in freeing his people, he should be allowed to do so."

It was this sort of frivolous debate that made me miss Greece. There was a rebellion at our doorstep, a knife at our throats, and we were still too busy arguing over the egos of individuals.

Marius's jaw dropped and he prepared to launch into another relentless tirade. He stopped when I stood to my feet.

I wasn't expecting to be heeded so easily, but the senators were surprised to see a relatively unknown junior senator standing up without being summoned. They all turned to watch.

"You have something to add?" Scaurus said.

"Senators." I wanted to remain silent, but could not. "We stand here discussing credit for Rome's achievement decades ago." I altered my tone. "All of us know that both of you men have won glory unmatched by almost any Romans before you. There is no need to squabble over who receives credit. All Rome honor and revere you both." I remembered the proper stance of an orator then and raised my right hand. "Yet the credit for the Numantine War, as any war Rome has fought or will fight, truly belongs to the legionaries. The men who fought, bled, and died for our Republic. It is to them we owe the most reverence."

Both sides of the senate house stood, clapped their hands, and stomped their feet. The first thing all of us could agree on this day. The response was forceful enough that Sulla and Marius were forced to match them, and the discussion of statues was effectively over.

When the applause died down, Scaurus said, "In any case, we have other matters to attend to. Rest assured, both of you will have a chance to speak on the matter further."

I hoped that wasn't true.

He began the day's proceedings with the same dull conversations about grain supply, which typically suffocate most meetings of the senate. The heat made matters worse. Corpulent senators waved ostrich-feather fans to cool themselves, togas clinging to wrinkly skin like wet blankets.

During a rather innocuous debate, I leaned down to Didius and whispered. "I've heard rumor that I've been elected as a quaestor. Do you know of this?"

He crossed his arms. "How could you not know you've been

elected in Rome, Sertorius?" he said. "I've been wondering how you campaigned for office while leading the men."

So, he'd heard of it. How was I the last to know? If he wasn't behind it, who was?

Jupiter, I thought, *please don't allow Marius or Sulla to be behind it.* They'd expect my gratitude and service for the rest of my life.

A familiar face rose from the crowd and caught my attention.

"I think, conscript fathers, we are not considering the issue with the Italians with enough urgency," he said.

It took me a moment to place him. My first experience in Rome had been within the home of the Caepiones. Regardless of how that time ended, I reflected fondly on the small boy who lived there. Now, Marcus Caepio was commanding the attention of Rome's most august body. I couldn't help but smile.

Sulla rose. "Lucius Caesar is raising a substantial force in the south as a display of force. I will leave to join him as soon as . . . I've resolved certain matters here." The surrounding senators laughed, and Marius glared.

Marcus Caepio stepped down to the senate floor and said, "A display of force is no longer enough. A single army is not enough. While you and Gaius Marius have been squabbling about statues, my family has been focusing on the threat looming—"

An old senator I didn't know jumped to his feet. "It was your family who brought Rome to the brink of destruction against the barbarians," he shouted.

Caepio spun to address him. "These are not barbarians we're dealing with," he said. "And I believe every man in this senate house bears some responsibility for that."

His father did lead Rome into one of our most catastrophic defeats. The Battle of Arausio took my eye. It cost the life of so many of my friends. It stole the life of my brother. They would hound Marcus for his father's errors all the days of his life. I admired him for rising above it.

The two men continued to glare at one another until Scaurus

SCROLL II | 23

intervened. "What is it you would like to share with us, Praetor Marcus Caepio?"

He lifted his right hand in an orator's gesture. "The one thing which has kept the Italians at bay for so long was the sheer diversity among them. The Marsi share nothing more in common with the Umbri than the Carthaginians do with Gauls, the Samnites no more with the Picentes than the Greeks with the Persians. But the gap between them is growing smaller each day."

"And how do you come to this conclusion?" Scaurus asked.

"My cousin is currently in Asculum. He's seen leaders from tribes across Italy gathering there." When this didn't illicit the response he was hoping, he continued. "He has witnessed an exchange of hostages."

An anxious murmur sprung up across the senate house.

Didius leaned back and whispered to me, "Why would they trade their own men?"

He was an accomplished politician and an intelligent man, but I learned in Greece there were many things Didius didn't know about warfare.

"An exchange of hostages symbolizes an alliance," I replied. "It ensures all parties involved will remain loyal, or their own hostages will be slaughtered."

Didius's eyes flickered.

"Conscript fathers, order. Order!" Scaurus said, his fragile voice barely cutting through the clamor. He stepped toward Caepio, his eyes narrow slits. "What proof does your cousin provide for this declaration?"

"The honest word of a Roman noble," Caepio said.

That meant nothing to me, but it seemed to suffice for the other senators.

Sulla gestured for the surrounding men to quiet down. "What would you have us do?"

Caepio nodded. "Thank you for asking. You say we have an army in the south, and that is good. We have the veterans returning with Didius who can muster in the north. This is good. But we have been straddling the wall for too long. Half preparing for war, half pretending like nothing will happen. Conscript fathers, either this war will take place, or it won't. If we can avoid war, we should disband our troops presently and save the state coffers. But this war *will* happen, and it will take place on all fronts. Tribes will spring up all over Italy with forces bent against us. The legions we have currently will not be enough to win the war once it arrives, and then it will be too late to muster new legions! We must not delay in levying troops."

"Warmonger!" someone shouted.

Several senators on both sides of the Curia stamped their feet.

Scaurus tapped the uneven mosaic floor with his walking stick to hush them. "And where would we levy these troops from? City dwellers? They've no more practice with a sword than they do with a plow. And they are not farmers."

Caepio smiled. "In Mutina. Devoted citizens, loyal Italians, and hardy Gauls fill those lands, and they will rally to our aid," he said. "Quintus Sertorius, join me on the senate floor."

I was still considering his proclamations when Didius nudged me.

"Come, join me," he said again.

I heard hushed whispers throughout the Curia as I made my way toward him. He placed his slender arm around my shoulder and gestured to the surrounding senators.

"We have elected Quintus Sertorius as quaestor, and I can think of none better to manage our recruitment efforts in the north," he said.

He didn't say it outright, but now I knew who had orchestrated my election.

"Look at his scars, gentlemen! A young man still, and already he's lost an eye in service to Rome. See the scars?" He gestured to my arms. "This is a noble and faithful servant of Rome."

Senators on both side of the senate house stood and

applauded. Most of them had never even met me before, but as a returning veteran, it was their duty to feign patriotic support.

Scaurus tapped his walking stick close to my feet. I met his gaze.

"And what say you, Quaestor?"

The senate house silenced, waiting on my response.

I thought of Arrea. After so long away, how could I abandon her again so soon? What would become of us?

Perhaps we could leave. Voluntary exile. I'd saved much of what I earned in Greece. We could buy a farm. A few horses to breed. A handful of sheep and chickens. I could work in the evening while she weaved new tunics to replace my dirty ones. My mother could visit for dinner in the evenings, and Apollonius could regale us with his poetry recitation after.

I would be damned as a coward for all history, cast out from my country and my comrades. But I would have my family. I would have peace.

In my heart, I knew this wasn't possible. My father hadn't raised the sort of man to abandon his country in its time of need.

As a young man, I'd made a vow to serve Rome. The thought of sacrificing my life was never frightening. But sacrificing my marriage? My family? Was there nothing I wouldn't be required to sacrifice on the altar of Rome's glory? I was beginning to believe there was not.

I stared through Scaurus, straight ahead at the Altar of Victory at the head of the senate house. "I will do my duty for Rome."

The senators applauded again, louder now. They were faceless blurs of cheering and shouting as I made my way back to my seat.

By the conclusion of the meeting, we voted unanimously for the levying of new troops. We voted men of rank and probity for position and placement throughout Italy. The senate gave the two consuls supreme command. One in the north and the other in the south, with men like Marius assigned as legati—or Marcus Caepio as praetor—with authority under them.

Scaurus dismissed us, and dozens of senators formed a line to congratulate me. My hands were damp with sweat by the time I addressed them all.

Some gave me trite advice, others promised to sacrifice to my health and success in Mutina. A few of them told me of the dangers of taking on too many lovers while in province, reminding me I couldn't bring them all home.

Titus Didius stood beside me with his arms folded. "It's rare they welcome home the legatus with more praise than his general," he said.

"It's not praise, general," I said.

He seemed to soften a bit when I said that.

He stepped in front of the next man who wished to greet me so he could have my full attention. "What is it, then?" he said. "If you'd only let me know you planned to campaign for office, Sertorius, I would have given you my full backing." I could see there was genuine jealousy in his eyes. "Why would you keep something like this from me? Only the gods know."

I exhaled. "I had not heard a word about it until yesterday."

Senators continued to scuffle alongside us and pat me on the shoulder.

His faced scrunched, perplexed. "You're serious?"

"I am. This was not my doing."

He shook his head before turning and fixing his eyes on Marcus Caepio. "I guess we know who is responsible, then. Go." He nodded toward Caepio. "Go to him."

"We'll reconvene soon," I said.

He gave a sour laugh. "We'll see."

I had too much on my mind to worry about the jealousy of men like Marius or Didius.

Rome was going to war, and with our closest allies. Men I'd fought beside my entire life. I was going to be separated from my wife once again—duty calling me to something I wanted no part of but couldn't avoid. My son was under the command of a dangerous, ambitious man who would use him as leverage to ensure I did not disrupt his plans, whatever they were.

And I needed to know what all this was about.

I stood patiently behind Caepio as he greeted his own crowd of well-wishers. The moment he noticed me, though, he didn't hesitate to turn from them.

"Brother Sertorius, just the man I wanted to see." He embraced me with a kiss on either cheek.

"Marcus Caepio," I said. "It's a pleasure." I halfway meant it.

"Rome's newest quaestor," he said, getting to the nub.

"Yes, and the most surprised one," I said.

He smiled and nodded. "Let's step outside, shall we? It's sweltering in here, and the blathering of these senators is overwhelming."

He led the way out of the Curia. Sunlight bathed the cobblestone Via Sacra, casting a warm glow on the sprawling forum. The Temple of Saturn cast a long shadow over the plaza, where men and woman clamored to find safety from the heat.

"Much nicer out here, isn't it?" Caepio inhaled the afternoon air.

"Yes, but not much quieter," I said.

The air buzzed with the hum of voices, echoing off the majestic columns and statues that line the perimeter. Pockets of men in flowing togas of rich hues argued about the senate's decision, their animated debates blending with the sound of sandaled feet against the stone.

I said, "I suppose I should thank you for helping me get elected."

He laughed. "It was an expensive venture, Quintus Sertorius, but one worthwhile. There was none worthier of the position."

Old veterans and homeless vagrants shuffled about in the shade of marble archways in search of someone willing to spare a few coins. The sour smell of their soiled tunics juxtaposed with the scent of fresh herbs and fruits on display by nearby vendors.

"I'm honored by the position. I'd often thought I might run for magistracy one day," I said. "But I was not ready."

He spun toward me. His youthful face bore the smoothness of marble, unblemished by the scars of battle. Well-groomed, meticulously combed dark locks accentuated and framed his gentle features. His piercing eyes, though never tested in battle, revealed a keen intellect and shrewd understanding. Try as I might, I could scarcely see the wild-haired boy I once knew in his gaze.

"Whether or not you know it," he began, "I've done you a great favor."

I waited until he turned from me again before I shook my head. "You helped me get elected to the position of quaestor. A great honor."

"But?" he said. "You were going to say *but*."

"But I've been gone for eight years." I ran a finger over an old scar on my forearm. "I've missed my home."

He raised his chin but eventually nodded. "Would you join me for a drink?" he said.

"My wife is expecting me," I said.

"She waited for eight years. She can wait a little longer."

I disliked his comment, but I was in no hurry to break the news to Arrea. And perhaps . . . perhaps if I spent some time with Caepio, I could find a way out of this situation.

Caepio moved easily in his toga. It was as natural as skin to him now. I took the steps down from the Curia more carefully, not as comfortable in a toga as in my breastplate and armor.

I followed him to the Basilica Aemilia and entered through two ornately carved doors.

Unlike any tavern I'd visited before, there were no depictions of fellatio on the mosaic walls and no dice-rolling gamblers in the back of the room. The tiled floor was not sticky with spilled wine or body fluids.

Instead, a marble statue of Apollo stood in the center, an overturned basin of water serving as a fountain trickled from his masterfully sculpted shoulder. Intimate clusters of couches were spread out equidistant from it. Senators and other opulent citizens were lounging on these with silver chalices of wine in hand.

The proprietor greeted us and bowed low. "Praetor Marcus Servilius Caepio, an honor," he said. "Falernian grape as usual, *domini*?"

"Yes, Claudianus. Enough for my friend and me," Caepio said. "And bring some figs and cheese as well. My friend looks famished."

He reclined on a nearby couch, and I sat rigid and upright like a legionary on the one across from him.

"Would you care to join me in a game of latrunculi?" He pointed to a board game on an oak table between us with thirteen black and thirteen white pieces.

It was a ridiculous game based on the premise of warfare. Take the *Dux*, or leader, or claim all the other twelve pieces. In war, you need only take a few of the pieces and the rest will flee. The victors slaughter them as they retreat, and then take the enemy king in turn.

"I better understand strategy on the battlefield than in games, I'm afraid."

He chuckled. "Nonsense. A novice commander like me is surely at a disadvantage against an experienced veteran like yourself."

He made the first move. "I decided to elect you as quaestor while thinking of your family," he said.

I stared back at him blankly.

The proprietor himself poured us each a chalice of wine.

"That's what you're concerned about, isn't it?"

"Of course it is," I said.

I took a sip of wine, and nothing had ever tasted sweeter. I had some fine wine in Greece, but nothing compared to a Falernian grape.

"It's your move, Quintus Sertorius," he said.

I was no fan of games depicting war, whether in the arena or on a board made of oak. I had enough of battle. I moved one of the pieces four squares forward.

"This is in their best interest, Quintus." He made his move without deliberation.

"You've not met my wife if you think she'll be pleased about my leaving again, Marcus," I said.

I wondered for a moment if my use of his first name might irritate him, but he didn't seem to mind it. He took a larger sip of his drink than I did.

"War is upon us," he said. "I did you a favor. War is coming to us whether or not we like it, and every noble son of Rome will be called to arms. Your options were to fight on the front lines again, or go to Mutina, raise a few troops, and endure the duration of the war in pampered comfort. Perhaps you would have liked some say in the matter, but I trust you'll agree the choice I made for you was the best one."

I'd served in enough wars to know there was never a campaign so peaceful or without bloodshed. He underestimated this either because he hoped to convince me or because he hadn't experienced any of this himself.

Unsure what to say, I made my next move and stalled by sipping my wine.

"What makes you so sure the Italians will really rebel? As I was leaving Greece, Titus Didius told me the rebellion had begun. But it was one army, raised by one rebel, and Rome turned them away and back to their senses before any blood spilled."

He shook his head as I spoke, distaste on his lips, and I knew it wasn't the wine.

Perhaps Marcus was simply hoping for his opportunity to win glory for himself, to redeem his family name. Without a war of dire consequences, he could never do that.

"Help me understand," I said.

He sat up on his couch, rigid now as a Roman eagle. "You know many things, Quintus Sertorius." His lithe jaw flexed. "But you have been gone for a long time. Too long. The Italians had one hope, a fool's hope, but one hope regardless. And his name was Marcus Drusus. The man who attempted to give them the citizenship they deserve. And he was murdered for his efforts."

Marcus Caepio was years younger than me, far thinner, and much less imposing, but his rhetoric was still powerful when he spoke on matters he cared about.

"And for this one man," I said, "allies that have followed us since the wars against Hannibal, and before, would wage war against us?" The words tasted sour in my mouth.

My own people, the Sabines, were gifted citizenship by the Romans hundreds of years before my birth, but there were many others like us that weren't so fortunate. I couldn't believe any of them could betray Rome. We'd all fought together for so long . . .

"It isn't about one man," he said. He focused for a moment on the game and moved a piece laterally. "He was their hope, Sertorius. And he was one of them. One of *us*, I should say. He was a Roman noble, heritage stretching back to the founding. And if he could be assassinated only for his desire to help the Italians receive proper citizenship, who else can do it?"

I'd wanted to see the other Italian tribes receive citizenship my entire life. I'd fought and bled beside so many of them. It seemed inevitable to me. I always assumed it would happen before it would be my own cause to bear.

But still we refused them citizenship. Even after centuries of bleeding for Rome, they had no one to vote for them. And if all these neglected allies of the Republic united in one cause, they would utterly surround us. Italy would burn. Bodies of Italy's sons would litter the peninsula from Genua to Rhegium.

I began to reply, but he cut me off.

"Any sensible Roman knows we should acquiesce. We should give each and every one of the Italian tribes citizenship." He cleansed his pallet with some wine before continuing, "Now. But we won't. The senate is too afraid of the power one man might achieve if he champions their cause. Too many loyal followers, loyal voters, they think . . . so, for fear, we threaten to let the Republic die." A deep sigh escaped his lips, his face etched with more concern than his years should allow. "Say any of this in the senate house, and they'd bar you for treason. Throw you into the Tullianum or off the Tarpeian Rock. So, war *will* happen. And it will happen soon."

I tore my mind from these ruminations by focusing on the game. I was seeing through his stratagem. He attempted to distract me by moving pieces at the flanks, while positioning two pieces to capture my *Dux*. "What does this have to do with me and my family?" I made my move to block his attempt.

He laughed at me then. "So many things, Quintus Sertorius. So many things," he said. He finished his wine and held it out for more. "You are a legatus. Before that, what did they call you? 'The 'Hero in Gaul'? Or no . . . the 'Hero in the North'?"

"Yes," I said reluctantly. "But—"

"Well, Hero in the North . . . when the war starts, you *would* be called to service. And the senate *would* send you anywhere in Italy they desired. And you *would* die on the battlefield with your men. Regardless of your desire to remain with your family."

He drank deeply from his wine now. I could tell by the elevation of his voice that he was feeling the effects. He moved another piece, unaware of the trap I'd laid for him.

"So you moved preemptively?" I said.

He nodded. "You can go to Mutina and raise troops. Take your wife with you if you'd like. Stay safe. Away from battle and bloodshed. I did this for you."

Even if he meant those words, I knew they were untrue. Blood would be shed, and I would see battle again. And even if he did this while thinking of me, I knew Rome too well to believe anything is done as a simple act of charity.

I took another gulp of wine and moved my *Dux* as if I was thinking nothing of it. "Is there anything you hope to gain yourself?"

This could have been considered an accusation, but he didn't appear to perceive it as one.

"I can trust you, Quintus Sertorius," he said. He sat up on the edge of his couch and looked me in the eye. "I can't say the same for anyone else in the senate."

"Marcus, you barely know me," I said. "I reflect fondly on the memories of my living in your grandfather's home. At least some of them. The ones with you. But I cannot believe you would trust me over any of your friends and relatives at a time like this."

He rubbed his eyes. "Even so, Sertorius, I trust you more than all of them." He moved another piece across the board, exposing his *Dux*. "And I remember those days more than you think I would. I remember how it all ended."

I told his father and grandfather I would see their ruin. That was how it had ended.

He continued. "You hated and opposed my father, and yet you still saved him from assassination."

When Marius planned to have Quintus Caepio, Marcus's father, killed, I wrote a letter to warn him. He'd been in voluntary exile, but very much alive, ever since.

I peered around to ensure no one was listening. If word reached Marius that I warned his enemy all those years ago, only the gods could cool his wrath.

Caepio reached out and took my hands in his own. "That's how I know I can trust you. You did the right thing even when you did not want to."

"I did only what a good Roman should," I said.

He burst out laughing, disrupting the quiet senators seated on couches throughout the room.

"Perhaps you don't know as much about Rome as you think you do, then," he said. "You are better than Rome, Quintus Sertorius." He chuckled again. "Perhaps we all are, but you most of all."

His words were becoming more slurred the more he drank. I longed to join him in the release of intoxication, but I had my wife to return to.

"Know this," he said, sobering a bit. "You can trust no one. I mean no one. This war will pit brother against brother, father against son."

On the board, I sprang my trap and moved a piece to surround his *Dux*. "Surely you don't expect Romans to join the rebel cause?" I said. "Few are so altruistic or care so deeply for the cause of others."

He did not laugh. "I think many are smart enough to know this will be our ruin. Some will see the Italians as the future and betray Rome for their own protection," he said. "Hard to blame a man for defecting to the winning side."

He looked down, chuckled, and shook his head when he saw how he'd been defeated. "See," he said, "looks can be deceiving. In games, as in war, you never know who you can trust." He flicked over his *Dux* in concession.

"I still remember walking you to the market to get you a new pair of sandals," I said. "You'd torn them while we played in the garden."

His eyes narrowed as he laid back on the couch and laid a hand on his forehead. "You asked me what I hope to gain for myself. I want you to raise the finest legionaries imaginable. Bring them to me, and I will lead them to victory. We will save Rome from the snares of defeat." His voice lowered then, as if he were talking to himself. "And I will restore my family name."

Once again, I was being called to war, as much for other men's ambitions as for my duty to the Republic. But this time, if Caepio was correct, there was no avoiding it. If we did not levy enough legions, if commanders like Caepio couldn't "save Rome from the snares of defeat," the Republic itself might crumble.

SCROLL III

Pollux greeted me at the door when I returned, tail wagging and nose wet. He jumped up as if to give me a hug, leaving two paw prints on my white toga. I didn't mind. He'd been a source of comfort on our long sea voyage from Greece, and I could use some comfort now.

I followed the smell of burning pastries to our bedroom, where Arrea knelt by the family altar. She must have convinced Apollonius to make his famous Greek pasteli—honey cakes with sesame seeds—something she claimed to miss terribly in her letters.

But she was pious enough to at least sacrifice one of them to the household gods.

I leaned on the doorframe and watched her. Fixed in beside a mattress and the wall, she had little room for prayer. I could hear the softness of her whisper, like bubbling water trickling over the stones of a brook, but I couldn't make out the words.

The light of a small candle flickered on her soft cheeks. The sight of her was peaceful, soothing. But I feared that wouldn't last once I delivered the news from Caepio.

"Do you pray to your own gods or the Roman ones?" I said when her prayer concluded.

She tamped out the smoldering embers of the simmering pastry on the altar. "Any god that will listen." She stood and brushed off her tunic.

"What do you ask when you pray?" I said.

She smiled, but there was sadness in her eyes. "Today I ask for nothing," she said. "I sacrifice only in gratitude. To have you home."

Pollux pranced toward her, his unclipped nails clicking on the travertine floor.

"And that this young man has joined us," she said.

I massaged my neck. It ached from the burden I was carrying. "We should talk."

I led her to the peristylum, which I hoped would give her some measure of solace. The spring flowers were blooming, as they always had as a result of her tender care.

"How was the senate?" she said. "Dreadfully boring as I hope?"

We sat beside each other on a stone bench beside a trickling fountain. I enjoyed the gentle chirp of the birds before responding. "Most of it. Usually is."

"But not all of it," she said. I couldn't see her moving, but she seemed to be farther away on the bench now.

"Not all of it." I sighed. "War with the Italians may be inevitable."

Her hands moved instinctively to cover her stomach. She said nothing, but I could see her chest begin to rise and fall harder.

"I don't know what to believe," I said. "About any of it. I saw Marcus Caepio, and he was rambling on like a madman for most of our discussion . . . but he seems to believe word of total rebellion to arrive any day."

After a moment, she shook her head. "We already went through this while you were gone, Quintus. The Italians raised a group of disgruntled farm hands and were marching toward Rome. All it took was a stern reprimand from the consul, and they turned right back around."

I nodded. "I hope this is more of the same."

The look in Caepio's eyes returned to mind. There was no doubting the sincerity of his belief. And he wasn't the type to believe something with no weight. "But . . . regardless . . ."

She could see I was struggling to speak. "By all the gods in Gaul and Rome, out with it, Quintus," she pled.

I swallowed. "My position of quaestor—one I did not ask for, remember—is to be served in Mutina." Her lips tightened, so I spoke faster to get as much out as possible before she offered resistance. "I'll be away from war, away from fighting. My task is to help levy the locals, to form a legion other men can lead into battle."

She leapt to her feet and spun toward me. "Where is this *Mutina*?" she spit, the name like poison on her lips.

I held out my hands to comfort her. "Less than two weeks journey. No more than ten days if you take a boat up the coast. It's . . . in the Italian side of Gaul. Your kinfolk," I said.

Her anger was unmitigated. "One night, Quintus. One night in our bed together, and already you speak of leaving."

"I did not want this, Arrea. I told Caepio as much and he swore I'd be called for service one way or another, and this way I can be kept away from battle." I pled. "Isn't that what you want?"

She looked away from me. "What I want is a husband."

I stood and Arrea's birds fluttered off. "Do you think I like being away from you? Do you think I prefer the cold company of fighting men to the warmth of my wife?"

She inhaled. "Sometimes I do not know what you want," she said. "Do you think our love can survive this?"

"It's six months or so, Arrea, nothing more."

The louder I raised my voice, the more hers lowered. "We barely survived the last campaign, Quintus. Can we survive another?" Her voice was a whisper.

"Yes. We've survived wars before and we will once again."

Tears welled up in her eyes. "No. Our marriage is eternal, just as we vowed. But *love* is a fragile thing." She pointed to the budding petals of a blue poplar. "It must be nourished, with water and light."

"Arrea, I cannot reject my duties. I cannot disavow the Republic and run in shame to hide."

"There is no shame in being a husband. In being a father. What is the point of battle if you lose what is most precious to you?"

"You are the most precious thing to me. You—"

"Bring me with you," she blurted out.

As we grew quiet, the pigeons returned to the garden and filled the space with gentle chirping.

"You want to come with me?" I said.

"Of course I do, Quintus," she said. "Like when we met, in a burnt down village in Gaul. Let me share your burdens. Let me suffer with you. Let me see what you see, so I might understand."

She fell into my embrace, and I held her head close.

"Do not part yourself from me again," she said.

"Shh." I ran my finger over her shoulder. "You will come with me."

"Vow it," she whispered.

I pulled away so she could look at me. "As long as it is within my power to choose, I will never leave you again."

I could almost hear the clatter of arms and horses and dying men. Things she would see if I kept my vow. What a foolish thing to promise. But the shimmer in her eyes was enough to bind any man forever.

Out of the corner of my eye, I spotted someone peeking around the corner and disappear just as quickly.

"Apollonius," I said. "I saw you."

He popped back out. "Quintus, I thought that was you," he said with a nervous smile. "Was wondering when you might return."

"I've returned, now join us." I would have to inform him as well, of course. He'd been nearly as close as a spouse to me over the last several years, after all.

"Perhaps we should begin discussing dinner." His eyes darted tentatively between Arrea and me.

"There's something more pressing we should speak of first," I said.

He winced. "I believe . . . I may have overheard."

I began to tell him about my commission as quaestor, but he interrupted.

"When do we leave?" he asked.

I smiled. "I rather thought you should have some say in the matter before I assumed you'd be joining me."

"My friend," he said, taking one of my hands between his own. "I've told you this once or twice before, I believe. Where you go, I go."

"Then we'll all go together, then," I said.

I didn't want to leave for war again. But I'd rather be in the mud of Mutina with my people than in a palace in Rome without them.

All I needed was to ensure a few more people would join me. I set out the next morning to find them.

In the back of the tavern, dice rolled around in a cup, cracking like knuckles before they poured out over the table. Straw covered the concrete floor, which stuck together in clumps from spilled wine. A few clucking chickens ambled around the room, pecking at the ground for bits of food.

The room had no windows to hide the nefarious activities within. The only light came from a few crackling fires. A cauldron of stew cooked above one, and meat roasted above the other, the grease hissing as it dripped.

I reclined on the edge of a couch in the center of the tavern, surrounded by my oldest and closest companions who'd just returned from the war in Greece alongside me.

Lucius Hirtuleius had joined me on every campaign I'd ever been on, from the kind with fake wooden swords in my father's fields to the ones where fields were overflowing with the slain. Once chubby and awkward, he was now the consummate Roman, in both appearance and character. Storied scars lined his flesh, but the deepest were those of his hands, where he shed his own blood in offering to the gods before every battle. Sandy hair—trimmed to regulation—framed a strong jaw and dimpled chin. He was shorter than the rest of us but built like a bull. There was no better man to have beside you in a fight.

Reclined on either side of him were the Insteius brothers, Spurius and Aulus. One wouldn't suppose they were twins by looking at them. Spurius was taller and darker, the one Nursia's girls chased when we were boys. Aulus was notoriously undisciplined in his diet and exercise, and now in his thirties, it was beginning to show. Regardless, his infamous grin and his charming laughter led to him being more successful with women than all of us combined. His witty rhetoric led him out of many precarious situations over the years.

"Our childhood friends are terrible influences," Lucius Hirtuleius said, rubbing his eyes. "I think you should leave while you can."

I was the only one not sick from the night before. Although, the smell of warm fish wafting in from the Aventine hill docks threatened to change that, not to mention the decidedly more human stench coming from within.

"Nonsense," I said. "I think they're just the type of influence we need." I clapped Aulus on the shoulder, and he groaned dramatically.

I hadn't seen them since we completed the triumph, and we'd celebrated our return differently. While I returned home to see my wife, they'd been all over Rome in taverns and gambling dens, as if they'd never been in the city before.

"I may disagree," Spurius said, devoid of color in his face. "I never want to taste Aventine wine again."

Steam rose from the freshly baked, torn open loaf the tavern proprietor brought us.

"I must say, you are officers of the legion now." I concealed a grin. "You'd likely be admitted to more savory establishments. Except maybe Aulus."

Lucius laid back on his couch and covered his eyes. "Never. From the dirt we were wrought, and in the dirt we'll remain."

The Numidian proprietor drew closer and slapped a dirty washrag on his shoulder. "What will you have this morning, *domini*?"

"I'll have the same wine as last night," Spurius said in defeat.

"I'll take the same," I said. "But make sure it's well-watered."

"*Gerrae.*" Aulus shook his head. "Bring him some milk too. The man's forgotten how to celebrate."

It was good to see them again. They'd been my home during those long years campaigning in Greece, and they felt like home still.

Lucius said, "I don't know if it's my imagination, but I believe it's easier to get drunk with a missing limb." He raised the nub where he'd lost his arm in Greece, the skin pulled taut and tucked into a deep and doughy pocket. He nearly lost his life in the incident, but my friend Lucius wasn't the type to die easily.

"Of course it is," Aulus said. "That was the arm you used to pleasure yourself. You built up a considerable amount of mass in that forearm."

Lucius threw an empty cup of wine at Aulus.

One of the other tavern patrons must have rolled something fortuitous as a clamor rose from their table. Lucius and the twins rubbed at their temples and groaned.

A young man stumbled down from the boarding rooms upstairs.

"What day is it?" His eyes were askew as he kneaded his temples.

I burst into laughter when I realized who it was.

"Aius Hirtuleius, what are you doing here, of all places?" I stood and threw my arms around his shoulders.

Lucius's little brother had been living in my mother's home since he was a child, but he wasn't a child any longer. Hard to remember everyone continues to age while we're away and fighting.

"Welcoming my brother home," he said. "Although I'm beginning to regret it."

"Came in last night," Lucius said. "We showed him how the Roman Legion drinks."

I sized him up. He was barely recognizable. His boyish curls were now shaved down to the skin, and he sported a finely trimmed beard, like a statue of Hercules.

"Just like the old days," I said. "Like back in Nursia, aye? Quintus, the Hirtuleius brothers, and the Insteius twins."

"I don't recall losing a thousand denarii on dice games in Nursia," Lucius said.

"Lucius! How could you be so reckless?" I wagged a finger at him.

A stray cat rubbed up against my leg, and I was duty bound to give him a scratch behind the ears.

"Reckless?" His face contorted like he was pondering a question of philosophy. "Some might call it 'daring' instead. It's a much nicer word, isn't it?"

My typically stoic friend was no gambler, nor was he a heavy drinker. It wasn't his typical method of celebration, but one could hardly blame him after all we had endured.

"Besides, I have no wife or children to return home to like you all. What else have I to spend my hard-earned denarii on?"

"*Cac*," Spurius said, bloodless in the face. "My wife. She'll skewer me when I return home like this."

Aius turned suddenly and emptied his stomach in a pisspot.

I tried to draw attention away from him. "Heading back to Nursia, then?" I said.

Spurius and Aulus nodded.

"Leaving as soon as we sober up," Spurius said.

"Tomorrow afternoon sometime," Aulus added.

The sound of footsteps and horse hooves poured in from the street outside.

"Well, before you all go, I have something I wish to speak with you about." I stood as the tavern keeper brought me my wine. It was far less watered than I liked, and it was nothing compared to the Falernian grape I'd enjoyed the day before, but it made me feel like a soldier again. "If you can steel yourselves for but a moment."

Spurius tried to blink himself awake, Lucius sat up on his couch, and Aulus took a swig of Spurius's wine.

"I have been elected quaestor," I said.

They showed the first signs of life in the morning, as each of them congratulated me with a pat on the shoulder or a kiss on the cheek.

"Well deserved, Quintus," Aius said, the last to show his support.

"It's a junior magistracy, but I'm to be stationed in Mutina, a few weeks' ride north," I said. "The fortunate news is that the provincial governor is on the far side of the Alps, so I'll have autonomous command. I can even choose and assign my own staff. I'd like to ask each of you to serve alongside me once again. And that includes you, Aius."

Spurius nodded with a smile on his lips. Aulus raised a fist in triumph, but the Hirtuleius brothers said little.

"No obligations, of course," I said.

"Of course we'll join you," Aulus said. "I'd like you to vow I'll sleep and eat better, and receive twice the pay, but we'll join you."

I looked to Lucius and swallowed. "And you?"

He glanced at Aius for a moment before responding. "I was actually waiting until we were all together to share the news," he said. "Gaius Marius has named me tribunus laticlavius of his forming legion, and Aius will join my staff."

We all celebrated for a moment, happier for Lucius even than they'd been for me. This was an incredible opportunity for both. Their future prospects were boundless with a commission like that. Even still, I could feel the hollow of disappointment in my gut.

"I had no notion," Aulus said.

"Didn't take long." Spurius shook his head in amazement.

"Marius sought me out shortly after he met with the senate yesterday. I'd had a few cups of wine by the time I agreed, but I assume the handshake is still binding."

"Well, congratulations are in order, I suppose," I said, forcing a smile and standing to embrace him.

I envied him. Not for his new position of authority—he deserved it as much as anyone—but for his blind devotion to Marius. Unlike myself, he had no quarrel with Marius's politics. I remembered what it was like to trust in Marius so completely, as if he were a god sent to save Rome from all her enemies. It was an empowering feeling, intoxicating to be in his presence. But I could never feel that way after what happened ten years before. He nearly cast the Republic into a civil war with his political maneuverings. Blood still stained the marble columns of the Capitol.

He clapped me firmly on the back.

"I am sorry I can't go with you, Sertorius," he said. "You know I would follow you through the fires of Vesta."

"I do. But your place is wherever you can serve Rome best," I said. "And congratulations for you as well, Aius." I turned to Lucius's younger brother.

He still looked green in the face, but he couldn't help but grin.

"First time in the legion?" Spurius asked.

"It is, and long overdue. Can you pass me that wine? My mouth tastes like an ox's hooves."

Aulus passed him Spurius's wine, and Aius drank deeply. He only held it down for a moment before he vomited again.

"So where are you rallying?" I tried to ignore the acrid stench.

Before Lucius could answer, there was a great clamor and shouting outside the tavern.

"Have you swords?" I said.

"Never without it," Lucius said.

We burst out into the sweltering morning heat and blinding light as a crowd stampeded past us.

"The Italians have rebelled! The Italians have rebelled!" a crier shouted. He burst into every open shop and continued to shout, "The Italians have rebelled!"

Was this a ruse? More fearmongering? I didn't believe him yet, but still we fell in with the crowd and followed the crier to an open market square before the Aventine docks.

Fishermen with sun-weathered faces etched with lines of toil, ceased peddling their day's catch. The Aventine poor, shrouded in frayed tunics and tattered cloaks, pressed in, their eyes fixed on the crier.

He ascended the steps of a small platform, a haze of salt-tinged mist looming overhead.

He turned to face us, inhaled deeply, and began. "The citizens of Asculum have openly rebelled! They've killed the emissary Opiter Caepio and slaughtered every Roman citizen within the city walls."

I knew Marcus Caepio would mourn the loss of his cousin,

SCROLL III | 47

but if this news were true, there were far greater concerns than one man's life.

War would begin immediately, and just as Marcus feared, we had not levied enough men in preparation. It would force Gavius into battle. Italy would burn.

The crier continued to reveal the horrors and atrocities within Asculum. A Roman noblewoman stripped naked and beaten in the marketplace, her hair cut with dull knives before they nailed her to a cross. A Roman shopkeeper with his hands cut off and his eyes gouged out. A baby boy dashed against rocks.

The words crashed over me like an angry sea. An unyielding blow, as if they placed an entire legion on my shoulders. Time slowed. My heart pounded like a war drum, drowning out everything around me. I could see only Gavius, as he was when he was a wild-haired, adventurous boy. His innocence was stark against the impending horrors.

Aulus crossed his arms. "These atrocities are unconscionable, but this does not mean all of Italy will rebel," he said.

"Where one goes, more will follow." Spurius frowned.

"It's their city," Aulus said. "We should never have been there."

I considered his response strange but assumed he simply had no wish to return to battle, especially against our kin. We'd been gone so long, and although he'd grown into a capable officer, he was no soldier at heart.

"Regardless, our mission is more dire than ever," I said, raising my voice over the shout of the crier and the wails of his listeners. "You may still return to Nursia if you like, but travel light and swift. The roads may be unsafe for Romans."

Aulus shook his head. "I have no fear of the roads. We'll be fine."

"We should plan to meet in Mutina no later than the Nones of April."

The crier continued, spittle flying from his lips. "These gorgons plucked a happy couple from the altar of their wedding day and crucified them to the rapturous applause of all Asculum's dwellers!"

Spurius turned to me and placed his hands on both my shoulders. "No, we will go with you," he said for them both.

Aulus did not object.

"Let us leave with haste, then," I said. "I need no more stories like these to prepare my sword for war."

So, Caepio was right. We were going back to war after all. But this was about more than my own return to battle. This time, my son was going to war too. And I had no way of protecting him.

SCROLL IV

GAVIUS SERTORIUS—FOUR Days before the Ides of March, 664 Ab Urbe Condita

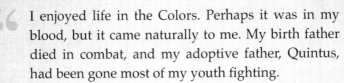 I enjoyed life in the Colors. Perhaps it was in my blood, but it came naturally to me. My birth father died in combat, and my adoptive father, Quintus, had been gone most of my youth fighting.

I never begrudged him for this. Nay, I admired him all the more. I just wanted to be out there with him. In Greece, fighting the traitors alongside him.

Now that I was serving, I hoped he'd be proud all the same. No, I didn't start as a legionary as he had, but that's why he made those sacrifices right? So I wouldn't have to?

I served on the staff of Lucius Cornelius Sulla, one of Rome's brightest young officers. He held me to a high standard, but that made me work all the harder. I rose early and stayed up late, shining my gear and practicing my movement drills. I doubted they'd come in handy any time soon, but over and over I imagined what it might be like when my father arrived and I might show him what I'd become. He was missing an eye, but I imagined he might cry from the other, embracing me with his strong arms and tell me how proud he was.

Vague visions serving as memories told me he loved me. But did he? It'd been so long. Did he resent having no children of his own? Did he provide for me just because I was all he had left?

Arrea always told me this thinking was wrong. While he was in Greece, and I was having night-mares, she'd hold me tight, and tell me about Quintus Sertorius. She said he was brave and unwavering in the face of danger, but what made him stand out from the rest was his heart. She said it was good, and expressed that the word didn't truly convey what she meant, but there was no better alternative.

Sometimes, especially on nights when the night-mares were particularly bad, I asked if he truly loved me. She would smile, tuck the covers beneath my chin, and reiterate over and over that he loved us both more than anything in the world, no matter the distance or time between us.

What a strange concept, love. I could barely remember what he looked like. But I believed the shimmer in Arrea's eyes. He loved me.

But my hope was waning. He was back in Italy now. He'd already celebrated in the Triumph. Every day he didn't arrive to greet me was another I doubted he ever would. Perhaps I was only a burden after all.

"Gavius, you bear a weight about you," my friend Cicero said.

I looked up from my mother's letter and feigned a smile. "You're too smart for your own good, Cicero."

He was another young officer like me. We even shared the same birthday.

Cicero leaned back on his couch in the praetorium, as he'd often done since Sulla left for Rome. The praetorium was nominally the general's tent, but we junior officers spent as much time there as in our own quarters. Sulla's tent smelled of fresh parchment and the eastern incense he insisted on burning. The tent where I, Cicero, and the three other junior tribunes stayed, on the other hand, smelled like sour wine and unwashed balls. This particularly repulsed Cicero, and I was happy to join him in the praetorium whenever I could.

Candelabra and fallow candles illuminated our faces and old letters when we took time to read them. When Sulla was present, he would dictate dispatches to us, or have us reviewing any military correspondence before bothering him with it. But even with Sulla gone, we stole as much time away from the rigors of camp life to enjoy the peaceful ambiance of the praetorium whenever we could.

"Intelligence is often overstated. Perception is not. Whatever you're studying over there has you troubled, and I think it would do you some good to speak of it." He brushed a boyish curl from over his eyes.

We were unlike, Cicero and I. Although we were the same age, to the day, he seemed infinitely younger than I. He wore the smallest size of chain mail provided to an officer's aid by the armorers, but still they were too large for him.

"It's an old letter from my mother," I said, rolling it back up.

Cicero sat up on his couch and dabbed at his nose with a white cloth. "Your birth mother or the one who raised you?"

"The one who raised me," I said.

My birth mother, Volesa, took her own life and left no letters behind for me.

He rubbed at the few scraggly hairs on his chin. "I'm sorry I had to ask," he said. "My own parents are . . . well, your trials are not ones I've had to endure."

The loud cadence of marching legionaries swallowed up the silence between us.

I waited until he met my eyes, and then smiled. "You have nothing to apologize for," I said. "I was born to two parents who loved me, but they did not last in this world. The gods favored me by giving me Quintus and Arrea, who raised me as their own." I repeated the phrase I'd been told, but it felt less genuine than it usually did.

He considered what I'd said, dabbing at his nose. He seemed to have a perpetual cold.

"That doesn't explain the weight you hold in your chest, Gavius," he said.

Moments like this reminded me that Marcus Tullius Cicero was not a child, even if he looked like one.

"My father has not come to see me," I said.

Cicero nodded to affirm me, but it was clear this wasn't something he could relate to.

Light flooded into the praetorium as the tent flap burst open. Our commander, Sulla, entered.

He was panting, and there was sweat on his

brow. "Gentlemen," he said, trying to maintain a calm composure.

There was a basin of water in the middle of his praetorium, and he knelt by it and splashed water over his face to cool himself.

I collected myself after a moment and jumped to my feet. "Imperator!" I offered the proper salute.

He wasn't an imperator, of course. He was serving under the consul Lucius Julius Caesar rather than in an autonomous command himself. Regardless, it was the proper response to his entrance, and one I hoped he'd praise me for.

Cicero did the same soon after, but he was far more reserved in his delivery.

Even stained with the soot of hard riding, his golden hair radiated. His icy eyes were stark against the dirt on his cheeks. He was a patrician, an elite, yet he was young and strong. He balked at social conventions even by the way he wore his toga loose around his shoulders, but there was no mistaking his noble lineage.

Sulla, head still dripping water, said, "How are you, boys?" He dabbed himself with a towel.

"I am adequate," Cicero said without hesitation.

"I completed the missive to Capuan delegation, legate," I said. "The messenger should be delivering it presently.

He dried himself off quickly and said, "Leave us."

I stood to leave, but it became clear he was speaking to everyone *but* me.

Cicero and a few slaves in the praetorium quickly departed.

"Did I say something wrong, commander?" I said. "If so, I apologize."

"You apologize too much, young Gavius."

I almost apologized again but caught myself. Finding nothing else to say instead, I remained silent.

"Actually," Sulla said with a wily grin, "I've just returned from Rome. And I have word of Quintus Sertorius."

I swallowed. "How is he?" I said as stoically as I could manage.

He chuckled, seeing right through me. "He is well. Healthy, although larger than you last saw him."

"Has he grown his other eye back?"

"Not quite yet, but he did ask about his son."

The words warmed me like a campfire. Had he really called me his son? I hoped so. Certainly he did. Or perhaps he called me his adoptive son, or even nephew, and Sulla refused to say it.

"And you told him I was the fastest rising star in the southern legions?" I said. I learned quickly after joining the legion that playful boasting was part of the language essential to daily living.

"Something like that." He winked. "He wishes to come see you, but he is an important and sought-after man these days."

Deflated, I sank back into my couch like Cicero had been before he left. Rome mattered, the senate mattered, glory and *dignitas* mattered. But did they all matter more than me?

I chastised myself for thinking such things.

I tried to summon a little dignity. "Did he have anything to say about me joining the legion?"

Sulla looked up, lost in the memory of whatever moment my question summoned. "You should have seen his face," Sulla said. "Had he the courage, he would have wept on the spot. I've never seen a man so proud."

I couldn't hide the parting of a smile on my lips, but I couldn't believe the words fully either. "And you wouldn't exaggerate with me would you, imperator?" I said.

Sulla placed a hand over his heart, wounded. He sat on the couch beside me. "What have I to gain by deception?"

"I don't say that you have anything personal to gain, but perhaps you wish to spare me disappointment," I said. "I wish only to hear the truth," I said.

"Gavius, I would not lie to you," he said. He sobered and turned from me. Deep in contemplation, he said, "I was born on the Subura to a debauched man and an unremarkable woman. They both died when I was young. I was fatherless, like you."

His eyes shimmered as he spoke, and I wondered why he spoke to me so freely.

He continued. "Life is hard. Cruel. And I would not lie to someone so like myself just to help you find comfort. You are young, yes, but I see you seek only truth."

I nodded. "Yes. I desire no coddling."

He seemed to delight in the statement. He clapped me on the shoulder as if I passed a test.

"And I'll give you none," he said. "Quintus Sertorius asked of you, and he was very proud to hear you've joined the legion. He promised to visit you when he's able."

I sighed. "Is he not able now?"

Sulla exhaled and rubbed the back of his neck, massaging the muscle as if it were sore from all his troubles. "Traveling throughout Italy is not as easy as it might have been a few months ago."

"And why might that be?"

"Italy is at war, young Gavius. Tribes around the peninsula are rallying together in rebellion."

My gut felt hollow. The color drained from my face and I knew it. I joined the legion with a vow to fight for and serve the Republic. But, for whatever reason, I never thought my services would be required, not yet at least.

"So you are brave enough to traverse the Italian countryside during war, and he is not?"

Sulla shook his head and placed an arm around my shoulder. "This isn't a matter of bravery," he said. "If he'd tried to visit, I might have repri-manded him for his foolishness. Single men with no sons may be reckless. Quintus Sertorius is neither. He should keep himself alive, I think."

He continued in his attempt to comfort me, but his words did nothing but wound me. All my life, I'd heard nothing but the tales of bravery of my father. I had not yet seen them.

Surviving Arausio with a stone in his eye, charging the Cimbri at the Battle of Vercellae, protecting the Acropolis with nothing but a few men when the rebel Greeks surrounded them.

And yet he wasn't brave enough to venture through the easy countryside of Italy to see me?

"I understand," I lied. "I hope he is well and healthy."

Sulla nodded. "I understand your confusion and your frustration. He will come to see you soon."

"I would like that, imperator," I said.

Sulla stood. He reached out and helped me to my feet.

"I need to address the men," he said. "I'd like you to join me."

"I'll rally with the rest of the junior staff."

He shook his head. "I'm asking you to join *me*, Gavius Sertorius. Will you join me?"

I blushed with pride. "Yes. I will join you."

"Delightful," he said. "Let's waste no more time then."

While Sulla had been gone, the legionaries were slow to accomplish their daily tasks. Now that he'd returned, it was remarkable how fast the 4,800 men could assemble in formation.

Sulla led us to a hill before the aligning forces. The air was alive with the scent of freshly tilled earth, intermingled with the aroma of wildflowers that always made me think of Arrea. The Tyrrhenian Sea lay to the west, and salt wafted toward us in the gentle breeze.

A hapless shepherd was guiding his bleating sheep in the distance but increased his pace away from us now. Birds chirped overhead and fluttered into the patchwork of cypress trees along the hilltop. It was a brief reprieve before the inevitable.

He stared out over his gathering troops with a glimmer in his eye. "It's a beautiful sight, isn't he?" he whispered.

His loyalist and most senior tribune, Lucullus, nodded. "They will fight hard for you, legate," he said.

The centurions continued to shout orders until the men were drawn up into perfect formation.

Lucullus tapped me on the arm. "How do you feel?" he whispered. The fair-haired tribune had been exceedingly kind since I'd arrived, so much so that I wondered if Sulla ordered him to do so. But there was no deception in his eyes.

"A bit hot at the moment," I scratched the inside of my arm, where my freshly smithed *musculata* breastplate continued to chafe me.

Lucullus nodded. This was his first campaign as well, and he likely knew exactly how I felt. "Lucius Sulla has won many great battles against many powerful foes. Greater than these stepsons of Italy. Have no fear," he said.

When the men were organized to his satisfaction, Sulla stepped forward and we followed behind him.

"Romans, I salute you," he said.

The men slapped their chests with a fist and offered him a sturdy salute.

"I bring grievous news from Rome," he said, his voice effortlessly and powerfully carrying over the centuries. "The city of Asculum has rebelled against us. They've taken every Roman man, woman, and child within the city and put them to the sword."

Cries of fury and indignation began to rise through the ranks of the legion.

Sulla raised his voice over them. "They have slaughtered a former consul."

The legionaries shouted wildly now, unswayed by the orders of silence from their centurions. Sulla didn't seem displeased by the display, but when he raised his hand, all noise ceased.

"Worse yet, tribes around the peninsula have voiced their support for Asculum and rallied to their cause," he said. "We are going to war, my brothers," he said.

Their anger turned to joy then.

"Lead us to them!" some shouted.

"We will kill them all!"

I could not see his face but could hear the smile in his voice.

"We will, we will kill them all," he assured them. "But first, we must prepare ourselves and continue to train. Our cohesion is everything. We will either die or conquer together." He raised his hand and snapped a finger. Two wagons rumbled to the front of the formation. The legionaries on board jumped off and opened up a chest in the back, revealing white tunics within.

"We will all don white tunics. Officers will bear white plumes on their helms. This legion, our legion, will stand out from all others so that when the enemy sees us coming, they will know who they are fighting!"

The men applauded, least of all because they were generally required to purchase their clothing themselves.

"This was a considerable expense, but one I was happy to make. We are no longer *Legio IX Gemina*. We are Sulla's Fist, and that name will strike terror into our enemies!"

I leaned closer to Lucullus so he might hear me over the rapturous applause of the legion.

"How will the proconsul feel about this?" I said, fearing Sulla's attempt at autonomy might place him in trouble with the commander of the southern armies.

Lucullus considered it. "Lucius Caesar is a pragmatic man," he said. "He cares only for results. If we win, he will allow Sulla to take the credit for his part. If we lose, Sulla might be tried for sedition." He shrugged, unconcerned.

As the men shouted Sulla's name, I looked out over the Italian countryside. There were no shepherds or chirping birds now. I attempted to catch a whiff of the flower scent but could no longer find it.

I'd heard my father speak of the horrors of war. Soon I would experience them for myself.

SCROLL V

Quintus Sertorius—The Ides of March, 664 Ab Urbe Condita

I was born 628 years after the founding of Rome.

My people were not among the first citizens. They were in the south, herding their flocks and tilling their fields. They called themselves the Sabines.

The first men to lay the bricks of Rome's foundation were cast-outs and runaways. Criminals. Among those seven hills and the swamp in the middle, these men congregated and built a place to call their own. They had no dreams of grandeur, of conquest. The early Romans only wished to survive.

Hard to do that without women.

The story goes they invited tribes from around Italy to a festival in their newly founded village. They spared no expenses and let the wine flow freely. Once their guests were good and drunk, the king of the Romans, Romulus, gave the signal. The Romans led the Sabine women away. They slaughtered the Sabine husbands and fathers.

My people called this event the "rape of the Sabine women." That's much too harsh a term for the likes of city dwellers. Romans prefer "abduction of the Sabine women." Legend says Romulus gave the women more rights and freedom then they'd ever held in the homes of their oppressive paterfamilias. It says they eventually fell in love with their counterparts. Accepting their fate, they bore the Romans sons and daughters, and built homes with them on the muddy slopes of the Palatine.

The Sabines couldn't accept it, of course. Perhaps my ancestors were among those who rallied together to destroy Rome, kidnappers and thieves that they were. Perhaps a former Sertorius held the battering ram or clambered onto the walls. Perhaps there was a woman inside he'd missed all that time.

When the Romans formed up and met them in battle, it was the women who rushed into the fray. Holding the two forces at bay, they pleaded for both sides to lay down their arms, lest one side lose their daughters, and the other their wives.

The Romans and Sabines complied, but neither ever forgot the insults they'd endured at the other's hands.

The Romans and the Sabines continued to fight for five hundred years before Rome eventually emerged victorious. Conquered and humiliated, Rome bestowed us with the rights of citizens. We were Romans now, whether we wanted to be or not. And from what my father told me, most of our people didn't.

But we were the lucky ones. Other tribes were not so fortunate. The Romans called these tribes "allies" after they vanquished them. Each year, the allies were required to send the best yield of their crops, hordes of gold in taxes, and their ablest young men, all to serve the glory of Rome.

Forgive me the history lesson, but these things were on my mind as we traveled to Mutina.

We passed through the lands of the Umbrians and the Etruscans, both of whom had a past with Rome like ours. How might they be feeling now? With Italia at war, and many of their people still lacking citizenship and rights of their own, why wouldn't they revolt against us?

Why wouldn't they swarm us on our path and make an example of us to Rome, the way Asculum had days prior?

We stayed on the main roads when we were able. We took the Via Cassia north. I spent five hundred denarii for a carriage to make Arrea's journey more comfortable, but there was little to be had in the way of comfort on this journey.

The scorching sun bore down on us at all hours of the day, mercilessly searing the parched earth beneath us. The marching cohort kicked up a swirl of powdery dust, which clang to our sweat-soaked tunics and dirtied our armor. Insects buzzed incessantly. Flies, gnats, and mosquitoes tormented both the men and my horse.

The monotonous rhythm of stamping feet and clopping hooves filled our days. Creaking of saddle leather and the jingle of bridles became the marching cadence that accompanied our journey toward the impending storm of war.

The flora—despite the oppressive heat and overdue rainfall—displayed a vivid palette of greens. From the sturdy cypress trees to the delicate leaves of the occasional olive grove.

I'd traveled the Via Cassia many times before, as well as most of the other roads in Italy. Never had I seen one emptier. Where were the travelers? Where were those on holiday?

No one was leaving the safety of their homes now. Not since the rebellion began. Their homes weren't truly safe either—nowhere was now—but I couldn't fault anyone for remaining where they felt comfortable. I'd have stayed in Rome if I could've. With my wife, and in the safety of my home, until the bitter end if I had to.

Aulus rode up beside me. "Sertorius, you ought to read this."

"What is it?" I wiped away a bead of sweat from under my helm.

Spurius galloped up toward us as well. "A messenger met us at the back of the formation."

"Who sent him?" I said.

Aulus looked at the wax tablet in his hands and furrowed his brow. "The senate and people of Rome, or something like that. Not quite sure?"

I shook my head and accepted the tablet from him.

It wasn't much of a message. Only three words.

Marsi

Vestini

Samnites

I said sarcastically, "Bona Dea, I can't believe what I'm reading."

They looked back at me blankly.

I sighed. "Perhaps some context would do me some good."

Aulus pushed his horse up next to mine, the beast snorting in response.

"Italian tribes that have joined the rebellion," he said grimly.

I looked at the list again. The Marsi and Vestini were in central Italy, to the north and east of Fucine Lake, respectively. They were also neighbors with Asculum, the city that started the war, so it didn't surprise me.

As I read the final tribe again, my stomach sank. I forced the tablet shut.

"I know." Spurius rode up on the other side of me, shaking his head. "The Marsi could be at Rome's gates within two days. The Via Valeria would be a brisk walk for them."

I shook my head. "It's not them I'm concerned about," I said. "The Samnites. They're in the south, where my son is now stationed."

Aulus audibly exhaled. "Don't you see the other tribe on the list?"

I'd forgotten, so I forced myself to open the tablet again. "The Vestini," I said.

"Yes, the Vestini," he said. "They have Sabine blood, Quintus."

We all fell quiet for a moment. The gentle clopping of horse hooves and the centurion's cadence calling filled our ears.

"They're Sabines, yes," I said. "The Vestini. I remember."

"We probably have cousins and uncles among them." Aulus shook his head.

"I believe I'm aware of all my cousins and uncles, Aulus. And they're all dead," I said, a poor attempt at humor.

Aulus released the reins and threw his hands up. "You know what I mean, Quintus."

"Aulus," Spurius whispered through clenched teeth. "Call him by his proper name when the men can hear us."

Aulus raised his voice. "We bathed naked with him in Nursia's rivers when we were boys. I'll call him 'acorn penis' if I like."

His audacity and disrespect was probably worthy of a firm reprimand, but I couldn't stop myself from laughing. I brought my oldest friends along with me for this very reason.

"Call me what you'd like," I said. "You are right. They are Sabines, and our ancestors were likely intertwined with theirs."

Aulus sobered, much older now in his eyes than he'd been when we departed for Greece all those years ago. "Does that not bother you?" he asked.

"What gives you the impression I'm not bothered?"

To find some comfort, I scratched my steed behind its ears, as I often did.

Spiky thistles and prickly shrubs guarded the edges of our road like sentinels, a firm reminder not to stray from the path.

Aulus pursed his lips. "It was more of a question, I suppose."

"Aulus, we are Romans. We fight for Rome. We don't get to choose our enemies, and if we could, the Vestini and those like them would be the last . . . but . . ."

"But what?" Aulus said.

"But they chose us. There is nothing left for us to do."

At length, Aulus nodded. "I wish it were not so."

Our voices soft now, I said, "Me too, *amice*."

Spurius cleared his throat. "The messenger conveyed more than the tablet."

"Tell me then," I said.

I stared off at the green countryside around us, and the golden flowers flourishing around them, trying not to imagine those hills set ablaze.

"The Italians are revolting in unison. They are part of an alliance."

"That seems rather obvious." I swatted a mosquito biting the back of my neck, just beneath my helmet.

"They have established a capital."

My gut went hollow and cold. I kept my composure for the sake of anyone listening.

"What do they call it? Where is it? How did they do this?"

Spurius unbuckled his helm and ran his fingers through the dark sweaty locks of his hair, the heat finally getting to him. "It was a city called Corfinium."

"Corfinium, I've been there," I said. The city was innocuous and peaceful. I couldn't imagine it as the citadel of a rebellion.

"It was called Corfinium, yes. But they've renamed it. They now call it Italica."

These people were so like me, so like my ancestors. And my job was to raise an army to destroy them. They called their new Rome "Italica," a derision of the name we all shared.

I could only feel like more of a traitor if I betrayed Rome and joined them.

"This league of Italian rebels is only made up of Asculum, the Marsi, the Vestini, and the Samnites, correct?" I said.

"Yes, Sertorius, but this is only the beginning," Spurius said. "There will be others."

I refused to reveal it to them or any of the legionaries who might be listening, but I prayed silently that the others who joined wouldn't be in the south. Not those near Gavius.

I looked back and forth between them.

"Something else is bothering the two of you," I said. "I would have you tell me."

Aulus sighed. "My wife can be a plaguing harpy, but I would have liked to return to her before we departed."

Spurius gasped. "Well, mine isn't. And I would never speak of her that way. But I wish I'd been able to see mine as well."

They were missing their wives, and rightfully so. Yet mine was with us, and I'd been ignoring her.

"When we arrive and begin raising troops, I can assign a cohort like this one to escort them to you safely."

"Yes," Aulus said without hesitation.

Spurius said nothing for a moment. "It's too dangerous," he eventually said. "Nursia will not rebel against Rome, and it holds no strategic value to the rebels. They'll be safe there."

My mind was on Arrea again. I wanted to hold her now.

"Sertorius," Spurius said. "We need to be careful."

I frowned and looked at the cohort marching before us. Were they enough?

Spurius nodded. "We will cross the mountains through Paeligni territory. They are kin to the Vestini and buttressed up to each other. They could join the rebellion any time."

"But they haven't yet," I said.

"No," Spurius said. "They haven't yet. But each rebel tribe has made an example when they joined the rebellion, an example of spilling Roman blood. Few of our citizens live in the hard country of the Paeligni. We don't want to be their example."

The Apennine Mountains loomed in the distance. I couldn't help but imagine spearmen rushing over those hills.

"You're right," I said. "We'll double the watch. Come with me a moment?"

Aulus shrugged and matched my speed as I hurried up in the formation until we reached the carriage.

Arrea was asleep within, Pollux nestled up beside her.

"Hold the reins, will you?" I passed them off to Aulus.

I caught a glance from Apollonius, my old friend who was driving the carriage. I gave him a wink to ensure he was prepared for my entry, stood, and jumped onto the carriage.

"Quintus," Arrea cried. "You scared me half to Hades!" She slapped my shoulder as I laughed but pulled me in beside her immediately thereafter.

Pollux looked up, shaking all over from wet nose to bushy tail. He drooled and vomited on his dark coat, just as he had when we sailed back from Greece. Growing up a stray, I'm sure he'd never traveled far.

"Why would you do something like that?" Arrea asked, her voice as sweet and sleepy as her eyes.

I snapped off my cloak and wrapped it around Pollux. He continued to shiver despite the blazing heat.

"I failed to make an entry when I returned from Greece," I said as I scratched behind Pollux's ears. "I'll keep trying until one of them lands."

Pollux, enjoying the affection and desiring some kind of protection from the evil wagon we rode on, quickly pounced onto my lap. Drool, vomit, and all.

"It was your decision to bring him," Arrea reminded me.

"You're right. This is clearly more effort than it's worth. I'll just let him off here," I said, scooting with Pollux to the edge of the carriage. "Come on, boy. Don't make this difficult."

Arrea rolled her eyes. "Stop, Quintus, you fool."

She'd already become attached to Pollux more than she let on.

Once she had Pollux and me back in her embrace, she seemed awake and suspicious.

"You joined us for a reason," she said. "Why?"

I sighed and laid back on the pitifully flat cushions of the carriage.

"Why can't we just enjoy a few moments' peace?" I said.

Arrea sat up and looked at me. "We can, but only when I know the truth."

Her eyes revealed she would not relent until I spoke. Even once I accepted this, I still struggled to find the words.

What a fine balance one must strike between truth and cruelty.

"Many rebel tribes are joining the war," I said. "We need to be cautious on the road."

She looked disappointed by the answer. "That's it? I assumed it was dangerous when I heard we were at war."

I laughed and shook my head. "Yes, that's it," I said. "I simply want you to put on a lorica of chainmail. Just precaution."

"What about him?" Arrea pointed at Apollonius.

I could hear his smile. "Don't worry, my lady," he said from the driver's seat. "I have followed your husband through many of his fearless escapades. I know just how to make myself disappear when I ought."

She pointed to Pollux. "And him?"

"We'll have to forge a special garment for him," I said.

She sobered and took one of my hands in her own. "We'll wear them, Quintus Sertorius. Have no fear."

But how couldn't I fear for her? I'd been ready to accept my own mortality since I was a young man. It was part of life. But being unable to protect Arrea? Unacceptable.

The carriage continued closer to the Apennines toward the tribes of the Paeligni.

I brought her with me to save our marriage. But what a fool I'd be if I lost her life in the process.

Mutina was on the other side of the mountains, and there was only one way to cross them. Through the land of the Paeligni.

The mountains were familiar to me. They were the same ones running through the village of my birth, Nursia, the same my ancestors watered with their sweat and blood for generations.

All Sabines knew to never cross into the lands of the Paeligni. But with no ships at our command or access to the sea, I had no choice but to lead my men right through those steep passes. They were a cloistered and uninviting people. We had no indication whether or not they would stay loyal, but I hoped we would make it out from the mountain pass and all the way to Mutina before we found out.

The *primus pilus* called for a halt and walked back to our carriage as we reached the foot of the mountain pass. "The way may get rough from here, quaestor."

"I'll return to my horse." I stood but left my shield beside Arrea.

"As you wish, quaestor. I'll get the men moving on your orders." He patted the side of the carriage and returned to formation.

"Arrea, if you sense that anything is wrong at all, get low and cover yourself and Pollux with the shield. We'll be all right," I said.

"We will be just fine," Arrea said. "Take care of yourself." She held on to my hand until I stepped down from the carriage and reclaimed my horse's reins from Aulus.

Spurius said, "You should move to the center of formation." His eyes scanned the mountain peaks. "And dismount. If we're attacked, you can fall into the center of the cohort's *testudo*."

"Nonsense," I said. I would not admit it, but this sense of impending threat was very familiar to me now. I'd almost missed it. "We're going to lead from the front."

I led my horse to the front of the resting legionaries, Aulus and Spurius following me. I met the eyes of as many men as possible, remembering many of their faces from Greece.

"Centurion, you may give the order," I said.

The *primus pilus* swallowed, unsure what to do. I could see by the hesitation in his eyes he would have agreed with Spurius. The center of formation would be much safer for us in the event of an attack. But I fixed my gaze, and he likely remembered me from Greece as well. He knew I wouldn't have my opinion changed.

"*Cum ordine seque!*" the centurion shouted, and the stamping of legionary feet began.

I and the Insteius twins led the way at a slow trot.

The rugged faces of towering cliffs loomed over us. Jagged peaks pierced the sky. Winter's snow still powdered their crowns, a stark contrast to the green valley below us. The air grew crisp and thin the higher we marched. The oppressive heat gave way to a chill. Apollo's sun retreated over the mountain peaks to the west.

If it wasn't for the impending danger, this would have been a fine evening for a gallop in the hills or perhaps a hunting excursion for the roe deer so abundant there.

But there was nothing peaceful about this trek. The smallest spark could ignite the flames of revolt in this land, and our passage was the test for their loyalty.

The path narrowed. The wind howled through the crags and crevices. Each stomp of the legionaries seemed to reverberate throughout the mountains, an audible declaration of our intrusion into the realm of the Paeligni.

Aulus's whisper cut through the echo. "Sertorius." He kept his gaze fixed forward but nodded gently. "Front left."

I maintained my posture as well, but Spurius and I both turned to see what Aulus had spotted.

Indeed, there was a man, no doubt a Paeligni tribesman, standing on a mountain ledge above us.

His long dark hair blew in the breeze, unrestrained by a helmet. His chest was bare too, and old scars lined it. Only a leather skirt and an iron shield covered him. A long spear was tucked beneath his arm.

"Eyes forward, Spurius," I chastened him as much as myself.

The man was standing tall, not attempting to conceal himself in any way. But he stood so still, I almost wondered if it was a trick of the gods.

Aulus gritted his teeth now. "He is not alone," he said. "Look carefully."

That familiar rush consumed me. It started deep in my chest, twisted through my stomach, and then shot through all my limbs like an archer's arrow.

I pretended to be looking up at the waning sun, even pointed to it and said something about its color, but in fact I was analyzing the hills.

I regretted the loss of my left eye now more than ever, but even with my impaired vision, I still counted a dozen or more Paeligni warriors, standing some twenty feet apart. Each stood as the first, frozen and still as Medusa's victims.

"What are your orders, quaestor?" Spurius said.

A circling hawk screeched above us.

I listened to the legionaries behind me. The centurion continued to call cadence, and the men echoed their reply, bored but happy, as they focused on remaining in step.

Our men didn't see the Paeligni. Not yet.

"Sertorius, orders?" Aulus said.

I lifted my arm to the mountains where the Paeligni warriors were perched.

"*Salvete!* Greetings, friends of Rome!" I shouted.

Aulus turned to me with eyes bulging from a red face. "What in Jupiter's name—"

I ignored him. "We salute you," I said. But in the brief silence between, I listened in again to the legionaries. They marched in silence now. They were focused and would be ready if something happened. "Your homeland is beautiful. The gods surely favor you," I continued to shout. My voice alone echoed along the mountaintops, as the Paeligni remained silent as the dead. "I come from a land not far from here—I'm a Sabine."

Spurius nudged his horse closer to mine, and he was

panicking just like his brother. He whispered. "Quintus, is this altogether wise?"

One of them disappeared in a flash, leaving only a cloud of dirt and a few errant rocks to tumble down the cliff.

I lowered my voice and addressed the twins. "They're seeking orders. They can't attack without permission from someone else." I spoke quickly. I spun toward the *primus pilus*. "Centurion!"

"Shields out!" He bellowed.

The men on the edges of the formation swiveled to the exposed side and crouched behind their shields.

The others stamped their foot once and lifted pila for the enemy to see.

The Paeligni maintained their statuesque composure.

"Are they mindless or what?" Aulus unsheathed his sword. "If they're going to fight they should come on and fight."

I tugged the reins until my horse swiveled toward the Paeligni warriors.

"We mean you no harm. We mean your neighbors no harm. I am leading this contingent of men to Mutina. If you wish to impede us, we will fight back, and much blood will be spilled this day. If you turn now, we will pass through your lands and not return soon. Perhaps when this is all over, we can share a cup together."

Spurius whispered for my attention and nodded to the far right. The young Paeligni runner was returning with orders from whoever commanded them.

My horse jerked her head against the reins, sensing the tension rising like the clouds of dust on the mountain path.

A whistle pierced through the air, and a single arrow landed a few feet before me. That was their signal.

One of their men shouted in Latin, "*Percute!*"

Warriors from every direction spilled over the small, worn-down goat paths of the mountain toward us.

The mind begins to race. There were thousands of strategic

decisions one could make in that moment. Thousands of orders to give the men, or the twins. Thousands of ways to conduct myself and lead my horse. Some of them would result in my death, and Arrea's too. Some would result in our survival and victory.

But I could only choose one.

I gave the hand signal, and the centurion relayed the orders.

"*Torna Mina!*"

My legionaries charged the mountain walls on either side, swords drawn.

It was the best I could do. We were naked and exposed here in the middle of this treacherous pass, and I most of all, for I left my shield with Arrea.

My gladius sang as I ripped it from the scabbard on my hip, the edge glistening in the evening sun.

The horse beneath me seemed to favor the left side of the path, and I chose not to fight her. She led the way, and the twins followed me.

The Paeligni warriors bared their yellow teeth. Booming, methodical war drums sounded from the mountains. The warriors ululated and raised their spears as they continued to flood down the mountain, like water over rock.

I was determined to reach the first one. I would spill first blood. A few were gathering near. Their hungry gaze cast on me.

They steadied themselves and balanced their spears above ox-hide shields, ready to strike.

I let out a war cry of my own, and rode toward them. Their jagged spear tips jabbed wildly at us, even from a distance. But I pushed on, determined to protect my men and my wife at all costs.

But I felt a tremor of fear ripple through the powerful frame of the horse beneath me. Her muscles tensed. She hadn't seen combat since Greece, and she wanted no part of it now.

She bucked, reared, and took flight, resisting and ignoring my commands. I tightened my grip on the reins, the most immediate battle now between man and beast. The world blurred around me. The battle began without me.

Once again, I had to decide. I released the reins and flew off her hindquarters, sword and all.

I landed hard. Mostly in the dirt, but a jagged rock clashed against my ribs. My breastplate bore most of the force, but I still found myself coughing.

Before I could grab my sword and scramble to my feet, Paeligni spearmen were above me.

"Protect the quaestor!" I heard someone shout.

One of the men above me raised his spear, preparing to plunge it into my heart. Before he could, a sword slashed through his neck. What remained dangled by a few tendons as he collapsed beside me, Spurius on the horse behind him with blood dripping from his sword.

My fingers fumbled through the dirt until I found my sword. I lifted it just in time to deflect a spear. I kicked the assailant and swung to my feet.

Another Paeligni was attacking from my right. I feigned to the side and grabbed the thrusting weapon. I wrenched it away as I brought the sword down on his arm, severing it before the wrist.

With a scream he fell back. I thrust my sword through his exposed belly, pushing forward until the hilt reached his navel.

I turned to face two more warriors racing toward me, but a powerful force propelled me back. It was my *primus pilus*, who'd hauled me back into his formation.

The legionaries opened ranks and allowed me to enter. I heard the scream of a dying horse. To my relief, Spurius and Aulus rushed into the ranks beside me. Dismounted, but otherwise unharmed.

Rocks continued to tumble down the cliff. It sounded like the mountains were whispering, speaking to us, warning us. We should never have come here.

I stole a glance at the silent carriage where my wife, dearest friend, and dog were now hiding. The warriors had so far ignored them, but I needed to end this before that changed.

"Send a message to all Italia!" I shouted. "Hold your ground!"

The traitors crashed into our shield wall. They did not fight like us, in formed lines. They fought man to man. Sword against spear and with no apparent instinct for self-preservation.

I braced against the shields before me. Thrusting my sword over them, I found the mark in between the ribs of an attacker. As soon as he fell, three more were there to replace him.

These legionaries under my command were some of the finest Rome had. The Paeligni didn't have the strength to break our shield wall. But we didn't have the numbers to repel them either.

This battle would wage on until long after the sun had completely set.

But suddenly the avalanche of spears against us stopped. The Paeligni backed away.

They slowly disappeared into the mountain paths they'd come from, leaving their dead and dying behind.

We hadn't defeated them. They were simply saving the battle for another day. They'd made their allegiances known. The Paeligni were joining the rebellion.

Some of my men lost their composure. "Where are they going?"

"Is the battle over?"

"Silence," the centurion commanded, and looked to me at the center of formation for orders.

I didn't have answers to any of their questions, but I knew one thing for certain. We needed to get over the mountain. Fast.

"Double time, march!" I shouted.

The men, breathless and trembling though they were, joyfully complied.

Before we made it very far, one of the Paeligni warriors

shouted, in crisp, clear Latin, "We will see you again, Romans. Hear our drums and fear our coming."

SCROLL VI

QUINTUS SERTORIUS—TWO Days after the Ides of March, 664 Ab Urbe Condita

The color of our scarlet tunics and cloaks was barely discernible by the time we reached the other side of the mountains the next morning. Hard marching left us caked in soot.

Unlike the Paeligni, I refused to leave behind my dead. We passed along the fallen from man to man so that each might share this burden until we arrived and could bury them.

The horses drawing Arrea's carriage somehow freed themselves during the tumult on the mountain. We tracked down a single horse, so Arrea alone remained mounted as we continued our journey.

Apollonius joined us on foot. He was no young man, but he bore the journey and his creaking bones with the dignity I'd grown to expect of him.

Pollux was inconsolable, refusing to take another step. I ordered a legionary to carry him, but Pollux refused to be held by anyone but myself. Rather than riding into Mutina on a steed with the glory and dignity of a Roman commander, I marched with mud on my sandals and a dog in my arms.

The city of Mutina loomed in the distance, its walls high and powerful. We continued our march toward it, but it seemed to draw no closer.

Ancient cypress trees flanked the stone road to the city gates. Fortunately, there was an open glade off to the side, surrounded by peach trees. It was here that I ordered the men to form up. I ordered the centurion to form up the men and tally our losses. I convened with my allies while awaiting his report.

Pollux was—mercifully for my arms—willing to take a few steps on his own, clearly invigorated by the prospects of leaving his scent on so many trees.

Apollonius looked haggard, older than he'd ever appeared before. He was still breathing heavily, dirt and spittle clinging to his beard.

None of us really knew what to say.

"Are you well?" I asked Arrea.

She nodded and smiled. She was the least disturbed of us all. She'd had a horse for the last several hours of our march while we remained on foot, but I doubted that was why.

Aulus sighed. "I'm fine, too, thanks for asking," he said. "Think they have good wine in Mutina?"

"It's famous across Italy from what I understand," Spurius said.

I ignored them. Arrea distracted me. Her hair was windswept and wild, her skin sunburned and wind-bitten. I found her no less beautiful than when she was dressed up. In fact, it reminded me of how she appeared when I first met her in Gaul. Still, the responsibility for her comfort weighed heavily on me.

"When we get in the city, we'll find you somewhere to take a hot bath," I said. "And I'll buy you the best dress in the city."

She laughed, a joyful sound I hadn't expected. "I may be a

quaestor's wife now, but I was a slave for twenty years," she said. "I'm fine."

The twins shuffled and looked away, but Arrea wasn't uncomfortable speaking of her past.

"Tribune . . ." came a voice from behind me. "Apologies. Quaestor, the men are assembled."

The centurion approached, formal and rigid in his stance and salute.

"Very well, centurion. Your name is Leptis, is that correct?"

"Aye, Quaestor."

Years of legionary life tanned and toughened the centurion's face like old leather. Deep lines etched their paths across his dark skin, rivulets carved by a lifetime of toil. Thick black hair covered the flesh of his arms except where bulging pink scars remained. Crisscrossing his skin like a map of his service, these scars carried with them a story of many battles won and lost. His nose was bulbous and crooked like an old boxer's, and I imagined there was a tale or two there as well.

We had interacted little during the Greek campaign, but his reputation for bravery was widespread.

"What's the count?" I asked.

"Eleven dead. Six with grievous injuries, the rest are minor. Two missing. No one saw them leave. They were with us until the mountains. Whether they are lost or absconded isn't clear yet."

I said, "Either way, we'll find out. We'll send out scouts to survey the mountains when we're certain the Paeligni have departed."

The centurion's eye twitched. "Are we certain that's wise, Quaestor?" He remained rigidly at attention.

"At ease," I said. "The Paeligni needed to display their loyalty to the rebel cause. I shouldn't think they will disrupt a few scouts collecting those left behind. We do not leave Romans behind."

The centurion pursed his lips and nodded but fiddled with

his necklace. He wasn't the type to disagree with an officer, but it was clear he wanted to.

"I can't help but notice your sense of fashion, centurion," Aulus said, pointing to Leptis's phallic necklace.

I noticed then that he wore a phallic ring as well. This wasn't uncommon, of course, but Aulus wasn't the type to fail mentioning it.

"They help ward off the Evil Eye," Leptis said. He exhaled hard through his nose, but it came out as a whistle.

"Perhaps we could avoid battle entirely if we all draped ourselves in penises," Aulus suggested.

The centurion's jaw flexed. "Your callous attitude discredits you, sir. They retreated, didn't they?" he said. "It's that sort of disrespect that brought us to this sad pass."

Aulus puckered his lips and looked inquisitive. "I thought it was refusing Italian citizenship that 'brought us to this sad pass'?"

I waved for Aulus to cease his antics. "Centurion, look at me. I can't say what or who caused all this. I can't say what caused the Paeligni to retreat. But when you address the men, I need you to convey confidence and strength."

The *primus pilus* lifted his chin. "Always, Quaestor."

"I'll address the men if you're ready."

He gave a final, informal nod and returned to the unflinching, rigid posture expected of a centurion.

"Officers afoot!" He bellowed at the cohort.

They stomped their right foot to acknowledge their readiness.

I gave Arrea's hand a gentle squeeze before moving to the front of formation. "Legionaries of Rome, we traveled from Rome to Athens once. We were nearly shipwrecked. Fought in pitched battles and held our own in ambushes. Some of you may have helped me defend the Acropolis from an army of traitors," I said. I allowed a smile to crease my lips. "This all might have been a stroll through the Bay of Naples, no?"

Their laughter rang out through the peach orchard.

"Our new task is no less important. Different, yes. But no less important. Enemies of Rome and all we stand for are at our very doorstep."

I thought I heard a scoff behind me, but continued.

"Rome needs fighting men. If the senate could spawn more of you, they would. Unfortunately, most of your sons are in Greece, and aren't yet old enough to wield a sword!"

They laughed harder now, basking in their first taste of relief since we reached the mountain pass.

"Mutina has been loyal to us. Even as our supposed allies gather in droves to betray us, they remain loyal," I said and prayed it was true. "We will be raising and training troops here. Men will come from miles and miles away to join us. They will want to be heroes of the republic, like you."

They lifted their chins a little higher and straightened their sagging shoulders. We all still looked like ox shit, but some of the Roman Triumph pride was returning to them.

"We will be forming two legions. And you, you will be serving as the First Cohort!" They cheered, relishing both their chance for glory and increased pay. "I need you to be ideal Romans. Show them loyalty. Show them discipline. That is all I ask of you. That, and don't sleep with any of Mutina's daughters."

They groaned as I expected.

"Serve well, and you'll be given leave to enjoy the venereal brothels. But before anything else, we lost eleven good men today," I said. "We must see these faithful sons of Rome to the afterlife properly. Your first task today is to gather wood for their pyres."

Even after the long, arduous days behind us, they stamped their feet to show they would do so happily.

I said, "Afterward, we build a fort."

They deflated at the prospect of several more hours of work before we could rest.

Gaius Marius once taught me that simple acts of discipline can be a vital reprieve for the men when things get hard, one of the many leadership lessons I obtained from him.

Perhaps one day they would thank me.

"Come on, men. I will work alongside you," I said.

Primus pilus Leptis ordered the men to fall out, and I joined them in the gathering of wood.

It's remarkable how much is required to properly cremate eleven men. These orchards would be barren by the end of the war.

SCROLL VII

Quintus Sertorius—Five days before the Ides of April, 664 Ab Urbe Condita

The first three weeks of any military command can be a strenuous one. The foundations needed to be laid, not just for a legionary fort but for logistics, command structure, and the training regimen. Tribal elders needed to be addressed, their thoughts heard. Relationships needed to be established with local leaders, from important priests to wealthy merchants. We would come to rely on all of them before our time in Mutina was over.

But on the twenty-fourth day, I stole a few moments for myself. The peach orchard was inviting, not just for the sweetness of its fruit but for the silence of its seclusion. It was here I found rest.

I rested against the sturdy trunk of a tree, the sweet scent of the peaches mingling with the earth aroma of the surrounding soil. The vibrant hues of pink and white petals against the azure sky were more beautiful than any mosaic I'd ever seen in Rome.

If I allowed myself, I might have been able to forget about the war effort and hungry legionaries for but a moment. Unfortunately, as most soldiers can attest, the quiet moments are often the most troubling ones.

My mind turned to Gavius, and I imagined what he was doing in Sulla's camp. I hoped he was well. I prayed he was safe. Unafraid. I fought with myself about whether Sulla was reckless enough to put him in danger. I never came to a satisfying answer.

I attempted to turn my mind to other things. My father's philosophy, perhaps, or mother's new horses she'd written me about. No use.

Sighing and stretching my legs out in the dirt, I retrieved the parchment from the leather capsule on my hip. It was a delicate roll of papyrus, a gift from one of Mutina's merchants who hoped our legionaries' propensity for spending would make him rich. It was more expensive than I would ever use for military missives, but it was perfect for a letter to my son.

I brandished a stylus and dipped it in ink. With the sharp tip poised above the delicate paper, I knew I must be as careful with my words as with the force of my hand.

Gavius,

My boy, how I've missed you. Not just since I arrived in Rome but all these years. Sometimes I still think of you as the boy who waved as I sailed away. I know you are grown. A man by all accounts. I wonder what you are like, who in our family you might favor. Do you still have those dark curls? I lost mine when I was about your age.

These are just a few of the questions that wake me up at night. There are many others. I wonder what kind of man you've become. What makes you laugh, what makes you angry, what makes tears well up in your eyes.

I long for our reunion. To see all this with my own eye (I only have the one if you remember). I intend to make this reunion happen as soon as possible.

If I could, I would be there already. I've been elected as quaestor, despite not offering myself for the position. The senate has sent me to Mutina to levy troops. It is no easy task. Our supply lines are inadequate, and the people are restless. Fearful of the rebels and us. One wrong move and I could end up recruiting for the enemy. So, I am forced to remain here until our grain supply is better established and our presence in the north is solidified.

But rest assured—the moment I am able—I will be there. At your camp.

In the meantime, I will continue serving the Republic, as you are. If you can believe it, Arrea has joined me on this campaign. For her own safety, she is staying in the city with a wealthy family. You know her— she would rather be out here with me, in the mud. But every time I visit, she speaks of you. Of how she misses you and wishes you were here with us.

We both do.

Please write to me soon, as your duties allow. Answer all my questions, or none of them. I simply look forward to seeing that your handwriting has improved since I last saw you.

I miss you, my son.

Roma Invicta
Your Father

The soft light of early evening filtered through the canopy above, casting dappled patterns upon the papyrus, as if Gaia herself bore witness to the weight of my parental love and my apprehension.

For I wanted to say much more. I wanted to tell him that Lucius Cornelius Sulla was a snake. He was using him, as he did everyone else, for his own ends. But to do so could have placed him in more danger. I refused to do that.

Satisfied with the letter, I sealed it in the leather capsule and stood. Disinterested in sitting with my thoughts any longer, I made back for camp, stopping only to hand off the letter to my finest envoy.

"Take the safest road. Haste is not the object, but arrival," I told him.

"Understood, Quaestor." He saluted and spun on his heels, his scarlet cape fluttering behind him as he departed.

I returned to my praetorium—the commander's tent at the center of a legionary fort—where the Insteius twins, Apollonius, and the first spear centurion were waiting on me.

I'd spent countless hours in commanders' tents throughout my time in the legion. Now I had my own. It wasn't as orderly as I'd like. Our current situation didn't afford us that. There were half-finished pila in a pile by the tent-flap entrance, and a mound of unpolished helmets littering the foot of my oak desk. On top, endless piles of parchment were stacked as high as a forum arch.

I took my seat behind the desk, lit a fallow candle, and accepted a handful of scrolls from *primus pilus* Leptis.

I'd been an officer for most of my time in the legion. Clerical work came with the role. But nothing could have prepared me for the sheer amount of documentation required of a quaestor in command of a small territory.

"2,641 recruited as of this morning," centurion Leptis said.

Spurius said, "*Gerrae*! How many? That doesn't seem possible."

"We've turned down several hundred more," he said. "I've never seen the registrars so busy."

Aulus plopped down on the corner of my desk. "Perhaps we need to improve our standards for entry." He nibbled at the nub of a peach seed, and I wondered when he'd found the time to pluck it.

Leptis's leathery skin wrinkled when Aulus spoke. It was clear he was still bristling over the comments about his phallic jewelry.

"It's all in the documentation. They've met and exceeded

every standard the Republic holds. We've even had thirty head of cavalry join, each man landed and literate."

I looked over the list provided to me:

A. Plautius
   Good manners
   Healthy teeth
   5.8 feet fall

Not literate
   Small hands

                                                        Enlisted

Q. Mascius
   Strong physique
   Throws pila well
   5.10 feet fall

Stutters
   Poor marching

                                                        Enlisted

Mam. Laelius
   Prior service
   Good sense of humor
   5.7 feet tall

. . .

Bad teeth
   Not literate

                                                        Enlisted

Spurius looked over my shoulder and must have noticed what I did. "Sense of humor is something worth noting?"

"Look around you," the centurion said. "Life has presented us with little to laugh about in the three weeks we've been here. If a man is resilient enough to keep smiling now, he'll have what it takes to make it through a campaign. I'd know. I've been on thirteen."

"How many of these are enlisting as legionaries and how many as auxiliaries?"

"341 legionaries," the centurion said, pleased with his own recollection. "The rest aren't citizens. Most of the recruits have been refugees from around Italy."

"At least they're inclined to fight well. They stand the most to lose from rampaging rebels," Apollonius said from the far corner of the praetorium, almost to himself as he was still diligently pouring over the documents in his lap.

Spurius crossed his arms. "I think we all stand to lose a great deal."

"The goal is two Roman legions and one auxiliary legion," I said. "15,000 men. 2,600 is a good start. The question is, how are we going to feed them all?" I said. "Has the grain supply arrived from Rome?"

Primus pilus Leptis frowned. "No, Quaestor. The envoy said they left two weeks ago. They could be running late, or . . ."

"Or the Paeligni captured them," I said.

Spurius shook his head. "How could the senate be so foolish?

We reported the ambush immediately. And they proceed to send our supplies via the same route?"

Leptis swallowed. "And with only thirty armed guards."

"Men in togas should have no place conducting wartime logistics," I said. "But that isn't within our control to change. We can only focus on what to do now. How can we feed these recruits until we receive a new shipment?"

Leptis slid a second scroll across my desk.

Tunics from Sardinia – 406
    Wheat – 316 libra
    Vinegar – 60 urna
    Wine – 20 urna
    Salt – 21 barrels
    Hard fodder – 80 libra
    Soft fodder – 67 libra

Aulus crossed his arms. "Centurion, I must ask. Can you really breathe out of that nose of yours?"

Leptis snorted, but again it came out as a whistle. "As well as the next man."

I slapped my desk. "Give me a moment's silence, for Hermes's sake."

Wheat – 211 libra
    Vinegar – 21 urna
    Salt – 16 barrels
    Posca – 56 urna
    Soft fodder – 14 libra

. . .

I exhaled and looked up. "We may be able to feed the men we have right now. But I can't see how we can afford to bring on another recruit without someone going hungry." I continued to knead my temples, the headache growing worse.

Aulus sighed. "If we aren't recruiting, we might as well leave. It's our entire purpose here."

I said, "We aren't going anywhere, and of course we'll keep recruiting. We just need to find more grain. I'll write to Rome and—"

Spurius grunted. "How will Rome send us grain? By what route?" he said. "The Paeligni will grow fat on our supplies by the end of this war."

"We have no choice but to try. Maybe the senate can order the governor of Cisalpine Gaul to send a shipment our way," I said.

Leptis placed his hands on my desk. "Quaestor, we've also just received a large shipment that isn't on that manifest." He smiled, as if he'd rolled a 'Venus' in a dice game of *Tessera* none of us had expected. "Thirty head of donkeys, two full carts of grain, a month's supply of salt, and vinegar enough to last an entire legion two weeks."

I exhaled. "I'm relieved to hear. Where is this shipment?"

"Arriving at the west gate as we speak. Everything was being tallied and recorded when I came to report, Quaestor."

"That reminds me," I said. "I am going to place Apollonius as our head of supply moving forward."

Everyone stared at me like I'd gone mad. Important positions like this were to be given out to the sons of senators, a favor one could collect on when needed. Not for freedmen or good friends.

Apollonius himself was just as surprised. He said nothing but peered into me, searching for my intentions.

Leptis balked. "I mean no offense, sir. But is he even a Roman citizen?"

I met the centurion's gaze. "He is. His name is Apollonius Sertorius by law, and he is as much a Roman citizen as you or I. He's twice as educated as any man in the legion. He understands mathematics and arithmetic better than any two of us put together."

The *primus pilus* leaned closer. "But is he loyal?"

"Have you ever been a slave, centurion?" Apollonius said coolly.

"Of course not."

"Well, if you had been, and you tasted freedom again only because of one man and one republic, the one thing you'd never question is your loyalty."

"I meant no disrespect . . ."

"None taken." Apollonius returned to his documents.

Leptis's old eyes looked genuinely contrite. "Well, sir, if you'd like, I'll show you to the arriving shipment. I'll give you the new manifest directly."

Apollonius stood, slower than he once did. "Lead the way," he said, friendly as could be, as if he hadn't been insulted.

I followed along as well, hoping to enjoy more time in the sun before it faded for the evening. I nodded for the twins to join us as well, which they did, but not without an amphora of wine in Aulus's grasp.

As we walked, I took a moment to admire the camp my legionaries had constructed. Tents, arrayed in perfect rows, formed a labyrinth of canvas and wooden frames, their simple yet sturdy structure a testament to the resourceful nature of the Roman legion.

"Centurion, you've done a fine job with the recruits thus far," I said. "If we can raise fifteen thousand men like these, the rebels have a better chance of escaping Tartarus than defeating us."

The unmistakable scent of fresh leather, mingling with the porridge cooking between each block of tents, created an aroma that felt as much like home to me as any domus in which I'd ever laid my head.

"I'm quite proud of them, Quaestor," Leptis said. "Perhaps I've just gone soft with age. For whatever reason, I find myself actually caring for these bands of *balatrones*."

Here and there, groups of half-armored men sparred with wooden swords. Nominally, they practiced that day's training. In reality, they were fighting boredom and enjoying themselves.

Their laughter reminded me of a time when I was a mule like them rather than an officer. I hoped Gavius was making memories like this.

Apollonius's steady voice cut through my reflections, "Centurion, what would be burning near the west gate?"

We looked where he was pointing. Smoke billowed up over the crenellated battlements.

It was then we heard the clang of swords, and it wasn't legionaries sparring.

The centurion was the first to take off in a sprint, surprisingly agile for his age and size. We hurried after him.

Noxious fumes poured in through the western gate. We passed through them.

On the other side, I could see men fighting in the smoke.

I drew my sword. "Sound the alarm!"

Spurius shouted and word traveled back until trumpets blared from the fort walls.

Fear or duty compelled me forward. I didn't know what we were facing.

Pockets of men were fighting to the death, but both sides of combatants looked like legionaries under my command.

"Stop this at once!" Centurion bellowed, but I think he realized as quickly as I had that this was not the simple scrapping of a few legionaries. This was an attack.

I tripped over something and nearly lost my footing. Looking down, I saw it was a donkey. Its head was severed, and warm blood spurted out from the wound.

A careful glance around revealed several other slain pack animals, some still braying violently with a leg missing or an arrow in their haunches.

"Flee back to Rome you dogs!" someone shouted.

I turned to the voice but saw instead a cloaked legionary with a dagger raised over his head. I extended my sword, but the dagger sliced through my arm. I felt nothing but a searing heat as I stabbed back at him. Beneath his cloak was the chainmail of the Roman legion. He stepped back, the wind driven from his lungs, but he was uninjured. When he charged me again, I kicked him in the knee. He buckled, and I thrust my sword into the exposed flesh of his neck.

"Protect the quaestor!" someone shouted. I think it was Spurius.

"No, protect the grain. The grain!" I said, just then realizing what was happening.

The attackers were scurrying off. I never knew for certain how many of them there were, but it wasn't many. They weren't trying to defeat us. The cutthroats had achieved whatever they sought to achieve.

"Hunt them down!" I shouted.

"Every last one of them!" Spurius added.

I turned.

Burning. Two full wagons filled to the brim with life-sustaining grain.

Legionaries rushed to fill their helmets with water or fan the flames with their cloaks.

It was no use.

"Who is responsible for this?" Leptis shouted, something in his voice revealing he still couldn't comprehend what he was seeing.

Only one legionary ran up to answer. "They acted fast. Two dozen or more."

"Why did they wear our armor?" the centurion asked.

"Perhaps they stole it, centurion?"

I knew already this wasn't true. I stumbled through the smoke until I found the man I'd slain.

His lips were still twitching, and I hoped he was still alive. But there was nothing in his eyes but a dim and fading light.

I searched through him as a final rattle escaped his chest. Within a leather satchel on his hip, I found two documents.

Straining through the smoke, I determined the first was a letter. Written, I believed, to a woman he loved. I chose not to read it. The other was a military diploma. I could recognize it anywhere.

I'd composed several just like this.

The scroll listed his name, the names of his parents, and the dates of his service. He'd served two years in Gaul during the wars against the Cimbri and Teutones. He fought in the battle of Vercellae, as I had. There were a few notes in hastily scribbled Latin about a few acts of bravery throughout his time in the auxiliary.

At the bottom there was the seal of approval from someone with Imperator's authority.

Spurius crouched beside me. "What did you find?"

My voice was weak. "He was a Roman citizen."

I passed him the document but couldn't clear its contents from my mind.

Apollonius, a cloth raised to cover his mouth and nose, said, "Sertorius, there is something I think you should see."

He pointed toward one of the burning wagons. Beneath the billowing flames, the words *"Filii Remi"* were scrawled. It was impossible to tell for certain, but it was the same color and texture as the blood of the fallen pack animals.

His voice was as heavy as the smoke. "Does this mean anything to you?"

"Sons of Remus," I said. "Remus was the brother of Romulus. His brother murdered him. History has forgotten Remus, while Rome venerated Romulus as our first king and as a god."

He needed no clarification. We both understood what this meant.

"Centurion!" I shouted. "Send out riders. I want every perpetrator captured. Search the bodies of the dead. I want to know who organized these 'Sons of Remus'."

"Understood, Quaestor," he said, finally accepting what happened.

Apollonius and I stood in silence and watched half our grain supply and livestock disappear in the flames. In the fort behind us, more than two thousand hungry men waited to be fed, and ultimately, it was my duty to ensure they were.

SCROLL VIII

ARREA—THREE DAYS before the Ides of April, 664 Ab Urbe Condita

> I might have written sooner if I'd known how, but I never learned until my husband was away fighting in Greece. Writing was one of the many things I learned how to do during that time.

I taught myself the basics of weaving so I might fit in with the pleasant society of other Roman wives. I toiled endlessly with plucking a harp, but eventually abandoned it, cursing my callused fingers as the cause. I eavesdropped on Gavius' lessons with his tutor, and thereafter considered myself well-versed in arithmetic and astronomy, although I knew that was far from the case.

While the air in Rome was fetid and sweltering, we stayed with my mother-in-law, Rhea. Nursia, my husband's birthplace, was cool and crisp by contrast. She taught me the basics of caring for a horse, how to birth a foal, how to break them into submission without losing your teeth in the process.

It was a shame I could put so little of this to use now, in Mutina. Quintus said I could accompany him on his recruiting campaign in the north, but he felt as distant as before. He said the safest place for me was within the high, fortified walls of Mutina itself rather than his legionary camp. The men were prone to drunkenness when there was no battle on the horizon, and there was always the threat of rebel activity, he said. I obeyed like a dutiful wife and stayed within the domus of a local official and his wife.

Theirs was an impressive home, larger than most that could fit within Rome. Some might say the tastes were gaudy, with more statues and Greek mosaics than were necessary, but I'm told provincials with more money than power or children often acquired and hoarded such things.

They gave me free access to their home, apart from the men's quarters, but I generally kept to the guest room assigned to me. There was a feather mattress on a raised bed of woven metal, and a household altar in the corner by a bronze mirror. The altar was all I truly needed, though. I spent much of my time there in prayer. I spoke most often to my own gods but never forgot to offer sacrifices to the Roman ones on Quintus's behalf. From time to time, I even said a prayer to the one God Apollonius worshipped, although I did not know His name and wondered if such a God would listen to a foreigner like me.

My heart gladdened to be nearer to my husband, and I much preferred it to staying in Rome without him or Gavius, but sometimes it felt more like a prison than a home. Boredom was something life never afforded me, either as a slave or a Roman matron, but I experienced it now seven-fold. I idled my time away with my newly developed skill of reading.

I borrowed a book called *On Agriculture* from my host. Some venerated old Roman named Cato wrote it over a hundred years before. Whenever someone would find me reading it, they'd grin and say *"Carthago delenda est,"* but I never knew why.

Dreams of a different life haunted me when I read that old tome. A fantasy. Moving somewhere to the hills, to farm and live off the land like my ancestors had. Neither Quintus nor I knew anything about agriculture, but we could learn it as well as I'd learned to read and write, I supposed. Cato was teaching me how to harvest crops, raise chickens, and care for goats. We could do that, my Quintus and I. Away from war, away from the constant distance, in space and in our hearts.

But I never uttered a word of it. I'd married a fighting man, and I would uphold that vow no matter what. I reminded myself that Rome needed him.

He came to see me when his responsibilities allowed it. But after the burning of his supplies, he placed the legion on high alert. His presence was required most hours of the day. He made light of this attack, to me at least, but I knew him well. The etches of concern and sleepless nights lined his face before my eyes.

When he could visit, he would stay for dinner, perhaps long enough to make love, but not much longer.

After such a time, he once said, "Your heart

doesn't stir the way it used to. Your lips don't kiss the way they used to."

I sat up in my rented bed and pulled the sheets to my breast. "Have you ever made love to a stranger?"

He fastened on his helm, the signal he was preparing for departure. "That's a dangerous question to ask your husband." He attempted levity, but I was unamused.

Besides, I knew he hadn't. But it's how I felt now. I still loved that man, the one deep within, but everything about him was different now. And the chasm of time and space between us dulled my heart's beat to a slow thud. It protected me while I was gone. It hindered me now that he had returned.

"I could send for you tomorrow if you'd like," he said. "You can ride through camp and see how the men are coming along."

"If you'd like." I didn't bother to add I'd happily go anywhere outside of that domus.

He kissed me on my head and lingered then. "Our time will not be long here. By the time the first snow of winter arrives, we will be home," he said.

I'd trusted every word Quintus Sertorius had uttered to me since the moment he stumbled, bloody and injured, into my master's hut in the village the Romans called "Burdigala." But I couldn't believe these, even if he meant them.

Apollonius visited as well, but with less and less frequency. There was an uncommon burden in his gray eyes. Even when he was a *servus*, they always shimmered with life, imagination, and curiosity. Not so now.

We sat in the domus garden and chatted quietly so as not to disturb my hosts.

"I once translated the entire Torah, my dear Arrea, and now I can hardly remember its contents," he said.

"Is that like the Sibylline book the Romans seek for prophecy?"

He smiled. "Something like that. It is a book of laws, of promises . . . and yes, of prophecy."

"It must have been quite a feat to translate the entire text. I imagine it was long to contain all that," I said.

His smile faded. "I assume most of my fellows would consider me an apostate now. Perhaps they always would've, with a Greek father, and not a very good one at that."

I took his hands and peered into his eyes, wondering what was causing such consternation. "A man as good as you could never been considered . . . that word," I said. "Perhaps you could start taking that rest day, the way you used to?"

"The sabbath." He nodded, sighed, and shook his head. "There's too much work to be done now. Perhaps as much as this old man can handle."

The birds twittered and bathed in a fountain at the center of the garden.

"Can I help? Is there something I can take from your shoulders?"

He patted my knee. "No, my dear. These are my burdens to bear. But your enthusiasm and willingness to help gives this old heart some joy yet."

He left then and came less often afterward.

In my solitude, I thought of Gavius often. Was he safe, well-fed, shaving often enough? Did he keep himself warm and dry, or was he still running around in the rain with his mouth open to catch a few drops, nothing but a sopping tunic on his back?

I offered thanks he was with Sulla. Despite the misunderstandings or differences between him and my husband, Sulla had been good to us, and Gavius in particular. Perhaps at times he was want of proper boundaries, but I took it as his jovial and warm nature. He'd been a great comfort to us both while Quintus was fighting in Greece and even protected our home with armed men when there were riots in the city.

But just as kind and charitable as he'd been with us in the city, I knew from his reputation he would be fierce and protective in battle. He would look after Gavius and see him safely home.

The only thing to distract me from my reading and brooding thoughts, aside from the infrequent visits of Quintus and Apollonius, were my gracious hosts.

They were kind enough to invite me to dine with them in the evenings, and although I took little joy in their company, I couldn't bring myself to refuse.

Flickering candelabra illuminated their triclinium, the Roman dining room. The pungent aroma of exotic spices lingered in the air with the scent of roasted dormice and baked cheese. Cooks prepared fresh *garum*, a fish sauce the Romans loved—and I detested—and brought us each a dish of our own.

Silk draperies caressed marble pillars rising to meet a ceiling painted with stories of the Roman gods. Statues of long-dead but ornately carved men lined the perimeter. Richly clad *servi* were spread around the room, waiting as silently as the statues for their next orders.

The husband, an old codger by the apt name of Tranquillus, was a dull man with poor table manners and even coarser words. Fortunately, he rarely offered them. Instead, he smacked his gums as he chewed *garum*-slathered bread, never pausing to swallow before taking his next bite. Blood-red wine dripped over his chin until he'd belch and wipe it on his sleeve.

His wife, Tullia, was a third of his age and as opposite as a woman can be from her husband. She was barely older than Gavius, delicate and pink like a chrysanthemum. She was brimming with excitement and life, and not just from within her pregnant belly. Still, she was little better company while her husband was present.

Eventually, he would rise without comment and waddle off toward his bed, which he took to early on account of the unwatered wine he drank.

Then, his young bride would come alive. "Tell me about your husband." She bristled and sat up on the edge of her couch. "He's quite a striking man, if you don't mind my saying." She had a habit of talking until I stopped her. "Some might consider his missing eye a mar on his appearance, but I think it's rather mysterious and adventurous."

She'd seen the eyepatch Quintus wore, but not what was underneath. But then again, he rarely let me see either. Oh, how I longed to see him in his complexity, his brokenness, his fullness. But he slept with his wound concealed. He bathed and made love with that leather eyepatch too. He was cautious, lest his mutilation be seen fully, but it was part of what made him, and the quick glimpses I received neither repulsed nor shamed me. Rather, it made me eternally grateful he'd lived to return to me at all.

I didn't begrudge him this, though. My scars were of the internal kind rather than of the flesh, but I understood the desire for concealment.

She said, "He must be a rugged lover, like a wild animal."

I sipped my willow water and forced a smile. "Quintus is a good man. Better in his heart than appearance, even."

"But surely it must be thrilling to be with such a . . ."

"Perhaps at first. His strength comforted me. It still does when he is around to offer it."

She continued to watch me, waiting for more. "You can speak plainly," she said. "No men are around to overhear." Her eyes shimmered with furtive delight.

I glanced at the two male *servi* standing behind her with ostrich-feathered fans in hand, cooling her off despite the pleasant temperature of the room.

"Oh, don't mind them. They're just *servi*." She clapped her hands together in a demand for more.

I wondered what she would think about sitting across from a freed slave. Would she respect me at all? Care for my conversation any longer? I doubted it. Most Roman ladies wouldn't.

My Quintus said nothing of it, though. Perhaps his senatorial colleagues laughed about it behind his back, but he showed no signs of regret or embarrassment at having married his freed *servus*. My heart warmed at the thought, remembering how he proposed to me and how he kissed me when he said his vows "when and where you are Gaia, I then and there, will be Gaius."

"Is he good to you, at least?" She tired of waiting. "A man such as that might be the sort to beat his wife regular."

"He's never laid a hand on me," I said. "Another might've, with the way I'm apt to talk."

Her eyes downcast by my answer, perhaps thrilled by the thought and attaching some form of romance or eroticism to the act of violence.

"I should like to get a beating from time to time, if only it meant my husband would pay me attention," she said, almost to herself.

I'd been beaten by men enough to know she was a fool.

"Not with that wee one inside you," I said.

Tullia smiled and cradled her belly. "It'll be a boy. This is my first, so some say I can't tell, but the priests confirmed it, and the soothsayers too."

She ran her hands over the developing mound.

I felt compelled to move beside her. Perhaps it was envy that drove me.

I'd but once felt a child within me, and when my master found out, he took measures to eradicate the child. I nearly lost my life as a result, and I was spared no work while mending.

When he sold me a few years later, my next owner wasted no time trying to impregnate me. The cheapest way to acquire a *servus* was to have one already owned rear one, he said. He failed in his task, and I knew my former master and his deeds had cursed my womb.

I cast the thought from my mind. "Can you feel him move?" I asked.

From time to time, I could still feel the shadow of a foot with little toes pressing inside me, a ghost of the child I never knew.

"The flutters started earlier than most. That's how I know he's a boy. Wake up little fellow," she whispered to her belly and the child within. "He's usually quite active after we sup."

She took my hands in her own. They were soft as flower petals and unmarred by hard labor. I wondered if the calluses of my own would reveal the nature of my past, but she paid them no mind. She placed them on her swollen belly.

The child did not kick, but I could feel it pulsing within. I closed my eyes and promised not to shed a tear before Tullia or anyone else.

Her marriage to old Tranquillus was unnatural. She should be married to someone like my Quintus. She was young, beautiful, and likely from a good family. Brimming with vitality and life. She could bear him a child. He should have married a girl like her.

I gasped when a little foot raised up to greet me, rolling over its mother's belly. "I believe you have it right," I said. "Perhaps it will be a boy, a strong man like his father."

Her lips pursed now, but she soon turned her attention back to the baby and began whispering a Roman's song to it.

I returned to my couch and pretended to pick from the remainder of my roasted dormice and baked cheese.

My heart desired a child, but it also swelled and beat when I thought of the son I'd raised, Gavius. He was not mine by flesh or blood, but I'd reared him like any mother, and I loved him like I imagined I would love my own.

And now he was off with Sulla in the south,

training to be a warrior like his father. I thought of him often, but especially now, as I was painfully reminded—I would have no child other than him.

SCROLL IX

GAVIUS SERTORIUS—IDES of May, 664 Ab Urbe Condita

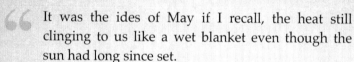

It was the ides of May if I recall, the heat still clinging to us like a wet blanket even though the sun had long since set.

Over the past month, tribe after tribe of Italian allies declared war against us. Some did so because they desired rights and freedoms that had been unavailable to them since Rome took control of Italy. Others desired power and entered war with a lustful eye to take Rome's place as conqueror and ruler of the Mediterranean. Some entered war because they sought to punish Rome for transgressions over the past half millennia. The Romans had abused and humiliated ancestors they never knew, and at last these descendants saw an opportunity to exact retribution. Others rebelled simply out of fear —being surrounded by these other rebelling tribes, they knew they'd be surrounded and destroyed unless they joined the cause.

SCROLL IX | 109

Even so, here we were, watching a play as if we were in the forum on a peaceful evening. Even with so many hostile tribes surrounding us in southern Italy, Sulla was determined to entertain his legionaries. It wasn't the quality one might find in Rome by any means, but the actors were passionate and dramatic, and Sulla believed the theater would raise morale.

"Did you drink much wine in Rome?" Sulla asked. I was seated in the chair just to his right, a position I regarded with great pride.

"As much as the next man," I said, deepening my voice as I often did in his presence. "Although my mother . . . Arrea, made sure it was well-watered."

A legionary fortress like ours had little room for this sort of activity, so legionaries were packed in like galley slaves before the hastily constructed wooden stage. The whole place reeked of sweat and flesh, but somehow the sweetness of Sulla's perfume rose above it all.

Sulla snapped his fingers for my cup to be filled. "This isn't of the quality you'll find in Rome, but I had this batch brought in from Nola, bottled in the year of Numidicus's consulship. The spice is adequate, and I won't measure how much water you include, so drink up." He winked.

The wine was thicker and stronger than any I'd tasted before, but I was determined not to reveal it. The spice settled on my tongue and made my eyes water. I was quick to blink it away.

"How about the theater?" he said, crossing his legs gingerly. "Did you visit the forum's productions often?"

I raised my voice over the laughter of the

legionaries. "No . . . well, not often. Sometimes I did." I wanted to say the right thing. "I never quite understand the humor."

A young man entered the stage to a cacophony of whistles and catcalls from the men. He wore a tall blonde wig and a dress as sheer as insect wings. Mercifully, he tucked his manhood between his thighs.

I attempted to continue the conversation as a convenient distraction to the lewd performer on stage. "My mother wasn't from Rome, and they didn't have plays where she was from."

Sulla laughed with the rest of the men, in utter delight.

I forced my attention back to the stage, and conjured a laugh of my own, although I did not understand the scenario of prostitute and Roman consul being played out on stage.

Sulla wiped a tear from his eye and leaned closer to me. "This one here is an old friend. His name is Metrobius. Finest actor in Rome, and possibly the bravest as well since he and his cortege had to brave the Italian roads to get here."

Cicero, who'd been reading something silently in the chair to the right of me, leaned forward. "Is it not unwise to maintain friendships with actors?" He rubbed at the errant, wiry hairs on his chin. "You're a patrician after all."

The smile did not fade from Sulla's lips. "My dear Cicero, you'll someday find that politicians make for the most boring dinner guests. Not so with thespians."

I was inclined to agree with Cicero but couldn't help but admire and envy the way Sulla balked at social conventions, the *mos maiorum,* and the opinions of others. I could only dream of being so confident.

Tribune Lucullus—still in full fighting kit unlike the rest of us—stepped cautiously in front of us. "*Legate*, I apologize for interrupting—"

"Nonsense! Take off that turtle shell and join us." Sulla gestured to the open chair to his left.

Lucullus frowned. "I would, sir, but . . . we have a few individuals seeking an audience with you. They say it cannot wait."

Sulla's eyes flashed and his smile faded. "I'm not accustomed to being summoned, tribune."

Lucullus's jaw tightened. "With your permission, legate. I'll tell them to *ede faecam*."

Telling whoever it was to eat shit would have been a bold and potentially dangerous move, but I have no doubt tribune Lucullus would have done so if Sulla asked him too.

Whatever flashed over Sulla passed quickly. He smiled again, his dove-white teeth glowing like a fire in the stage-side torchlights. "Nonsense, I'm rather curious now." He stood and clapped Lucullus reassuringly on the back. Before he got very far, he turned to me. "Well, come on then. You need to see what excitement awaits when it's your turn to lead," he said. "Oh and bring the wine. These sorts of performances are also better enjoyed with something to drink."

I inflated like a bireme's sails with a good wind, pleased to be invited along and equally as happy to be away from the theater.

I intended to invite Cicero, but he said, "Enjoy yourself. Plato and I will be retiring to my quarters for some quieter reflection." He rolled up his scroll and gave me a nod as I departed.

Sulla didn't bother to put his legatus's regalia back on. Instead, he followed Lucullus in a simple white tunic and soldier's sandals. Might have mistaken him for a legionary, if not for the gravity of his presence.

The men waiting for us stood on the parade ground, which was still uneven from that day's battle drills. The sun was setting behind them, but already the pale white moon and thousands of tiny stars sprinkled the azure sky.

"*Ave*, legate," a centurion with a bovine face anxiously stepped forward and saluted.

Sulla's blonde brow raised. "*Salvete*, centurion. What seems to be the problem?"

I took note that Sulla didn't return the salute.

The centurion's eyes flickered about. "Right, I'll just get right on with it then."

I noticed the centurion's accent was rural and thick. He was likely from somewhere like the countryside we now occupied.

He reached back and pulled forward a young legionary with tightly trimmed auburn curls.

Sulla turned to us with a furtive grin, as if to suggest what was about to happen would be humorous indeed.

"This man, *decanus* by rank, has been . . . well, he's been . . ."

Sulla said, "Formulate your words like you're giving battle orders, centurion."

"He's been bedding other legionarii."

"One legionary," the *decanus* corrected with a snarl.

I realized then that his lip was split and a swollen bruise shadowed his right eye.

Sulla held back his cup of wine, and I stepped

forward to refill it. One of his *servi* came rushing from the shadows and beat me to it.

"Do you deny the claim, *decane*?" Sulla asked.

"I do not. But I have 'bedded' only one man." He lifted his shoulders, bracing for whatever punishment he might receive. "I love him."

The centurion scoffed and shook his head. "Legate, do not be swayed by his pathetic mewling. He's been filled with a lustful—"

Sulla snapped his fingers rapidly and the centurion fell silent. He drank deeply from his wine and took a moment to enjoy the silence. "What is it you desire, centurion?"

"Arbitration and a ruling."

"Forgive me if I'm wrong, but aren't matters of punishment squarely within your realm of authority as this man's centurion?" He pointed to the *decanus's* face. "I can see you've already begun deliberations."

"They are, sir. Indeed. But given the personal nature of the grievance, I thought it best to bring him to someone else."

Sulla let his head back and laughed.

The centurion bristled. Unused to being mocked like this, the veins on his head threatened to burst.

Sulla, holding his belly, said. "Are you in love with the same fellow?"

"Of course not!" The centurion shouted. "Uhh . . . sir."

"What makes it personal then?"

The centurion cleared his throat. "When I accosted him for his behavior, he said, verbatim, *'es mundus excrementi'*."

Sulla nearly spit out his wine.

"And are you?" Sulla said. "Are you a pile of shit?"

The centurion spluttered like he was choking on a bad oyster.

"Regardless," Sulla said, sobering. "You have broken the chain of command, I believe. Should you not have brought this very grievous situation to your first-spear centurion? Or the camp prefect after him?"

The centurion finally closed his jaw and nodded. "They were both indisposed . . . at your . . . theater."

Sulla turned his attention to the battered young man. "Tell me, lad, this love of yours is consensual?"

"Of course it is. We love each other."

"Will you fight harder with your love beside you?"

"I would destroy the entire rebel army to protect him."

Sulla nodded. "Good. You'll receive no punishment."

The centurion raised his voice now. "Legate, I remind you, it is against Roman law to—"

Sulla approached the man with both grace and purpose, like a lion in the arena. He buried a finger in the *lorica* protecting the centurion's chest. "Out there . . ." With his free hand, he pointed beyond the scope of our fortifications. "The law may say that. But here I am the law. You seem to forget that."

"You aren't even the commander of the southern armies! That's Lucius Caesar!"

Sulla shook his head. Somehow, he appeared to grow then, towering over the centurion and threatening to swallow him whole for his insolence.

"I am Caesar's legatus. And this is my camp. You are a centurion, so you cannot claim ignorance."

Only when the centurion lowered his gaze in surrender did Sulla step away. He tilted his head back and analyzed the stars with ease, his deliberations concluded.

After an awkward moment or two, the centurion and *decanus* saluted and turned to leave.

"Wait," Sulla said. "Centurions are *immunes*, are they not?"

Since joining the legion, I'd come to learn that the term meant any man of the legion who was exempt from partaking in physical labor. Centurions were obviously on that list.

The centurion's jaw dropped, already sensing what Sulla might say. "Of course, legate."

"Not tomorrow. When the sun rises, I want you digging battlements. Understood?"

The centurion eventually nodded.

"I need to hear you say it."

"Understood, legate."

Like a whipped dog, the centurion retreated toward his tent, in the opposite direction of Sulla's theater.

Sulla turned to us and finally allowed himself to laugh again, this time clapping his hands with delight.

"Infallible as always, legate," Lucullus said.

Sulla finished his wine and shrugged. "Yesterday or tomorrow, my ruling might have been entirely different." He came and placed a hand on both our shoulders. "But this should keep the officers in line for a while. Perhaps another time I'll have a legionary whipped and scourged for some minor offense to ensure their fidelity as well. The trick is, gentlemen, to keep them guessing."

"You have one more petitioner." Lucullus pointed.

Behind Sulla stood a single man in his mid-fifties, if I had to guess, but absent the careworn wrinkles of hardship, he appeared far younger. There wasn't a single sunspot on his alabaster skin. Gold rings adorned his soft hands. His wealth was apparent from the quality and color of his toga.

"Lucius Cluentius! You're alive!" Sulla threw out his arms and hurried to embrace the man.

I'd never met him before, but I recognized the name because I'd written reports on him at Sulla's dictation. He was the chief magistrate of Pompeii, a prosperous Italian city nearby. Thus far, he and his city had not openly declared which side of the war his people would support.

Cluentius accepted Sulla's embrace, but with a furrowed brow and slack jaw. "I beg your pardon?"

"I sent for you weeks ago! When I hadn't received your official response, I assumed you must have gotten yourself killed." Sulla laughed.

Cluentius did not. "The roads are treacherous. I couldn't leave until I secured a guard." He gestured to the twenty armed men standing off behind him toward the gate.

Lucullus clicked his tongue and nodded for us to move closer. He must have sensed something he didn't like.

Sulla shrugged and gestured back to the roaring theater behind us, which must have been reaching the finale of the performance if one could tell from the applause. "If actors and prostitutes could make it, I'd wager you could as well."

Cluentius combed a strand of silver hair behind his ear. "They're peasants. Who would bother to harass them? You understand I would be targeted."

I couldn't see Sulla's face, but I felt that the same suppressed rage that passed over him earlier had now returned.

When he spoke, his voice was still audible and commanding, but little more than a whisper. "I sent an official summons, dear Lucius."

"I arrived as soon as I could." Cluentius lifted his chin and stared straight forward, but it wasn't difficult to see he was uncomfortable or intimidated by how close Sulla now stood to him.

"Mm-hmm." Sulla nodded. "And what news do you bring me?"

"I have brought official word from the people of Pompeii. Although deliberations are ongoing as to whether we will join the war effort, we want to express that we seek no conflict with Rome. Your people are safe to come and—"

As Cluentius continued to ramble on, Sulla walked over to a nearby legionary on guard duty and took one of the pilum from his back.

"I refuse to tolerate any poor treatment of Roman citizens or legionarii. We ever remain a loyal and fastidious friend of Rome—"

Sulla began drawing a circle with the pilum in the dirt around Cluentius.

When at last the monologue concluded, Cluentius looked down to see what Sulla had created. "What's this?"

"It's a circle," said Sulla, cheerfully. "And I

expect you to come to your decision by the time you step out of it."

Cluentius's skin became ashen. "I'm just one man. I am not able to make decisions unilaterally or—"

Sulla nodded. "Certainly. But by the time you step from that circle, you must have an answer for me. Rome has spoken."

If the centurion's jaw had dropped before, Cluentius's was now on the Italian soil beneath him. His eyes followed Sulla in the moonlight, incredulous.

Lucullus and I continued to watch. Both of us were enraptured, taking notes in our mind.

The fortress gates off in the distance groaned open as riders galloped through them.

Sulla seemed to notice this as well, and said, "Very good! Our scouts have returned. Remain in your circle while I deliberate."

He took only a single step to the side and waited for the riders to come to him.

I wrote the dispatches myself, so I knew it wasn't true, but the whole thing couldn't have gone off better for Sulla's display of power than if he choreographed it himself.

The first rider to reach him dismounted quickly. "Legate, the loyal city of Aesernia has been besieged by the Samnites. They call for our aid," the man said with his last breath before placing his hands on his knees and regurgitating.

Sulla turned back to Cluentius, who remained in his circle. "See? A city not a day's march from you has now been besieged by the rebels. You may think me unfair, but I force you to make a decision for your own safety."

Cluentius hung his head. "You ask me to do something I cannot do."

"I ask you to do the thing you know you *should* do," he said. "But refuse to. Why should Pompeii side with nefarious rebels? Your people are too leisured and intelligent for such barbarity."

Cluentius struggled to swallow. "The Italic League . . . the rebels have offered us more than Rome ever has. If I drew a circle around you and asked you to decide whether to give us citizenship before you step out, could or would you do it?"

Sulla's back and shoulders tightened through his white "Sulla's fist" legion tunic.

"Rome will reward those that remain loyal." I could tell from the sound of his voice that he spoke through clenched teeth. "You have done nothing to prove your loyalty."

Cluentius exhaled and stepped from his circle. "Pompeii will join the Italic League then."

Lucullus drew his sword, ready for a fight. I brandished my own, but hoped not to use it.

Sulla, however, was unperturbed. He slammed the butt of the pilum into the ground. "Very well, Cluentius," he said. "Eventually, and mark my words, your head will one day sit upon this spike." He pointed to the top of the pilum.

Cluentius looked like he might join the rider in his vomiting. "We're free to go then?"

"Of course you're free to go!" Sulla threw his arm around the man's shoulder. "Go and go with Fortuna's blessing. Drink, eat, and make love to your wife. Advice from a friend, enjoy this time. Truly. Soon you will be disemboweled, chopped up, and burned to ash," he said, walking the man back toward the gate. "The terror you'll endure will be . .

. well, terrible. But it will be temporary, I assure you. So enjoy this time that's left to you. You may reflect fondly on these days when you're in Tartarus."

Cluentius said nothing, at least which I could hear, until Sulla released him and he rejoined the ranks of his security guard. Whether he refused to speak or could not speak, I do not know.

Sulla returned to us, but this time he was not laughing.

Lucullus snapped to attention, and I followed his direction.

"What are your orders, legate?" Lucullus said.

Sulla inhaled and exhaled, slowly and deeply. He tilted his head back and looked up at the heavens again. "Do you ever try to count the stars, tribune?" he said, but did not allow time for an answer. "No orders tonight. Let the men enjoy the finale of the show. Tomorrow, we ride for battle."

My gut seemed to hollow with those words, but I steeled myself by finishing the rest of my wine, which now went down much easier than it had when I first tasted it.

Perhaps Sulla noticed my angst.

He placed both hands on my shoulders and forced me to look at him. "You're about to earn more glory than you could possibly imagine. Your father will look on with his one eye in envy."

SCROLL X

Quintus Sertorius—Four days before the Kalends of June, 664
Ab Urbe Condita

The blade sliced through my skin as easily as silk. I ground my
teeth and strained to not make a noise, refusing to give him the
satisfaction. Now I regretted not accepting that wooden peg to
bite down on.

The old doctor, Albinus, spoke in a thick accent native to
those of the subura. "You'll not faint, will you? Some of the more
feminine among your men do."

I grunted. "To *Dis* with you, old man." Beads of sweat
formed on my head as I heard the blood dripping into the pail
beneath the table.

"There, it's already over," he said. "I will report to your wife
what a brave legionary you were."

I looked at my arm, which was sliced right at the bend of the
elbow. Red blood was rushing over like a flood. My vision was
hazy and my hearing muted, so I glanced away and returned to
the straw pillow he provided.

"You're sure spilling a little blood will solve the problem?" I said. If this is what it takes to get rid of a fever, I might just choose the headache, cough, and chills.

He scoffed. "You're sure spilling a little blood from your enemies will solve *your* problem?"

"I guess it depends on how much blood."

He nodded triumphantly and wiped his surgeon's knife on an old cloth. "And so it is here. The body doesn't just generate new blood now, does it? The old blood remains stagnant for too long, and you become sick. Read some Hippocrates if you don't believe me."

"Perhaps I should simply be more reckless in combat?" I said.

"I didn't cut off the arm now did I?" he smiled, his gums caving in from the absence of teeth.

"When can I get up?" I asked.

"When I give you the order, Quaestor," he said with a flourish of his dried knife.

"Yes, *domine*," I jested. I rather liked the old doctor. His wit and eternal cynicism made him a good fit around legionaries.

Arrea entered then and was quick to take a step back.

"He's done quite well, my lady," Albinus said with a bow.

Arrea shook her head. "You know, in Gaul, the men sometimes have barbers shave their pubic hair in public. And yet I still find this practice of bloodletting barbaric."

With Arrea now here, I found the courage to sit up on the table, though careful to leave my arm hanging off the side.

"Don't worry, my dear," I said, my ears ringing. "This is literally the *cutting edge* of medicine. Dear Albinus constantly reminds me."

He snapped his fingers. "It's six denarii. I suggest you let a little blood *before* you get sick next time, rather than after."

I brandished my coin purse and counted out a few pieces for him. "Here's seven. The extra is for putting up with my men."

He quickly pushed the extra back into my hand. "I'm compensated adequately, thank you very much. If you expect me to make those *balatrones* into actual *medici*, however, you'll be sourly disappointed."

"We have paid you to make them *medici* and make them *medici* you shall."

"The quality of a potter's work reflects the quality in his clay. In this case, you have given me clay mixed with horseshit."

I laughed and quickly laid back down on the table. "They cannot be all that bad."

"Ehh . . . you're not the only one with a fever in camp, you know. They've become adequately experienced with the spilling of blood, but I guess that was already true, wasn't it? Ask them to splint a broken limb, and you'd be just as well off asking your dog, Pollux."

I sighed. "I'm aware of all the sick men. Forty-three was my last count."

"Your last count is antiquated, then. I believe the most recent number has reached the hundreds."

I rubbed my eye and was about to respond but began to hack and cough violently before I could do so.

"Perhaps he's got some bad blood left in him?" Arrea said.

I wiped the spittle from my chin. "Don't encourage him, Arrea. He'll leave me a hollow husk if given the chance."

Albinus chuckled and began wrapping up my arm. "That's more than enough for now."

"Why did we not stop at *just* enough?"

"The cough, the fatigue, and the fever itself will subside in a matter of days. Never fear."

"Mightn't that have happened regardless?"

"It might've. Or you might have died." He shrugged. "Who knows? Consider that and cast your die next time before you bother an old physician."

I smiled and held out my hand—the one attached to the arm not bleeding. "Thank you, Albinus," I said.

He accepted my hand and said, "Get well, *amice*."

With that, he departed, leaving only Arrea and me in my praetorium.

She's visited more often since I became sick, but it was both more and less often than I desired. I knew she was growing quite bored within the confines of the city, but I didn't want her to see how bad things were becoming. When we were apart, I longed only for a quiet moment alone with her. Whenever we had a bit of solitude, I was completely at a loss for what to say.

Fortunately, I fell into a fit of coughing again. She came and placed a hand on my forehead.

"I think it's better. Truly. Although I give no credit to your doctor friend."

I cleared my throat of the phlegm collected there and spit it into my bucket of blood. "You say that because your hands are burning as hot as my forehead. You've been in the sun too long."

"Not much to do here but watch your men play legionary. It's quite entertaining when the centurions get angry."

I coughed again, and this time I ensured it was forceful enough to purge whatever was in me that wanted to get out.

"You've lost some weight at least," she said. "You look more like the wounded man who stumbled into my master's hut in Gaul."

Perhaps it was the fever, or the loss of blood, but her voice was just as soft and divine as it was the day she saved me. I thought I might say that, but when I looked up at her, the words were lost to me again.

So beautiful. So tender. My heart begged me to tell her many things, but perhaps the articulation spilled out with my blood.

"Are the men really as bad as Albinus said?" There was one thing I could always talk about, and it was camp life.

She lowered her head, now running her fingers through my hair. "He doesn't strike me as the type to lie."

Her words and the look on her face frightened me. I sat up on the table and swung my legs off to the side. "I've been confined to my bed for too long. The men need their commander."

She helped me make it to my feet and held on in case I capsized. She released me when she realized I wouldn't.

"I should make an appearance," I said.

"Of course." She nodded.

I thought she might try convincing me to stay, perhaps to lay down and hold each other like we used to. I would have stayed if she did.

We remained in a few moments of silence, and still she said nothing.

"Would you like to come with me? Keep me on my feet?"

She considered it for a moment, but it seemed to me as if she was searching instead for a reason to decline.

"I should return to Tullia," she said. "A good Roman wife should be sequestered with the other women, right?" She smiled, and even knowing it was forced, it warmed me.

"My wife can do what she likes."

She said nothing else, so I leaned in and kissed her forehead. "If I don't return within the hour, assume I've died from Albinus's experiments and have him executed immediately."

She laughed. "We'll put on a funeral for you like Rome has never seen before," she said.

There was a spark of familiarity there in the way we jested. Just enough to remind me of how warm and safe it felt to be close with her. Enough to remind me how rarely we experienced it. I yearned for it as much as anything else. But like trying to catch a feather in the wind, it always seemed out of grasp.

"I'll come see you in a few days."

I exited into the camp, nearly blinded by the midday sun. None of the legionaries seemed to be bothered by the brightness, but I'd been stowed away in bed like an ancient relic for days. The only light I'd seen was the sunshine afforded to me in my dreams.

I stifled another cough. I tried to walk as if I wasn't sick and woozy from blood loss but couldn't find the proper stride.

Blacksmiths hammered relentlessly in the shade of tents all

around me—we had a lot of armaments to produce. Centurions barked orders, and the legionarii echoed them. Even so, I could hear coughs rising from several directions.

No one seemed to notice me as I walked through camp. Perhaps I'd lost weight like Arrea suggested, or perhaps everyone was too fixated on what tasks lay before them. I was pleased with the results either way. I wanted to see how they'd been performing while I was out of commission the past few days.

I knew it couldn't be good. The first two thousand men joined within days of our arrival, and since then, we'd had only a trickle. The reason was clear. Because the displaced citizens of the rebellion had few options other than to join, they did so without hesitation. But the rest, those fortunate enough not to be forced by circumstances into our ranks . . . what was their incentive?

They wouldn't be joining for sustenance. I know how rumors spread in the legion and with those considering whether to join. All Mutina and half of Italy knew we were short on grain, wine, olive oil, salt, and anything else a legionary might desire.

They weren't joining for opportunity. Why would they? Our most faithful allies never received the compensation (in the form of citizenship, equal pay, and fair rights) they deserved after fighting as auxiliaries for centuries. Why would anyone else seek to join us in vanquishing them? What hope did they have of receiving what our enemies had not?

Would they join for patriotism? Devotion to a country that neither recognized nor desired them? The senate might believe people around the Mare Nostrum would flock to our ranks just to serve our "cause," but legionaries live in the world of practicalities. This would not happen.

I had a fine line to walk. If I was too easy in pushing for recruits, we would not raise the legions the senate ordered me to levy. If I was too harsh, I would alienate the locals and end up raising an army for our enemy. If I made no promises of wealth, status, or freedom, why should they join? If I made promises on the behalf of the senate they would not tolerate, I would face exile or worse upon my return to Rome.

And the shortage of grain and the pervasive fever made all of this worse. News was slow to reach us from the rest of Italy of the initial phases of the war, but I hoped things were going better than they were in Mutina. If the legions were genuinely relying on the quantity and quality of the troops I was levying, I feared for what would become of Rome.

"Quaestor!" I heard a voice shout as I walked, distracting me from my ruminations.

I turned to find Leptis jogging toward me, beads of sweat collecting on his forehead like a jeweled diadem.

"Centurion, it's good to see you," I said.

He didn't fail to salute me properly, but he was jovial and more familiar in his mannerisms than I was used to. I don't believe I'd seen him smile before, but he was smiling now, revealing a jaggedly chipped front tooth.

"I'm relieved to see you healthy, Quaestor."

I was taken aback by his happiness but decided it was a genuine display of relief at my improving health.

"I've seen better days, Leptis, and I'll hope to see better days again. But I'm recovering," I said. "Apollo strikes down the proud, but he restores them all the same."

He chuckled and shook his head. "Prideful? Not my quaestor. If any man in this legion had accomplished half of what you have, their *dignitas* would be so inflated it'd have to be carried about on a litter."

I looked beyond the centurion and found a formation of men he'd been training. They were waiting patiently at attention, but more than a few had altered their position to watch us.

He remained there, as if he wanted to say something, but instead he just kept smiling like a schoolboy. He did have a certain childish element to him, something not uncommon to legionaries.

"Is there something I can do for you, Centurion?" I said.

"Oh, yes. I thought you might want to speak to the recruits?" He gestured toward the formation.

Over half of them had twisted their heads to look at me now, so I had no other recourse.

"Of course. I'd be happy too," I said. I always wanted to be the sort of leader who addressed his men, but on this occasion, I would have rather remained at the rear. What if I fainted? One can hardly imagine the stories of Apollo's curse that would spread throughout the legion if I did.

He ushered me to the front of the formation and ordered everyone to stand properly.

"Your commander is about to address you," he said.

"*Salve, legionarii,*" I said.

They stomped their right feet.

I'd become accustomed to speaking before legions by now, but in this moment, I felt woefully inadequate. My head was swimming and my voice felt weak. What could I say to these understandably concerned soldiers to assuage them?

"I apologize for my absence of late," I said. "Mutina's cooking has left me stranded on the *latrina* for days."

The men chuckled. We all knew there was more to what was happening with the sickness in our camp, but there was nothing to gain by addressing it.

"I'm pleased to see you've been progressing well despite my recent holiday," I said and a few more laughed. "You are the luckiest recruits I've known in some time." I clapped Leptis on his shoulder. "This is one of the finest centurions and the most resolute leaders of men that I've had the pleasure to serve with. Follow his instructions, and you might one day find yourself on the same list."

Leptis beamed, breathing in whistles through his busted nose. The recruits all nodded. I'm sure they had mixed feelings about him at the moment, as legionary training is mostly chastisements with a little bit of instruction, but soon they'd know exactly what I meant.

I let my smile fade, and they matched my sober expression. "You have endured much, even in these few weeks you've counted yourselves among Rome's *legionarii*. We've had scant food, a lack of wine, and a fever that won't seem to leave us be. That's what it means to be a legionary. Some days you eat and drink like a king, the next like a *servus*. Sometimes, the victories come cheap and easy, and others come only after much toil and bloodshed. That is what it means to be a legionary."

They nodded, almost prideful at their plight, as I and my comrades had once been when I was a mule like them.

I only hoped their story would turn out better than mine had. I prayed some of their companions might live.

"But better days lie ahead. You are counted among Rome's finest now, and when the dust settles, she will compensate you well." I meant it, but when I considered our current enemies, I realized the hypocrisy of the statement.

One of them broke rank and shouted, "We'll spend it all on wine and women, Quaestor!"

As the men laughed, I turned to the centurion. "Leptis, I'd like to speak with you privately for a moment."

"Fall out, men," he said. "I'll be testing your water skins when I return. I want them to be half-full. No excuses. And Critus, you'd better fix that stubble on your chin or I'll order the century to shave you."

It was nigh impossible to find anywhere in camp that legionaries wouldn't overhear us, but as we neared the black-smiths' tents, the sound of clanking hammers drowned out our voices.

"What is it, Quaestor?" he asked.

"Have we any updates on the Sons of Remus?"

Uttering those words, the memories of their screams returned to mind. We'd captured three of the attackers after they burned our grain supply. Even after hours of torture, they refused to name any one leader. I believed them when they said there wasn't any particular man in charge. The Sons of Remus was a secret organization of Roman citizens—true born or earned—that stood for the rights of the Italians. Their aim was to disrupt us long enough that we'd be forced to acquiesce and relent to the rebels' demands. Failing that, they would ensure we lost the war.

He scratched at his leathery forehead. "The torture detachment has gained a considerable amount of training working on those men. They refused, or are unable, to share anything else."

Hot steam rose from the tent of a nearby blacksmith, the air thick with scorched iron.

"They've suffered long enough. Have them executed."

He nodded. "Should we have them crucified? We can display their corpses as a reminder outside the fortress walls."

I remembered hearing the crier mentioning how the rebels did this outside Asculum.

"No," I said. "They are Roman citizens. Traitor or not, I will not have these men crucified. Cremate them and spread their ashes. That is enough."

"Quaestor, I—"

"The gods will give them exactly what they deserve in the afterlife. Nothing more, nothing less."

Part of me wondered if the gods might even reward them. If they were on the right side of this war, and we were in the wrong. Who knows what the gods think of mortal affairs? I thrust the thought from my mind."

Leptis was a religious man, as many are who survived so many years of battle. That was enough for him.

"As you command, Quaestor."

"I want the scouts devoted to finding out more. We must discover if there's any way to identify these traitors. To catch them *before* they destroy our supply lines and not after."

A shadow grew between us. Apollonius was approaching, his silhouette dark with the sun behind him.

"It's good to see you in better health, *amice*," he said.

We embraced, and I kissed his cheek. I was just as relieved to see him, but perhaps for different reasons.

"How are you?" I said.

Centurion Leptis took a few steps away to inspect the craftsmanship of the blacksmiths.

"Older than yesterday, younger than tomorrow." He smiled, but weariness strained his eyes like a fever. "And you?"

"Old Albinus spilled an aqueduct's worth of my blood earlier, and he promises me I'm as strong as Vulcan now." I stifled a cough. I wasn't well, but after speaking about the Sons of Remus, I was resolved to become well soon.

Apollonius said, "Hopefully you won't have his limp leg. You're already missing an eye, it's best if our commander keeps all his limbs intact."

We joined Leptis in the blacksmith's tent, where he picked up a red-hot gladius and tested the weight in his hand.

"The counterbalance is the most important thing. More so than even the sharpness," he said.

Leptis knew nothing more about forging weapons than me or Apollonius, but centurions can be quite particular.

"Would it disrupt your work if I tested the weight myself?"

The blacksmith bowed. "No, Quaestor. I hope they are to your satisfaction."

I took a gladius directly from the anvil. It was still bent, requiring more hammering, as heat billowed out from its blade like a furnace.

"How are our supplies?" I asked Apollonius. "Any improvements?"

He ran his fingers through his white beard, as he often did when in contemplation. "Improvement is a relative concept, I suppose. Better than a few weeks ago? Yes. But are we where we should be? No. Not by any means."

Leptis set the gladius down with a clamor and said, "Cisalpine Gaul is sending two months' worth of supplies."

Apollonius nodded. "Yes, but grain only. We're already two weeks behind on wine and oil for the recruits. We have nothing to give as an initial payment to those who join, and our registrars have slowed to a halt since that became the case."

"The men do love their wine," I said. I turned to the black-smith and returned his blade to the anvil. "The weight is perfect, I believe. Make a thousand like this, and we will conquer the world."

I stepped away from the insufferable heat of the blacksmith's forge, Apollonius and Leptis following me.

We walked through the orderly tent rows of one of my centuries as we continued to discuss.

Leptis said, "If you believe the men are ready, Quaestor, we may have to begin sending out foraging parties soon."

I admired a cohort standard waving before a row of tents and said, "I trust you've prepared them to wield a sword. My concern is that pillaging any land nearby, Roman or otherwise, could alienate the locals. If we lose their support, if men stop joining us, we will fail."

Apollonius added, "This is not like fighting in Gaul or Africa. Requisition is an important part of military command, I under-stand, but doing so in Italy could be disastrous.

There was a collective movement throughout camp, dozens of legionaries heading in the same direction.

"What do you suppose that is about?" I asked.

Leptus's jaw flexed. "I don't know. But I intend to find out."

I searched for smoke above the fort walls in the direction they ran. Fortunately, I found none. Instead, only cheers and applause rose in the air.

"It's been weeks since I've heard laughter in this camp," Apollonius said.

"There are few sounds more refreshing to a commander than the laughter of happy soldiers," I said.

"And few noises more intolerable to centurions."

"Quintus," someone shouted behind us. The voice was

masculine, and there was only one man familiar or insubordinate enough to call me by my praenomen in front of our legionaries.

I turned to find Aulus riding toward us on a painted horse.

Primus pilus Leptis said, "It's Quaestor Quintus Sertorius, commander of Mutina's legions."

Aulus slowed his horse to a stop before us and cocked his head. "The two of us used to bathe naked in creek beds and rivers. I saw his pitiful first attempt at a kiss. I'll call him what I like until he tells me otherwise."

"Quiet, both of you," I said. They were both right in their own way, and both were wrong. "What is it?"

Aulus brushed back his shaggy blond hair and smiled that wide smile that won him so many female companions back in Nursia. "It's good to see you awake and well, *amice*."

Perhaps the few days away was the cause, or perhaps it was the blood loss and the growing weakness in my chest. But I marveled at the sight of him. He wore a black breastplate with silver trimmings and a blue-plumed helmet. He looked far more like the commander than I did with my bandaged arm and sunken cheeks.

"What can I do for you, Aulus?" The strain of a pending cough grew in my chest.

He shrugged. "I think the opportune question is, what can Aulus do for you?"

"My lungs burn, and my head is on fire. Speak plainly."

Aulus shrugged. "Come with me. I'll show you."

Leptis said, "Quaestor, I beg you to chastise him for speaking so informally to you."

"First Spear Leptis, I appreciate and duly note your concern for my prestige," I said. "But let all your men know this, if they display courage and aptitude in battle, as Aulus did in Greece, they may call me anything they'd like."

Aulus flashed a charming grin. "I'll lead then. Come along, centurion."

We parted as Aulus trotted passed us. It was clear almost immediately we were heading to the same place the legionaries had been gathering.

As we rounded the row of tents, I could see hundreds of legionaries gathering there before a few wagons. Barrels were being hauled down and passed around.

"What is this?" I asked.

Aulus jumped from his horse and extended his arms to the wagons. "A gift. A bountiful gift."

"From whom?" Apollonius questioned.

"A loyal old farmer. Called himself Flavius Rufus. Said he hoped to support us and our efforts," Aulus said. "You'd never believe it. He told me he feared for the lives of his wife and daughters, living out there on a plot of land in the foothills near the Paeligni. Said for us to end the war soon."

"This should have been added to the supply manifest and doled out accordingly, Aulus," Apollonius said.

Aulus deflated, his eyes hardening that his great fortune hadn't impressed us as he expected. "I ordered the carts to be brought in. The men saw to the rest and the centurions did nothing to stop them."

"Aulus, what was in those barrels?" I said.

He crossed his arms. "Wine. A lot of it. Mostly *posca*, so we wouldn't have kept it for ourselves anyway. Too sour for your tastes, Apollonius," he said. "Nothing to be concerned about."

"You see a thousand happy young men," Apollonius said. "I see two-thousand men who will be thirsty again tomorrow."

Aulus threw his hands up. "This alone wouldn't have solved our supply issues. Our battle now is not with logistics but with soldier's hearts. Nothing boosts morale like a belly full of wine."

A few of the men near the wagon were laughing and wrestling over a skin of *posca*. Those around them beginning to cheer and cast out wagers on who would be the victor. Others sang songs about defeating the rebels.

I swallowed. "Aulus, what did you say that man's name was?"

"Who? The man who gave me this? Flavius Rufus. I doubt you'd know him."

I sprang toward the wagons. "Stop! I order everyone to stop!" I shouted. "Do not drink the *posca*!"

"What? Why?" Aulus shouted after.

But Apollonius and Leptis joined me in rallying the cry.

I prayed I was wrong. I asked Jupiter for this to be a moment of fever-induced paranoia. But such a bountiful gift, and for nothing in return. Rarely had Fortuna favored us so. And the man's initials . . . *Filii Remi* shared them.

I heard a violent fit of coughing nearby. I knew where the *valetudinarium* tents were located. These coughs weren't coming from them.

More coughing sounded from another direction. One of the legionarii closest to us began violently regurgitating the *posca* he'd just drank.

Some of the legionarii were too preoccupied with their own drinking and singing to notice. Others were cackling at the misfortunes of their comrades.

"What is happening to them?" Aulus asked, eyes glassy and mouth open.

"Aulus, go and fetch Albinus immediately!"

He wasted no time. But I feared we were too late.

"All of you who have drank the *posca* must purge yourselves immediately," I bellowed. The strain forced me to cough into my arm, but I fought through it. "Now!"

"Waste of good wine," a few of them grumbled, but most of them complied and began emptying their stomachs with the rest of their brethren.

A trembling man cried out from the ground. "Where am I? Where am I?" He clutched his ribcage like it was tearing apart.

Centurion Leptis began chasing down a few men who hadn't forced spilled out their wine. The rest of the officers and men were running around in a blur, looking for somewhere safe to vomit or collapse outside the judgmental eye of their comrades. Perhaps most of them didn't realize their friends were just as sick and doing the same thing.

I ordered for fresh water to be brought out and helped fetch some myself. Wool blankets and torches for the chills. What else could we do? I needed Albinus, fast.

But moments later Aulus returned without him. "Sertorius." He tucked his helmet beneath his arm, his face ashen and crestfallen. "You should come quickly," he said.

I followed Aulus to the *valetudinarium* tent from where Albinus worked. He was lying on a cot with his legs tucked to his chest. Vomit and blood flowed freely over his chin, soaking his shirt. His eyes were wild and dilated, his flesh colorless and waxy.

"*Amice.*" I knelt by his side and took his trembling hands within my own. "Tell me what to do and I will do it."

He sputtered and coughed, blood droplets splashing my face. "Nothing to be done now." His breath was labored and shaken like a reed in the wind. "I've seen this before. It's *Conium maculatum.* Hemlock."

I placed a hand over my mouth, my eyes wide now. "Can we stop it?"

He shook his head. "I can already feel my heartbeat slowing. It's over."

I hung my head. "How? . . ."

He frowned. "So little time, and you ask questions you already have the answer for." I followed his gaze to an empty skin of *posca* on the floor beside him. "One of the helpers—" he broke out into a fit of coughing and I held him to my chest. "One of the helpers brought me a cup. It reminds me of the filth I drank in the Subura."

"What of the others?"

"They're younger and . . . more robust than I am. Perhaps some will live. Others will die." He closed his eyes. "And I never even tasted it. Must be getting old." His limbs trembled violently, then fell still. At first, I thought he'd breathed his last, but he said, "Not the worst way to go, is it? To die like Pole-marchus and Socrates . . . I can think of worse ways to . . ."

A guttural moan escaped his lips, and his limbs went slack in my arms. He was dead.

I closed his eyes with the back of my hand and laid him down softly. The moment I'd released him, I leapt to my feet and ran back into camp. There would be time to mourn later.

Leptis and the other centurions were doing the best they could to restore order, having partitioned off the healthy and the sick. Leptis ordered the sick to be splashed with water from the horse troughs.

I found my old friend Aulus standing helplessly amid the chaos.

"Aulus, send out riders. I want that Flavius Rufus found and brought to camp immediately."

His voice was little more than a whisper. "Twenty head of cavalry are already moving in his direction, Quaestor."

Leptis rushed to me. "We'll need to have this man crucified and made an example of."

My flesh burned. "Send out another ten riders. I want this man found and brought before me on his knees!"

Italy was at war, my son was in the thick of it far away from me, we were drastically short on supplies, and now my own men were dying before my eyes with no remedy available.

But I would reestablish order. I would regain control. And I'd do it the only way I knew would work: the sword.

SCROLL XI

LUCIUS HIRTULEIUS—NONES of June, 664 Ab Urbe Condita

Finding Marius in camp was never a simple task. Legati spend most of their time in their praetorium, huddled over scrolls and wax tablets requiring their signature and seal. But not Marius.

Sometimes I found him in full-kit training alongside the legionaries like he was one of them. Other times, he was inspecting the stables and the quality of the hard and soft fodder available to our horses. It wasn't uncommon to find him inspecting the strength of a random suit of chainmail or the sturdiness of freshly constructed shields in the *fabrica*. He defecated in the same latrines as the rest of the men, and took his time there, as he found it an excellent location to speak with the men on equal terms and gauge their morale. I often found him at the camp altars, where others would gather to watch his generous and fervent sacrifice and prayers.

This time, six days before the Ides of June, I found him outside the camp walls, overseeing the trench digging and earthwork creation of the legionaries.

"Legate, how are you this morning?" I said. "The scouts have arrived with news from across Italy."

The rhythmic clanging of shovels striking the dry earth reverberated through the air, clouds of dust rising with it.

He crossed his arms. "They can wait."

We'd been at war with the rebels for over three months now and still hadn't met them in pitched battle. Several other Roman forced had, and few of them had been successful. One of the closest legions under a man named Perpenna had been massacred. The survivors joined our ranks, and they brought with them a sense of dread and fear of the rebel armies.

Many of our men declared that the waiting was more grueling than combat ever could be. Marius knew better. He was the primary reason we'd avoided battle thus far. If it wasn't for his advice, the consul Lucius Caesar would have certainly already charged headlong into battle several times.

Marius was just as restless as the rest of us. But he refused to jump into battle, so he jumped into the ditch beside his men and snatched a shovel from a nearby legionary.

"Dig, you whoresons!" he bellowed.

They laughed and dug harder, inspired by his presence. The scouts continued to stand awkwardly behind us. I refused to stand idly by while Gaius Marius himself dug a trench, so I hopped in and joined him.

Marius was an enigma to me. He was in his midsixties. Most of the men his age were leisured and refined, relaxing in Rome while the young and ambitious waged wars on her behalf. And they certainly weren't digging trenches with the legionaries. But that was Gaius Marius. Even in his old age and with a larger belly than before, his arms were still thick and sinewy. His voice was booming, and his hands were shaped like mallets.

"Tell me," he said, his voice quieter now, but not in any way labored by his exertion. "Have you already spoken with the scouts?"

"Briefly." I blinked stinging sweat from my eyes and trained to maintain Marius's pace beneath the oppressive sun.

"Prepare me then. Is the news good or bad?"

I hesitated. "Some honey, some vinegar."

There were four separate scouts with reports from all over Italy, and indeed some of the news was good for Rome. Most of it, however, was dreadful. As a patriot and soldier of Rome, I was concerned about all of it, but most haunting of all was the crestfallen eyes of the man who returned from Sertorius's camp in Mutina.

"I expected nothing but vinegar." He sighed. "Let's get this over with."

We crawled out of the ditch to find a massive stallion gallop to a halt before us. It was black as a raven, and a gold-fringed ceremonial tarp hung over its back. As I craned to see the rider, I was perplexed to find a child.

"*Ave*, rider," Marius said, shielding his eyes from the sun. He was curious, but perhaps also irritated by the disturbance.

"Do you not recognize me, uncle?" the boy said

with a grin. He handed off the reins to a nearby legionary and gracefully leapt from the massive black stallion.

Marius's jaw dropped. "Gaius Julius Caesar? Can it be?"

"It is I," he said. He wore a breastplate and helm like an officer's cadet, although they were the size of a child's imitation.

"What a pleasant surprise to see you here," Marius said, even more confused than before.

"I come bearing a gift." He gestured back to the horse. "A steed befitting Rome's Third Founder."

Marius marveled at the offering. "What a fine beast he is."

"My father purchased him from the Parthians. I'd wager it costs as much as our home in the Subura," he said, his voice refined and slow, like a man twice his age. "He was inclined to have a handful of slaves bring it to you, but I was determined to usher this gift to you myself."

Marius craned his head. "It wasn't prudent of your father to send you through Italy with such a fine prize."

The young man shrugged. "I had twenty armed guards to escort me. I had them wait outside the baggage camp."

Marius approached the steed and patted its haunches. "I will ride this beast into battle and win many wars. I will compensate your father, I assure you."

"We all benefit by your winning this war. That is all any Roman could expect in compensation."

The boy's use of language and keen understanding impressed me. Perhaps he simply looked younger than he was?

"Oh, let me introduce you to my tribune. This is Lucius Hirtuleius. Tribune, this is my nephew, Gaius Julius Caesar."

I extended my hand. His were soft and small, but he gripped with the strength of a man.

"*Salvete*, Gaius." I smiled.

He nodded. "Caesar, if you will," he said. "I'm too young to be called by my cognomen exclusively, but it pleases my mother when I use it. It is an honor to meet you, tribune. I trust my uncle always surrounds himself with the finest Romans, but it's a pleasure to see it for myself."

"I must ask, Caesar, how old are you?"

He lifted his chin and straightened his shoulders. "I'll turn ten next month," he said. "If I was any older, I'd be pitching my tent here in camp and helping you punish these traitors."

Marius chuckled, the first time I'd seen him do that since the war began. "I have no doubt. Tell me, what news from Rome?"

Young Caesar shook his head. "It's ghastly, uncle. Some plebeian tribune named Hybrida passed a law that allows the legal prosecution of anyone who 'diminishes the majesty of the Roman people.'"

The scouts continued creeping toward us, likely eager to give their missive and get out of the sun for a few hours.

Marius stared at his nephew blankly. "And what exactly does that mean?"

Caesar shrugged. "Everything and nothing. It's essentially been used by politicians to bring forth charges against their rivals. Already, men like Memmius, Calpurnius Piso, and Marcus Scaurus have been dragged through the courts."

Marius smiled for a moment, but it quickly faded. "Leave it to the politicians to squabble among themselves while the Republic is falling apart."

Caesar sobered, his eyes revealing a depth and understanding uncommon even among grown men. "I regret to inform you that my grandfather, Aurelius Cotta, has also been prosecuted. To avoid condemnation on these flagrantly false charges, he has voluntarily exiled himself."

I was uninformed on most of the relationships and machinations of Rome's politicians. I was simply a soldier. But I did know Aurelius Cotta and his allies were no friends of Marius. Regardless, they were distant relatives through marriage to the Caesar family, so this was an insult to Marius as well.

Marius's powerful jaw twitched. "When I return to Rome, I'll have this addressed."

Caesar smiled at last and nodded. "Of course, uncle. Until then, know that our family is protecting your interests in Rome."

"Will you be staying with us for the night?" Marius said. We were expecting battle sometime soon, so this seemed inappropriate to ask a child, but this nine-year-old boy seemed perfectly capable of handling himself in camp.

Caesar frowned. "Unfortunately, I must return. My mother has procured a Greek tutor from Athens, and his lessons are to begin immediately." He stepped forward, half the height of his uncle, and extended his hand. "It's a pleasure to see you in such good health, uncle. I will wait in anticipation for your triumph when you return."

Marius accepted his hand joyfully, like he would

a man's. "I'll have you beside me on the chariot if I'm able."

Caesar bowed and turned to leave.

I shook my head and let out a laugh. "I think there are a few Mariuses in that boy," I said.

Marius frowned for a moment, perhaps insulted, before understanding me. "Fortunately, he takes after me and not the other men in his life. His father has the ambition of a sardine, and his uncle is a treacherous little snake."

From the look in his eye, I inferred he wanted to discuss this topic further. Disinterested in having any conversation even nominally political, I pointed back to our scouts. "Perhaps we should receive our report now?"

He grunted and strode toward the patiently waiting messengers.

"Report," he said.

They saluted. One of them swallowed. "Should we convene in your praetorium, legate? Out of the earshot of your men."

Marius crossed his arms. "They're distracted with their work. I like the sunshine. We'll meet here." He pointed his finger like a dagger at the scout on the left. "You. Report."

The most haggard among them stepped forward. Soot covered him from head to toe, the result of hard riding, but his face was still ashen beneath it. His lips were cracked and his eyes downcast. Still, he offered a salute and took a deep breath to summon up some composure.

"Legate, I have returned from Mutina, where forces are being mustered by the proconsul Livianus."

Marius grunted. "Livianus is on the far side of

the Alps. Quaestor Quintus Sertorius is mustering those troops under his own authority. We all know it, and you can say so for the rest of your briefing."

The scout's eyes fluttered as if he were remembering something terrible. "Quaestor Quintus Sertorius was indeed commanding this levying operation. He presumably still is if he's still alive."

A gnawing ache developed in the pit of my stomach and spread throughout my limbs. My fingers instinctively clenched into fists, as if trying to hold on to some semblance of control. I wanted to pummel the messenger.

Marius's voice deepened and wavered on the edge of anger. "And why would Quintus Sertorius not be alive? He hasn't even seen battle as far as I know."

The scout nodded. "Fortuna has hounded his efforts." He was slow with his delivery, lingering on every word to ensure he spoke true.

I waited breathlessly for something hopeful, offering a silent prayer that my oldest friend was safe and well.

The scout continued, "When I arrived, his army had just suffered severe poisoning at the hand of rebel spies. There was a sickness, too, a fever. They barely permitted me access to see him, and he was bedridden. His teeth were chattering, and his one eye was sunken. Some of the camp believed Orcus would call his name soon."

I bent over and placed a hand on my knee.

Marius, for once, had no sharp response. His voice was low and filled with sorrow. "He should have never been in Mutina. He should be here with me," he said, almost to himself.

The scout continued despite our grieving.

"They've raised several thousand able-bodied men to aid in the war effort but lost"—he pulled out a wax tablet and untied its leather thongs—"237 men as a result of the poisoning and other illnesses."

Marius placed his hands akimbo on his hips and shook his head. "Did they at least apprehend those responsible?"

"Some, not all," the scout said. "They captured and executed the man who delivered the poisoned wine. He was a wealthy but simple farmer—a Roman citizen, even—who was sympathetic to the Italian cause."

I said, "Another member of the so-called Sons of Remus?"

Only a few days before, Marius ordered the execution of three Roman legionaries who were conspiring to send a schematic of our fortress defenses to a nearby rebel army.

"That's correct. Their 'forces' seem to have infiltrated most of the armies mustering around Italy."

"Unless you have anything else to share, I'll hear the word of our other scouts."

"Only that, even if he does survive, the legions mustering under Quintus Sertorius are on the verge of mutiny," he said. "It's best if we do not rely on their reinforcements."

"You lie!" I barked. "I have served on the staff of Quintus Sertorius since I was too young to grow a beard. He's one of the finest young officers Rome has. His men will never betray him."

The scout swallowed and shrugged sheepishly. "Hard to lead men from a tent cot," he said. "Between a lack of supplies, the poisoning, the sickness, and the unrest in Italy, I'm sure keeping the recruits in line is an impossible task for any commander, no matter how brilliant he is."

"Enough. Eat, drink, and bathe. I'll give you your next assignment before nightfall," Marius said. He turned to me. "I grieve with you, Hirtuleius. I know he is a brother to you."

I couldn't speak, not even to express my thanks. I tasted bile in my throat and my stomach felt sick. Quintus Sertorius was supposed to be impervious. I couldn't believe what I was hearing but had no way to confirm or deny the scout's report.

"You." Marius pointed to the next scout. "What is your report, young Hermes?"

The scout snapped to attention and offered a salute. He brandished a long scroll and unfurled it. "The rebels have besieged the city of Aesernia. An army under Sextus Julius Caesar entered pitched battle with the besieging army. The rebels defeated them. Four thousand legionaries died in the ensuing conflict. Sextus Julius Caesar is dead."

For a moment, a spark of excitement flashed before Marius's eyes. He soon recalled himself and summoned a more appropriate expression of solemnity.

"The army of Lucius Cornelius Sulla now rides to the defense of the Roman colony."

Marius balked at the mention of Sulla. "What makes him think he'll fare any differently than that debauched wretch Sextus Caesar?"

The scout was unqualified to answer, so he continued, "The city of Nola has fallen by treachery into the hands of the Samnite rebels under the command of Papius Mutilus. He rounded up all Roman citizens and sympathizers and crucified them outside the city gates."

It was remarkable how casually the envoy rendered those words. One could barely fathom seeing all your loved ones herded up like cattle and nailed to a piece of wood, hung up to starve and suffer for days before the birds picked all of you clean.

The scout continued. "This display reportedly horrified the cities surrounding Nola. They now flock to join the rebels in droves. Stabiae, Herculaneum, Salernum, and Pompeii have all sworn their allegiance to the Italic league."

Marius grunted. "If they think a few crucifixions are something to fear, they clearly don't remember what it's like to taste the wrath of Rome," he said. "Justice will be served."

"In this manner, Mutilus has gained ten thousand fighting men, and one thousand head of cavalry," the scout read.

Marius had no quip in response.

"Mutilus, thus reinforced, marched on Acerrae. The army under Lucius Caesar joined the fray. The Samnites advanced on his camp, and almost broke through, but the Consul Caesar bravely flanked them with his Campanian cavalry, routing the rebels and killing six thousand of the enemy forces. Rome has ordered a three-day festival to commemorate the victory and has permitted citizens to wear their togae, as they've been banned from doing since the onset of the war. Thus diminished, however, Caesar's army was forced to retreat and abandon the city of Acerrae to the rebels. The siege is ongoing."

The scout rolled up the missive, saluted, and stepped back.

The silence that followed was eerie, as if all the spirits of the recently slain were crying out to fill the absence.

Marius's face was twisted like he'd sipped a cup of *posca* and expected *passum*. He shook his head and cursed under his breath. "Three days of festivals? Celebrating a victory . . . what victory? The man had to retreat!" He threw up his arms in disgust and pointed to the third scout. "You, go on before I say something imprudent."

This man was the youngest of the three and appeared the least rugged. I assumed he'd not traveled the same distance as the others. Although he wore the same light armor as the other two, there was something about his posture that made me believe he possessed a more noble lineage.

"The Marsi tribe has beaten the legions of Pompeius Strabo back from the siege at Asculum. He has retreated to the coast."

Marius laughed. "Who? I guess we're giving an army to anyone these days."

"Marsi 'consul' Poppaedius Silo is now marching south to interrupt our efforts to relieve the siege of Alba."

My head was already spinning in circles, both from the generally horrific news and the sheer number of armies and commanders to keep track of, but this latter forced my attention. Our forces were just a few days' march from Alba. Silo would be upon us soon. And he was the rebel consul as well. I'd heard whispers of both his brilliance and his brutality.

"Fantastic scouting," Marius said. "You'll need to tell Lupus immediately. We can waste no time.

We need to rally the forces and retreat without delay."

The scout shuffled. "Actually, legate, I just returned from his camp."

"Very well. Where does he plan to retreat?"

The scout frowned. "Consul Lupus is marching to meet the Marsi. He commands your armies to continue the march and to cross the river south of his location. Thus, we can divide their forces and hit them from two fronts."

The famous look of rage came over Marius, his face turning as purple as Nursian turnips, the veins in his neck and forehead bulging. "He comm . . . he . . ." he stuttered. He clinched his hammer fists, and I feared for a moment he might throw one of them into the scout's teeth. "I have expressly told him *not* to engage with the enemy. We are not ready."

"All due respect, legate, but Lupus is consul. He is in command of the northern armies."

Marius balked. I stepped forward in preparation to halt his assault.

"Command? What has he ever commanded but a cortege of slaves in his bathhouse?"

The legionaries nearby were listening in carefully now.

"The senate and people of Rome have—"

Marius shouted. "Spare me the senate and people of Rome, legionary. Spare me. And why isn't Caepio being called on to reinforce this ill-advised assault? Why should I be required to partake in a battle so remarkably foolish?"

The scout exhaled. "Because Praetor Caepio is fighting the Paeligni in the mountains and cannot be reached," he said. "And because the Consul of Rome has given you an order."

"Get out of my face," Marius said. "Go, now, before I lose my patience."

The scout saluted and mounted a nearby horse, presumably to ride back to inform the consul of Marius's response.

He stood in stunned silence for a long moment. I considered leaving him with his brooding. The Third Founder of Rome, victor over the Numidians, the Cimbri, and the Teutones, the six-time consul, now taking orders like an officer-cadet. Perhaps it was his greatness that he served Rome despite this, or perhaps it was not. All I knew was that dissension among commanders was hardly ever a fortuitous thing before battle.

"Rally the men," Marius said to me, barely audible. "Burn down the fort. We're moving out. Go on, refill those trenches!" he bellowed. He shook his head and walked past me. "We shall see who knows more of war: the senate's playthings or Gaius Marius."

After serving with Marius for so many years before, I knew the answer to the question. But for once, I hoped he and I were both wrong.

 We departed fast as Zephyr's wind but marched slowly. Not because Marius intended to delay our arrival or because he didn't plan to assist the consul but because he refused to march us into an ambush.

Still, many murmured about the legate's cautiousness. Some said he was a coward, probably those too young to remember him for his heroic deeds only decades before. A few others said he was losing his nerve in his old age. Those who served with him in Gaul or Numidia said no such thing.

We made camp near a fork in the river. We would cross the next morning, but in addition to the bridge, Marius ordered the men to construct our camp to full legionary standards.

"I'll not let these stepsons of Italy catch us with our tunics around our ankles," he said.

That night, my brother, Aius, came to my tent. He was still in full-kit, despite most of us already downgrading to our tunics. I knew why. It wasn't so long ago I was preparing for my first battle, and the armor, no matter how heavy or chafing it might be, brought great comfort in those moments.

His voice was higher than usual when he said, "Care to share a little wine with me?" His eyes fluttered.

"Have all you'd like. I'll take a cup or two, well-watered, nothing more," I said. "I want my head clear tomorrow morning."

He wasted no time pouring us two cups. "Tribune Aquillius says it's a good idea to drink the night before battle. He thinks it's good for your nerves."

My tent was far from hospitable, but I did have two backless oxhide leather chairs with a folding oak table between them, so we sat there.

I said, "Aquillius is a good man. He was a legatus with us in Gaul. All of us have different prebattle rituals. You'll find out what suits you best."

My own ritual consisted of a simple blood offering to Mars and Bellona. The cut through my palm still stung from the latest sacrifice.

He shrugged. "If I live long enough to taste battle more than once."

In Rome, Aius appeared at least my age, perhaps older. He knew all the customs, how to behave anywhere from the forum to the bath-houses. But here, in the legion, he appeared infinitely younger.

I was grateful to have him with me, but part of me now regretted bringing him along. He was intelligent enough to be an orator, a public advocate, or even a politician if he could make the right friends. He had no need of the legions.

And while my grandfather's harsh rearing hardened me, it made Aius soft and kind. The legion probably didn't need him any more than he needed it. But what is service to Rome if it comes with no sacrifice?

"Having visions of grandeur and a glorious death, are you?" I attempted to jest.

He smiled. "I'd rather stay alive and be glorious, if I may."

"You'll be fine. Just obey the orders and stay close to me. Marius is the ablest commander Rome has ever seen."

"Bold praise," Aius said. "But it's Marius's own disposition that frightens me. If he fears battle, why shouldn't I?"

We both knew he would have been just as frightened otherwise, but I refused to mention it. "Marius isn't afraid. He's cautious. Serve under him long enough, and you'll be able to distinguish the two."

Aius took a long pull of his wine. "I wish my first battle wasn't against the Marsi," he said.

"Don't believe all the tales you hear of their

brutality," I said. "They spread these messages like carrier pigeons to sow fear into our ranks. We've beaten better than them."

Aius played with the fringed edges of the red ribbon wrapped around his breastplate. "That's not it," he said. His eyes glazed over. "I visited the Marsi lands with Rhea for the festival of Magna Mater a few years back, when you were in Greece. They're a hardy people, but they were festive and welcoming. Merry. They enjoyed good wine and song, and friendly company." He hung his head. "I'd rather not fight them."

I sighed, having no interest in discussing this. I sympathized with the Italian cause, as did many who'd fought alongside fine auxiliaries throughout their careers. I'd prefer to avoid contemplation of it altogether. It's easy to kill when the enemy is a faceless, nameless entity.

"None of us wish to fight the Marsi. Perhaps we won't have to do so much longer. The politicians in Rome may find a remedy for this quickly. We simply must hold on until then."

He smiled sadly. "You've been gone on campaign too long, my brother, if you think the politicians in Rome will accomplish anything quickly."

I exhaled and took a sip of my wine, just to satisfy him. "I think it's about time to visit Somnus, don't you? Tomorrow will be a long day."

He finished his wine and lingered for a moment. His eyes were wet and strained when he looked up at me again. "Perhaps I could stay in your tent tonight? I'll bring my cot and lie on the floor." He straightened. "You know how much trouble I have rising in the morning, and I don't want to be late to formation."

I patted his knee. "Of course. Get your things and I'll clear a space for you."

 I rose early the next morning. Aius slept fretfully if one could tell by his constant shifting, so I stepped over him and allowed him to rest.

The sky was cobalt, with the sun just beginning to peak over the Apennines in the east. Rich women would have paid vast sums for jewelry the color of that sky, but it was foreboding and threatening on this morning.

I made my way through camp, passing by the legionary tents, which were usually ringing out with snoring and farting. This morning, the only sound from within was the quiet murmuring of legionaries who'd barely slept.

The sentries saluted me and opened the gates as I exited, ambling down to the river with an empty skin of water and a bronze razor in my only hand.

The rippling water was freezing to the touch, despite the oppressive warmth of the June morning. It flowed from the bottom of the Fucine Lake if I remember correctly, so it stayed that way year-round. Regardless, I didn't mind. It reminded me of thawing a skin of water in Gaul just to have a few drops to shave with. Besides, battle would be hot as Vulcan's forge that day, and the water was refreshing.

I scraped the razor over my cheeks and chin, the

stubble quickly falling away. I refilled the skin and took a few sips as I went along. Crouching by the bank, I dipped my razor into the water to wash off the oil and stubble. Even with nothing but the early morning sun for light, I could see a mist of blood surrounding the knife.

It would be my luck to nick myself on the day of battle. Sertorius laughs at my superstitions, but one should not spill any blood before battle that isn't consecrated and offered to the gods. It's a bad omen. All the priests agree.

As I patted my damp face, I found no cuts or blood. Yet the water continued to run red.

I looked up the river and thought I could see a bulky object in the water I hadn't noticed before. I assumed it was a log, or a discarded carriage wheel, but I hurried up the riverbank to get a closer look. It didn't take but a few steps before I could clearly see that the object was a body. And from the helmet still fastened on, I knew it was a Roman.

I sprinted back into the camp. Marius needed to hear of this immediately, even if it was nothing more than a drunken-night-before-battle incident. Before I could reach his praetorium, where I assumed he'd be, I found him exercising shirtless in the fortress courtyard.

"Ah, come to join me, young Hirtuleius? Let's have a match of Greek wrestling and I'll show anyone awake why I'm still feared by nations and tribes across the Mare Nostrum."

I offered a quick salute. "Legate, there's something you must see."

Marius knew his officers and men well. He trusted I wouldn't request his presence if it wasn't dire, so he nodded for me to lead on and we rushed back to the river.

By now, there were dozens of bodies bobbing down the river, and the water was as red as our tunics.

Marius's face revealed nothing as he looked on, bending down to inspect them further.

The headless corpse of a Roman *aquilifer* washed up on the bank right where I'd just shaved.

"These are Lupus's men." He dabbed at the waxy flesh of the corpse with two fingers. "He's not been dead for more than an hour."

"I'll send out riders immediately," I said.

"We have no need." He shook his head. "The battle was lost or is being lost."

"How do you know, legate?"

He pointed around the river. "Do you see any Marsi among these corpses?"

To be honest, their armor was so like ours, I'm not sure I could tell the difference without inspecting them closer, but I trusted Marius.

"We can't defeat the Marsi without them," I said. "I'll rally the men and sound for a tactical retreat immediately."

"No," he grunted. "No. The Marsi camp is undefended. We must act swiftly. Rally the men, but for battle."

I felt a flood come over me with those words. Was it relief, dread, or desire? I don't know. But I was ready to follow the orders.

"Moving, legate," I said.

"Send a few men down here to collect these bodies. After we've vanquished our foe, we'll see that they're honored properly. Perhaps the gods will look after them better than their commander ever did."

Marius made up for our previous delays with godlike speed now. We put our freshly constructed bridge to the test as the legionaries crossed over four abreast, leaving only a single cohort behind to protect the fort and baggage camp.

Aius and I were mounted and waiting for the legionaries to file over before we crossed, groaning and developing another bead of sweat with each creak and shift in the bridge's wood.

The Hirtuleii were a fairer stock than Sertorius's people, but I'd never seen Aius so ashen. His eyes glazed over, and he blinked rapidly. And I knew it wasn't just the bridge that scared him.

"You don't have to shed blood today if you don't want to," I whispered. "You're on the staff of a tribune. No one expects you to join the fray."

He turned, hands trembling on his steed's reins. "Would you avoid battle, brother?" he said. "I didn't think so. And I won't either."

Our turn to traverse the bridge was upon us. Marius lifted his sword to the heavens and began the cavalry crossing.

I kept my eyes forward as we passed over, unwilling to look down at the scarlet river beneath us. It was deep and swift. Under the weight of all my gear, one misstep and I'd sink like a stone to my watery grave. I exhaled with relief the moment we touched grass again, but there was no time to thank the gods. Marius and his black warhorse shot off like a bolt of Jupiter's lightning, and we rushed to follow him.

I wrapped the reins around the nub of my left arm and held on tightly with my right. Battle would be difficult from horseback with one hand, and I was no gifted rider to begin with. But I'd faced greater tasks than this. The gods would see me through, I told myself.

"Double time, march!" the centurions bellowed as we galloped past them.

We followed the bank of the river upstream, more bodies and thicker blood in the stream apparent with every step. Marius lifted his sword again and swung it toward the left, the directional cue we all followed. Part of me wanted to ride directly to Lupus's fortress and avenge our fallen comrades, but we had another objective first.

The sun was nearly at its zenith by the time we spotted the Marsi camp in the distance. The walls were built like ours, but they constructed it poorly. Little more than a fence to keep in their pack animals when compared to the high walls Marius ordered us to construct.

Marius did not halt us for any speeches. The bloated and dismembered corpses of our brothers were all the motivation we needed.

We were nearly two hundred paces away from the Marsi camp when their sentries scrambled out to line up a defense. They poured out in the hundreds, but they were no match for our ranks. The Marsi would suffer for the arrogance of their commander the same as Lupus's men had this morning.

Marius wheeled the cavalry to the right, allowing the legionaries to engage in the initial assault. The whistling of a pila volley sounded behind us, followed by the thud of spear-tip against Marsi shields and the bloodcurdling cries of the wounded.

The Marsi cavalry was hurrying to form up out of a second gate. Their commander was barking orders for them to form up, but they were no more organized than a gaggle of geese by the time we reached them.

I stole one final glance at Aius. His mouth was agape and his breathing erratic. His sword still sheathed.

"Stay with me!" I shouted, but I doubted he heard me over the stamping cavalry.

Marius led the assault as we crashed into them. Horses darted in every direction, some absent their rider and others with the rider slain and limp in the saddle.

I slew the first foe to meet me without hesitation. He stabbed at me once, but I parried and stabbed down into his neck. I looked into his wild, perplexed eyes.

The Marsi had neither the fair skin of the Cimbri nor the beards of the Greeks. Their armor was chainmail like ours; most used short swords identical to the gladii we wielded. They looked like us. It felt like I was killing one of my own people. My brothers.

I'm certain I became as ashen as Aius while I watched the screaming Marsi convulse and collapse from his horse and under the trampling hooves of our cavalry.

I felt a nick across my good arm. Before even turning, I sliced my blade to the right. It ricocheted off the warrior's sword. The reins slipped off my left arm, and my steed wheeled about my enemy. I steadied my blade before me and waited for a moment to strike.

"Come and let me remove your other hand, Roman!" the warrior shouted in crisp Latin.

He stabbed down at my horse's head, but I batted it away. In his brief recoil, I swung and sliced through his shoulder. The wound was deep, but he was lost in battle and felt none of it.

My horse jerked her head back and forth and resisted the direction of my legs. He was in control now, but he stayed close to my foe, as if he wanted to see him fall as much as I did.

I met his eyes and saw him deliberating his next strike. I leapt in preparation, but before the sword stroke came, a spear wedged through his belly, small rings of his chainmail lorica bursting.

He let out the breathless groan of a man who's lung was punctured. He collapsed in his saddle with the spear still wedged in his gut, his sword slipping from his fingers.

The cavalry was in chaos. I swung my head like my horse, trying to find another enemy to face. I could barely tell the difference between their men and our own, and couldn't fix my gaze on anything long enough to distinguish the two. I'd completely lost Aius and couldn't spot Marius either.

A nearby rider shouted. "Kill these Roman whoresons! For the Italic League!"

I kicked my horse toward him, but he refused me. Still, I caught the Marsi warrior's attention, and he instantly galloped toward me.

I recognized him as the man barking orders at our arrival. A formidable foe, with scars of his own all across his exposed forearms, probably earned in battle for the Republic.

"For Rome!" I shouted back at him.

He bared his teeth as he reached me. He wasted no time, belting out a flurry of strikes I narrowly blocked. The strength of his arm was enough to nearly force me to lose my grip, but I held on tight. I knew my life depended on it.

With the last strike of this volley, my horse proceeded and moved me from the path, perhaps saving my life. I swung down and cleaved off the rebel's hand at the wrist, the blade still wedged in his grasp.

He let out a wail that rose above the tumult, grabbing his bloody nub. I knew the feeling, but he wouldn't have to live with it long. I thrust my sword into his gut, all my weight behind it. I struggled to keep my balance as I bore harder to get through the breastplate, and then the easy release as it tore through the soft tissue of his stomach. Lifeblood spilled through his stained teeth and over snarled lips. The last look he gave me before his eyes rolled back was one of defiance.

There was no order for retreat, but their remaining cavalry were scurrying off in any direction they could for safety. Most didn't make it far.

"Do not give chase," Marius bellowed from somewhere in the chaos. "Into the fortress!"

He let out a victory cry and rode into the Marsi camp. The surviving warriors were seeking shelter in vain within their tents and camp structures, all laid out exactly like a Roman camp. Our riders hunted them down like rabbits and swiftly put an end to their cries for mercy.

I searched for Aius in the stampeding cavalry but could see nothing.

The booming crack of splintering gates resounded through the air as our legionaries burst into the camp. The battle—or, more appropriately the slaughter—was over.

"*Roma Invicta!*" Marius shouted, and echoes of the victory cry sounded from all over the Marsi camp.

Torches spun toward the smoking fortress. The acrid stench of burning leather and fallen warriors rose through the air.

In the distance I saw Manius Aquillius, one of the other tribunes, capturing their granaries, the camp followers already on their knees in surrender. Already legionaries were brandishing iron chain to shackle them.

"Aius!" I cried out but knew I couldn't be heard.

I dismounted and walked my horse to a hitching post. He complied without a fuss, just as relieved the battle was over as any of us.

I searched throughout the camp as our forces captured slaves, burnt down buildings, tested out the Marsi weapons and armor to see if they were worth keeping, and used their daggers to carve out gold teeth or cut off the ringed fingers of the fallen.

"Aius!"

Nothing. I ran out of the fortress, where the slain cavalrymen were baking in the June sun. I spotted his armor then, as he had a red ribbon tied around the breastplate. Aius was on his knees with his hands in his lap and his head bowed.

My heart sank, I feared him dead with the rest

of them, but even from a distance I could see his trembling. He was the only living man among them.

"Aius, Aius," I said. "Are you hurt?"

His eyes were not blinking at all now, he stared at his hands, as if in wonder of them.

His voice was hoarse and little more than a whisper. "My steed died," he said. "Is that my fault?" His gaze remained fixed on his hands.

"No, of course not, brother." I attempted to help him up, but he didn't budge, so instead I knelt beside him.

His voice was flat now, like he was responding to a bad joke. "I killed a man." He swallowed. "I cut off his leg at the knee like, like . . . like it was nothing more than cabbage."

I pulled him toward my chest. I found myself staring at his hands as well. They were covered in blood spatter, but otherwise unharmed. They were shaking so much that his belt was jingling beneath them.

"You don't have to talk about it now," I said. "We've won the day."

"The bone was harder to get through than I imagined," he said. "More resistance. I did not know the bone was so stark and white when seen on a severed limb."

I reached over and calmed the trembling of his hand, finding them slippery with the blood on each of them.

"Grandfather would be proud of you," I said. "I'm proud of you."

He looked at me. "Not as glorious as they say," he said, still nothing but a blank fixture in his eyes. "Nothing to it, really. Just try not to die."

I rubbed his shoulder as I heard footsteps coming from the gate.

"On your feet, tribune," Marius said. He noticed Aius and his face hardened in a moment of understanding. "The day is not done yet. We set out for Lupus's camp."

I looked at Aius and back to Marius. This skirmish would be nothing compared to a battle against the full army of Poppaedius Silo, and I couldn't imagine Aius making it out alive in this condition.

Marius seemed to know my thoughts. "I'm leaving behind two hundred men to secure all the supplies and armaments. I order him to stay with them."

I exhaled with relief. "Thank you, legate."

Marius nodded. "Mount up, we're leaving presently."

I managed to get Aius to his feet and walked him into the camp. He was unharmed other than a bruised leg resulting from the fall off his horse, but his mind was elsewhere and had no sense of direction or purpose.

I held a skin of watered wine to his lips and forced him to drink before I returned to my steed and joined Marius. We left immediately.

Halfway to Lupus's camp, we met the celebrating Marsi on the road. They were formed up for marching, not in battle array. The sound of their cheering and victory songs vanished when they caught sight of us.

I saw the rebel "consul" and rebel commander, Poppaedius Silo, at the head of the formation on a tall horse to match Marius's.

Both forces remained at a halt, less than a mile

apart. By my eye, they outnumbered us three to one. That they hesitated was interesting. But perhaps they'd already quenched this day's thirst for Roman blood.

Marius remained still; his fist raised. With the flick of his wrist, he could send us forward to battle, or back toward our camp. His gaze was fixed on Silo, as if to see the choice was his.

A hawk screeched above. Standards whipped and cracked in the wind.

Silo cupped his hands round his mouth and shouted, "Go and greet your comrades! We've left you a gift."

"Shall we pursue them?" I asked Marius, wrapping the reins even tighter around my nub this time.

Marius's eyes narrowed. "Sally forth if you have the stomach," he shouted.

He led his horse to the opening between us, and I followed with a few other riders. Silo deliberated but eventually met us in the middle.

The expanse between the two armies seemed to shrink compared to the palpable tension between the two commanders.

"I will repay what you did this morning. Tenfold. Remember my words," Marius said.

Silo was tall and commanding, with broad shoulders to match the rippling muscles of the towering warhorse beneath him. He wore a weathered cloak that billowed in the wind, revealing glimpses of a bloody sword on his hip. A strong jawline and long nose accentuated his piercing gaze, eyes flickering with the embers of defiance. A neatly trimmed dark beard framed his seasoned face, revealing both nobility and a rugged stoicism men desire in their commanders.

He had seen many battles before, that much was clear. They were almost certainly battles waged for the Roman Republic.

The rebel commander's words were measured and calmly rendered. "Justice will be served, of that I have no doubt," Silo said. "Frankly, general Marius, this was long overdue."

Marius's lips twisted like a pair of angry snakes. "You speak of justice as a fish speaks of flying. Rome offers justice, and no one else."

Silo's horse carried him a few steps closer. They could reach out and strike each other now if they desired. My knuckles tightened around my hilt.

"Rome had the power to extend justice, instead they denied it. I will rectify that."

His Latin was refined like a Falernian grape wine. He'd clearly spent much time with the Roman elite. He would be indistinguishable in a room of senators.

"You will cause the deaths of thousands of men on both sides of us. And in the end, you will die as well. I will erase your name from history."

Silo smiled. "History may not remember me. You may not remember me. But I remember you, Gaius Marius. More than any other Roman, I will delight in seeing the light fade out of your eyes," he said. "Mighty conqueror, six-time consul . . . dead at the hands of a rebel."

Marius drew his sword. "Let us not delay your gratification any longer, then," he said. "Fight me."

I brandished my gladius, as did every man present except Silo. He alone kept his hands folded in his lap, unconcerned by the sword tip poised a few feet from him.

"Not today, Gaius Marius. But soon enough. We will meet on the battlefield. Perhaps then you will remember me. I will be the last face you look upon."

He slowly wheeled his horse around and cantered off back to his army.

Marius led us back to our formation. His knuckles whitened on the firm grip of his reins.

"Forward," he ordered.

We passed the Marsi as they marched eastward, almost a stone's throw away from us. Watching them leave, Roman blood still dripping from their swords, the cause of all the dismembered corpses flowing down our river—we all wanted to attack. I can sense the heart of a legion by nothing but the stamping of their feet, and I could tell they desired to punish Silo and his men.

Marius's voice was loud enough for the entire legion to hear, and perhaps our enemies as well. "Let us not delay," he said. "They will soon taste the fruits of their victory. In this life, they'll receive torture, death, and dismemberment. In the next, the gods will repay their treachery with eternal torment."

We reached Lupus's camp within half an hour and halted before the smoldering walls. The smoke billowed higher than any temple in Rome. Nothing but the crackling of fires sounded from within.

The legatus ordered only a handful of us to ride forward, as I'm sure he knew the sight awaiting us might have destroyed the morale of our less hardened recruits.

I wrapped my cloak around my face as we

entered, but still coughed from so much smoke. Marius alone appeared unperturbed.

The grotesque display awaiting us made the Marsi camp look like a small skirmish. Headless bodies were strewn about, so packed in it appeared they all died simultaneously in formation. A row of spikes stood before the burning praetorium; the head of a Roman officer placed on each.

My eyes were watering, and I told myself it was the smoke. The horses were becoming skittish. Most of us dismounted, as it was nearly impossible to ride with so many corpses about us.

I wandered aimlessly through this horror. I peered into legionary tents to find men dead in their cots, each with a deep red gash through their throats.

What kind of treachery, what kind of evil led to this?

Everyone silenced around me. I searched for the cause, and it was then that I found it.

I noticed the feet first. Blood dripped from the toes. The fine leather of the sandals was caked with mud. And a single nail pierced them together and onto the piece of wood behind them.

Consul Lupus had been crucified.

I found Marius beneath the cross, staring up at the man he'd once stood beside and against in the senate house, the same he'd worked and coordinated the war effort with since the rebellion began.

The consul's eyes stared blankly down at us. A crumpled scroll was nailed to his chest. It read 'Filii Remi'.

Marius looked up with nothing but disgust in his eyes. "There is no punishment mentioned in all the tomes of history and all the gods befitting this crime." The veins of his neck and forehead bulged. "Cut him down. You three, find any cart that isn't already in ruins. Gather up the bodies."

I said a silent prayer for the fallen consul and all his men, asking Proserpina to see them rewarded in the afterlife for their sacrifice.

Marius turned to me. "I'm taking them to Rome," he said. "Let's see if the people still want three days of festivals."

SCROLL XII

GAVIUS SERTORIUS—IDES of June, 664 Ab Urbe Condita

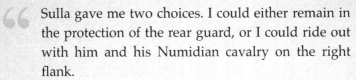 Sulla gave me two choices. I could either remain in the protection of the rear guard, or I could ride out with him and his Numidian cavalry on the right flank.

I thought only for a moment about what my father might have done.

"I'll join you," I said.

Perhaps compelled by his own *dignitas*, or forced by my decision, Cicero sighed and said, "Marcus Tullius Cicero will not remain behind the line while our brothers fight to defend us."

I stifled a grin. I couldn't imagine my dear friend riding into battle, even after all our training, but I found his presence comforting. If he could do it, we all could.

The air was cool and crisp as we rode out on the morning of battle. Rainfall watered the fields during the night, and a white mist rose and spun around us like smoke from a campfire.

Sulla was a cheerful person by nature, but he was in remarkably good spirits as we approached the open valley beneath Aesernia.

A wisp of golden hair danced above his brow. Paired with his grin and the playful way he bounced on his steed, he almost appeared boyish. But there was no mistaking that the Roman leading us was a warrior. The muscles in his arms were defined and unrestrained by the toga he usually wore, even in camp and in his armor. I'd never seen him prepared for battle before, but now the stories of his prowess and skill were easy to comprehend.

The historical depictions on his breastplate were inlaid with gold. Despite being surrounded by an entire legion of legionaries clad in white, he seemed to stand out from the rest from the sheer starkness of his cloak.

The formation was determined the night prior. Sulla ordered the reserves to line up behind the left and right flanks, exposing our center if the frontal assault was violent enough. One of his officers said this was a madman's gambit, but Sulla smiled and said with our superior cavalry, it was a roll of the die worth betting on.

As the men formed up, the cavalry followed Sulla out to address them. It was now that I saw just how vulnerable our center was. I knew nothing of warfare, but our frontlines seemed pitifully thin compared to the flanks. It felt like a stone lodged in my throat. Despite myself, I couldn't look away, couldn't stop imagining the center failing and our lines breaking. A rout. Slaughter. Death.

But I was close enough to see that Sulla was

looking the same way, and there was nothing but a smile on his face.

"This is a glorious day, brothers!" he shouted, his voice carrying seamlessly through the valley. "A glorious day! For this is the day we begin reconciling with our misguided allies."

The comment surprised me, and I imagine it did the men as well, for there was no applause.

Beside me, Cicero's hands trembled and clutched his reins with a grip uncommon to him.

"Feel no remorse or guilt for what we're about to do today," Sulla said. "When wolves leave their pack, it is the role of the others to find them and swat them back to their senses. To walk them— battered and bloody though they may be—back to their father's tribe." He became serious, but not sullen. With pride, he looked out over our legion, Sulla's Fist, as he called us. "That is what we must do today. Let us make the *swatting* memorable enough that our wayward countrymen do not tarry much longer."

I peered over my shoulder and saw the rebels beginning their advance.

"Let us remind them—let us remind all of Italy —we are Rome."

Finally, the legionaries let out a collective war cry, and began bashing their swords against their shields. I'd never heard anything like it.

"Fight well. Protect the man beside you. And spare none," Sulla shouted. "*Roma Invicta!*"

"*Roma Invicta!*" the entire formation bellowed.

Sulla lifted his sword to the morning sun and set off toward the right flank.

"How do you feel?" Tribune Lucullus asked me as we found our position.

I almost said that I was fine or that I was excited to begin the day. Or that I was only bothered by the ceaseless blinking of my eyes. In the end, I said nothing.

"Mars and Bellona will keep you," he said. "The first battle is always the hardest. But remember, that's all it is. The first. We will live to see many more." He'd seen no more battles than me, but the confidence with which he spoke was inspiring nonetheless.

The air was cool, but my flesh was burning. My face felt like sunbaked brick. All I could do was nod, lest I make my fears known.

The rebels were advancing now. And moving swiftly. Orders were given, and our legionaries moved forward, but at a quarter the pace of our enemy. They moved silently save the determined and collective stamp of their feet. We remained in position, waiting on the order from Sulla.

"You are nervous?" said a Numidian horseman before me. I looked away for the shame of it, but I could feel the man's smile.

I nodded.

"Nothing to worry, Roman," he said. "Sulla is great commander. Why we followed him from my country. We win today."

I took a deep breath and looked up again, this time summoning a quick smile. I dared not look to Cicero, knowing our collective fear might have sent us both riding off to the coast in treachery and cowardice.

Forcing myself to look out over the advancing enemy forces, I said a silent prayer. Arrea told me my father's favorite of the divinity was Diana, for she had saved him in battle once before. It was to her I prayed.

But my mind refused to stop when I made my final vow of offering.

The faces of the Italian rebels began to grow into view. They looked so familiar, so . . . normal. Hearing tales of battle as a young man, I imagined my first battle would be against unnatural men who looked as strange and contemptible as the monsters Odysseus fought.

But they were just like me. Like Cicero and Lucullus. Perhaps like my father. They might have had wives or mothers like Arrea.

I shook my head to stop the thoughts. My father's resort in distress was philosophy. He'd been absent for many years, and I'd been unable to benefit from his wisdom since I was a boy, but I knew enough to steel my mind.

Maiming and death might await me.

A disturbing thought, but to name my fears, even as the enemy drew nearer and nearer, seemed almost comforting.

On the other hand, I might be about to maim and kill others.

Somehow that felt no better.

The whistling of vaulted javelin filled the morning air as our first and second rank sent out a volley of pila. The faint cries of the fallen rose, but the clash of arms quickly snuffed it out as their front line broke against ours like water on rock.

This was my duty. I would make Sulla proud, I would make my father proud.

I felt something rising in my throat. Sour bile poured into my mouth, but I swallowed it down.

Sulla's voice was cool and crisp as the morning air. "Forward!"

We followed him far off to the south, and for a moment it felt as if we were fleeing the battle entirely. I'm ashamed to admit I wouldn't have minded it. But in a terrible and decisive flick of Sulla's wrist, we wheeled about, heading directly for the enemy infantry attacking our right flank.

I would be protected, I told myself. Mars and Bellona would keep me, like Lucullus said. And so would Diana. I'd made a very generous vow of twenty pigeons, after all. At least I thought that was generous. Perhaps it wasn't enough. I hoped it was enough.

The Numidian cavalry was light and swift. Shouting out curses in their own tongue, they broke away from the rest of us and crashed into the enemy line first.

Panic set in as I realized I remembered nothing of my training. Junior tribunes received little combat training. I cursed myself for not joining the legionaries in more of their exercises. What did I do with my sword?

Brandish it first? I did so now, and it sang from my scabbard. It felt thin and weightless in my hand compared to the wooden ones we'd used in training. I couldn't imagine how it could pierce through a chain-mail lorica. But of course it did. Right? How else could the rest of our men ride into battle so carelessly?

I reached the enemy infantry before my mind caught up to itself. The horse beneath me took control and leapt over and onto them before their swords could find a mark.

Flesh burning now. More than before. Breath in

my lungs scorching, like a sun burn. Legs were exposed, and I was keenly aware of it now.

I was surrounded by the angry infantry of our spurned allies. I could not fight them all. I could not defend myself from them all. I did not want my horse to die. I did not know what to do.

Just keep riding.

I heard a voice. It was in my head. It was Diana. Or Bellona. Or Mars, perhaps, but I believe it was female.

My horse carried me forward, and once I heeded the voice, I pushed her harder.

I saw so much, I saw nothing. Men on both sides. Italian and rebels. Angry. With me. Why me? There was violence in their eyes, and I did not even look at them. I felt it.

Before one stabbed at me, I swung my blade down to meet it. I felt the ricochet up my arm. My horse kept moving, and she didn't cry out.

I felt mounds of human flesh under her hooves. I heard the bones snap. Whether it was alive or dead I did not know.

Our infantry troops were to my left. They were fighting tirelessly. At first they were winning and pushing forward. The closer I got to the center, the less this was the case. They were further away with each stride. More of the enemy filled the gap.

Sulla said this would happen. The center was supposed to collapse. Then we would envelope the enemy as they advance. I knew nothing of war except the stories my father had told me, but it looked bad.

I ignored the dying—ally and foe—and kept pushing my steed forward. I swung my sword errantly to my right. I felt reverberations as it clashed into sword or shield. Perhaps into flesh.

"Mars be with us!" I heard Sulla cry. Or at least I think I did.

Suddenly, and I mean suddenly, I was in the air. I heard my horse screech. She did so right before, I think, but I didn't hear it until I was in the air. I hit the earth with a thud, the mud created by the previous day's rain billowing up around me.

Violent eyes stared down at me.

I saw the shimmer of a sword tip, just above my eyes. The man wielding it opened his mouth and roared, but then a blade dissected his face. He screamed and fell back, his cheek bloody and split by a Roman gladius.

Another stabbed down at me. I batted it away. I saw the olive flesh of a leg beside me. I sliced at it. The knee shifted and for a moment I thought I missed, but then the leg split.

I bellowed out like the legionaries had before, not seeking to kill but seeking to live more than ever before. I stabbed at the gut of a distracted enemy warrior. He recoiled from the force, but I failed to split the rings of his chainmail.

I tried scrambling to my feet but slipped in the mud and the blood.

The violent tip of an enemy sword careened toward me. I rolled over before I even perceived it. Perhaps that was Bellona's doing, or Diana's.

As I recoiled, I swung my sword and severed his arm at the wrist. I heard the man cry and it neither delighted nor horrified me. I stabbed him in the bicep. Blood burst out in spurts like a half-clogged fountain in the forum.

How am I still alive? I wondered.

As if the enemy heard me, several swords appeared above me, ready to plunge.

Be proud of me father. I thought, and I was speaking to Quintus Sertorius when I conjured those words.

I closed my eyes and awaited my fate. Finality might be relief in the chaos of battle.

But I felt no pain. When I opened my eyes again, the white clad legionaries of Sulla's Fist were stepping over me.

I felt a force behind me, propelling me to the air once again.

"On your feet, sir," a voice said. It was a legionary. "The fight isn't over."

"Onward and at them!" I felt myself shout.

I had no shield, but I fell into line with the rest of the legionaries, and they protected me with theirs.

Sulla's Fist. My eyes felt open now for the first time that day. And we were exactly what Sulla said we were. Conquerors.

"Kill them all!" I bellowed, and somewhere inside I wondered where it came from.

I felt invincible now. Perhaps divine. I pushed my way toward the front of the formation, despite the resistance of the legionaries closest to me.

Lucullus's prophecy had proved true. The gods protected me. I would live to see nightfall, and now I needed to prove myself. Whether anyone would see it, whether my father would know of it. I wanted, I *needed*, to prove that I was like them. And now I felt the courage to do so.

I arrived at the front line. The faces of the rebels were now intimate and personal, so close before me, but I felt none of the apprehension I did previously.

"Retreat!"

I heard the words but didn't comprehend them. I continued fighting my way to the front ranks and was nearly there. Just one. I needed to know I killed one man that day, at least.

But a swift river of retreating legionaries carried me away. The enemies seemed to be doing the same, the gap between us and them growing ever wider.

"It's over, sir," a legionary said, placing a hand on my shoulder.

I wrenched myself away before I even processed what he was saying. "Get off of me!" I bellowed.

He released me. I advanced to the gap left between the enemy forces and ours. There was an incomprehensible amount of bodies there, both theirs and ours. But I felt nothing about the loss in that moment.

I needed to find my horse. That was the only thing I needed.

It took me only moments to spot her in the carnage. She was three times the size of the surrounding bodies. Her tongue hung out and touched the bloody mud. Her eyes were open.

All the strength faded from me then. I fell to my knees. I climbed over the broken bodies to reach her.

I finally perceived the terrific screams all around me. The dying from both sides. And no one was coming back for them.

I watched the enemy descend toward Aesernia where they were setting up siege, and Sulla's Fist retreating the same way back to our own camp.

No one won this day. A stalemate. Just bloodshed.

"Come on, girl. I'm here now," I said. But I knew in my heart she wasn't waking up.

I laid her head down softly against the mud and forced her eyes closed. Standing, I checked myself to make sure there were no other injuries I was unaware of. There was nothing but the superficial. I hobbled over the mounds of corpses back toward to the camp.

When Sulla saw me, he jumped off his own horse and ran to me. *Dignitas* says no Roman man of stature should ever run, but it did not sway Sulla this day.

"My boy, I thought we lost you," he said.

I swallowed, but eventually found the right words to say. "I lost my horse. I could not return until I said goodbye."

"Young Gavius, I would sacrifice all the horses in Italy if it means you are safe," he said. "You did well today. I am proud."

Something flooded out of me then, and I collapsed in his embrace. I wept and didn't attempt to hide it.

"Battle scars all men, in one way or another," he said. "But at least you did not turn out like poor Cicero."

He nodded over toward the battlements, where my young friend crouched and vomited. Lucullus knelt beside him, patting his back.

I laughed, but it was not at Cicero's expense.

"Let me go offer some comfort," I said.

Sulla smiled and clapped me on the back one last time. "When you're done, we'll share a cup in celebration."

I struggled to find my balance, but eventually made my way to Cicero and knelt beside him. "We made it, my friend."

He turned to me, ashen white and just as reproachful as he ever was when we discussed philosophy.

"Do not ever let me do that again," he said. "I think I'll remain in the rear guard moving forward, thank you."

He barely got the last words out before he vomited once again. I looked at the older tribune, wondering if we might share a silent laugh at our friend's expense, but there was no humor in Lucullus's face.

"A terrible thing we must do," Lucullus said as he patted Cicero's back. "All for the glory of Rome."

"All for the glory of Rome," I echoed.

I stood then and watched as the remaining legionaries funneled into the fortress.

I felt as if I left something on that battlefield. Something I needed to go back and retrieve.

I'm not sure I ever found it.

SCROLL XIII

 "Bring me another cup, and more spice this time," Tullia ordered to any *servus* listening.

Dining with my hosts became increasingly uncomfortable as Tullia's pregnancy advanced, but she was particularly uncomfortable on this night.

"In Gaul, women often drink milk when they're pregnant." I picked at a few figs left over from our first course and leaned up on my couch.

Tullia leaned back and allowed a slave to dab her forehead with a damp towel.

"And where has that gotten the Gauls?" she said. "They're barbarians are they not? Roman women drink wine. It civilizes the baby."

She struggled to rock herself to a seated position so she could drink more comfortably. Tullia's gulps were becoming as uncouth as her husbands, who sat across from us with an open mouth full of food and ears not listening.

"Perhaps if the little fellow becomes drunk, he'll hurry and get out of me," she said, her voice more shrill by the hour.

I forced a smile. "He may not be ready yet," I said. "Do you know exactly when you conceived?"

She snorted and shook her head. "My husband couples with me so rarely I can mark the exact day. It's been long enough."

I crossed my legs and shrugged. "You've created a warm and safe home for the child. Perhaps he just wants a while longer with you."

A pang of jealousy ran through my chest.

Her words slurred. "Well, he certainly hasn't asked my opinion on the matter." Tullia's eyes narrowed as she looked at Tranquillus. "Have you nothing to say, husband? You did this to me. Look at my ankles." She pulled up the hem of her stola, something she would have never done sober or undisturbed by the discomfort of her pregnancy, revealing swollen knots where thin, shapely ankles had been recently.

Tranquillus stood with a grunt. "Too much women talk . . ." he mumbled.

She shook her head as he waddled off. "I pray he's a better father than he is a husband."

I thought about Sertorius. Despite the difficulties we'd endured throughout our marriage, I could not imagine a more dutiful and loving husband. Still, he would be an even better father. My face blushed at the thought of him with a newborn, of how he would tend and care for me as I carried it in my womb. The image of him holding a tiny babe to his chest made my stomach leap.

"Men are often uncomfortable with such matters," I assured her. "We will help bring your child into the world, and when Tranquillus sees your child for the first time, he will love you more than you ever thought possible."

She finished her wine, laid back on her couch, and placed a hand dramatically on her forehead. "Dear Arrea, what can you know of birthing if you've born no child of your own?"

My skin bristled. I reminded myself the pregnancy had overwhelmed her, and she'd drank too much wine. "You are right, I haven't given birth myself. But I've helped countless women bring life, and I'll do the same with you."

As a slave, one of my many responsibilities was to serve in the position of midwife, both to my fellow slaves and the various mistresses who owned me.

Suddenly, and without provocation, she burst into tears. "Oh, Arrea. I'm afraid it will be a difficult birth. The way he kicks, I fear he'll fight the entire way out."

I hurried to comfort her, but my words were firm. "Steel yourself, girl," I said. "He senses you, and your tears and fears startle him."

She sniffled and embraced me.

My breasts ached the way my beating heart did beneath.

A shadow parsed through the flickering torch-light, and I knew from the determined stride it wasn't Tranquillus.

"It's akin to the battlefield. Just a different type of war."

I turned to find my husband there, strong and handsome in his officer's armor. The muscles of the breastplate were nearly as defined as the ones he contained beneath it.

One of Tranquillus's slaves rushed into the triclinium behind him.

"Quaestor of Rome, Quintus Sertorius, commander of Mutina's legions!" he shouted, a bit too late for a formal entry.

Tullia wiped her tears. "We are so glad you've come, Quaestor," she said. "You've been absent of late."

Quintus exhaled and nodded. He looked into my eyes and there was something of an apology there. "I wish it were not so. The situation in camp has been difficult."

"Bona Dea, I hope it's nothing too serious." Tullia placed a delicate hand on her chest, recomposed.

Tranquillus came shuffling back into the dining room. He lacked personality, but he was most animated when my husband was around. Tranquillus was the type who wanted to be surrounded by powerful men, which was likely the reason he volunteered to host me.

Quintus extended his hand and nodded to Tranquillus. "Not so grievous," he said. "The complications one might expect from this sort of position. Nothing more."

Tranquillus nodded with a thoughtful look on his usually dull face. "Traitors I bet. They're everywhere."

Quintus swallowed and eventually nodded. "We're exploring that possibility, yes."

"Check for markings," Tranquillus said.

"I don't take your meaning."

"Check for markings. They give themselves

tattoos like the Gauls. Heard it from a cousin who lives in Capua, where they caught some traitors."

This was the most coherent sentence I'd heard my host utter, and the look on my husband's face revealed he was equally impressed.

"Thank you, Tranquillus. I will certainly do that." He turned his attention back to me. "Could I speak with you for a few moments?"

"Certainly." I stood, both eager and hesitant to have a few moments alone with my husband.

"Forgive me, I have not properly embraced you." His muscular arms enveloped me, and he kissed my head. His chest expanded against me as he smelled my hair.

He apologized to our hosts and promised to share a drink with them soon, before leading me away, to the peristylum.

Their garden contained more expensive statues than flowers, but Sertorius knew greenery and bird song would set me at ease. It was a tactic he often employed, and one I was now aware of.

I assumed he brought bad news.

We sat on an ornately carved marble bench beside a trickling water fountain.

"Tell me, how are things really? I've barely seen you the past few weeks."

"Unfortunately, my dear, I must always be cautious of listening ears." He glanced around the room, but there was no one present, not even *servi*.

I took a deep breath.

He seemed to notice my disappointment.

"How have you been here? Are your hosts kind to you?"

There was little to share about my monotonous time in the home of Tranquillus and Tullia, aside from her delayed pregnancy and growing frustration. He likely knew that.

"All is well, Quintus," I said.

He opened his mouth to reply but I interrupted him.

"When I've assisted Tullia in her birth, I'd like to leave. I . . ."

"Where would you like to go?" he said. "To join me in camp, or back home?"

"I don't know," I said. I hadn't given it much thought until now, but I spoke truth. I was ready to leave. This venture afforded me little more time with my husband than I'd have waiting for him in Rome. Something needed to change about the arrangement.

"I understand," he said, but his eye revealed deep concern. "But the camp is unsafe. The rebels have infil—" He caught himself and lowered his tone. "The camp isn't safe. Tranquillus is right that Roman traitors are within our midst. Whispers of mutiny continue to spread despite our constant effort."

"I will face the danger with you then," I said.

He sighed. "If only I could permit that, my love. But I am already risking so much. My life is threatened. The lives of all the men who serve under me are at risk. And Gavius's life too. I need you safe. I need to know I can sleep at night without worrying your wine has been poisoned or there is a dagger at your throat."

He spoke more freely now than he had in months. The stress of his situation or the genuine fear for my life must have caused it.

I wanted to say something more, but simply nodded. How could I argue against that? How could I willingly make matters worse on my husband when he was already dealing with so much?

But even as I embraced him and whispered, "I understand," I knew it was untrue.

I would leave the home of Tranquillus and Tullia soon enough. One way or the other.

SCROLL XIV

QUINTUS SERTORIUS—THREE days before the Nones of Quintilis, 664 Ab Urbe Condita

My father taught me when a man feels he's losing control of everything around him, he can find solace in hunting.

The hunter can't control whether he returns with a prize, but he can control all the elements that contribute to a successful hunt.

I focused on proper tracking and observing the terrain. I was careful to string my bow properly, not too loose, and not too tight. I remained downwind of my prey, so it didn't pick up my scent prematurely.

To be honest, I didn't much care whether I found the buck I'd been tracking. Its hoofprints in the mud were nearly the size of a bear's, and I knew we could use the meat. But more than anything, I needed some time away from camp. Time to clear my mind.

Pollux sat contentedly beside me. The wind ruffled the shaggy hair of his ears and forehead. His black nose twitched as he attempted to pick up the scent of our prey.

He was no hunting dog, like the Laconians bred for that singular purpose. He was neither large nor ferocious enough to serve as an efficient guard dog in the event we found ourselves near a predator. But I found his company remarkably comforting, so I brought him along any time I stole to the woods.

Despite my pleasant surroundings and calming company, my mind continued to swim like a violent rapid.

I visited my wife far less than I wanted. I told myself there was nothing else I could do, but I knew in my heart her sadness directly resulted from my choices. I wondered how much longer she could bear it.

Since my arrival in Mutina, I'd written Gavius six letters, and sent them with my best couriers. I still hadn't received a reply.

A chasm had developed between me and the Insteius twins. I reprimanded Aulus for bringing poisoned grain into camp so flippantly, but despite the encouragement of several other officers, I did not punish him formally. Despite that, he ceased calling me by my first name and seemed to avoid speaking with me unless his duties required him to do so.

Spurius lectured me on the flaws of my lenient policies, at least toward everyone but his brother. He encouraged me to bring down an iron fist on the people around Mutina and make stronger displays against traitors. I thought execution was enough.

For the first time since he became my companion, I found little refuge in Apollonius. He was as dutiful and caring as a friend can be, but his own burdens overwhelmed him. And these were burdens I cast upon him with the unrequested promotion. I couldn't bring myself to trouble him any further.

And then there were the legionaries. Hungry, recovering from fevers and poisonings, and doubtful of our cause. Mutiny seemed to linger in the air. Even beyond that, I didn't know who I could trust, who might secretly sympathize with the rebel cause.

Sunlight poured in through a tall canopy of trees above

Pollux and me, but it was otherwise cool and dark. The leaves continued to rustle, but I knew it was nothing more than the wind for the time being. I sat with my back against the rough bark of an old oak, Pollux by my side and my hand on his back.

I didn't know if the buck was still in the area, but I had no intentions of leaving until I knew for certain.

While waiting, I daydreamed about retiring from my position. I could take Arrea and leave this place. We could find somewhere untouched by war, find rest, rekindle the love we once knew.

But Rome needed me, now more than ever. The responsibility left knots in my back and shoulders. I couldn't fail. I couldn't leave.

But perhaps my good fortune was at an end. Perhaps the gods no longer favored me.

Pollux perked up his floppy ears. He craned his neck, and his nose began twitching with increased vigor. He crept to his feet and his body went rigid. One paw lifted, as did his long tail, as he pointed toward whatever awaited us.

My heart stirred like it did when I'd gone hunting with my father as a boy. He would have told me to be still and watchful, but just as when I was a child, I was too eager to remain seated.

I swung myself to my knees and grabbed an arrow from my quiver. I hadn't used a bow in years, as the sling and javelin were the only missile weapons used by the legion, but I knew if I had a clear shot, I wouldn't miss my opportunity.

Pollux crept a few paces with the same repressed excitement I was feeling, and I trailed him closely. I strained my eye to see what he was smelling but could see nothing for the brush and overgrowth of the surrounding forest.

I heard some twigs snapping in the distance, right where Pollux was aiming himself. It was our buck. It would feed one hundred men or more.

At first, I could only see the antlers. They had more points than the barricades outside our fortress. I notched an arrow and held it close to my cheek.

I recalled my father's instructions on breathing and almost heard his voice reminding me to raise my elbow properly.

The buck came into view in a distant clearing. The sunlight dappled his beautiful chestnut coat, his eyes shimmering jewels in a majestic face. I would honor him after his death, as my father taught me.

I waited for my breath to steady, and on the next full exhale, I would release.

"Quaestor," a voice echoed through the trees.

The arrow released and ricocheted off the side of a tree nearby. I could see nothing of the deer now but the trail of dirt and crumbled leaves left in his wake.

"My apologies, Quaestor. I . . . I didn't know."

No matter how alone I might feel, there was always a contingent of guards nearby. They were told expressly to avoid interrupting me unless it was urgent. I knew from the sheepish look on the young legionary's face he wouldn't have done so otherwise.

"What is it?"

"I've been told to bring you quickly," he said. "Urgent news, I'm told."

I slung the bow over my chest and looked down to Pollux. His ears were pinned, and he whined in disappointment.

"Sorry, boy," I said. "We'll get him next time."

"I'll take you to them straight away, sir." The legionary waved me on.

Typically, no one else was bold enough to interrupt me in my few moments of rest. I knew at once he meant one of the Insteius twins, or both.

Once we reconvened with the ambling guards posted at the edge of the wood line, I saw the horses of both the Insteius twins.

"I suppose your father's hunting skills were wasted on you?" Aulus said.

"Perhaps he should have spent that time teaching me how to choose my friends more carefully," I said.

Aulus chuckled but Spurius found no humor in it.

"What's that supposed to mean?" he said.

"I spoke in jest." I accepted a towel from a nearby legionary and dabbed my forehead. "What is it you needed so urgently?" I said.

"Just a few moments away from listening ears," Spurius said as he leapt from his steed.

"Fortuna may offer some mercy to us at last," he said.

"And how might that be? If it's more recruits, her blessing rides side-by-side with a curse, I'm afraid."

"Not more recruits, although others may be inclined to join us after they hear of our good fortunes," Spurius said.

It'd been some time since we'd received positive news.

"Speak plainly then, brothers," I said.

Spurius stepped closer to me and placed a hand on my shoulder. "There was a battle near the River Reno. Neither the rebels nor the Romans were successful, but both forces were driven off."

I said, "Fortuna surely favors us!"

Spurius shook his head and sighed. "You don't understand. The rebels were on the march to supply the city of Asculum. They were taking rations enough to last them the fall and winter. In their retreat, they had to abandon it."

"A great blessing for the Roman army who fought them, I'm sure. Shall we write them a letter and ask for a measure of charity?" I asked.

Aulus smiled and clapped me on the back. "You really are a dull one, aren't you?"

Spurius massaged the knotted flesh of his neck. "They abandoned the supply train. My scouts reported this at sixth hour.

The pack animals are dead. There was no sign of enemy rein-forcements to recover the lost supplies."

I looked up at the sky and tried to get a sense of what time it was. I could tell from the sun it was at least the eighth hour.

I rubbed my forehead. Pollux was lying by my feet, panting, and peering up at me with his wet, innocent eyes.

"What if they poisoned it like the Sons of Remus?"

"I considered that," Spurius said. "We'll have a small tasting before doling anything out to the men. We can use *servi* or the locals, whatever you like. I'm sure the hungrier among us would revel in the opportunity, even with the lingering threat of rebel tampering."

"Besides," Aulus said. "Why would they poison food that's meant for their allies in Asculum?"

I looked at him blankly. "If the whole thing is a ruse, it was never meant to reach them."

His jaw dropped as if he'd never considered the possibility.

I turned my attention to Spurius. "But what if the carts are empty? A taste-test does nothing to solve that."

Spurius reached into a leather satchel at his hip. From it he drew a fistful of grain, trickling through his fingers. "It's full, Quintus. And I'm no expert on poisoning, but I see no sign of tampering here. Have a look if you'd like."

He sifted some grain into my hands, and it looked as pure as any I'd ever seen. Still, I'd seen nothing wrong with the supplies Rufus left us either, so I couldn't be too certain.

"There is always the threat of an ambush," I said.

"They likely expect us or another Roman force to sally forth with a single contingent of guard and a handful of oxen to pull the carts," Spurius said. "Of course, we can't afford to be so care-less. But if we march out with a cohort or two, we can repulse the ambushers, if any exist."

"I'm certain this is a trap." I let the last of the threshed grain fall to the earth. "But we aren't in a place to ignore oppor-tunities."

The twins nodded.

Aulus asked, "Shall I rally the men for mobilization?"

Pollux jumped up with renewed vigor, noticing the excitement of my companions.

"No," I said. "Tonight. Under the cover of darkness."

Spurius furrowed his brow, and then lowered his head. "Quintus . . . I admire and commend your caution, but the supplies may very well be gone by then."

"Then so be it," I said, and I said it with coldness, without any of the familiarity I generally shared with the twins. "If this is an ambush, those lying in wait for us will be gone by then. If not, then the grain may very well still be there. Regardless, we will go tonight. I may end up being the man who failed in his duty to raise two legions for the war efforts, but I will *not* be the fool who marches his men to their deaths over the promise of a goddess's bounty, especially one who has shown us no favor in so long."

Spurius stared back at me with baleful eyes. I knew he wanted to contest the issue further, but I made it clear there was no room for argument.

At length he nodded and said, "I'll ride back to camp and alert the officers."

"Ensure none of the men are made aware of our plans until nightfall," I said. "We do not know who we can trust."

Spurius saluted before mounting up and departing.

Pollux began barking and wagging his tail at the sudden burst from Spurius's horse.

"Shh, boy. Nothing to worry about," I said.

Aulus chuckled. "My brother is passionate, I'll give him that," he said. "One campaign in Greece, and he thinks he knows better than you."

"I'm not concerned with what my officers think, so long as I can trust them."

Aulus turned to me. "What do you mean by that?"

I sighed. "After everything we've endured in Mutina, I just don't know who I can trust."

His brows were furrowed, but it wasn't anger in his eyes now, but sorrow. He crossed his arms. "But you trust me?"

My silence was enough of a reply.

He cleared his throat. "Let me make something clear, my old friend. I am here for one reason, and one reason only," he said. "Look at me."

I met his gaze.

"You. You are the reason I am here. This is a war I don't want. I suppose I've made that abundantly clear. There is a part of me, a majority perhaps, that wants the rebels to whip our pompous asses from here to the Pillar of Hercules. A part of me that thinks, if all those deserving were considered equal in the eyes of Rome, our Republic would be the stronger for it."

"Aulus, I—"

He raised his hand to stop me. "But I am here, raising troops and preparing to fight alongside you once again because I believe in you . . ." he said. "I believe in you more than I believe in any Republic. More than Rome. And I would follow you into Pluto's arse if you asked me to."

He turned away for a moment. "I had nothing to do with that damned grain supply. If I could go back and change it, I would. I was careless, foolish, reckless . . . but always loyal. Punish me if you want, as the other officers implore you. But I beg you to never doubt that I am ever your friend and ally. Like when we were children. Playing pretend in Nursia's fields. You'd instruct us on who to be and how to act. We all followed you without question then and loved you for it. And we love you now."

He whistled his horse to him and mounted up. "I'll rally with Spurius and the officers. And I'll prepare for tonight." He slid his helmet on over his blonde hair and buckled it beneath his chin. "I'm prepared to kill as many rebels as we need to."

For all his many charms, deception wasn't one of them. I

knew from the look in his eye, he told the truth. I could trust Aulus. Could I trust everyone else?

Spurius pled for me to stay behind—it was an unnecessary risk, he said. Aulus could remain in camp too. He could lead two cohorts and come back with our prize.

As much as I appreciated this, I declined. I assured him it wasn't a lack of confidence in his abilities, but I wanted to be present. I wanted the men to know their commander was there alongside them. And I wanted three cohorts, not two.

The stars were as numerous as all of Rome's legions as we marched out, and the light reflected off the steel chainmail of our fifteen hundred men.

Our scouts put the distance at eight miles southeast from Mutina before we left. We covered three times that much ground in training every day, but it felt different when marching in unfriendly territory, when the sun was no longer shining, and the watchful eyes of our sentries were not there to guard us.

We'd been marching for half a watch, at least, and seen nothing. No travelers on the road, no hastily made camps off to the side. Even the fauna seemed silent this night. Insects chirped in the overgrown weeds surrounding the stone road, and frogs croaked whenever we approached a bog. Otherwise, all was still.

I broke off from my guard contingent at the back of the formation and galloped to the center where the Insteius twins were riding with another thirty head of cavalry.

"Any word from the scouts?"

Aulus did not look at me, but Spurius did and shook his head. "You'll know as soon as I do. They'll be here any moment."

"Do you think they were slain?" Aulus asked.

Spurius said, "Not my scouts. They're the best in the legion, I assure you. Even if they met resistance, they wouldn't have been spotted."

Right on cue, three scouts galloped over the hills before us.

They didn't look distressed, at least in the shimmering moonlight, but they certainly moved with haste.

"Halt!" I shouted, and Leptis echoed the orders from the front of the formation.

Spurius rode out to meet them. I considered joining, but they departed as quickly as they'd arrived.

"What's the report?" I asked Spurius when he returned.

Spurius stared straight ahead, sweat on his brow and beneath his helm.

"Spurius?" I said.

I saw his jaw tighten and his eyes blink. "They said they saw nothing . . ."

"You don't believe them?" I asked.

He wiped away the sweat and rubbed at his eyes. "Maybe we should turn around," he said.

Aulus whipped toward him with an incredulous look on his face. "Why? We're this close, and they said they saw nothing. Let's keep moving."

"Aulus says we should continue. Spurius . . . do you truly think we should turn around?"

Only half his face was visible in the moonlight, and I could see that it was pale and careworn. Still, he said nothing.

"We'll face it together," I said, and gave the command for our march to continue.

I knew we were nearly there. And as if the gods had been listening to us, only moments passed before we spotted a dark obstruction in our path.

"This is the abandoned supply train?" I said.

"Right where the scouts told us it would be," Aulus said.

"Half-time, march!" I shouted. "Shields out and up." We neared the abandoned wagons. "Halt!"

I could smell the slaughtered pack animals before I could see them.

"Oxen!" Spurius shouted and a few legionaries strained forward from the back of formation with some stubborn beasts of burden.

They took an exceptionally long amount of time to free the slaughtered pack animals and to bind our own.

As the legionaries continued to work, I leapt from my steed and handed off the reins to Spurius.

"What are you doing?" he asked.

I hopped up the side of one wagon and opened a chest. Inside, the earthy smell of fresh grain greeted me. I scooped my hands through it, breathing deeply, as if I might detect some kind of impurity with my nose alone.

There was a crackle then, a sound like fire. I turned toward the disturbance but saw nothing. I strained my eye in the darkness to see something, anything, but nothing appeared.

I hopped down from the wagon and returned to my steed. "Spurius," I said. "I spent months in the camp of our barbarian invaders a decade ago, and this might have been the most admirable reconnaissance I've ever seen."

He nodded. But I knew he wouldn't be entirely relieved until we were all back in camp safely. "Just trying to do my part, Quaestor."

"More oxen!" I shouted. "Let's get each of these carts taken care of and head back to Mutina. I don't think we'll have any difficulty at all enlisting the rest of our legions with supplies like this."

I heard the crackling noise of a fire again, and it was stronger now. I turned to my left, where a ball of burning brush rolled down toward us.

"Shields left!" I shouted, but it was already upon us.

I heard the wails of several Romans as their flesh roasted inside their chainmail.

The same crackling sound developed on the other side.

"Shields right!"

Shapes materialized on the hills on either side of us. Men bent on our destruction.

I ran to the ranks of our men.

"Rally to protect the quaestor," Spurius shouted.

"No, no. Keep your spacing!" I said, but it was too late. Our three cohorts were collapsing to protect me.

"Shields out!" I tried to shout before the clash, but I don't know if I was heard or not.

Our ranks seemed to squeeze inward, and then we expanded outward.

"Push back," I shouted as I felt the surge.

I thrust myself through the ranks of the legionaries, fighting to the front ranks. Aulus's words swirled through my mind. Whoever these attackers were, they'd fought beside us before. The same who helped me fight the Cimbri and Teutones, the same who had expanded the name of Rome all over our vast Republic.

But now, they sought to kill those I loved. They didn't even know that they'd just cursed Spurius. I didn't want to think what they'd do to Arrea, or my son if we lost in the north and they could get ahold of him.

"Rotate!" centurion Leptis shouted, and our lines swapped. And the second line was thirsty for blood. They kept their shields just as confidently before them as the first rank, but their swords were fresh and unbloodied.

"Move!" I pushed myself to the front ranks.

Some rebels gasped when they saw me. Perhaps the eyepatch gave it away. The Hero of the North was there to destroy them.

"Stand firm and remember your training." I reached the front line, fixing myself between the sturdy shields of two legionaries, sword poised at shoulder height.

The dark shapes of enemy soldiers continued pouring over the hills. How our scouts failed to find them was beyond me, but the results were the same. We were surrounded.

Moonlight radiated from gladii all around us, as they stabbed down and over our shields. Oscan war chants began and were rallied by their troops.

I lunged forward with my first strike and found the mark on the unprotected flesh of a rebel's neck, just above his chainmail. The fact that they wore armor fashioned just like ours was discouraging, but I knew every weakness, every unprotected inch of flesh on the bodies of our foes. And I would find them.

Blood sprayed across my face as the man cried out and crumbled. He was quickly swallowed up and others took his place.

The legionary to my right stabbed over his shield as I had, just as the centurions taught him. But it was an inopportune moment to strike. A rebel severed his arm beneath the elbow.

He shrieked as he fell back, dropping his shield and grabbing the stump of his arm.

The legionaries behind him hauled him back by his chainmail, and a few rebels struggled to wedge themselves into his place.

Spotting me, one of them roared and lifted his sword above his head. Before he could bring it down to sever one of my own limbs, I stabbed the exposed flesh of his armpit. The blade found its way through his ribs and to his heart. The warriors eyes rolled back and he collapsed into the ranks of his comrades.

"Restore the line," I shouted.

Legionaries behind us pushed forward.

"Second rank, *pila*!" Leptis's calm but booming voice rose above the tumult.

Instinctively, I and the rest of the men on the front rank dropped to a knee, lifting our shields to cover ourselves.

Javelins whistled above our heads as the front ranks of the rebels cried out or dropped their splintered shields if they were fortunate enough to have lived.

"Strike now!" I bellowed as we leapt back to our feet and cohesively stabbed at the unshielded rebels.

Our line pushed forward in the momentary advantage, but a

new whistling sounded from above. I looked up to find blaze arrows crashing down above us like shooting stars.

The legionary to my right shouted out as an arrow ripped into his cheek, flames billowing out from the wound.

"Spurius." I turned. "Spurius!"

I found him atop his horse with the other contingent of cavalry, surrounded on both sides by our faltering line.

"Quaestor," he shouted back when he spotted me.

"You must break free." I pointed toward the front of the formation. "You must scatter those archers on the hill!"

"Moving!" Aulus shouted, as he and his brother galloped off with the rest of the horsemen.

If they couldn't succeed, we'd all end up in a sea of flaming arrows.

I cried out as I felt a searing pain envelop my left arm. An arrow wedged into my shoulder. I broke it off where I could and stabbed its broken shard into the eye of an advancing rebel.

In his terror and confusion, he swung his sword around him wildly, connecting with friend and foe alike. I ended his suffering with a swift slice of his thigh. He fell forward into our line and was immediately engulfed in swords.

I turned toward our cavalry and saw rebel horsemen riding out to repulse them. They were fewer in number—they hadn't expected us to bring so many. I said a silent prayer to Diana to cover and protect Aulus and Spurius. I knew our lives now depended on them.

"Jupiter!" I bellowed.

"Optimus," a few of the men grunted out in reply.

"Jupiter!"

"Maximus!" more of them echoed.

"Jupiter!"

"Optimus!"

There were no more rebels pouring over the hills. Their numbers were dwindling, but so were ours. Already the number of wounded dragged to safety between our flanks was equaling the number of their defenders.

Another volley of flaming arrows pelted down on our ranks. Most of our men had their shields raised to protect themselves now, but the panic it caused was still palpable.

The weight of the arrow tip in my shoulder seemed to drag the entire left side of my body down, but my sword arm was still strong. The man beside me was in a pitched conflict with the rebel across from him, his shield buttressed up against the other man and both striking without finding the mark.

I sliced through the flesh and sinew of the rebel's arm, and in his moment of recoil, the legionary thrust his blade through the gaping mouth of his opponent.

The flaming arrows ceased. Atop the hill, the twins and our surviving cavalry swept through the ranks of the fleeing rebel archers. Their cries sounded throughout the valley.

The rebel infantry turned in terror, finding themselves now surrounded between our line and our cavalry, their own horsemen and archer reserves scattered like rabbits.

Their Oscan war chants and insults vanished as their men scampered away from the fray.

"Forward," Leptis shouted. The line advanced while I rushed to support our other flank, where the fighting continued.

"Our commander is with us!" one centurion shouted, and the men rallied around me.

"*Pila* on my signal." I lifted my sword and brought it down fast. "Now!"

The first rank crouched again, and the volley of javelins swept over them.

Turning to the other flank, our cavalry was swarming over the rebels now, slaughtering every man who attempted escape.

The other rebels must have seen it, too, for as the dust of the pila volley settled, they were fleeing as well.

"Let them run, let them run!" I bellowed.

We'd had enough ambushes for one day, and I wouldn't allow us to charge haphazardly into another.

We won the night.

I stood alone on the hill among the corpses of the fallen rebel archers, gazing down at the carnage of the battle we'd just endured.

My wound demanded attention from a *medicus*, but it could wait. The cries of our survivors reminded me there were many others who needed more attention than me.

Spurius and Aulus rode up toward me.

"If that arrow were only a few inches away, you might have lost your other eye," Aulus said.

"You need to see a *medicus*." Spurius inspected the wound.

"I will. Fortunately, the flames cauterize the wound. I suppose I'll thank the rebels for that." I pressed on the tender flesh around the broken arrow shaft. "Do we have a report?"

Spurius shook his head. "Leptis is still tallying up the dead and the wounded."

"The eye test tells me . . . it is not good." Aulus sighed. "But they failed to slaughter our oxen, so at least we can return with the grain."

I shook my head. "These rebels are either idiotic or profoundly arrogant. Why on Gaia's earth would they leave actual supplies for an ambush?"

"Perhaps they knew you'd be too cautious to sally forth otherwise," Spurius said.

Aulus shrugged. "Or perhaps they felt certain of their victory?"

I watched as legionaries were piling up the corpses of the dead and gathering wood for a pyre.

I sighed. "War is the most unnatural thing," I said.

Spurius frowned. "If it were unnatural, man wouldn't have been waging war since before time."

I shook my head. "War isn't natural. Violence is, perhaps, but not war. Fighting to protect your home, your family . . . settling disputes with another. But young men fighting a war they know very little about, that is unnatural. How many of these men, how many of those who started this war at Asculum really know anything about it? How many truly believe this was the best course of action? All it takes is a few powerful politicians or rhetoricians. A handful will rally to the cause because they seek blood. The rest have no choice but to comply. How can they not enter the fray when their fathers, brothers, and friends have already done so?"

I was content in our silent melancholy until Aulus said, "We have won the day, and will return home with a great gift from the rebels. Perhaps that's enough for now, nay?"

"Perhaps," I said. "But we still have one problem."

"I'd say we have more than one," Aulus said. "Which do you speak of?"

I turned to them. "We have a traitor among us. The rebels couldn't have known we would march out tonight otherwise." The throbbing in my head now matched the intensity of the pain in my arm. I rubbed wearily at my temples. "I have heard that the Sons of Remus mark their bodies with a kind of brand or tattoo. We must find them."

"Oh, we'll find them," Aulus said.

"Have we found a leader among the fallen?" I said.

Spurius nodded. "We believe so," he said. "His breastplate crest designates he was an officer of some distinction."

"We can burn him with the rest or leave him out to rot. Your decision," Aulus said.

I nodded. "Let the men decide. But first," I said. "Bring me his head. I have use for it."

The sun was rising by the time we returned to Mutina. I instructed the wounded to be taken into camp, and for the rest of the men to follow them. However, I gave instructions for the wagons to remain with us on the road.

"We're going into the city," I said.

"You can't mean to give the grain to the city?" Aulus said, his eyes fixed on the severed head dangling at my horse.

"No," I said. "The grain will be for our men. But first, I have use of it. Call up the bugler."

"Should you not bathe yourself first?" Spurius asked.

"Or have that arrowhead extracted . . ." Aulus said.

I shook my head. "This is exactly how I intend to present myself."

"And you intend on taking the severed head of an Italian into the city? Even the barbarous among those in Mutina may find this too savage for their liking," Spurius said, a bit of distaste on his own lips.

I turned to him. "Since we've arrived, you've encouraged me to display Rome's strength. That is what I'll do today."

We said nothing else as we waited for the musician to join us.

"Forward," I said.

The oxen grunted as they were pulled to a walk. The city gates opened before us as we entered the marketplace, three carts of grain and a handful of bloody Roman officers.

Drowsy eyed shopkeepers were opening their stalls, their children splashing in the center fountain. Their skin blanched as they caught sight of us.

"Sound the horn," I said.

The bugles rang clear and crisp throughout the marketplace. Heads popped out of insulae windows above the shops. Mothers hurried to usher their curious children from our path.

The heavy, almost tangible smell of the sheep pens and their molding hay. Unbathed gatherers. The sweet, pungent aroma of both fresh and rotten fruit available for sale in the rickety wooden stalls around the marketplace.

Before us on the path was a pile of still-steaming donkey excrement. A shopkeeper hiked up his tunic and ran to sweep it from our path before we arrived. Everyone parted before us but quickly took a knee and bowed their heads. Women swooned at the sight of the arrow in my arm and the severed head clutched by a tuft of hair in my hand.

"Make way for Quaestor Quintus Sertorius!" the bugler shouted between the clearings of his instrument.

I could hear the scurrying of footsteps behind us as the shop-keepers abandoned their stalls to follow.

"Louder," I told the bugler, and he complied.

Crowds were flocking in behind us as thick as the sheep were in their pens. Perhaps they simply desired to see the content of the wagons in a hope they might receive a share, but I think they desired most to hear what I had to say. They would soon find out.

I led us toward the Temple of Jupiter, where a speakers' plat-form like the rostra looked out over an open courtyard. It was nothing in size compared to Rome's forum, but it would serve my purpose.

I lifted my fist for our procession to halt and strode alone to the center of the platform.

I took my place there and watched the crowds flooding into every open space available, like the slushing of a broken aqueduct.

"Citizens and allies of Rome," I said. "I bring you news of victory."

I'd never seen a crowd of provincials so silently waiting for the words of a Roman. The bleating of sheep from the market-place could be heard in the distance, but nothing else.

"You are aware of the shortages, sicknesses, and cowardly poisonings we've endured, otherwise many more of you would have joined us. I'll not lie to you, citizens. This has been a long and arduous journey since we arrived in Mutina over three months ago. Some may have believed Fortuna cursed us, and our days here were numbered and doomed to fail," I said. "If so, you were wrong."

I raised the head of the rebel leader and tossed it from the platform. The groaning crowd scurried to avoid it.

"No matter what the rebels attempt, no matter how much adversity we are dealt, Rome will conquer. Rome will *always* conquer."

Pigeons fluttered from the rafters of the ancient temple beside the speakers' platform.

I pointed to our wagons. "This is a shipment of grain." A few of my legionaries hoisted themselves up and opened the chests to reveal its contents.

"This grain was meant for the rebels in Asculum. They will not receive it."

The legionaries scooped up a few handfuls of grain and tossed it into the crowd.

"Without this, Asculum will fall. And with it, the rebel cause. With the grain in our possession, my legions will grow, in strength and in numbers, and we will join the other legions in the total annihilation of our enemies. Rome will always conquer. This war will be over soon. And you, citizens, have only to decide which side you would like to be on.

"Rome will remember the citizens who serve with land and bounty. She will reward the allies who stand up against this rebellion with citizenship and plenty. Rome, you may know, has a good memory. But in this one instance, She may be willing to forget. We will forget those who have stood by while others fought and died to protect this Republic. She will even forgive those who have sacrificed for our destruction and served the cause of our enemy."

Eyes widened and mouths opened as the crowd listened to every word carefully.

"But this is the last time. We will not forget again. Rome will remember those who value security over loyalty. And those who seek to antagonize us will be destroyed, like the rebel whose head now lies before you.

"For those also willing to forget the past and join our cause today, you will receive an enlistment bonus of a month's supply of grain, for you and your families here in Mutina or wherever they are throughout Italy."

The legionaries continued to shower the crowds with grain.

"Today is the last day to decide which side of history you want to find yourself on. I look forward to fighting alongside you."

I climbed down from the speaker's platform.

"Rome! Rome! Rome!" the cheering began.

It was subdued and spread out at first, but soon the entire courtyard was echoing the chant. I exhaled and lowered my head, as depleted and weary as one feels after battle.

"Quite a speech, Quaestor," Aulus said, barely audible over the chanting.

"Without substance, words mean nothing."

The lifeless rebel head was hoisted up on a spike by some of the more passionate men in the rabble.

I turned back to the twins. "I must see the *medicus*. Assign twenty additional junior officers to the registrars. They'll be busy today, I think. The rest of the officers, rally them to my praetorium."

"What should we tell them is the reason?" Spurius asked.

My jaw flexed. "Because there is a traitor among us." I looked him directly in the eye. "And I'm going to find out who it is."

There was little light in the *valetudinarium*, but I could still see more than I wanted to. Sackcloth cots were pushed up against one another and filled the entire length of the room. A wounded legionary occupied each of them.

The stench of blood and open wounds swirled through the air like smoke, mixed with the buckets of seawater used to treat burns.

I walked aimlessly through the narrow passage between a few rows of cots. Some plied themselves with unwatered wine or opium and now snored in a deep sleep. A few of the luckier men laughed and played *Tessera*, a game of dice usually reserved for more pleasant surroundings.

But the rest were crying out. For mercy, for a medic, for their mothers.

Despite that, I could hear the soft but constant trickle of blood running off the cots and operating tables.

I winced as a rotten stench overwhelmed me. The man to my right was lying on his back, staring up and muttering beneath his breath. His intestines were exposed, some of them spilled out and lying in his lap. He ran his fingers over them, seeming to feel nothing.

I covered my face with the mud-soaked hem of my toga. "*Medicus*," I shouted. It blended in with all the other cries for medical attention, so I gave an order. "*Medicus*, post!"

The toiling *medici* huffed at my distraction but one of them hurried to me, surgical scissors still in hand.

"Quaestor," he said.

"Why is this man not receiving attention?" I demanded.

The young *medicus* swallowed and lowered his gaze. "Because he is going to die, Quaestor. We cannot divert resources and our precious, precious time to helping him. When the critical but hopeful legionaries have been tended to, we will put him out of his misery."

Perhaps it was the stench, or the sight, or the constant dripping of blood. Perhaps it was the realization gained by the *medicus*'s words. But I found nothing to say, my gaze still fixed on the legionary and his rhythmically chanting lips.

"I apologize, profusely, Quaestor . . . I had not seen your

arm." He began to squirm. "I'll fetch our *medici optimi* immediately."

"No, you will not," I said. "There are many worse than me. They'll be seen first."

His mouth hung agape.

"That's an order," I said. "Is there a free cot?"

He nodded vigorously and led me toward the back of the *valetudinarium*. "Shall I clean it for you, sir?"

The sackcloth was still damp with blood. "No. Tend to the others. I won't be going anywhere."

I plopped down on the cot. Pain reverberated through my arm and back.

The grinding of an amputation saw began, quickly followed by the muffled screams of the wounded.

I rolled over and pressed one ear into the cot.

"Quaestor?" I heard a soft voice.

I opened my eye to find a young legionary lying on the cot beside me. I may have known him, but even if I had, he was unrecognizable now. From his now hairless head to the bottom of his feet, his flesh was burned and black as the volcanic rock. His scarlet tunic was melted into his flesh. The only thing human about him now was his shimmering hazel eyes, and even one of these was covered by charred flesh.

"*Ave, amice.*"

"I'm honored to be here beside you, sir," he said, his voice wavering on the edge of a sword point.

"I'm honored to be here beside you," I said. "You fought bravely today."

I think he smiled as he looked up, his breath shaky and weak. "I'll be better prepared for our next battle. I . . . I will bring glory to Rome."

"You already have, legionary."

"I just didn't see . . . see that ball of flame. I'd never seen anything—"

"Shh . . . rest now, lad. Think of home. How proud your family will be."

"Will you tell them the tale of our victory?"

I said, "I will tell all of Rome. I vow it."

His blackened lips formed a sad smile like an upturned archer's bow. "I helped win a battle."

He rested easier on his cot and fell silent.

I bit my knuckle and focused on my breath. For how long, I do not know. The next thing I knew, the *medici* surrounded my cot.

"Tools?" one said.

"Barbs too large to cut. Split reed pens."

"Won't be easy to extract," the first *medicus* said.

"No punctured organs or arteries to avoid. This might be the easiest today."

I said, "Where is Albinus?" I braced as they poured acid vinegar over my arm.

"Albinus is dead, Quaestor. The poison got him some months ago," the elder *medicus* replied.

Realization returned to me then. In my haze, I'd forgotten his last moments in my arms. I would have enjoyed his care then, even if it was accompanied by vulgar manners and an insult or two at my expense.

"Would you like some opium before we begin?"

I shook my head. "No. I have a meeting with the officers as soon as we're finished."

They looked at each other, but neither said anything.

"How are the others?" I asked.

They passed me a wooden peg to bite down on while trying to decide how to respond.

"Not well. We've run out of treatments for the burn victims," the younger *medicus* replied.

"We've used up all the sea water. Collected breastmilk from every nursing woman in the baggage camp. We've just a bit of honey and lemon slices left."

"Send the rest of the wounded into Mutina. Promise payment for any doctors who will help."

I placed the wooden peg between my teeth.

The elder *medicus* shouted something in Greek to one of his subordinates and placed the scalpel against my arm.

My teeth nearly shattered as they ground down on the peg, and soon after I was no longer present to feel anything.

My hazy thoughts drifted to Gavius, where he might be, what he might be doing. Was he safe? Was he eating enough? Did he think of me often?

"Copper alloy skewers," the elder *medicus*'s gruff voice stirred me.

I could feel nothing in my arm now, and the wooden peg in my lips was now lying in a pool of drool on my cot.

"Is it over?"

"Just a bit of stitching remains."

The sensation in my arm returned just in time to feel the searing pain. My eyelid fluttered, but I maintained my composure now.

Soon enough, the *medici* stepped away, rushing on to the next man who needed attention.

The officers had been waiting long enough, and only Jupiter knew what accusations were being thrown around in the attempt to locate the traitor. More blood would be shed soon if I didn't hurry.

I wasted no time rocking myself to my feet, despite the blur of my vision and trembling in my knees.

Instinct helped me navigate the camp, directly to my praetorium. The twenty or so officers within were mumbling and restless when I entered, but all froze in silence when they caught site of me.

"Evening, gentlemen," I said. "Someone pour me a cup of wine."

They split before me as I quickly found a seat at my desk.

"I'm fine," I said, the words muffled by the ringing in my ears.

"You're still bleeding," Apollonius said.

I looked down and saw that he was right. "The stitching will hold. It will clot soon enough."

I accepted the cup of wine from a *servus* and quickly drained it. Nothing had ever tasted sweeter, but I tried to block out the image of the dripping blood of the *valetudinarium*, and the similar color of the wine.

"Are we all here?" I asked.

Aulus stepped forward, with a bloodless face. "We were. Spurius got tired of waiting and returned to his quarters. Said he needed to write a dispatch."

"You," I pointed to a junior officer. "Go and fetch him. Let's get this over with."

He snapped a salute and spun toward the exit.

"You all know why we are here?" I accepted another cup of wine. "The same reason the rebels ambushed us last night. There is a traitor."

A second-spear centurion said, "How can we be certain? Couldn't they just have been lying in wait, knowing a Roman army would come for the supplies eventually?"

"It's that kind of naivety that makes me suspicious," another centurion barked with a pointed finger.

"You don't mean me? I've fought for Rome for eleven years now, and saved your sorry hide a time or two, Domitius!"

"Enough," I slammed my cup down, the wine spilling down over my hand. "There is a traitor. But that doesn't mean we can betray one another. There will be no baseless accusations tolerated. The traitor will be determined by evidence and dealt with swiftly," I said.

"And how can we be certain? How do we obtain this evidence?" Aulus asked, a bit of his color returning. "I doubt this traitor will simply name himself."

"We will wait for Spurius to arrive," I said.

We waited in uncomfortable silence as my dizziness worsened, until the junior officer returned.

"Is he behind you?" I asked.

He frowned and shook his head. "He was absent, Quaestor," he said. "There was a letter. It's addressed to you."

I hesitated, already knowing in my heart the contents within. At length I accepted the letter and cracked open its seal.

It was never supposed to end like this. I never intended for you to be harmed. I didn't intend for any of this. Everything went so wrong. Please take care of my brother. He will need you now more than ever. Until Elysium,

Spurius Insteius

"What does it say?" Aulus asked.

But I continued sifting over the words, hoping there was some hidden meaning, something to decode. Something, anything.

"Well?" a centurion said.

"Officers . . ." I rolled up the scroll. "Tribune Spurius believes he knows how our information is leaking to the rebels," I said. I held fast to my cup with both hands, hoping the ripple in my wine didn't give me away. "He is seeking out the traitor."

"Where did he go?" Aulus asked, his gaze piercing, the longing in them incredulous.

"I cannot say. It will jeopardize his mission." I swallowed.

Aulus slammed both hands on my desk. "Mission be damned, I'm his brother and I'm going with him."

I jumped to my feet, allowing my backless chair to crash onto the floor.

"All of you will need to undress."

"Excuse me?" the camp prefect sneered.

"The Sons of Remus brand themselves with a marking. If any

man here bears the mark, we'll know who is responsible," I said. "Only the guilty have anything to fear."

A few raised their arms to offer an objection, but knowing how suspicious that might seem, none followed through. Men began unbuckling their breastplates or shimmying the chainmail over their heads.

Soon, my praetorium would be filled with twenty naked but innocent men.

The only traitor was the one I let go free.

SCROLL XV

Lucius Hirtuleius—One day after the Ides of Quintilis, 664 Ab Urbe Condita

" Over a month had passed since the rebels had crucified consul Lupus. Gaius Marius had led us to destroy their camp, but his greatest contribution to the war effort was returning to Rome with the bodies of the slain, including Lupus himself, the nails still wedged in his hands and feet.

The senate immediately passed a decree requiring all those fallen in battle to be buried or cremated on the battlefield. They wanted to see no more of corpses. But Marius's display already achieved the desired effect. Those same citizens who'd been celebrating with games and festivals a few weeks prior were now wearing black and sprinkling ash on their heads. The rest of us knew the gravity of the war, now those in the city did too.

When he returned to our camp, he was less grim

than when he'd departed, as if he'd transferred his own concerns to the populace.

Marius was no good at keeping secrets, however, and it was only moments after his return that he revealed the purpose of his improved spirits.

"I am to be given full command of the north," he said with a familiar glimmer in his eye. "Now we can finally send these bastards to *Dis* and finish the damn war."

I exhaled in relief, but not all the officers joined me. Most, including Aius, only stared back blankly.

"Well, come then, let's share some wine and contemplate our stratagem."

He snapped for cups to be brought to myself and the other senior officers in his praetorium, but several declined.

Marius hmphed. "So glum and gloomy. And for what? Your sour disposition does nothing to deter the rebels." He finished his wine, and rather than extending his cup for a refill, he snatched the amphora from his *servus* and turned to me. "Let's ride out and survey the area. The rest of you can sulk in private."

I nodded but lingered a moment to place a hand on my brother's shoulder. Aius hadn't been the same since his first battle. He no longer discussed history or politics nor read poetry during the few quiet moments camp life afforded him. He didn't talk to me.

Any soldier can understand why.

"Hirtuleius, let's move," Marius grunted.

I followed him out to the stables, where we both mounted up. We sped through drilling centuries toward the gate, where legionaries struggled to open them just in time for us to part through.

He led us to an open hilltop overlooking the camp and surrounding area of the Liris River valley.

"Not a terrible place to fight, is it?" He shielded his eyes from the sun with the back of his hand.

"Here or in Pluto's arse. I'm ready to fight wherever we can meet them."

"The men aren't ready. We'll have to abandon the valley if the Marsi advance," he said. "So be careful what you wish for. Pluto's arse might be just where we're forced to meet them."

I considered whether he might want me to object and attest to the men's preparedness. I declined. He was probably right. Our own men were raw and mostly untested, and those we assimilated from the survivors of Lupus's camp were battle-scarred and wounded. Thanks to years serving in Rome's auxiliary legions, our enemy had no such concerns.

The thumping of horse hooves in the distance interrupted us.

"We should return to camp." I instinctively placed my only hand on my hilt.

The general crossed his arms. "Even our enemies are not so devoid of honor they'd kill Gaius Marius by treachery."

I strained my eyes to see the riders more clearly. There were at least twenty of them, one bearing a legion standard.

"They look like Romans," I said.

"Hmph. They all do." Marius shook his head. "These rebels are absent the ingenuity to create anything of their own."

Marius clicked his tongue, and his horse took a few careful steps toward them.

One rider cried out. "*Salvete*, Romans."

Marius declined to respond, and so did I.

"They're definitely Romans," I said beneath my breath.

"I'm not blind. I can see that," he said.

The horsemen met us at the base of the hill and called for a halt. One rode out from the rest, his silver breastplate radiating like a god's in the afternoon sun.

"Legate Marius, it's a pleasure," the young man said with a curt bow of the head.

"Marcus Caepio," Marius said.

"I'll admit, I'm surprised. I've heard many tales of the bravery of the esteemed Gaius Marius, but I had not expected to find you in rebel territory without a guard present."

"I need no guard to protect me."

Caepio untied his helmet and handed it to a rider behind him. He brushed a boyish curl from his forehead and smiled. "And what would you do if the Marsi sent two thousand riders out to kill you? I doubt you and your one-armed friend could hold them off."

My commander grunted, in the way only he could. "I am Gaius Marius. I saved not just Rome but all of Italy from the Cimbri and Teutones. Our enemies have more respect than to assassinate me."

It was one thing to say this to me but another to say it to Marcus Caepio. I winced at his words.

Caepio's men laughed, but the younger leader only nodded. "You have great belief in the honor of our foes then. I think your faith may be misplaced."

I cast a sidelong glance at Marius, and saw

vehemence in his eyes, as if he were looking upon an enemy. And I didn't understand why.

"If I'm wrong, I'll happily die for Rome."

"How very honorable of you," Caepio said.

Marius grunted again, but somehow the inflection indicated something different than the others. He was becoming disinterested in conversation. "Perhaps I should be more careful now," he said with a shrug. "I am the commander of the northern armies, after all."

Caepio contrived a look of bafflement. "Commander of the north?"

"Tell him, tribune," Marius said.

I nodded. "The Senate and People of Rome have given Gaius Marius supreme command of the northern Roman forces for the duration of the war against the rebels."

Some horsemen snickered.

My fist tightened around the reins.

"Where did you hear that?" asked Caepio.

Marius straightened and lifted his chin toward Olympus. "I just left Rome two days ago. After Lupus's death, they gave me full command of the northern Italian theater."

Caepio frowned, looked down, and shook his head. "I am grieved."

Marius grunted, and this time it revealed amusement. "You'll have your time," he said. "The old breed like me will be dead soon enough."

"I'm grieved that you've been so misinformed." Caepio looked up, and despite his frown and furrowed brow, there was a glimmer in his eye.

"Misinformed, eh? Enlighten me then." Marius released his reins and crossed his arms.

"You are not sole commander of the north. The two of us will share the command."

Marius's lips twisted like he'd tasted sour fruit. "You reek of entitlement. Like only a noble can be who's been told how special he is his entire life."

Caepio seemed unperturbed by the insult. Instead, he extended a wax tablet.

"Give me that." Marius sallied toward him and snatched it from the young praetor's hand.

"When was this recorded? I left Rome two days ago. Two days. And they gave me supreme command."

Caepio allowed himself at least a moment to smirk in triumph. "Perhaps you traveled slowly." He nodded toward one of his cavalrymen.

"I left this morning," the rider said. "Rode without stopping for food, water, piss, or shit. The senate's extended their decree not but seven hours ago."

Marius continued to analyze the wax tablet with the grief one might if it contained news of a loved one's death.

His words were barely audible through teeth clenched so tight. "Why did they change their minds?"

Caepio lifted his chin now. "My victory over the Frentani. They see the value in keeping me autonomous for the time being."

Marius slammed the tablet shut.

Caepio smiled then. "Don't worry, Gaius Marius. Once us young breed have died off, you'll have your chance again."

My commander spoke then, and for once his voice was neither gruff nor harsh. "I can take no solace in this, knowing so many Romans will die as a footstool for your ambition."

Caepio shrugged. "It will be far less than the number who've already died for yours. Well, I have delivered the news. We'll return to camp, then. Perhaps we can meet tomorrow to discuss strategy?"

Marius lingered in silence. I almost nudged him when the silence became unbearable, but eventually he nodded his head.

Caepio reclaimed his helm and buckled it under his clean-shaven chin. "Very well. I look forward to learning from the great Gaius Marius and forging a battle plan for the road ahead."

The riders wasted no time on pleasantries, and quickly swung and rode off the way they'd come.

I sat as still as I could upon my horse, waiting on my commander to issue the first statement.

Eventually he pushed his horse to move, barely a trot. I followed him, keeping my mouth shut as I figured he wanted.

"You know, Hirtuleius," he said. "I'm not sure how much longer I can endure young men and their ambition. I'd almost rather die now than wait and see when it comes to fruition."

"Sir, that's nonsense," I answered as I thought I ought to. "Rome needs you now more than ever. Do not let the spoiled sons of senators steal you from your path."

A nod. "True. Besides, I'll be dead before the worst of men like Marcus Caepio really take over. It's your generation who must truly worry."

"If you take your cavalry and move them around the left flank like so . . ." Caepio moved his stick through the sand as if he were a great artist. "You may take out the Marsi artillery before they have a chance to disrupt our front lines."

We'd been stuck in this praetorium for hours. They said we were planning for battle, but I realized quickly it was a hypothetical battlefield with hypothetical troops. Marius never organized that way. I felt uneasy about the entire process.

Marius snatched the stick from Caepio and shook his head. "Let me educate you, boy. Learn from me. I have seen many battles. You have not."

"His fathers have seen many battles," someone in the tent said, under their breath.

"Yes." Marius straightened like a sword. "His father saw battle. The one they call the Battle of Arausio. He abandoned fifty thousand of his men to slaughter."

Notably, Caepio said nothing. He neither agreed nor disagreed with the legionary who spoke up for him or retaliated against Marius.

One of Caepio's men shouted a rebuttal, but Marcus Caepio himself lifted his fist to shut them down.

"If I am wrong, simply tell me how and where in my analysis I have failed," he said. "And spare me the insults of my father. No one is more disgusted by Arausio than I am."

Marius raised his bushy brows and nodded. "Perhaps you can be educated after all." With Caepio's stick, he continued to draw lines in the sand. "We outmatch our enemy in cavalry, it is true. But they have slingers. Have you ever fought slingers, Marcus Caepio?"

Caepio gnawed at the already mangled end to his thumbnail. The rest of his fingers were well manicured, so I knew this was a recent habit. The arrogance of the young officer the day before was now completely absent.

"I have not," he said.

"Slingers can pierce the armor of a man at two hundred paces. They can splinter shields. They can pierce a man's heart if they desire to."

Marcus shook his head. "And you know this because you have fought slingers before, I assume? If that's the case, you could defeat them. Spare me the anecdotes and tell me what to do so we can conclude this tedious meeting."

Marius grunted. "I know this because I fought *with* slingers, and I saw what they accomplished."

As if that wasn't a portent, a messenger broke through the leather flap of the praetorium then, struggling to catch his breath.

"Out with it, legionary," Caepio said.

"Sir, there's . . . there's . . ." the man held his chest and sucked air like a fish out of water. "A man who wants to speak with you."

"Who is this man?" Marius raised his voice and plunged his stick into the sand table.

The messenger looked to Marius and shuttered. "Apologies, sir. But he desires to speak with Marcus Caepio specifically."

Marius spit into the sand. "The man's desires be damned. I am co-commander of the northern legions and I demand to know who is deserving of such an interruption!"

The tent flap opened again.

Only one man stepped inside. His tunic was disheveled and his hair a dirt-clod mangled mess. I

assumed for a moment this was some priest for a
far-flung god or a beggar who wished to exchange
information for food.

"You have interrupted us," Caepio said. "State
your purpose and begone."

"My name is Poppaedius Silo," the man said.

With a swift and practiced motion, Marius
unsheathed his sword, the metallic hiss of steel
slicing through the air. "We should cut off your
head then," he said. He pointed the blade at the
rebel commander's throat.

"Hold," Marcus Caepio commanded. The confidence he'd displayed the day before was apparent
in his eyes once more.

Silo's mouth hung open, and he breathed heavily. His lips were chapped and cracked to the point
of bleeding. He nodded. "You have every right to
kill me. I deserve nothing less," he said. "But if I
may have one last moment of fatal hubris, could I
request a cup of wine?"

Caepio's eyes remained fixed on the man, as we
all waited to see how he would respond.

"Place him in shackles and then give him what
he wants," Marius said. But this was not his camp,
this was not his praetorium. This was Caepio's
camp, and the rebel consul was his guest.

None of the legionaries obeyed Marius.

"Bring him wine," Caepio said. "Are you cold?
You are shivering."

Silo exhaled and hung his head. "I am many
things, young legate. The trembling, I believe, is
from starvation."

"Bring him some figs and cheese then as well,
and a loaf of bread."

Marius threw up his powerful arms. "Bring me

another cup as well then. It might be the only thing to keep me from strangling this man where he stands."

His lack of tact disappointed me.

Silo's voice was hoarse and lingered on the edge of a cough. "I thank you," he said. "You display more courtesy than I deserve."

"That goes without saying," Marius said, hands akimbo on his hips. "How many Roman sons now lie dead because of you? How many wives have you widowed and how many children have you orphaned?"

It was true. Poppaedius Silo helped start this war, and he had been leading it as a 'consul' since it began. And in battle after battle, he was victorious. Leaving fields of hundreds, thousands of Roman dead and left to rot. We'd seen it firsthand in Lupus's camp, Silo's brutality on full display in our consul's crucified body.

Silo's face was blank, but his eyes were wet and the eyelids heavy. When he spoke, it was little more than a whisper. "I know," he said. "That's why I've come. I know Rome will have me executed. It's what I deserve. I wish only to make this right before my death."

He accepted the cup of wine with both hands and placed it against his cracked lips. Beads of purple wine dripped down his chin as he finished the cup, eyes closed and overcome with relief.

"I apologize. I am parched."

"You apologize for your bad table manners," Caepio said. "And yet you say nothing for the lives you've stolen. The war you created."

Silo nodded. "Because an apology now means nothing." His eyes glazed over as he stared through

Caepio, into his own mind. "There's nothing I can do to bring the dead back. Nothing I can do to comfort the grieving wives or shelter the mourning children. Nothing."

Caepio's cold eyes narrowed. "What can you do then?"

Life appeared in Silo's eyes for the first time. "I can help end this war."

"The war you started," Marius was quick to add.

Silo nodded. "Yes, the war I started. It's only right that I help end it."

Servi brought out two chairs, one for Silo and another for Caepio. This was their discussion now, and we were simply spectators.

"Refill his cup," Caepio said. "Your mind has clearly been altered, then. And it is not yet the wine. Why would you seek to end a war you felt passionate enough to start less than a year ago?"

Silo rubbed at his forehead, smears of mud and sweat streaking with fingerprints. "Because this was never what I wanted," he said. "I thought once we created enough trouble, defeated a few armies . . . showed Rome how much they needed us . . . that legislation would be passed, and Rome would welcome us back as citizens and brothers."

Marius laughed now, an unpleasant, raspy, forceful laugh. "You cannot expect us to believe you are so foolish."

Silo scratched the stubble on his chin, as broken as any homeless veteran I'd ever seen in the forum. "If you prefer to put more faith in my intelligence, then I am honored," he said. "I do not ask that you believe me. I am here only to tell you the truth and allow you to do as you please with that."

Marius crossed his scarred arms and turned away to signify his resistance.

"So you've come to us to help us end the war." Caepio had a cup of wine in his hand, but it remained untouched. His eyes were locked on Silo. "How could you manage to do that?"

Silo gratefully drained his wine and threw a handful of figs into his mouth. He lifted a finger to apologize for his barbarity, then said, "I attempted to speak with my men before I absconded. They refused to listen, as if I was putting them through a test."

He paused as if that answer was sufficient, so Caepio said, "How is that helpful to us?"

His tactful response to Silo impressed me. He was cordial and played the part of a good host, but his posture and voice made it clear the man's attempts at pity did not yet sway him.

"That is not helpful. No." Silo shook his head. "That I left, however, is. My army is leaderless. They are spiraling without me. This, if wielded properly, can end the war."

Marius shook his head. "You think your defection alone will cause the downfall of the Italian cause?" he said. "Your arrogance knows no bounds. You may have created this war from the pits of your black heart, but it is much larger than you now."

Silo hung his head. "The Marsi, Paeligni, Vestini, Marrucini, Picentes, and Frentani are all under my command. Leaderless, they are a ship at sea without sails." He stood then and faced Marius for the first time. Despite his haggard appearance, the straightness of his back and the depth of his chest proved why he'd been a formidable foe. "And

I am not defecting. I will not fight against my brothers. Now or ever."

Caepio studied him. "What is it you propose then?"

Silo returned to his seat and accepted another cup of wine, although this one he did not finish immediately. "I would like to facilitate peace," he said. "Perhaps this is the arrogance legatus Gaius Marius accused me of, but I believe I'm in a unique position to help achieve that."

"How would you accomplish this?" Caepio clasped his hands in his lap.

"I know where they make camp," Silo said. "We can ride out to them with overwhelming force. They will form up to protect themselves, but without leadership, they will hesitate. Bind me if you will. Present me to them, and I will tell them to lay down their arms. And they will listen."

"*Faux*! All of it!" Marius bellowed, throwing his cup of wine into a table filled with documents in the far corner of the praetorium.

Caepio turned to him, calm but in control. "I ask that you mind yourself in my praetorium, legate."

Marius's mouth opened, surely to berate the young legate for his insolence, but I quickly reached out and took his arm.

He turned to me, lips twisted up like a snake, but he said nothing more.

Caepio turned back to the rebel consul. "And what is to stop you from turning on me the moment we arrive? What's to say this is not all a ruse?"

Silo nodded, understanding the accusation. He looked up at the young officer again, and his eyes glistened with tears. "I'm honored you think me so clever, even if dishonorable. But alas, this weary heart is too selfish, even still. If I felt there was another choice available to me, I would take it," he said. "I'm being honest because I have no other choice."

My heart began to race, and it didn't do so very often. I'd been preparing for war, at war, or just returning from a war, since I was a child. That hardens a young man. I knew to never trust a hope. But the thought of this war being over . . . the idea of reconciliation. It made my heart leap. Let us all reunite and take the fight to those who wished harm on us. Let us stop fighting brothers, cousins, kinsmen.

Silo turned to the messenger, who was just now catching his breath near the entryway. "Go and fetch them." He nodded. Turning back to Caepio he said, "I do not expect you to trust my word. You would be foolish to do so. Instead, I bring my three sons."

The envoy returned with three young men, all just as disheveled as Silo.

Silo continued, "Shackle them, bind them, blindfold them, if you must."

Caepio stood, his chest rising with the same fluttering of the heart and breath mine was. "And is there anything you ask in return?"

"I ask that you not harm them," Silo said, the shimmering of his eyes amplifying. He spoke again, but now his voice cracked, like a man's twice his age. "Please do not hurt them. And I will see this war ended."

Marius shouted, "They don't even look like you."

Silo smiled, cracked lips beginning to quiver. "Fortuna's blessing. They favor their mother," he said. "And perhaps none of us look as we ought after days traveling with nothing but the clothes on our backs."

Caepio strode over toward the sons and analyzed them. "What is your name?" he asked the eldest.

The young man straightened some, but his eyes were still fixed on the floor of Caepio's praetorium beneath him. "My name is Poppaedius Silo the Younger."

"And you?" Caepio asked the next.

"Gnaeus."

Caepio crouched to inspect the youngest of the three, a boy not yet old enough to shave. "And you?"

He made direct eye contact, and his face hardened. "My name is Marcus Silo," he said. "And I do not wish to be here."

Caepio smiled. "Marcus. We share a praenomen. And I appreciate that you do not wish to be here; I wouldn't want to be here either. But this is your lot. You, I think, will do many more great things than your father. Perhaps you'll even restore your family name and make history forget about all the harm your father caused."

The boy collected saliva in his mouth, and I could tell by his eyes he considered spitting in Caepio's face. Instead, he spit by his worn-out sandals on the floor of Caepio's praetorium.

Caepio seemed impressed by the display.

"Even if this man speaks true," Marius said, "do you really think even the defection of his entire army would end this war? Hardly. The Samnites will still be at large."

Silo drank deeply and smacked his lips to savor

the taste, but his cast-off gaze indicated he was considering the legate's words. "You're correct. But Mutilus will be stranded in the south once my armies have defected. Despite your beliefs in his wickedness, Mutilus is not a man who wishes to see the death of his men. He will lay down his arms because he will have no other choice."

Caepio crossed his arms. I'm no great interpreter of men, but I believe he was becoming more suspicious. "You've asked me not to torment your sons while they're left with us. Is there nothing else you ask for?"

Silo had a handful of cheese but put it back into the bowl. He swallowed and considered the question. "There is one thing. And it's the most important. If you deny me, I will not follow through on any of this," he said. "You must vow to spare the lives of my men. Spin whatever tales you need about how they were deceived by a demagogue and tyrant like Poppaedius Silo. Just let them go free. Let them fight in your legions once again. Rome will only grow stronger because of this."

"Ha!" Marius bellowed. "You know nothing of Rome if you think one such as Marcus Servilius Caepio can promise exculpation for ten thousand men."

"I have over thirty thousand men under my command," Silo corrected him. "But that's hardly the point."

Caepio clinched his jaw, and I saw his knuckles whiten. "I cannot *promise* their safety. But I can vow my willingness to speak on their half before the senate. As a patrician—as a praetor—my words have weight. And I have many advocates who will support me at my request."

Silo nodded. "That is enough for me."

"Then we will ride out tomorrow and end this war," Caepio said.

"I left three days ago with my sons," Silo said. "Soon my men will realize what's happening, and they will elect a new leader. I do not know how soon. But I fear the longer we wait, the more likely it is that we face resistance."

"What would you propose then?" Caepio said.

Silo made direct eye contact with him. "If you have the men and the capacity, I say we go now. Waste not a moment further. Let's end this war."

"You cannot possibly believe this!" Marius balked.

Caepio ignored him. "I have the men and the capacity. We will depart now."

Marius turned to me. "Take the three captives to our camp, along with the rest of our cortege. I will remain a little while longer."

"Excuse me?" Caepio turned to Marius, a violence in his eyes he'd never displayed toward the Italian rebel.

"You will be absent. These prisoners should be under the command of a legatus. I will keep them in my camp."

Silo looked up, and finally the first tear fell over his mud-covered face. "General Marius, I served under you in Numidia. I was there at Muluccha and Cirta." His jaw flexed. "Do you remember? I was there, an auxiliary commander."

Marius glared at the man. "I remember. You served under me, and yet you seek Marcus Caepio rather than me?"

Silo nodded. "He defeated the Frentani, a tribe under my command, and showed mercy to the survivors. We sacrificed years under you. Did you show us any?"

Marius found no words.

Silo shook his head and exited the tent with Caepio.

I said, "Come on." I ushered the three sons of Silo out of the tent. "Let's go."

"With pleasure," the youngest said.

I whistled for the rest of our guard to join us. We set off toward our camp. And I hoped this would be for the last time, praying to whichever god would listen that Caepio was right, and this war was at an end.

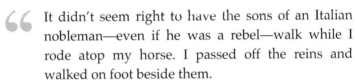It didn't seem right to have the sons of an Italian nobleman—even if he was a rebel—walk while I rode atop my horse. I passed off the reins and walked on foot beside them.

Ponds and bogs surrounded the road on either side. A fisherman's tent was set up. The man within snored loudly, likely waiting for first light to cast in his line. Fireflies flickered like faraway stars. Frogs croaked and occasionally leapt from their lily pads when the sound of our approach startled them.

The gentle flickering of a few legionary torches illuminated our path.

"How are your restraints?" I asked the prisoners.

The youngest snarled. "Tight enough, Roman."

"I meant to ask if they're uncomfortable." I sighed. "I'm happy to loosen them. There's no

SCROLL XV | 237

reason to make this night more uncomfortable than it already is."

The two older sons said nothing, marching on somberly with their eyes cast to the ground. The youngest squirmed.

"I wouldn't mind having the rope loosened," he said. "If you're offering."

The two older brothers shot him a look as I asked him to halt. I took out my dagger and cut the restraints entirely. We had thirty head of infantry and twenty riders behind us. There was nothing to fear.

He rubbed at his sore wrists and gave a slight nod as thanks.

The dirt beneath us contained as much moisture as a horse's brush. The crunch of the powdered earth under our sandals filled the air.

"We might as well fill our time with some discussion," I said. "We have several miles to go."

"There is nothing to talk about," the middle son said, and I detected an accent in his voice for the first time. I was woefully inexperienced with Italian dialects, especially compared to my friend Quintus Sertorius, but it wasn't an inflection I was familiar with.

"We can talk of war. Perhaps ones where we weren't fighting one another. You two seem to be of fighting age. Served in battle before?"

Neither of them said anything, but I assumed from their posture they had not.

"I joined when I wasn't much older than the lad here," I said. "They actually wanted to enroll me as an auxiliary because I was a Sabine, despite my being a citizen."

"You should be fighting for us then," the young man said.

I smiled sadly. "I wish only that the war wasn't necessary."

We seemed to agree on that and continued in silence. Some of our men hurried forward to collect a few fallen tree limbs in our path.

I looked up at the stars and wondered how far away they were, and if they were truly our ancestors watching over us. "My father served on a campaign in the Balearic Islands when I was still in my mother's womb," I said. "My grandfather told me many Marsi served in the war alongside him."

"It's a wonder that he does not sympathize with our cause then," the eldest said, and his accent seemed even more foreign than his middle brother.

"He did not survive." I frowned. "If he had, I believe this war would bring him greater pain than even his own death."

The middle son began, "My father—"

The elder and the younger brother simultaneously elbowed him into silence.

"You can speak of your father," I said.

"We will not bring dishonor to him," the youngest said. "Nor will we share anything useful to you, Roman."

I held up my hand and my nub. "There is no intelligence collection here. I've cut your restraints, and I'll do so for your brothers, if they'd like. We are simply talking as men. Passing time under Diana's full moon."

They offered no resistance, but neither did they speak.

"What kind of father is Poppaedius Silo?" I said.

"It's clear to me he cares for you. I've regretted not having a father of my own to raise me."

"My . . . our father was a good man. Is a good man. He does care for us," the middle brother said, almost to himself.

"Cease your mewling, brother," the youngest said.

"I'm certain he's frightened for you now, then." I nodded. "You'll receive proper treatment as long as I am around. But I know this must weigh on a father's mind."

"It's for the good of the Italian cause." The middle son looked at me, and in the torchlight's glow, I noticed something I hadn't previously. His eyebrows were red despite a black head of hair. Odd.

My response was calm. "Tell me about your real father."

His eyes widened, and I could see the realization in them.

"Quiet, weakling," the youngest boy used his free hands to clobber his restrained "brother."

The oldest turned to me with his bound hands clasped. "Please, he vowed to free us if we obeyed."

The youngest tackled his "brother" to the ground, and they rolled around in the Italian dirt, grunting and cursing.

"Enough," I ordered. "Poppaedius Silo deceived us both. He didn't send his own children because he knows Rome will execute you when his treachery is perceived."

The youngest cried out, "Lies!" He scrambled to his feet.

I held out my hand and a rider brought me my

horse. I wrapped the reins around my nub and hauled myself up.

"You are slaves?" I said.

"Not after tonight," the youngest said.

"They're going to kill us, you fool." The eldest shouted. "He's right."

The middle "brother" wiped his bloody nose against his shoulder. "The desire for freedom blinded us."

"Cut their restraints," I ordered.

The nearby legionaries looked among one another, but eventually complied.

"Go," I said. "Go and never forget this: it is Rome that casts judgment and offers mercy. No one else. Yah!" I spun my horse around and sped off the way we'd come, the fireflies flying past me like a shower of stars.

My only prayer was that I wasn't too late to save Caepio and his men.

SCROLL XVI

Quintus Sertorius—Six days before the Kalends of Sextilis, 664 Ab Urbe Condita

Seventeen days had passed since I gave a speech to the citizens of Mutina, seventeen days since I threw the severed head of a rebel commander at their feet. Thousands of men joined our ranks over that timeframe. Our registrars became quite selective about who we'd take, and eventually we closed our doors entirely. Our task was complete. We had levied three legions, two Roman and one auxiliary.

Supplies were still low, but with the gift taken from the generous rebels, we had enough for now. And our time in Mutina would soon be at an end.

I would take my army to Marcus Caepio and leave them under his capable command. Perhaps I could retire back to Rome with Arrea and Apollonius and spend a few months in my own home for the first time in nearly nine years.

Despite Fortuna's blessing on us, my heart still burned with the sharp pain of betrayal. Spurius's actions stung me like a snake's fangs. And like my veins were coursing with venom, I found it harder to breathe.

At times, I hated him. Other times I admired him. I questioned myself. Why hadn't I seen the truth? How could he do this? I could not reconcile the man I knew with someone who could betray his brothers and cause the death of his kinsmen. Why had he done this?

I found no answers to comfort me.

On many occasions, I composed a letter to Spurius, asking all the questions that plagued my mind, only to burn them lest someone discover them and learn the truth.

As haunted as I might be, Aulus was much worse.

His famous smile and infectious laughter evaporated like a mid-May rain. Spurius always hounded him to take care of himself and his equipment, to maintain his hair and stubble in proper regulations and shine his armor as a good example to the men. Now his hair grew shaggy and his beard unkempt, his armor covered in dirt from the movement drills we accompanied the men on each day.

He no longer called me "Quintus" in front of the men, but then again, he rarely addressed me at all. He could have called me *es mundus excrementi* for all I cared. I simply missed the sound of his voice.

But I believe Aulus resented me for not telling him where Spurius had gone off to. I accepted my exile from his inner confidence. This was much better than him knowing the truth. It might break him. Or worse yet, I feared he might run off to join the rebels himself, if that's indeed what his brother had done.

And I couldn't bear to lose two friends to treachery.

These thoughts plagued my mind like a swarm of locusts as I signed documents spread across my praetorium desk.

"Why is this man being paid more than the others of equal rank?" I asked. I rubbed my forehead. My eye felt strained from staring over so many lines of Apollonius's concise, small handwriting.

"He speaks Oscan," he said. "The senate offers three denarii extra to any man who can communicate with the Paeligni and Samnites."

"Very well." I scribbled out my name as a shadow grew over me.

"Leptis, I'll get the reports to you as soon as—"

A beam of light poured in as someone entered the tent. I looked up to find an ashen messenger standing before my desk.

He saluted, but there was little enthusiasm in it. Dirt from hard riding covered his face, but the bloodless color beneath his sunken eyes was still apparent.

"What can I do for you, Hermes?" I said.

"Envoy Artellius Varro with word from the Senate and People of Rome." He extended a sealed letter.

"Just set it there," I said. "I'm drowning in documentation, you might notice. Come, would you have a cup of wine? I can see you've been riding hard."

When he did not answer, I looked up again to find his lips quivering.

"This satchel here . . ." He raised a leather bag on his hip, "Two hundred letters to new widows and unfortunate parents fill this satchel. The centurions wrote them, but it's my role to deliver them. I cannot stay long."

"Two hundred men have died?"

He struggled to swallow. "Four thousand have perished," he said. "I am but one of many with this task."

I broke the seal of the letter and quickly unfurled it.

Quaestor Q. Sertorius,

Legio XII and Legio XVII have been defeated by the rebel armies of Q. Poppaedius Silo. Praetor M. Servilius Caepio was slain with his men. Following this defeat, we disbanded Legio XII and Legio XVII, and amalgamated the survivors into the legions under the authority of Legatus G. Marius. You, Quaestor Q. Sertorius, are to report to the command of Legatus G. Marius no later than the Ides of September with the legions you've recruited. You will remain under his command until the end of the year, at which time you will be resigned as the senate and people of Rome see fit. Roma Invicta.

Senate and People of Rome
Q. Lutatius Catulus

"Bring me a cup of wine," I said to anyone listening. I passed off the letter to Apollonius and placed a hand over my mouth.

I tried to picture the face of Marcus Caepio, praetor and senator of Rome. Only the child I once knew came to mind, running with abandon in torn sandals, stopping only to give a few coins to an old beggar and ask him about his life.

My voice was barely audible. Had the envoy not been so exposed to this sort of pain, he might not have heard me. "How did this happen?"

"Treachery," he said. "Poppaedius Silo laid out an ambush for the praetor and his men as they rode out under the guise of establishing peace. Silo killed Caepio himself, and afterward fixed his head on the tip of his spear and paraded it before the fleeing Romans."

I shuddered, the boy's gentle smile fresh before my eye. "Stories of battlefield barbarities are often exaggerated."

The envoy frowned. "Not this time," he said. "I saw it myself."

My gut hollowed when I imagined his mother, Junia, receiving the same news. "I admire your bravery, emissary." I drank deeply from the wine placed before me. "No man should bear this task alone."

He laughed sadly. "Better than having my head on a spike." His eyes glazed over as the image must have reappeared in his mind. "If you'll dismiss me, I should return to Rome with the remaining dispatches."

I thought of Arrea. Of our marriage. Of war and what lay ahead.

"Dismissed."

"*Vale*," he said, and left to deliver another letter.

After he departed, Apollonius sat down the letter and placed a hand on my shoulder. "I grieve with you, *amice*."

"I grieve with the two hundred wives and mothers," I said. "Will you have a little wine with me?"

I told myself this was a time to mourn for all the lives lost, but I couldn't ignore the concern for my wife. Caepio promised to take my legions and allow me to return to Rome with Arrea, but many things changed with the death of the praetor. The senate's letter made it clear they expected me to continue serving under Marius.

He pulled up a chair beside me and accepted a cup. "I guess we are returning to war sooner than we'd hoped."

"No matter how much I try to escape men like Gaius Marius, no matter how I attempt to avoid constant war . . . to give my wife the family she deserves . . . I continue to find myself right back in this chair, receiving this news and fighting in my mind to accept all the things I can't control."

He patted my shoulder, careful to avoid the still-mending wound. "The balm comes when we accept what we can't control rather than fighting it."

I smiled sadly. "For once, my old friend, I find your advice to be of little use to me. How can I not fight against this? If I don't, I will spend the rest of my life at war, the rest of my life at odds with the one woman I love."

He sipped from his wine and smiled. "Fighting doesn't seem to have helped you much thus far," he said. "Just as my constant fears over our supply did me no good. It was a blessing from my

God or one of yours, and the blunder of our enemy that made all the difference. Perhaps we need only wait."

"Apollonius, I don't know what to do," I said softly. "I am losing Arrea day by day, and returning to war might be oil for the fire."

I dreaded the thought of telling Arrea, the experience becoming all too familiar for both of us. What was there to say? What was there to decide? Rome decided for us.

We were going back to war.

SCROLL XVII

AREA—FIVE DAYS before the Nones of Sextilis, 664 Ab Urbe Condita

Tullia's labored breaths filled the room, their rhythmic cadence punctuated by the occasional gasp and moan. A priestess stood behind us. She rang a small bell and uttered the same prayer to Lucina repeatedly. Two midwife *servae* worked tirelessly, one grinding out herbs for another potion, the other checking Tullia's progress.

Her blush bedroom, usually a sanctuary of silken drapes and ornate furniture, had become a laborious battleground. The beautiful mosaic floor was now littered with rags, sodden and discarded. The air was heavy with the olive oil I slathered her with, but the undeniable musk of childbirth swallowed it up.

Dim light poured through the open shutters above the bed, revealing that the sun was rising. We began before it set.

"Courage, Tullia," I said. "It won't be long now." I took her soft hand in my own.

She squeezed with the strength of a dozen men, and with the other she crumpled up the sweat dampened sheets beneath her. Another wave of contractions. They were longer now and more frequent. When this one concluded, her strength evaporated, and she collapsed, her body trembling, back to her pillow.

Her voice was breathless and weak. "You said that hours ago."

The *servus* at the foot of the bed raised her head. "She's right this time, *domina*."

"Soon, you'll hold your child for the first time. Focus on this," I said.

The other *servus* brought Tullia a cup. "Honey water with dittany and catmint. It will help with the pain."

Tullia allowed her head to be raised, and she drank deeply. "I want more verbena root."

"I'll . . . fetch some," the *servus* said.

As she departed, I saw Tranquillus pacing like a caged animal beyond the threshold of the door, a panicked look on his face. For once, he was paying Tullia the attention she desired, even if custom and the priestess forbade him from entering. But she no longer seemed to care.

I pressed a damp sponge to Tullia's forehead and ran my fingers through her sweat-soaked hair. The dark tendrils were cool and slippery to the touch. The softness contrasted with the look of misery on her face.

I'd never seen someone in such consuming pain —not in any of the other births I'd assisted in or the countless times I'd stitched my husband back to life

SCROLL XVII | 249

after receiving battlefield wounds. Such agony, and I would have done anything to trade places with her.

It began again.

Tullia's groans echoed off the vaulted ceilings, rhythmic and relentless. The priestess continued the same short prayer but raised her voice. She flicked the bell quicker.

"Arrea, I cannot . . ." she said before losing her breath again.

"Yes you can," I said. "Look, Apollo's chariot is ascending." I pointed to the window above her.

She looked up at the nascent morning light and let out one last scream that surpassed all the ones before it.

"*Domina*, I need you!" the *servus* at the foot of the bed yelled.

This time, I knew she referred to me. I rushed to her just in time for the little head to fall into my hands. As slippery as an eel, bloody as a battlefield, and soft as a dove. Life, born into my hands.

"Hello there," I whispered as I continued to usher the child into the world. When it was free, I raised it to my breast and patted the back. "Shh."

Tullia fell silent. A new, primal cry emerged from the child.

"Oh," Tullia muttered and placed a hand to her trembling lips.

The midwife *servus* was quick to cut the cord and wrap a clean, silk cloth around the baby.

Light flooded into the room as Tranquillus thrust the door open.

"Is he safe? Is he healthy?" he asked. His eyes were frantic, darting from the child to my face, searching for reassurance.

I bobbed the child up and down gently and turned to reveal it to Tranquillus. "Healthy and safe, yes. But I believe he is a she. You have a beautiful baby girl, Tranquillus."

A shadow fell across his face, the lines around his mouth deepening into a hardened scowl. His shoulders slumped in the tacit admission of disappointment.

The baby's soft mewling broke the mirthless silence, a sound so full of life and yet clearly a disappointment to her father.

He backed out of the room and disappeared among his opulent statues, trinkets, and frescoes in the atrium.

My heart churned with a pang of protective indignation. Rage. Sorrow. I looked down at the babe. I couldn't imagine how those soft, cherubic features came from someone like Tranquillus.

"May . . . can I . . ." Tullia whispered.

I cradled the baby's head until Tullia took hold. My body ached when I released her, but I found joy in the spark of wonder in the young mother's eye.

"To Tartarus with him," Tullia said, a soft finger combing through the wisps of dark hair on the baby's head. "I don't care that we were wrong about you."

"She'll be strong, Tullia," I said. "Like her mother. We can only rejoice and thank the gods for this healthy child."

She didn't seem to hear me, continuing to gaze in amazement at the swaddled babe in her arms.

"I will give you some time," I said.

Blinking tears from my eyes, I exited to the atrium. I rubbed my forehead with a shaking, bloody hand. I wept but didn't know why.

All I wanted to do was return to the chambers and see the baby again. Count each of its toes and fingers. Kiss its wrinkled nose.

A man's shadow grew beneath me. I prayed it wasn't Tranquillus who was approaching. I would say things that no one should ever utter to their host.

"I hope that blood belongs to someone else."

The voice belonged to my husband. There was none other so strong but so gentle.

"If only it was the blood of Tranquillus . . ." I said.

He was never without his breastplate and legionary cloak, but I noticed this time he was wearing all his quaestor's trappings. A high, scarlet plumed helmet, leather wrist guards with brace nobs, and a sheathed gladius on his hip.

"Is the baby healthy?"

We embraced.

I nodded. "Yes. Healthy and strong. A beautiful baby girl, with more hair than Apollonius."

I observed his expression, but as I expected, there was nothing but delight in his eye.

"A joyous occasion," he said. "I'll sacrifice a white dove to Venus in the child's honor."

He took my hands in his as the lines of worry on his forehead seemed to grow.

"What is it, Quintus?"

"Would you like to sit in the peristylum?" he asked.

"No," I said. "We can talk here."

He nodded, understanding. "I suppose we've grown too accustomed to having conversations like this."

"Yes, we have."

He squeezed my hand. "Arrea, Marcus Caepio is dead."

Caepio had never done me any harm, but I'd never liked him. He was the one who gave Quintus his assignment in Greece which took him away from me for so long. And he was at the center of his current assignment as well.

But the sorrow in my husband's voice was genuine. I grieved with him. "I am sorry, Quintus."

He exhaled. "I'm sorry too."

I knew there was something more. I waited for him to say it.

His eye was downcast now. "After his death, the senate sent me a letter, assigning me and my forces to Gaius Marius. We will have to leave soon."

"Oh," I said. I retracted my hands from his and placed one on my chest.

"Battle is inevitable. And there is nothing I can do to avoid it. I don't know what to do, Arrea."

"Of course you do," I said. "Go and defeat them."

He looked at me strangely. With the initial force of the news now passed, I took his hands again.

"Go and defeat them. Rome has need of you."

"Yes, but you need me too . . ."

I raised to the tip of my toes and kissed him. "I do. But I will wait for you," I said. "However long it takes."

"This isn't what I wanted . . ."

"I know."

It isn't what I wanted either. But my Quintus was a good man. I was blessed, by his gods or mine, to have found him.

"Go and do what you must. I will sacrifice and

pray for you every morning and every night until you return."

"So you will not be coming with me? Of course you aren't . . . the risk is far too great. That was a foolish question."

I placed a hand on his cheek. "I would go with you, and I would risk my life to be by your side. Without a second thought." I looked back to Tullia's room, where she was rocking her babe. "But there are other places I'm needed. I can be of use. I can help, rather than wait."

"Where will you go?" he asked.

I thought about it for only a moment. "I will go to Nursia," I said. "Your mother could use some company and assistance; I have no doubt."

He took a deep breath before nodding. "If that is your wish." He rubbed his rough thumb over my palms. "I will come to you as soon as we conclude this war."

"We will both long for your return."

"I will assign thirty of my finest men to escort you to Nursia."

"Pollux is the only company I need, if you'll allow me to take him with me," I said.

He smiled for the first time. "I'll miss you both tremendously, but I think I can spare him." He released my hands and embraced me. "But Arrea, please take the guards. The roads are perilous, and I can't risk something happening to you."

I melted into his arms. "I'll take them, Quintus."

There were no more words to say, so we remained in each other's arms in comfortable silence. We hadn't touched like that since he arrived in Rome. This would keep me warm until he returned.

SCROLL XVIII

GAVIUS SERTORIUS—TWO days before the Nones of Sextilis, 664
Ab Urbe Condita

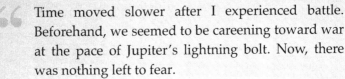 Time moved slower after I experienced battle.
Beforehand, we seemed to be careening toward war
at the pace of Jupiter's lightning bolt. Now, there
was nothing left to fear.

I knew from the stories my father and other
veterans told me that it could get much worse. I
understood this. But I had seen battle now. Blood
spraying like a water fountain. Severed arms and
legs as lifeless as fallen tree limbs. The stench of the
dying, the cries of the wounded, the cheers of the
victorious. I'd seen it, I'd been there, I was one of
them.

My disappointment still grew day after day
when my father didn't arrive to greet me. I received
no letters. But our reunion felt less urgent now.
When he did arrive, if he ever did, I could shake his
hand and salute him as one who had shed blood for

Rome. We shared that in common now. And if he didn't come, well, I cared less for that now too. I had Sulla.

My birth father died when I was a baby. My father, Quintus Sertorius, left for war when I was a child, and I hadn't seen him since. I knew little of what a father was supposed to be, but when I looked at my legatus, I decided he possessed all the proper qualities. He invested his time and energy in me. He encouraged me. He laughed with me. He let me struggle, but only when he was close enough to save the day if that's what I needed.

Despite this, I decided to share one thing with my father. After our first battle, the legionaries began to interact with me more. Whispers spread of my conduct in battle, and they respected whatever they heard. They wanted to include me in their inner circle but were unsure how to address me as I was a junior officer.

"The man who raised me was called 'stallion' by his men when he fought against the Cimbri and Teutones," I told them. "Apparently because of his skill as a rider."

The legionaries there found this serendipitous but humorous. "If he was half the rider you are, he was deserving of the title," one of them flattered me.

They debated among themselves while sharing a skin of vinegar wine. Some voted for the name "war horse," some for "bronco," but ultimately, they settled on "stallion," just as I'd hoped.

Cicero was less interested in engaging after the battle than he'd been before.

"My talents are clearly wasted on warfare," he said. "I shall devote myself to administration and rhetoric." He had dabbed his forehead with a damp cloth. "But you, dear Gavius, should continue to devote yourself to the art of battle. Each Roman ought to lend himself and his greatest strengths to the Republic."

I might have told Cicero beforehand battle wouldn't suit him. He might have known it, too, but I respected his bravery for trying. I only lamented it all because he treated me differently now. As if we were part of two different worlds. He no longer made eye contact with me, no longer spoke to me with the bombast or authority he usually did.

Perhaps he was ashamed of his own failures in battle. But it felt as if he saw me differently now. As if I was just another of the legion, the blood-spillers. When he spoke to me, his words continued to puff me up, but I wondered how much of it he meant.

I was writing these thoughts down when another junior officer interrupted me.

I was reclining on a green hill just outside our camp walls. I ran my fingers through the blades of grass—pondering how to articulate my words properly—when he approached.

"Meeting of the officers, time now," he said.

"I'm on the move," I said.

But as I placed the stylus back on the wax tablet before me, the junior officer said, "I mean it, Gavius. He asked me to fetch everyone this instant. It's important."

I considered telling him Sulla favored me and I could take as long as I liked, but his words intrigued me. If Sulla had something important to share, I wanted to be present. I dreamed about even being consulted; my words being respected by all. Perhaps they'd say I was "wise beyond my years."

"Lead the way." I stuffed everything I had in a satchel on my back.

We moved not toward the fortress and the praetorium where I assumed we'd be meeting but around the walls, where Sulla was standing with a few of his officers over a pit of dirt.

"Hold on now, you're saying . . . we're here . . . and they are camped . . . here?" Sulla directed a tree limb through the dirt.

"Close, legate," the man said, before Sulla handed him the stick. He kicked dirt over Sulla's obstructions and started again. "We are here, south of Alba. The enemy is currently located here." He drew a large circle in the dirt. "Just to the east of the Fucine Lake."

Sulla scratched his chin. "And where is Gaius Marius?"

"Right here, legate," the emissary said, drawing a line north. "Between Aesernia and Italica."

"Between Aesernia and what?" Sulla stamped his foot. "We do not use rebel terms here."

The emissary swallowed. "Corfinium. My apologies, sir."

Sulla towered over the man. "Don't apologize to me, apologize to your country. The rebels cannot rename things any more than you or I can."

The emissary bowed his head. "Right you are, legate. I meant only to . . . I should not have called the city of Corfinium the city of Italica."

The emissary drew in the sand again.

"I was not speaking rhetorically, messenger," Sulla said. "Apologize to your country."

The emissary stared back blankly until the

authority of Sulla's gaze forced him to his knees. "Republic of Rome, I ask that you forgive me my ignorance."

"Good enough, on your feet." Sulla flicked his wrist for the man to stand.

It was then that he turned. His eyes softened when he saw me.

"Young Gavius, come join me," he said. "I'm eager to hear your thoughts on all this."

I deepened my voice to match his. "I'm quite eager to know more myself." I adjusted the sword belt around my hips like I'd seen the older men do.

He placed his arm around my shoulders and redrew everything in the dirt for me to see. "This represents us," he said. "And the enemy forces are lining up here, not so far away."

"What's the distance?" I asked.

Sulla nodded. "Less than two days ride," he said. "Roughly forty-five miles."

I nodded. "And where is Gaius Marius?"

Rumors of Gaius Marius filled the ears of every young Roman, but I recalled hearing my father speak of direct interactions with him. At first he spoke of him with reverence and respect, and eventually profound disappointment and regret. I only knew I wanted to stay far away from him, lest I be caught up in the web of love and hate like Quintus Sertorius.

"This envoy claims he is here." Sulla drew a small circle between the marks designating the rebels and ourselves. "Less than a full day's march. We'll likely hear from his camp soon. The Marsi are the greatest threat to both of us."

"Do you think we could defeat Poppaedius Silo together?" I asked.

Sulla looked at me with a mixture of consternation and admiration. "I think so, yes."

"Then we should fight with Marius," I said.

Sulla smacked his lips, and for a moment, his eyes became stern. "You think we should fight with Gaius Marius?"

I felt my heartbeat now. It was heavy—hard even—but steady. "Yes. You are the better general. You've proven that, but now the world will know it. You have nothing to fear from the old relic."

Sulla stared at me with a posture as rigid as a statue. Eventually, he smiled. "Gavius Sertorius, you might be the wisest among us," he said.

"It's just faith in you and the Republic," I said. "That's all."

The emissary shook his head. "Legate, let me show you again . . . if we were to take position here—"

Sulla raised his fist. "Tell me, emissary. Am I stronger going into war with our Roman allies, or are we weaker?"

"I cannot say whether you are stronger or weaker going against your—"

"Then the one thing I needed you for has already been accomplished by a provincial named Gavius," he said. "You're dismissed, emissary."

There were a dozen other officers standing around us, arms crossed. None of them spoke up in defense of the messenger as he turned and sulked off.

"The same applies to the rest of you." Sulla turned to them. "The senate may favor the high-born and the old bloods, but in my camp, if you serve no purpose, I'll dismiss you and appoint someone more deserving in your place."

He took the stick he'd been using to draw in the dirt and plunged it into the earth. "Battle with the Marsi is swiftly upon us. Our swords could be bloodied by the ides, perhaps even sooner. There is no question about that. The only thing we must deliberate on is whether to fight alongside Gaius Marius and the northern armies who are hastening south," he said. "You all know how I feel about him, and most of you feel the same. But as Gavius so eloquently established, our odds of success are dramatically improved by fighting alongside Marius's legions."

The camp prefect, a bronze-skinned old officer who'd fought in more campaigns than I had years on alive, shook his head. He seemed reluctant, like the rest, to share his opinion, so Sulla called on him.

"What are your thoughts, prefect Opimius?"

"That Gaius Marius is a son of a whore," he said. "I served with you at Vercellae. It was we who won the battle, and yet it was Marius and his men who took every denarius of plunder, and it was he who received the triumph. He snorted and spat a glob of mucus. "You deserved more, and we did too. I have no desire to fight alongside him and his minions. Let us have a go at the rebels without him."

A few of the officers nodded but weren't so enthusiastic as to voice their support.

Sulla glared at him for a moment and then chuckled. "I have no doubts as to Marius's mother being a whore. I'm certain that's offensive to all the lovely women of the profession. And no one has more reason to loathe Gaius Marius than me—"

The prefect cut him off. "Exactly. I can't imagine how you'd even consider fighting with him after all he's done. To this day, he fights to steal the glory you earned against the Numidians and the Cimbri."

Sulla smiled and strode to the prefect's side, placing an arm around his shoulder. "If you plan on kissing my arse, Prefect, would you at least ply me with wine first?"

The old prefect stared back with his bushy brows furrowed beneath his helm.

"It's true," Sulla said. "I have more reason to hate Marius than any of you. Yet I consider joining forces with him for this battle. How can I not?" He bent over and picked a small yellow flower from the earth and twisted it in his fingers. "The Marsi alone outnumber us three-to-one. We have superior cavalry, it's true, but they have five times our skirmishers at least. And they have allies. Who knows how many tribes will join them on the battlefield. Their arrows and spears will blot out the sun, like at Thermopylae."

"That's why we have shields, legate," one of the junior officers said.

Lucullus barked, "Do not patronize the commander, or you'll have me to answer to."

Sulla held up a hand. "Never mind him, Lucullus," Sulla said. "He may speak to me how he likes, although I may place him on the front line to test out his faith in the protection of our shields."

The junior officer stepped back and lowered his gaze.

Sulla clicked his tongue and shook his head. "I'm surprised by you, gentlemen. Do you really detest the 'Third Founder of Rome' so much, or do you simply fear losing the spoils of war you so desperately desire?"

The prefect stepped forward and crossed his arms. "Legate, we only wish to see you receive the glory you're due. We know that bastard will steal it if given the chance."

Sulla towered over the old prefect. "Then we must make our part in the victory decisive, so there is no question who won the day."

"Legate, if I may," I said.

Some officers looked at me with a frown, but Sulla's smile maintained my confidence.

"Of course, young tribune. What are your thoughts?"

"My adoptive father told me of his first battle against the Cimbri and Teutones. There were two Roman armies in the north. One general was a noble, the other a plebeian. They refused to coordinate together because of opposing political ideologies, because of their perceived *dignitas*."

Quintus Sertorius had told me the story a hundred times, a hundred different ways, when I was a boy. Sharing a new detail every time he told it, as he swept through the haunting visions in his mind. It was no wonder I could recall the details.

"The Cimbri took advantage of this and forced a battle with one side before the other was ready. Both armies were completely annihilated. My birth father died among them. My adoptive father barely made it out with his life." I took the stick from the dirt pit and drew arrows from the circle representing our army and Marius's, pointing directly at the Marsi enemy. "We might be able to beat the rebels alone. Perhaps that's worth the risk if *dignitas* and personal glory is worth more than Roman lives. Otherwise, we should fight with Gaius Marius. He may be a whoreson, but the thirty thousand men who fight for him are not. They are Romans like us. And we can win this war together."

Sulla's pensive gaze was always a mystery to unravel, a fact I think he delighted in. But in this moment, there was no mistaking what lie behind those blue eyes. He was proud.

"Listen to this, men. Listen to the youngest among us, sharing wisdom beyond anything the rest of us have offered. Is there anything one can say against that?"

The prefect's nostrils flared. "I think the boy—"

"You'll address him by his title."

"I think the tribune has much to learn about warfare and about the nature of men. But we will follow where you lead, legate."

Sulla clapped his hands. "It's settled then. We'll send a delegation tomorrow. And if the old bastard doesn't want to fight with us, at least the blood will be on his hands."

The officers saluted and most of them departed. I decided to wait around and see if Sulla had any further morsels of praise for my "wisdom."

He turned to me and shook his head. "You surprise me more and more each day, Gavius Sertorius," he said. "I have come to look on you as the son I've never had."

I'd desired to hear this from Quintus Sertorius for so long. But perhaps this was enough.

I stifled any revelation of emotion. "Your leadership has made me who I am."

He clapped me on the shoulder. "One day, lad, you may surpass me. You may surpass both your fathers, and all their fathers before them. Keep the path. Maintain your composure. Rome has need of you," he said. "We ride out tomorrow."

SCROLL XIX

Quintus Sertorius—One day before the Nones of Sextilis, 664 Ab Urbe Condita

My fond memories of Marius were tarnished by his political maneuverings as consul ten years before, but warm nostalgia never failed to overcome me when I stepped into his camp.

It was like most Roman camps, I suppose, not unlike the one I'd been training and raising troops in for four months. But there was a peculiar way he ordered his camp to be organized. His men proudly displayed their century flags and cohort eagles at set intervals. The camp smelled of fresh leather, and centurions shouted orders in the rural accent of their commander.

There was one difference I noticed upon arrival, which I'd not seen before in a Marian camp. The men seemed unhappy. There were no dice games between the tents, no sharing of wineskins or the singing of vulgar ballads about their commander's sexual exploits. If Marius was known for one thing, outside of his booming and gravelly voice, it was his ability to keep his troops' morale strong even at the worst of times.

But this time, things appeared to be different. I scanned the faces of legionaries as I passed through the camp. They had the vacant, dead-fish eyes of those who'd fought in a terrible loss. Perhaps these were the survivors of the ambush that took Caepio's life. Others, from the slaughter of Lupus's camp a few months prior or the defeat of Perpenna's legion at the onset of the war.

I swept from my steed and took the reins into my hand. His tail swished happily, as he was relieved as I was that our days of riding were now over, and we were back in a proper camp. Horses could perceive battle as soon as any of us, though, or so I've always said, so I feared his playful clopping would not last long.

Marius was exercising in an open parade field at the center of camp. Couriers stood around and raised their voices over the groans of his exertion as he lifted a large stone boulder and flipped it.

"The delegates are waiting in your praetorium now, legate," one messenger said.

He ignored them completely, continuing to exert his dominance over the rock before him. His muscles were no longer sinewy or cut like a statue of Hercules, as they'd been when I first met him, but he was no less powerful from the looks of it. His old, sun-specked skin was stretched taut over bulging biceps and forearms, his legs still as thick as a horse's.

I stopped at the edge of the parade field but said nothing. I didn't want to make the same mistake as the emissaries and disturb Marius while at work.

But he noticed me almost immediately, as if he felt my presence the moment I arrived. He stopped rolling the stone midefort and stood. He placed his hands on his hips and stared at me.

At first, I thought he was catching his breath, but I could see now he couldn't find the words to say.

He took a few steps forward as the emissaries continued to clamor for his immediate attention.

Beads of sweat clung to his chest hair like dew on a spider web.

"My old boy," he said, with neither warmth nor malice.

"General Marius, sir," I said, and offered him a salute.

He was the type of fellow to embrace and offer a kiss to those he considered part of his tribe. I'd felt the strength of his arms this way many times before, but now he only extended a hand.

A sadness swept through me as his callused hand wrapped around my forearm with ease. I couldn't deny there was still a great deal of love and respect for him in my heart, and the rift between us saddened me. For a moment, I wished we could go back in time and remove all memories of the political upheaval he created ten years before.

"Reporting for service. I bring with me two full legions of Roman recruits at full capacity, along with a half-staffed legion of auxiliaries," I said.

He continued to search my eyes. There was sullenness, a seriousness to him now that was uncommon. I wondered if the war had weighed on him the way my efforts in the north had burdened me. But somehow, I knew the look in his eye was personal.

At last he spoke, and his gruff old voice was a welcome tone, despite my reservations. "I'd order the camp expanded, but we'll be on the move within a few hours."

Marius was many things, but a man of few words, he was not. I expected more somehow. I figured he might mention me sitting with Didius instead of him at the first meeting of the senate after our return. His childlike response to perceived slights was one of his most prevalent traits. He said nothing of it now, and I wondered if he'd given up on me entirely.

Perhaps that was good. It's what I wanted, in some respects. He was a dangerous and unpredictable man, particularly in politics, and his overreliance on me had placed me in danger time and again, and that wasn't the future I wanted for me or my wife.

Regardless of the past, he'd mentored me, almost like a father, for years. I owed to him my first military commands, my seat on the senate . . . there were no strands of my life I could not trace back to Gaius Marius, and the distance in his eyes felt unnatural.

"I kept the men in formation," I said. "We'll be prepared to march at your order."

The emissary cupped a hand over his mouth and shouted again. "I beseech you, General Marius, the delegates are waiting in your camp, and time is running short."

Marius turned with his characteristic and youthful vitality. "Mars's balls, man! I heard you. Go serve them some swill to drink and fatten their bellies. I will go when I damn well please."

His voice echoed throughout the camp, and the emissary gulped like he'd seen enemy cavalry riding on him. He departed without delay.

"You don't want to ask where we're going?" Marius material-ized a dirty rag from his legionary trousers and dabbed at the sweat on his neck and balding forehead.

"I will follow your orders wherever they lead," I said.

He grunted, his most frequent method of communication. "I have enough sycophants around me, Sertorius. I could always rely on your honesty before. Can I count on it now?"

The horse by my side caught a scent on the air and began sniffing Marius. He rubbed his bulbous thumb between her eyes but kept his own locked on me.

"You can rely on my honesty," I said. "You may know that it is not my desire to be here. But as always, I will follow you through the inferno of Orcus, if that's what's required."

He exhaled at this and shook his head. "We're going some-where far worse than that," he said. "We're joining the forces of Lucius Sulla."

I didn't care to fight beside Sulla, but my son was serving in his camp. Perhaps I could finally see him again.

"We're joining Lucius Sulla?"

I didn't believe what I was hearing. What had transpired that he would draw swords beside his most personal enemy?

"He's camped a half-day's march to the east." Marius crossed his muscular arms. He watched my response closely. "The Marsi army is vast, powerful, and more experienced than our own. We must fight together if we are to conquer."

"Understood, legate," I said.

His jaw flexed. "I assumed this news would please you."

"Why would I be pleased?"

"Your new friends in the senate are allies of Sulla's," Marius said. "I assumed you'd want to ride into battle with your colleagues."

There was the famous spurned Marius I'd been expecting.

I met his gaze. "Sulla is no friend of mine. I will ride into battle with whomever for Rome's protection and safety, but do not mistake my service to the Republic as an allegiance to any man. My allegiance is to the Republic itself and to my family."

His posture seemed to soften at that, but there was none of the backslapping common to Marius when he was completely at ease.

"Quintus Sertorius, you one-eyed demigod!" I heard a familiar voice from nearby.

My oldest friend, Lucius Hirtuleius, was sprinting toward me in full kit, his breastplate fixed so tight against his muscular chest it barely moved.

I'd waited a long time to be reunited with Lucius. We'd served together on nearly every campaign I'd ever been on, and this was the longest I'd been separated from him since we were little more than boys.

But I chose not to run to him. Marius was a man easily offended, and turning my back to him would not have been a good way to begin our reunion, especially with the question I knew I was about to ask him.

Lucius was as close to Marius as any man, though, and had

no qualms interrupting him. He threw his burly arms around my shoulders and patted my back with his nub.

"It's good to see you, *amice*," I said.

Marius watched our embrace with curiosity, but what was happening behind those dark eyes, I could not tell.

"From the reports, we thought you were half in hades." Lucius pulled away and sized me up. "But you look healthy as an ox."

"The gods are merciful," I said. "I'm sure I have your sacrificed pigeons to thank for that." I declined to mention the sickness, the poisonings, and the general struggle we'd faced in the north.

He punched my shoulder with his remaining fist.

I quickly redirected our attention to Marius. "We were just discussing the upcoming battle."

Lucius shook his head. "These Marsi are some tough bastards. You remember how they held down the right flank at Vercellae?"

Marius grunted, and I could tell from the inflection we were to speak no more of our enemy as former allies. Right now, they were the same as the Cimbri or Teutones. A foe we must defeat.

"The battle will be long, and it will be bloody." Marius's eyes hardened. "But, if we can defeat the Marsi—if we can nail that Poppaedius Silo to a cross—the rest of the rebels will bend their knee."

Marius was a brilliant strategist, a masterful tactician in battle like Scipio Africanus or even his great enemy Hannibal. But I doubted his prophecy. The Samnites and their allies were too entrenched to surrender now. Regardless, defeating the Marsi would be our first major victory of the war, and we desperately needed one.

"Before we begin preparations, I would ask something of you, legate Marius." I turned to him.

The look in his eye told me he was in no mood to extend favors, but he waved his hand for me to continue.

"I would like to ride into Sulla's camp. Before battle."

"Just arrived and you already seek to abandon me."

I shook my head. "It's nothing of the sort," I said. "My son, Gavius, is in his camp. It's nigh on nine years now since I've seen him. I wish only to embrace him before we do battle."

Marius collected bile in his throat and spit near my legionary sandals. "That angers me even further. Your son fighting under a man you claim is no friend of yours? Tell me, why is he not serving under me? Why was I not asked? My counsel not received? I would have made him an officer. I could have created a career for him . . . like I did for you."

I'd seen Marius push over tables and shatter amphorae of wine in a fit of anger, but never strike someone. I wondered if he was capable of it now.

"I was away, legate. In Greece. My counsel was sought no more than yours," I said. "Had I been, Sulla would be the last commander I would want him serving under."

Lucius sighed. "I'll bet he's keeping Gavius as a threat," he said. "He knows you'll have to play along, or your son could be in harm's way."

"That makes you a liability in command," Marius grunted.

"You know me, legate," I said. "I am as steadfast in battle as I've ever been, and more experienced." I held out my hands as if I was before an altar. "I just want to see my boy before swords are drawn and blood is spilt."

"Go." Marius pointed back the way I'd came. "Go. And when you return, you'll report to me. I will assign your legions at my discretion."

"If that is your order, legate," I said. I didn't know what he meant by that, but with the thought of seeing Gavius foremost in my mind, I didn't care.

Marius spun on his heels and made for his praetorium to entertain his guests, not bothering to dry himself any further or redress.

"I'm sorry," Lucius said, eyes cast on the glob of spit dissolving into the sand by my feet.

"You have nothing to apologize for." I exhaled. "I would sacrifice more than this to see Gavius. There is no guarantee either of us make it out of this battle alive, especially with Marius and Sulla controlling us like children's figurines."

"Marius will protect you." Lucius's faith in his commander was never wavering. Whether this was a flaw or virtue, I do not know.

"Unfortunately, *amice* . . ." I pulled myself back onto my horse. "I don't think even the gods can protect us in the battle to come."

Full of religious fervor as always, I could see him formulating a reprimand for my blasphemy, but he didn't offer it.

"Return to us safely," he said instead. "And give Gavius love from his uncle Lucius."

"I will," I said.

If only safety was something in my hands now. But even Lucius's pigeon sacrifices could no longer offer that. The fate of us all, the life and death of my son, now lay in the hands of Lucius Cornelius Sulla.

We rode hard, my horse and me. He nearly bucked me a time or two in frustration at the pace, but a moment in the shade pacified him.

The sun was setting by the time I arrived, but it was still burnt-orange and oppressive. Somewhere in the west, it would be resting on Rome's high walls like a crown. But in the morning, it did the same for the city the rebels now called "Italica."

An adage came to mind. More people worship the rising sun than the setting one, and I wondered if this was true now.

"Halt." The gate sentry held out his palm. "How do you enter?"

I assumed there was some sort of phrase used to verify entry into Sulla's camp. It was a common practice now, as so many Sons of Remus had wreaked havoc in Roman fortifications.

"I know not how I enter," I said. "But I am Quaestor Quintus Sertorius, sent by legatus Gaius Marius."

The sentry lowered his gaze. "Right you are, sir. I will alert the commander of your arrival."

"No need." I tapped him on the shoulder. "I'll go to him straight away," I lied.

"I'll lead you to him," the sentry offered.

"Legionary, remain at your post and fulfill your orders."

He gulped and nodded, before returning to attention outside the gates.

I had no intentions of seeing Sulla if I could avoid it. There was nothing to say. My only objective was to find my son.

Sulla's camp was not dissimilar from Marius's or any other legion's, but I was stunned by the white cloth of their tunics, cloaks, and tents. Where was the scarlet?

This new, white cloth must have been expensive to acquire, and I knew the senate would have never paid from the state coffers for such a luxury. Sulla was willing to spend anything to bind his men closer to him, to set them apart. I could see that immediately.

Most of the men gathered outside their tents as one of their mates prepared supper. Their helpings looked meager but sufficient, and their spirits were noticeably higher than those in Marius's camp. What defeats had they sustained, after all? What reason had they to fear a battle with the undefeated Marsi?

I unbuckled my helm and fastened it to my horse's saddle; the plume brushing his haunches. I wanted to fit in until I found my boy, and most of Sulla's legion had already dressed down to their tunics.

A training dummy sat in an open square between the tents,

and I hitched my horse there. My eye remained watchful for any officers, who might lead me toward the tribunes' quarters.

I wondered what I would find him doing. Would he be eating alone? Drinking with the men or playing a game of *Tessera*? Did he brood over the battle to come, or was he delighting in its arrival? Had he lost friends in previous skirmishes or heard the cries of the dying?

Would he remember me? Would he embrace me and call me father? Would he ask to join me?

A legionary passed by with a bowl of porridge in his hand.

"Soldier," I called to him.

He quickly set the bowl by his feet and stood to attention. Sulla's men were in fine order and of strong morale.

"Sir." He saluted.

"I am looking for a junior officer named Gavius Sertorius. Can you direct me to him?"

He seemed to soften. "You mean stallion? He's usually with the horses."

I tilted my head. Stallion was the name I went by on my first campaign. For a moment, I wondered if this was an old veteran confusing me with my son, but he was far too young. I realized my son had taken the title, as I had, and it filled my heart with warmth and increased my desire to find him.

The legionary continued, "Either that, or with legatus Sulla. He's become relied on."

A shadow grew and stretched out between the legionary and me.

"Gavius is not with me at the moment."

I turned. There stood Sulla, in a white ornate breastplate and a helmet with pale horse hair.

His expression was hard and unwelcoming for a moment, but then his famous grin stretched across his face.

"Brother Sertorius, how good of you to join us." He threw his arms around me. The smell of his perfume clung to him like a swarm of flies, so unnatural and uncommon a scent in legionary camps.

I embraced him in return and kept my voice light. "I have come to see my son," I freed myself.

His reaction to my arrival was the opposite of Marius's, but at least with the latter, I knew it was genuine.

"I feared you never would. The boy longed for your arrival, but I've feared he's given up."

Sulla was a master with words. He knew just how to twist them. He could sense every insecurity and fear in a man's heart and attack it like an enemy flank. I told myself not to listen.

"My efforts in the north were hindered. Poor health, rebel sabotage . . . I came as soon as I could."

He puckered his lips and nodded. "Of course, of course. The boy may not understand, but I certainly do. I reassured him often of your desire to reunite."

"Gratitude," I said.

That I should have to offer thanks to Sulla for his words to my son was reason enough to stir my anger, but I maintained my composure for the sake of Gavius.

"Anything for an old war companion." He smiled again.

"Could you point me in his direction?"

"I can do better than that." He swept his arm around my shoulder. "I'll lead you right to him."

I'd rather have found him alone, but the thought of reuniting with Gavius compelled me to comply.

"Lead on."

He flicked his wrists to dismiss the legionary who was still standing at attention nearby.

"Tell me, have you levied your legions?" he said.

His steps were slow and ambling, deliberately hindering our progress.

"I have raised the legions."

"And you have brought them to join us?"

I turned to him. "The senate has assigned my legions to the command of legatus Gaius Marius."

"Of course. That is what I meant. We will all be fighting alongside one another soon enough, dear brother. Old grievances are behind us, the glory of Rome before us. I hope you're capable of this?"

I cared nothing for old grievances with Sulla. My concern and distrust for him was squarely because of the capacity for boundless ambition in his heart.

"I can," I said, "for the good of the Republic and the safety of my family."

His lips thinned and his eyes narrowed. Something seemed to pass over him, and the arm around my shoulder even seemed to tighten. "You should be very loyal to me then," he said. "I am the best hope you have for both."

"Protect my son from harm, and fight well for the Republic, and you have nothing to fear from me."

He lowered his voice so the legionaries eating at their tents might not overhear. "You know I fear nothing," he said. "For the gods protect and guide me. I am their divine vessel. I seek only complicity."

"Complicity with what? What aims do you have that don't align with everyone else in the Republic?"

He ignored my question. "And with that out of the way, we can be as friendly as pigs in the forum." He stopped and took my hands in his own. The palms were soft and supple, recently rubbed with rose water and oil. Mine left dirt stains on him.

I craned my head to find Gavius.

"Do you not recognize him?" Sulla smiled, with almost a glimmer of pride in his eye. He pointed to a young man seated on a sown log just a few paces before us.

"Thank you, legate. I've waited a long time for this."

As I turned to leave, he squeezed my hands tighter. Those oiled, perfumed hands now revealed the same burning strength in his eyes.

"You know, when I first brought Gavius along, I found it amusing." His icy eyes fixed on mine now. "But under my care, he has become a valuable warrior. I think I shall keep him."

I met his gaze. "My son is not yours to keep," I said. "Nor is he mine. He is a Roman citizen. He will go where he pleases and serve whom he pleases."

His eyes narrowed. He leaned closer and whispered in my ear, "Be careful, Sertorius." He left a lingering kiss on my cheek before stepping away slowly.

He watched me carefully as I turned to my son.

SCROLL XX

GAVIUS SERTORIUS—ONE day before the Nones of Sextilis, 664 Ab Urbe Condita

There were two silver horses engraved on my breastplate. I paid extra attention to them when I cleaned my armor. I told myself they were my father's horse, Sura, and my grandmother's favorite mare, Stellatina.

They would bring me luck in battle, as Sura had brought favor to Quintus Sertorius.

I dabbed a rag on my tongue and began cleaning the silver horses, applying pressure to persistent smudges of dirt.

The crunch of dirt sounded behind me as footsteps grew near.

I didn't bother looking up. It was probably Cicero or another junior officer, needing my assistance in one of the routine things required of us.

"I am looking for Gavius Sertorius," said the unfamiliar voice.

"Can you come back later, mate?" I sighed. "I want this armor shining like Sulla's by nightfall."

"It's shining better than your father's, after he's ridden all this way to see you."

I stopped cleaning. Tried to make sense of the words. I spun around on the log I was sitting on.

The man before me might not have been recognizable, but no one could mistake that leather eyepatch. He made a replica for me when I was a small boy. Wearing it impaired my vision like his. I wanted to be just like him.

"Do you not know me, boy?" he said.

I did. I knew him. Larger and more muscular than I remembered, the stubble of a black beard evenly spread across chin and jaw.

His scarred, battle-hardened presence sowed terror into his enemies, and perhaps even to his own men. It filled me with peace and security, as it did when he'd tucked me in and helped me fight nightmares as a boy.

"I know you," I said. I set down my armor and stood.

He began to say something, but I threw my arms around his shoulders.

His arms were just as strong as they were when I was a child, just as comforting and protecting.

"I have missed you, my son."

He smelled of sweat, leather, and olive oil, such a familiar scent from my childhood.

Then I drew back. I'd dreamed of his arrival since he departed for Greece, even more since I joined the legion. I wanted to appear as a strong man, independent and confident in my own right. I was no mere boy to comfort. Not by him. Not any longer.

His arms hung open and empty before he let them fall.

Had he not thought of this moment? Thought of nothing to say to me after all this time? Perhaps an apology for all those years away or at least an explanation as to why he hadn't visited me sooner. Instead, he stood there like he was deaf or dumb.

"We're riding for battle soon," I said.

"I've heard." He nodded. "I'll be fighting as well."

"You mean to join us?" My heart leapt, but I resisted any impulse to reveal it.

He shook his head. "Not exactly. The senate assigned my legions to the command of Gaius Marius."

Sulla told me about this Marius before. The rumors of his grandeur were exaggerated or outright lies. Most of the glory he'd earned in battle, he stole from more competent commanders, like Sulla. Besides that, he was politically corrupt and likely should have been executed for the revolution he helped create when I was just a boy.

It shamed our family name to be aligned with such a man, but I did not say it.

My father laughed at himself and rubbed the back of his neck. "So much to say, and I can find none of the words. There's so much I want to know."

"You could have written." I crossed my arms.

His lips parted and his eye bounced around like he was attempting to solve a riddle.

"Gavius, I wrote. Early and often. I sent them by courier to this very camp."

I searched his face for the answers. Duplicity was not one of his strengths, at least according to Arrea.

"I never received them."

He exhaled, slow and long, and nodded as if he realized something. Perhaps he forgot to send them.

"I . . . I'm happy to find you well."

"I am." I looked down at my armor and wished I'd been wearing it when he arrived. "How is . . . Arrea?"

He smiled sadly at the mention of her name. "Well. She's on her way to visit your grandmother as we speak, if she hasn't already arrived." He paused before adding quickly, "She misses you. She speaks of you often."

I thought of her all the time. I missed her as much as I'd missed him, but for different reasons. Her comfort and strength brought me from childhood to manhood. I could have used her soft presence now. But perhaps it would have softened me, I thought. The distance was for the best.

"Have you fared well here in camp? Do the officers treat you well?"

"I am an officer," I said.

He nodded. "Yes . . . I meant—"

"Sulla has been good to me. I've not had a request denied or a need unmet. I've learned much. I've grown much."

He smiled and looked me over from my head to my feet. "I can see that. You're a man now in your own right," he said. "I am very proud of you."

The words rushed over me like a current.

"I . . . well . . . is there anything you would ask of me?" he asked. His words were filled with longing, but I did not know their intent.

"I have everything I need," I said.

His horse began stamping impatiently behind him, but he seemed not to notice.

His voice was little more than a whisper. "Good," he said.

"I have much to do," I said.

He nodded and gestured back to the log behind me. "Of course, of course. I'll let you return to your duties, then. I just . . . wanted to see you before battle," he said. "All grown up now."

"Perhaps we will celebrate our victory together," I said but spoke the words with formality and distance.

He smiled again, but there was sadness in his eye. "I would like that."

My father stepped forward to embrace me, but I stuck out my arm before he could. He accepted a handshake, one shared between colleagues or mere acquaintances. I feared for my composure if he placed his arms around me once more.

He accepted my hand reluctantly. His hands were coarse like old, sunbaked leather, his arms lined with more scars than I remembered.

"Be safe," he said.

"Gods protect you." I nodded.

He swept back onto his horse with the careless grace I remembered as a boy. My father gave me one last look before departing.

I wasted no time returning to my armor. Working with my hands could distract my mind. That's what Lucullus told me before.

I blinked away the wetness of my eyes and tried not to think of all the things I wished I'd said.

SCROLL XXI

QUINTUS SERTORIUS—ONE day before the Nones of Sextilis, 664 Ab Urbe Condita

My mind was on Gavius as I departed the camp.

The gate guard stopped me. "Do you know where Saturn's Hill is?"

I shook my head.

He pointed with his pilum. "Three miles that way. Surrounded by thick forest. We're meeting with Marian delegates there shortly. You can wait and travel with our officers if you'd like."

Declining, I clicked for my horse to trot through the opening gates. I needed to be alone with my thoughts.

I rode under the slate sky in the direction the legionary directed me. Clouds threatened a torrent of rain, and already a moist wind swished around me.

Why was Gavius so reserved? Why did he seem angry? My stomach twisted into knots. What had Sulla told him?

But I was proud. He was a man by all accounts, my brother's face reflected in his like in a pool of water. There was fresh

SCROLL XXI | 283

stubble on his chin. His build was lithe but his muscles tight. There was a resolve in his eyes that appeared randomly when he was a child. He was a warrior now. No mere boy any longer.

Joy and pain spiderwebbed through my mind as I took a lightly worn dirt path into the woods. Thorns and weeds covered the path, patches of poisonous berries grew on either side.

My horse snorted. The twisted, decaying tree limbs looked like snakes. I ran my fingers through his mane to calm him, but he remained alert, his eyes watchful and his gait restrained.

The forest opened to a hilltop scattered with yellow flowers. A roe deer scattered in the distance. This was Saturn's Hill, where Marius and Sulla would meet for the first time since their confrontation in Rome.

I fed my horse chunks of hardtack from the leather pouch on my hip and waited there for at least another hour. The trees and fallen leaves in the surrounding forest swished and spun around, a cacophony of rustling. Rainfall began about the time the sky darkened and the shrouded moon reached its zenith. There were no stars out.

Water droplets stung the bare flesh of my arms and ran off in streams from the crest of my helmet. I considered taking shelter beneath a tree when I saw horses appear from the wood line. At first, I thought they might be a wild pack, my heart stirring the way it did when my father and I would look for wild stallions in the hills above Nursia. But even in the darkness, the glimmer of armored Romans appeared atop the horses.

In the glow of torches, I could see the riders on one side wore white tunics beneath their armor, and the other side wore scarlet.

My horse stamped and snorted, billows of smoke pouring from his nostrils.

"Shh, boy," I calmed him. He'd seen too much battle for a colt less than three years. The sight of even our allies in battle array frightened him.

"Lo there, here rides Gaius Marius, conqueror of the Numidians and the Cimbri, the Third Founder of Rome!" a rider on one side of me shouted.

"Lo there, here rides Lucius Cornelius Sulla, commander of Sulla's Fist, scourge of the rebel armies!" a rider on the other side shouted.

I feared for a moment they might continue shouting out about their exploits and assumed titles, but they rode up and paused on either side of me.

I could see little from the swift, horizontal rain and the darkness, but I instantly spotted Lucius beside Gaius Marius, the latter being the only man who wore no cloak and seemed not to notice the rain.

"We go to battle tomorrow, old friend," Sulla said.

Marius said nothing. He and Sulla joined me on the center of the hill.

Sulla extended his hand. Marius eventually accepted it.

I thought I heard thunder in the distance, but perhaps it was a tree falling. So surreal, this might have been a dream, or a nightmare.

The sand-colored moon broke away from the clouds and shed light on Sulla's men. There was Gavius, atop a fine white mare, in full battle array. He did not meet my gaze.

Sulla lifted his voice above the whistling wind. "We have surveyed the battlefield. We will meet them six miles due east of here, in a valley near some ancient ruins from a forgotten people."

"I should like to see the battlefield myself before I agree," Marius said.

"There is nowhere else. We either meet them there or retreat," Sulla said.

Marius grunted. "Have you a battle map?"

Sulla snapped his fingers, and Gavius easily moved his horse to Sulla's side, and materialized a capsule.

Marius opened it and shielded the parchment. "Bring me a torch," he ordered.

One of his men complied, but the crackling fire roared in the wind, sparks flying everywhere.

"Where are you in all this?" Marius said.

Sulla leapt from his horse and strode to Marius's side. "Here. Northeast of your position."

Marius gasped and thrust out the note for someone to take it. I happily did so.

"Have you so little men?" Marius balked.

No one brought me a torch, but I strained my eye to make out the map as best I could on the dampening scroll.

Marius's forces did indeed make up most of the map, with a tick to designate every cohort. Aligned across from him were the rebels. The Marsi, the Paeligni, the Marrucini. Their legionaries were designated the same as ours, but slashes appeared to represent skirmishers and dots for slingers. Off in the top right corner was Sulla's name, with a fraction of the other armies.

Sulla said, "I have one full legion of the finest men Rome has to offer. One full legion of auxiliaries. And twelve hundred of the best cavalry in Numidia."

"Full strength?" I said. "Have you not seen battle?"

His helmet glistened as he nodded. "We were replenished."

Marius grunted, low and long. He'd received no reinforcements, just amalgamated more defeated legions into his ranks.

"Why do you suppose the enemy will arrange themselves like this?" I asked.

Sulla shrugged. "I don't."

I gave him back the scroll.

"I believe they will position their legionaries in the center, attempting to defeat us by overwhelming force. Their shock-troop skirmishers on the flanks to sow terror into our ranks, and slingers to assault us from the distance."

Marius said, "They'll not defeat me by a display of force."

No one commented.

"We are vastly outnumbered," I said, recalling the map as

best I could. "If I read the numerals right, the Marsi alone have nearly forty thousand men."

Sulla nodded. "And legatus Marius has thirty thousand."

Marius grunted. "I do not."

Sulla tilted his head. "You have six legions do you not?"

"Not at full strength," he said. "2,611 men in one, 3,723 composing two others, an auxiliary legion of only 1,897, as of muster this morning." He recalled this from memory.

Sulla made a sound somewhere between a gasp and a laugh. "Could you not combine the legions to create fewer at full strength?"

Marius snapped back, "No I could not." He bared his teeth. "I've been busy trying to win a war. Besides, pride in one's legion makes them fight harder. Strip away their identity, and they lose the will to fight."

"My legions are at full strength, my auxiliaries at half," I said. "A total of nearly thirteen thousand men."

Sulla snatched a torch from an officer behind him and bore over his own map. "Together you must have no more than . . ."

"25,300 fighting men," Marius said. "And six hundred head of Campanian cavalry."

Sulla was, for once, at a loss for words.

"Having second thoughts?" Marius questioned.

At once I knew the war of egos had begun. I'd seen this before, and I dreaded to bear witness again.

"No. We must . . . we only need to use the terrain to our advantage."

"I will place Sertorius's men in the reserves," Marius said. "They will reinforce the center at my order."

"Legate," I said. I knew I must be careful how I spoke these words or risk them being rejected out of spite. "We could divide my forces, one legion on the left and another on the right, with the auxiliaries in the reserves. This should still provide you with the reinforcements you require, but my men should be able to fight off the skirmishers and slingers on the rebel flanks."

Marius considered it, but he was smart enough to identify sound tactical advice. "Fine. Lucius Hirtuleius will command the left flank. You will command the right."

I didn't wish for my legions to be separated, but at least this way we could fight rather than wait for the battle to fall apart before us.

Marius continued; his eyes raised as if he were still seeing the battle map in his mind. "I will align my legions in the center, with my auxiliary unit in the front. Sertorius's auxiliaries, as he suggests, will remain in reserves under the command of . . ."

"Aulus Insteius is my second in command," I said.

"So be it." Marius flicked his wrist. "Where is this Aulus Insteius?"

"Here, legate," came the familiar voice. Aulus led his horse into the flickering torchlight. His eyes just as grim as they'd been since the moment his brother left us.

"You can command the auxiliaries in reserve. But understand this: your responsibility is to reinforce me in the center. Remain in position until I order you to advance. Under no circumstances are you to act otherwise. Understood?"

"Understood, legate."

Then Marius pointed to Sulla. "You will collapse onto their eastern flank. Combined with Sertorius's men, you should be able to roll them up like a carpet. But you must remain in position until you're certain you can envelop the rebels. Strike too soon and our entire stratagem fails."

Something flashed before Sulla's eyes. He was unused to being given orders. But there was no man alive with more experience in battle than Gaius Marius. From my recollection of the map, I saw no other options.

Sulla said, "My cavalry will take care of their slingers. They'll rout or die."

"Fine. And my cavalry will ride round their flanks and take out the Marsi reserves."

"Agreed." Sulla rolled up the map and handed it back to Gavius.

"And remember, men . . ." Marius raised his voice, cutting through the wind and rain with ease. "There is no time for revenge in war."

I could see Sulla's peculiar smile in the moonlight. "If it was vengeance I sought, I'd kill you first."

Both sides gripped their sword hilts. Everyone but Sulla.

Marius spit and shook his head. "Revenge for what? For digging you out of the gutter and giving you a place on my staff? For giving you food and wine and a place at my table? Handing you power, position, and authority, though you'd done nothing to deserve it? You ungrateful whoreson."

Sulla didn't appear the least offended. "Even if my mother were a whore, I'd still have better blood than you."

"Enough," I said.

"Besides," Sulla said, "my vengeance would not be personal. It would be for the revolution you fomented, for your corruption, ambition, avarice. For the damage you've caused to this Republic."

Marius let his head back and let out a raspy and uncharacteristic laugh. "You speak only of yourself."

"Gentlemen, enough." I ordered. "Tomorrow we ride for war. If only for this one day, we must put aside past transgression and political rivalries."

The humor fell from Marius's face. "As you wish."

"Tomorrow then?" Sulla said.

"Tomorrow."

Marius and Sulla both wheeled their steeds in opposite directions and led their men back to their respective camps.

"Gavius," I said. "Gavius!" The torrent of rushing leaves and the stamping of hooves drowned me out.

Tomorrow, six miles east of that wood line, we would kill or we would die.

I hadn't been in a battle this size since we defeated the Cimbri. We could only hope for a similar victory on this humid morning.

Marius's forces stretched nearly a quarter mile. Even from the slight elevation of the eastern flank where I was positioned with my men, I could barely see the rest of my men on the opposite side of the line, those under the command of my friend Lucius Hirtuleius.

The previous night's storm left the fields as muddy and uneven as a pigsty. Every step left behind a sloshy imprint and sludge clinging to the soles of our sandals.

Once the fighting set in, this would be a strain on our feet and ankles, making it nearly impossible to hold the front line. But at least our enemy would face the same obstacle.

Rain before battle was sometimes welcome, despite the difficulty of finding good footing. But not today. The month of Sextilis was upon us, and the moisture would coalesce with the heat, choking lungs and forcing legionary tunics to cling to us like wet blankets.

I stepped out from the ranks of my men and knelt. I plucked a blade of grass and rubbed it between my thumb and forefinger. Our ancestors, the Romans and Italians, had fought here before. Their blood watered this vast valley, in battles both against one another and beside one another, as brothers-in-arms. I wondered what they would think now. What would my father think? What about my ancestor who was awarded his citizenship and a gold ring by the Romans after fighting them for years?

Perhaps they would wonder why they shed all that blood if we were only to draw swords against one another once again.

I flicked the blade of grass, and an eastern wind carried it away.

"The men are steady," came a nasally voice from behind me. "Better than you'd expect from recruits."

Leptis was standing with his shoulders straight and his flat-tened, crooked nose lifted high. He was proud of the men, and so was I.

"They have their First Spear to thank for that." I stood. "You've led them well. And they will fight hard for you today."

He nodded, then shook his head. "Aye. I thank you, Quaestor, but you're wrong there. We all fight for you."

I patted him on the shoulder. "We fight for one another."

We stared out over the valley. It was shaped almost like an arena, a creation of the gods with the singular purpose of watching inferior beings slaughter one another. Forests surrounded the valley, but there wasn't a single tree, rock, or other obstruction on the field of battle. There was no elevation, no high or low ground. It would be strength against strength, sword against sword. And soon the dying and the dead would fill this empty, grassy valley. The conqueror and the vanquished.

"Something weighs on you," Leptis said, "and I don't believe it's the morning dew."

"I've fought in many battles, centurion. But never while knowing my son was somewhere on the battlefield doing the same." I gripped the hilt of my sword. It brought me comfort despite the sting of my words. "Have you ever fought in a battle with a son?"

Leptis pursed his lips. "Aye. I've got over four thousand sons here behind me." He nodded back to our legion. "I've got no wee ones of my own, Quaestor. I do not know whether to curse or thank the gods for that. Today, at least, I am grateful."

"I cannot allow it to cloud my judgment. My mind." I spoke as much to myself as the centurion.

He nodded, understanding more than a man without a child should be able to. He reached up then and unclasped the neck-lace behind his neck.

Leptis slid off the phallic necklace and extended it to me.

"I've worn this to ward off The Evil Eye since I was a child myself," he said. "I don't believe I need it any longer."

"Thank you, Leptis. You're a gracious man. But I would not take so precious a gift on the day of battle."

"Not for you. For your lad." He knelt and scooped up a handful of mud, much of it remaining under his fingernails. The centurion placed the pendent in the hole created and covered it up. He patted the mound a few times, and his hand lingered there for a moment, and I wondered if he was saying a silent prayer.

"I'm grateful, centurion," I said. "Truly."

He stood and stretched, almost as if a weight had been lifted. "I have all the protection I need. I have a one-eyed quaestor to protect me."

"I sacrificed this eye to ward off the evil one, actually."

He looked back with a mixture of amazement and admiration until he realized I was joking.

We laughed, and he clapped me on the back. I hoped the men were watching. Some levity might loosen their nerves.

"How much longer now, do you think?" Leptis asked.

I scanned the edge of the valley. Soon, nearly fifty thousand men would appear upon the horizon, chanting and howling for our blood.

"An hour at least," I said. There was still no reverberation on the earth, and I knew from experience we'd feel their arrival before we'd see it.

"These rebels take their time." He shook his head. The centurion was ready for their arrival.

But I wasn't. A part of me still hoped they wouldn't arrive.

I looked off to the east, where I could spot but a glimmer of armor belonging to the legions under Sulla. They remained ready and partially concealed by ancient columns, built perhaps by the same shared ancestors who once fought here. Gavius was somewhere among them.

I hoped a father's prayers and Leptis's sacrifice would be enough to protect him.

The earth tremored beneath my feet.

We would soon find out.

"Advance!"

Four thousand eight hundred men moved behind me. I knew from experience that several hundred had either pissed or shit themselves, some both.

A few hundred more had thrown up what little bread and wine they'd forced down that morning.

Thousands were thinking of women. A mother, a wife, a lover. The desire for one last embrace, a final touch of the lips, a flood of words never spoken, and an urge to run and deliver them like a letter. I assumed thousands spoke to their ancestors, asking for whatever strength their fathers' once had to dwell in them now. Most of them were probably praying, silently and to every god and goddess known to man.

But all of them—every last one—held a swiftly beating heart in their chest. Thumping, pounding beneath their chainmail like a starved, caged lion in the arena.

On the far end of the line, another four thousand eight hundred legionaries I raised in Mutina, just like these, were marching behind my friend Lucius Hirtuleius. Between us advanced the three battle-scarred legions under Marius's command.

The legion ranks behind me opened up, and I fell in with the rest of them. Our pace was slow and deliberate, while the rebels across from us were moving twice as fast to the tune of war drums and chants about Rome's downfall.

I raised my voice above the stamping of my men. "Whatever happens, hold the line," I said. "Men die in battle. Men are slaughtered in retreat."

I glanced toward the center of our line. Marius's auxiliaries were marching forward. I wondered if they knew they were destined to die, enduring the rebel's brutal assault. If so, they were heroes and more patriotic than most Roman-born citizens ever would be.

"Protect the eagle," I said. "Protect your standard. Protect the man beside you."

The mud beneath us would soon run red. Thick with viscera and entrails. The bodies of fathers, sons, brothers, and husbands would soon pile up like moray eels in a fishmonger's net. Humanity, life, all signs of individuality, vanished.

"Quaestor," centurion Leptis shouted from his post on the right side of the formation.

I made my way through the marching ranks to his side.

His old but sharp eyes scanned the enemy. "Where are the tanned-leather warriors of the Paeligni? Where are the pointed helmets of the Marrucini?"

One of the breathless legionaries spoke up. "Perhaps they fear defeat and abandoned their allies?"

I looked across at the marching rebels, the earth beneath us groaning with every cohesive stride they took. They were vast. More even than I expected. Our legions, so expansive and great to my eye that morning, were dwarfed by the enemy.

But the centurion was right. Every waving banner I saw belonged to the Marsi. Had their allies abandoned them?

Or perhaps they felt no need to enlist assistance. They still outnumbered us, but this was a good sign.

"Keep your eyes on the horizon," I said. "But for now, let's thank the gods."

The Marsi front lines were lifting their pila now. They launched them just like we did. Marius's auxiliaries braced against the bombardment, but I could hear their screams from so far across the battlefield.

Unarmored hordes rushed at us.

They ululated and swung slings over their heads.

"Shields up!" Leptis bellowed.

I peered through a gap in our shields and hoped a stone

wouldn't slip through and take my other eye. The rebel slingers were in place now.

Rocks flew. The sound of their barrage against our shields was like the war drums, but unsteady, inconsistent, and ceaseless.

Wood splintered and streams of light poured in through holes the stones left in our reinforced wooden scutum.

My men cried out. A young legionary a few ranks before me collapsed, writhing on the ground and holding on to a broken jaw, only connected now by a few strings of viscera and tendons.

"Centurion," I shouted. "Give the order."

I knew what the Marsi were doing. They were baiting us. Taunting our flank to advance past the bulk of our line. To give chase. And I knew their shock troops were interspersed and waiting behind them to ambush us upon our arrival.

The slingers continued to hail down on us. I could almost hear the crunch of bones, of wrists snapping and elbows cracking as the stones collided with us.

"Centurion," I said. "Give the order or I will."

We were stranded here on the eastern flank. With no cavalry to scatter the slingers, there was nothing else we could do.

"Advance!" he bellowed.

"Double time, march!" I added.

Those with intact shields lifted and extended them, but now we ran behind them with the speed of those tasting their own blood.

As expected, the slingers turned their backs and ran before we reached them.

Perhaps Sulla's men would give chase and rout them. But I saw no dust rising from the old columns where his men were waiting.

Lightly armored spearmen sprinted through the midst of the fleeing slingers.

"First row," Leptis shouted, "volley!"

We halted as seamlessly as we could, but the lines folded up and clashed into one another. Still, the first line lowered their shields, and lifted pila above their heads.

"Now!"

A gust of wind followed their whistling spears. They found their mark in the chests, throat, and feet of the Marsi shock troops, but still the remainder sprinted on.

"Brace!"

They crashed into our line. They spilled over the edge and into the formation like an angry current, spear tips flashing in the morning light.

I fixed myself behind the front wall of shields. We held the line with all our strength, but our feet dug in and slipped through the mud. Down the line, one man collapsed and with him slipped the men on either side of him. Spears swallowed them up and their sharp screams soon silenced.

"Fill the line, fill the line," I pointed with the tip of my sword. A spear bashed it aside.

The Marsi warrior lunged for me, but a gladius dug into his stomach and cut him from naval to sternum, the small bronze plate of armor over his chest doing nothing to protect him.

My sandals sunk deeper in the mud. My toes submerged. I steadied myself against the shield wall. The rebels weren't weighed down by the heavy chainmail and armor as we were, so they struck fast.

The jagged tip of a spear ricocheted off the cheek plate of my helmet. They spared me no moment to thank the gods. I thrust my gladius over the shield wall. It was a remarkably familiar feeling—my blade gliding through soft flesh and tissue, and the thud and reverberation of striking bone. I pushed until the blade slipped through the back of the rebel's spine.

I stole a glance over my shoulders at both sides of the line. We were holding. The recruits, many of whom were those trembling and vomiting only moments before, were clamoring to the front of the line. Others resisted and dug their feet in against the forward push, but those behind them gave no quarter for retreat.

"Second line," centurion Leptis shouted.

The first and second lines rotated, and the fresher troops bashed their shields against the violent current of rebel attackers.

Leptis's face already dripped with blood, his eyes wild and full of life. Reckless and daring but also tactful and a master of his craft. The men fought braver beside him, and I did as well.

The man to my left fell, muddy hands gripping tight to his throat and the gush of lifeblood seeping through his fingers. No time. I wrenched the shield from his wrist and stood over him.

I felt the men drag him off to a *medicus*, but it was too late. His mind was already on his ancestors, the gods, or a woman back home. And his last thought would be of them.

Two Marsi warriors bashed against my shield at once. The strength of those beside me kept me in place, but my feet slipped in the mud. I had to lower the sword. A spear tip dove over the shield before me and struck the chainmail at my shoulder. A few rings splintered off, but no blood spurted out.

The man to my right severed the attacker's arm at the elbow. His shrieking was piercing and animalistic, but it did not last long. I regained my balance and sent my blade through his throat. There was no resistance as he fell backward, with beads of red blood spilling over his lips.

I glanced again around me. We were holding. The enemy were numerous, but with little armor and lesser weaponry, we would soon force them to retreat. Their aim was to cause us to falter, not to defeat us outright, and they had failed to do that.

I knew the rebel tactics. They'd learned their fighting from us. I knew they were doing the same on the far end of our line, against the men I raised under Lucius.

I only hoped Lucius was faring well.

Deflecting the wild stab of a spear, I stole a glimpse over the rebel hordes at the ancient columns where Sulla's men remained. Gavius was there. And I prayed they'd stay there—and out of the fighting—for as long as they could.

SCROLL XXII

Lucius Hirtuleius—The Nones of Sextilis, 664 Ab Urbe Condita

The Marsi slingers scattered like rabbits before we even reached them, but their skirmishers were much more formidable. They spread out so thin they threatened to surround us.

The troops under my command were green, and they didn't know me from Pluto. I could see the terror in their eyes as the speared skirmishers leapt over our line, terror sowing through our ranks.

I lifted my sword. "Fight for your homes! Fight for your families, for your brothers! Fight for the Republic!"

Despite my desire to make for the frontlines, I'd tried to stay in the rear, where I could give orders and direct cohort movements more effectively. But as the cries rang out, I could resist no longer.

"Move," I ordered as I pushed through the ranks.

They needed to see me from the front. That's the way Sertorius always commanded.

As I sifted through the ranks, I looked over at our center, where Marius led his legions against those of the enemy. His troops were so identical to the enemy's it looked like he was marching into a mirror. But one could not mistake the degree to which the rebels outnumbered him.

The auxiliaries at the helm of his forces were already routing. They staggered over the bodies of the fallen toward the safety of Marius's legions, but most did not make it. Many of the fleeing auxiliaries collapsed with a spear wedged between their shoulder blades, the rebels proving to be just as effective with pila as we were.

Trumpets and buccinae rang out as Marius's legionaries collided with the rebels. There was no better battlefield commander than Gaius Marius, but how much could he expect to achieve when so outnumbered?

Sertorius and I needed to win on the edges of the battlefield, and fast. Then, without cavalry interference, we could flank the Marsi center and win the day.

"*Murum aries attigit!*" I shouted. "Send these traitors back to Dis!"

I arrived at the frontline. The sword in my hand was thirsty for blood, and I gave it the chance to quench that thirst.

SCROLL XXIII

GAVIUS SERTORIUS—THE Nones of Sextilis, 664 Ab Urbe Condita

We had been close enough to the Marsi skirmishers to smell the leather of their slings. We'd been waiting behind the ancient ruins of some old temples all morning, but certainly they'd seen us. Why did they not strike?

Instead, the Marsi slingers and skirmishers broke off in a sprint toward the south, a blood chilling cry rising from their throats. They were charging toward my father, but surely he was prepared for them.

My breath was slow and even. I felt in control, in command of my senses. I was ready to fight. Although, I couldn't stop the tremor of my hands, the weakness in my knees.

Sulla, perched casually in the saddle of the horse beside mine, was as calm as a cup of water. He bit into a peach, beads of juice running over his chin.

"Freshly harvested, if you'd like one," he said with a mouthful.

"I would accept some wine," I said.

"You'll have as much as you can drink soon enough." He tossed the pit behind him and stretched.

I trusted him. If he was unafraid, I shouldn't fear either.

But still, my hands shook.

I peered around a broken column. The rebels clashed with my father's men. The bloody dance had begun.

The tremor in my hands spread throughout my body.

"Legate, should we not follow them? We can flank them and turn on the Marsi center with our allies." I ran my fingers through the mane of my horse to find some comfort.

He smacked his lips, clapped me on the shoulder, and smiled. "In due time, my boy. We have a plan and cannot abandon it now," he said. "But do not worry about your father. He can handle himself. And we'll soon draw our swords and roll these bastards up like a carpet."

Part of me wanted to admit that I feared for my father's safety, that I did not want him to die. How my heart would break if my last words to him were so aloof and cold.

I bit my lip until it swelled to ensure none of my doubts and fears escaped.

I turned my attention back to the slingers, whose stones were now shooting through the air so fast they were invisible to the eye.

"In due time" was hardly comforting. How

much time did my father have? How much time did any of us have?

War horns sounded. And they differed from the ones we'd been hearing all morning. And they came from the north.

I was too short to see over the other riders. "What is it?" I asked. "What is that?"

Sulla craned his neck and leaned up in his saddle. For the first time, his jaw dropped.

The war horn sounded again, in violent bursts unlike anything I'd heard before.

"What do you see, legate?" I called.

"The Marrucini, those bastards are here . . ." he said. "Forward, march!"

My horse carried me off with the others. It wasn't until we passed our marching legionaries and left the ruined temple behind us that I saw the ambushing rebels arriving from the northeast.

All the plans and strategies prepared the night prior were now useless. None of us could have planned on another ten thousand rebels appearing after the battle began.

The fray where my father and his men continued to toil faded behind us as we followed Sulla to meet the Marrucini ambushers.

SCROLL XXIV

Quintus Sertorius—The Nones of Sextilis, 664 Ab Urbe Condita

Dust rose above the ancient columns to the east. But Sulla's legion and his riders were not coming to our aid. I stepped back in the formation and allowed a few legionaries to take my place. I strained my eye to see what was happening. I could hear distant war horns from the north but nothing more.

Sulla and his men headed north, moving fast. Away from the rebels. Away from the battlefield.

"Sulla's men are abandoning us!" one legionary cried out.

Others shouted, "Coward!"

"*Filius canis!*"

"Come back and fight!"

"Hold your positions!" I shouted above them.

For all Sulla's faults, he was no coward. Not Sulla. Not my son. Surely they didn't mean to leave us here to die.

I fixed my gaze on Sulla's riders as they departed, wondering which one might be Gavius.

The frontal assault slowed. Some of the rebel shock troops

stepped backward and away from the fray. One by one, they turned and ran back.

"They're retreating," some shouted.

"Hold, hold," Leptis steadied them. He scanned the legionaries until he found me. "Orders, Quaestor?"

"Hold the position." I pushed my way to the front, hoping to get a clearer vantage, which might help me understand what was happening.

But I could see well enough. That wasn't the problem.

Sulla's men were abandoning the field of battle, and the troops and slingers we'd been engaged with were now charging off after them. Why would they seek to attack a fleeing army when so many of us were remaining to fight?

The sun reached its zenith. The heat was rising like a mist, but the worst heat was yet to come. Our feet still sank in the mud beneath us, but dust was rising too. And the battle was far from over.

The pounding of war drums filled the gap left by the fleeing Marsi.

I knew the sound immediately. The same rhythmic thud we'd heard in the mountain passes on our way to Mutina.

The drumbeats echoed throughout the valley, and for a moment it was impossible to determine where they originated.

It sounded again, and closer now. South. The drums were coming from the south.

I pushed my way toward the back of the ranks, where the *optiones* were staring off at the bodies materializing from the southeast.

The Paeligni had arrived.

"About face!" I ordered. Our men spun in the mud.

The long-haired, leather armored Paeligni were charging like Olympic sprinters—spears, swords, and axes in hand. Less than a quarter mile away now.

How had our scouts missed them? How had no one seen the Paeligni waiting somewhere beyond the battlefield?

I knew the answer in my gut. Traitors. The Sons of Remus were striking again. This time it wasn't Spurius Insteius, but who knows how many of them infiltrated our ranks?

They grew closer. Lightly armored shock troops and slingers intermixed. There was no time to stop and prepare for either of them.

"Pila!" I shouted to the front ranks, their centurions all in the front of formation and too far away to give orders themselves.

The petrified recruits stumbled to lift the javelins above their heads.

The Paeligni chargers came into range.

"Let loose," I said.

My men vaulted their pila. Some found their mark. Others missed entirely. The rebels continued their charge.

"Second rank!" I shouted. The front row crouched, half-prepared for the order, as the second wave of pila were launched.

By the time they repositioned themselves, the Paeligni were upon us.

They hacked and slashed like mad butchers, caring nothing for the protection of their bodies or the preservation of their lives.

It made me wonder how they could hold so much hate in their hearts for Rome. But I didn't care. I couldn't afford to.

"*Roma Invicta!*" I charged to the front like a centurion.

Rocks began to rain down over top of us, their slingers apparently not caring at all if their own men fell victim to their projectiles.

"*Testudo!*" I bellowed, ducking under the shield of a nearby legionary.

I stabbed through the opening between shields. I hit something, but I could not see what. It wasn't a lethal blow either way, for the rebel shouted out and jammed a dagger through the opening.

I leaned back and away from the jagged blade as it stabbed

over and over again, from left to right, in search of anything and anyone.

My ears were ringing so loud I could hardly hear the curses coming from the Paeligni on the other side of our shields, but a piercing cry rang through. The dagger still sweeping toward my face, I turned to look at the formation. There were silent bodies lying face down, a few bloody arms attached to nothing but still gripping a sword.

The line was crumbling. We were losing.

I would have called for the second rank to advance, but there was no give in the Paeligni troops. They offered not a moment to think or to breathe or to react.

"*Condite Vestra Sponte!*" I shouted.

As I ordered, the men lowered their shields. I knew some of my men would die because of these orders, but it was the only option. Remaining in a defensive position would mean our destruction. We had to retaliate.

I turned down the line. "Strike now."

Shields down now, we were exposed to the Paeligni. But it also exposed them to us. As if it were one unified movement, the front line stabbed over the shield wall. A cacophony of cries rose from the wounded rebels.

More filled their place. But we had a moment now. "Second rank!" I bellowed in the brief reprieve.

Everyone else on the front line stepped to the side and back, and the second rank replaced them. They were fresher, and they were angry. Watching your comrades die and being unable to do anything about it has that effect on a man.

The man who stepped up to my left was immediately stabbed in the cheek, the flesh beneath his eye hanging down like a slice of pork. He neither cried nor shouted out. He almost seemed not to notice. Instead, he slashed his sword wildly, forgetting all his training and his discipline.

An axe hacked down on his forearm. He gasped now and

recoiled, his arm holding on now only by bone, stark and white against the spurting blood, and a few bits of flesh.

"Get him to the rear," I ordered, and pushed him back in formation.

But we were in the rear. There was nowhere safe for him now.

I vowed to give the man a military crown for his bravery if he lived through the day, but in my heart, I knew he wouldn't.

The man who had severed this legionary's arm turned his attention to me, thick, sticky blood dripping from the edge of his axe. He hoisted the axe overhead and cleaved down at me. I raised my sword and caught it, although the jagged edge still clanked against my helmet. With a flick of the wrist, I sent his axe flying.

Barely armored, disarmed, and unperturbed, he lunged at me with nothing but his fists and hate in his eyes. I stabbed through one of them, and his skull split around the edges of my gladius.

I kicked at the man to wedge him from my blade, but he was fixed there, still standing like the living but as absent as the dead. I continued to push and pull him to free my blade but had no success.

In a moment of exhaustion, I looked over my shoulder. In the far distance, the Marsi were returning. They must have abandoned their pursuit of Sulla, if that's ever what it was, and were charging right back toward us.

We were surrounded.

SCROLL XXV

Lucius Hirtuleius—The Nones of Sextilis, 664 Ab Urbe Condita

"Most battles would have ended by now, with a handful of casualties and a tactful retreat by both sides. It may have been an hour or two or more. It was impossible to keep track of the time aside from the growing weariness in our bones and the number of corpses at our feet.

Skirmishers—like those attacking us on the left flank—were supposed to strike and run. They couldn't defeat us. We were armored and in a tight formation.

I realized, probably too late, what they were doing. They only needed to stall us. To keep us focused on them. To delay any assistance to Marius and the center.

What could I do now? I cursed myself for not seeing it sooner, for not remaining at the rear of my formation and ordering a tactical advance or a tactical retreat . . . something.

"Tribune! Tribune!" a scout rode hard to the side of our formation, mud covering his legs from hard riding.

I stepped away from the front. "Where are Sulla's forces?" I demanded. "They should have attacked by now!"

Perhaps they had. I couldn't see across the battlefield over so many fighting men, but I knew the tide of battle would have shifted if our plans had come to fruition.

"We've been ambushed. The Marrucini attacked from the northeast, drawing Sulla's men out of position. They will be of no aid to us unless he defeats them."

I wiped stinging sweat from my eyes and tried to recall the numbers we'd discussed before the battle. Sulla had one full legion, another of auxiliaries, and something like twelve hundred cavalry. I couldn't recall the specifics of the report on the Marrucini, but I know they had more men than that.

Sulla would be lucky to survive, let alone defeat the attackers. They weren't coming.

I swore under my breath.

"Ride to the right flank. Tell Quaestor Sertorius this immediately. If we are to survive this day, we must push on the center and reinforce Legatus Marius at once!"

The scout dodged a slinger rock. "I'm sorry, sir. The Paeligni sprung a trap for us, appeared from the southeast. The eastern flank is surrounded."

A searing pain developed in my chest. For a moment, I feared I'd been struck, but the only wound was from the report.

I was on the far side of the battlefield, and there

was nothing I could do to help him. If we did not win in the center, and reach him immediately, the mixed armies of rebels would swallow him and his men up.

There was no more to glean from the scout, nothing more to communicate.

"Legionaries, wedge formation!" I ordered.

A risky tactic, one that would either lead us to Marius or to death.

The front lines thinned out to a single point.

"Charge!" I bellowed, and the centurions echoed the cry.

We pushed into the rebel line, and on toward Marius at the center. Exposed but lethal.

This was our only chance. Victory or death.

SCROLL XXVI

Gavius Sertorius—The Nones of Sextilis, 664 Ab Urbe Condita

"Sulla's Fist! Sulla's Fist!" the legionaries shouted in unison.

As Sulla, I, and the rest of the cavalry sped by them, I heard Tribune Lucullus shout, "Make five thousand sound like five hundred thousand!"

I was proud to count myself among those brave men that day, but I couldn't calculate how we could be victorious while so outnumbered.

Would this be like one of those stories I'd heard of as a child? I'd often dreamed about—romanticized—noble defeat. Martyrdom. The heroic death that inspires and unites a nation. Noble sacrifices like that saved Rome many times before.

But I did not want to see one now. I didn't want to die. The idea still seemed poetic. But not today. Not yet.

Sulla lifted his sword and directed our movement with its tip. We swung away from the colliding infantrymen.

I was glad not to be among them. But I knew my sword wouldn't be spared much longer. Or my flesh.

Hail suddenly rained down from the heavens. Grizzled Numidian cavalrymen were falling from their horses all around me. The gods must be angry.

But it wasn't hail. They were stones. Slingers. Violent slingers and their rocks shot through the air like invisible arrows. How could they move so fast? How could they kill with such precision? So small a thing . . . from a little strap of leather.

An enormous weight overcame the left side of my body. I slumped in my saddle, and looked down to see if someone was hanging on to me, trying to pull me from my horse.

But I was moving too fast, with the rest of our horsemen. There was no one there.

It was then I noticed the obstruction in my forearm. The blood billowing up and spilling out in every direction.

My horse carried me forward as I marveled at the sight. The stone, no larger than my thumb, felt like a pound of iron dragging me down.

I tried to lift my arm, to stretch my hand. I couldn't.

Men were screaming all around me then, and I realized we were amid the fleeing slingers.

They ran as fast as any man can, but to no avail. Without thinking, I slashed my sword to the right and cleaved a leather helmet from the head of a slinger. The helm went flying, and the man collapsed. I turned to see him.

His face was buried in the mud. Horses stampeded over him. He did not move. He was dead.

My first kill.

I needed to keep track. Not out of pride or morbid fascination, but the gods demanded precision in sacrifices.

I faced forward to find many more such men running. They dropped their slings and pouches of rocks. My horse bucked them left and right, my sword collided with their heads, necks, and shoulders.

The gods demand precision in sacrifices.

The horseman to my left shot up like a catapult's rock. The stallion collapsed and crumbled with a horrific screech I would never forget.

The same happened to the rider on my right.

Where was Sulla? Where was direction or purpose or meaning? I was lost.

Riders were falling and screaming and falling silent. The horses kept screeching, like the cries of mourners at a funeral that never stops.

The slingers were no longer among us. Skirmishers armed with spears were.

One of them stabbed up at me. He struck the chainmail but didn't have enough force to push through. I slashed my sword to sever his spear, but my horse carried me on before I could kill him.

There were fewer and fewer horsemen nearby. Panicked, I looked around and found Sulla's sword tip in the air, now dripping with fresh blood. He was swinging it overhead, and away from the skirmishers' ambush.

I jerked my reins toward Sulla. But without the use of my left arm, it was ineffectual. That, or my horse was too consumed to obey.

We charged on through into an open clearing, and somehow, I was still alive, and my horse was still safe. Finally, he listened to my commands and wheeled about, and carried me off toward Sulla.

It looked like we'd lost nearly a third of our men. But I could see my commander now, and that assured, confident look was back on his face. We would strike them again.

SCROLL XXVII

QUINTUS SERTORIUS—THE Nones of Sextilis, 664 Ab Urbe Condita

I could hear the muffled screams of the dying beneath the corpses of the dead. A wall of bodies surrounded us but did nothing for protection. Rebels continued to hem us in on all sides.

The sun beat down upon us like a molten hammer, painting the battlefield in hues of merciless gold. Every breath was a lungful of war itself—bitter, metallic, raw.

My sandals, once firm and supple, were sodden with the lifeblood of my men and my enemy alike.

On all sides, my proud legionaries were growing weary and weak. We didn't have much longer.

I somehow heard a single voice over the tumult. "Quaestor!"

A rider galloped up on the other side of the enemy. Once he spotted me, he began delivering his message. "The Marrucini have attacked the forces under Legatus Sulla! They are on the verge of collapse. Legatus Marius is holding but will be—"

A slinger's rock ripped through his temple. His lips moved

but rather than words, only blood spilled out. His eye hung from his face the way his body clung to his horse as it carried him off.

I batted the errant swing of a rebel's club as I tried to make sense of the messenger's words. The realization was setting in as I lunged forward and stabbed the Paeligni warrior in his shoulder.

Sulla had been ambushed. Gavius had been ambushed. And they were on the verge of collapse.

Without reinforcements, my only son would die. And we were in no position to reinforce anyone. It was only a matter of time before my own men would abandon their positions and die while routing.

I stepped away from the front line and pushed through the ranks of the men.

"Centurion! Leptis!" I shouted. I craned my head to spot him, but the fray was a bloody blur. "Centurion!"

I continued pushing forward to the other side of our surrounded formation, finding our ranks much thinner and easier to navigate than the last time I'd tried.

Leptis was there in the fray, chanting with the others on the front line. A broken spear was wedged into his stomach. Even in the chaos, I could see the blood oozing down his left leg.

"Fight! Fight till the last man!" he shouted.

"Centurion!" I did not want to lose another centurion, not today. I needed to get him away from the front immediately, even if only to stabilize his blood loss before he returned to the fray.

But he did not heed my call. He fought on, as he ordered his men to do. A Marsi warrior jumped into the air and slammed a spear down into his shoulder. Another did the same on his other side, the spear instead striking the side of his neck.

"The centurion is down!" some shouted.

I made it to the front and stepped past Leptis. The two rebel warriors who killed my centurion turned their gaze on me.

They lifted spears, dripping with Leptis's blood and glinting ominously in the oppressive midday sun.

One rushed me. I sidestepped the stab of his spear and brought my elbow down to snap it. Stunned, the rebel remained frozen as I charged him. My blade sliced through the side of his neck like a hot knife through snow.

The dying rebel's companion struck quickly. His lunge was too high, or it might have killed me. It connected with my helmet and sent it from my head to the mud.

Everything shrank to the point of a quill now. My senses focused entirely on the one man in front of me, the man who killed my centurion. He stabbed again, fast as a serpent's strike. The spear ricocheted off my gladius before I brought it down with a swift, merciless strike.

My blade carved into his shoulder and lodged itself in the bone. He stumbled back and fell to his knees with a guttural cry of unfiltered agony.

In one swift motion, I swept up my helmet from the muddy earth and bashed it against his head. Three blows were required before the warrior collapsed. I dislodged my sword and turned.

But this minor victory was ashen on my tongue.

The centurion was on his knees, balancing himself on the tip of his sword. Shallow, raspy breaths rattled from his lungs. His eyes blinked rapidly.

"The First Spear has fallen!" another cried.

By the time I reached him, there was nothing left to say. He was still breathing, still blinking, but chilling crimson painted his exposed flesh. His steely eyes clouded with the approaching veil of death. He was seeing an ancestor, a woman, a god. And saying those words he wished he'd said long ago.

I took up his heavy arms and dragged him from the front. When I stole a glance at him again, the chants on his lips had fallen silent and his eyes were still.

"Thank you," I said. It was all time allowed. I closed his eyes with my bloody hand and stood again.

I looked toward the front and back of our formation, both engaged with the rebels. I considered which side to join, where we had a higher probability of breaking through. I found hope on neither side.

There was no escape.

But it was then I spotted a tall rider moving swiftly toward the rear of the Paeligni ambushers. He raised his sword and extended toward the enemy. The plume of his helmet was red, and sweaty blond locks of hair covered his forehead beneath that helmet.

Aulus.

Marius's six hundred horsemen rode beside him. Charging furiously behind them were the three thousand auxiliary reserves I'd raised in Mutina.

I turned toward the northern end of our forces, engaged with the Marsi. "Defensive perimeter! Hold the line! We advance south!" I bellowed.

Panic struck the Paeligni line as they now found themselves surrounded, the way they'd so recently surrounded us. And their light armor and small shields were no match for a cavalry charge.

I pushed through the line again, toward the Paeligni, leaping over strewn corpses as I went.

The rebels turned from us now, facing the more immediate threat of the horsemen crashing into their weak line. They hoisted spears at the exposed bellies of the rearing steeds, but few found their mark.

I found a man doing the same and wrapped my arm around his neck. I placed the tip of my gladius at the small of his back and pushed until it ripped through his flesh and the sweaty tunic clinging to him.

Aulus had given the orders well. After the cavalry sowed terror into the Paeligni ranks, he wheeled about and rode around the formation, aiming for the Marsi engaged with us in the north.

They did not wait to experience what the Paeligni just had before them. Spears dropped to the mud as they turned on their heels and sprinted off in every direction.

The Marsi shock troops would not be returning to attack us a third time.

"*Roma Invicta!*" Aulus's voice rose above the warring valley. We all echoed the cry.

"*Roma Invicta!*"

"*Roma Invicta!*"

The Paeligni attempted to retreat, but there was nowhere to run. The auxiliaries were waiting for them wherever they went.

Turning again to the north, all the Marsi had either abandoned their posts or died while their companions ran.

"Flee to the ends of the earth, you cowards!" Aulus shouted.

I sprinted toward him. "Aulus, you saved our lives," I said.

He leapt from his steed before it fully came to a halt. He threw his arms around my shoulders and kissed my face, leaving blood on his cheek.

"I'm just relieved I wasn't too late."

"Marius told you to only reinforce the center . . ." I said.

He spit. "Marius be damned," he said. "Besides, we can move to reinforce them now. We should move." He took the reins of his horse.

"Sulla is surrounded. I must go to his aid."

His brows furrowed. Then he must have remembered where Gavius was fighting.

"Go to them," he said. "I will see you in victory, or in Elysium." He swept himself back onto his horse.

"Gods keep you." I placed a fist over my heart.

"Riders, auxiliaries. To Marius!"

The tides of battle can change so quickly. We'd won this engagement, but Sulla was losing his. And we would all lose the day if Marius could not win the center.

No time to celebrate our victory, no time to bury our dead. I reformed our line, and we marched toward Sulla. Toward my son.

SCROLL XXVIII

GAVIUS SERTORIUS—THE Nones of Sextilis, 664 Ab Urbe Condita

 I might die.

I'd never had the thought before, but it was present on my mind now. Not from the stone in my arm, although my eyes refused to cease looking at it except when a foe was beneath me.

But still I knew a more grievous wound could be awaiting me. Any moment.

We crashed into the Marrucini line, retreated, and then rushed in again, over and over. Yet they stood firm, their front lines still engaged with the legionaries of Sulla's Fist.

No matter how many we killed, more came, as if they spawned from the pits of Hades in infinite numbers.

I could barely see the blurry fray of the Marsi and Romans fighting to the southwest, but I could hear them clearly. Slaughter. Chaos incarnate. Cries in such numbers I'd never heard before. Whether they belonged to the Roman dying or the rebels, I did not know. Likely both. Marius was said to be a skilled commander, but the plan was for us to flank the Marsi line at the right time, and with over-whelming cavalry force we might have been able to rout them prematurely. That time had come and gone. How much longer could they hold? How much longer could we survive?

"Steady," Sulla shouted, his dripping, gleaming sword extended to the heavens. "Ride!"

We galloped off again. Slingers' stones show-ered us, so we spaced ourselves out. It spared us the worst of the missile assault but would expose us when we crashed into the rebels once more.

We collided with them again, among a chorus of Numidian war chants, curses, and admonishments.

Focus on breathing.

That's what Sulla had taught me.

But it was easier in training. I couldn't get the rhythm right.

I cleaved the helmet of a Marrucini warrior beneath me.

I needed to tighten my grip or the next time the gladius might fly from my hand.

The next I stabbed. I didn't have the power to impale him, but it punctured enough to cause him to cry out and collapse, writhing until he was swal-lowed up by a stampede of the Numidian riders behind me.

My right foot rushed with warmth. Blood covered it.

It was darkest above my knee, and I could see the white of bone there. One rebel had sliced me open, and I hadn't noticed.

A spear jammed up at me. I swayed to the side,

narrowly dodging it. I stabbed at the attacker, my blade clanking off his helm. I shifted my weight and slashed down before he could retaliate. My gladius glided through the soft flesh of the warrior's throat. It wasn't deep, but it was deep enough.

His eyes flashed by me as I continued riding, although I could still see them in my mind like an official seal stamped them there. The look wasn't hatred. More like intense surprise. Confusion.

The blood pooled on my foot and dripped from my heel.

What would happen now? How much blood had I lost?

I tried to recall the errant stories told by legionaries around campfires about their previous battles.

Would I grow cold? Would I lose my sight or the sensation in my limbs?

No time. My horse screeched as a spear wedged into her haunches. She bucked and kicked at the assailant, but it was a downward slice of my blade that severed his arm and sent him to the scarlet mud.

"Reform, reform!" Sulla's voice lifted easily above the tumult.

My steed, wounded though he was, navigated to freedom outside the Marrucini line with little help from me. He led us both back toward Sulla's cavalry a few hundred feet from the rebels.

I thought we'd killed more of them. It felt like so many had fallen. But their numbers looked undiminished.

I could not say the same for ours. The legionaries of Sulla's Fist continued to dwindle before our eyes, and there was nothing we could do.

My horse stamped his hooves. He was preparing, like me, for our next assault.

But Sulla was shouting, "Hold, hold, hold!"

The stragglers who'd begun the charge preemptively turned and retreated to the line.

Some of the Numidians questioned my legatus in their native tongue.

But I followed Sulla's gaze to the south.

And there was an image I'd conjured in my mind many times as a boy. The one they called "The Hero of the North," a one-eyed legionary commander capable of terrifying even the most formidable of foes.

"Charge!" he was shouting, and the men at his back rallied the cry.

They raced past us in a wedge formation and crashed into the flank of the Marrucini line, my father the first among them to draw blood.

"Sertorius!" I raised my sword and cheered him.

I'd missed the orders from Sulla, and we were already charging off, wheeling around the enemy line this time.

Sulla led us to the rear of the Marrucini, who were terror struck by the unexpected arrival of Quintus Sertorius.

Renewed vigor flooded my limbs, even my injured forearm and my wounded leg. My grip felt tighter.

When the order was given for us to crush them, I did not hesitate. My steed just as ready, despite his own wound.

He leapt over the edge of their line and crashed down onto several men, who were packed in tightly now. I swung my sword at anything that moved, the ricochet reverberating up my arm when I hit the mark, but not deterring me in the least.

The Marrucini banners were falling around us. Sulla's Fist pushed forward, my father's men broke into their line.

The rebels were scrambling now. They sprinted off toward freedom, but they would not find it. Sulla waved his sword overhead, signaling for us to loosen ranks, and track down every man we could.

Few made it to the safety of the wood line a quarter mile away, and these we did not chase. Let them live and tell the tale. Let everyone know what they could expect if they defied Rome.

"Rally to me! Rally to me!" Sulla shouted. "To the center!"

We'd planned to flank the Marsi, to crush them like hammer and anvil with Marius's troops. The delay cost us, but now we would do just that. My only prayer was that we weren't too late.

SCROLL XXIX

Lucius Hirtuleius—The Nones of Sextilis, 664 Ab Urbe Condita

" The heat was unbearable now. Exhaustion had set in. Swords moved slower than a leaf drifting listlessly on the wind.

The stench of the voided bowels and opened stomachs of the fallen was overwhelming.

We could not continue much longer. The wedge formation I'd used to assault the western flank of the Marsi was designed to rout opponents as quickly as possible. When it did not, casualties were high and chaos ensued.

The Marsi did not rout and gave no indication they were about to.

We lost all military bearing and fortitude upon the assault. Their line intermingled with ours. Men fought individual battles like the barbarians of Gaul. There was no shield wall to protect us.

"Reform, reform. Reform the line!" I ordered

over and over, but it was no use. Those engaged in combat could consider nothing but the enemy at their throats.

So the battle waged on. It felt we'd been fixed here in time for an eternity. If someone told me there was no life, no existence outside of this shattered line, this bloody fray, I might have believed them. No women, no wine, no song, no dance, no Rome. Only screams and orders and blood and dismemberment.

Aulus and the reserves had crashed into the right flank nearly an hour before, but it did nothing to slow the rebel advance. They were surrounded on that side of their formation. They should be routing. Standard battle tactics demanded it. But they did not. No matter how many men fell there, they always seemed to outnumber us.

I'd seen nothing of Sertorius and his men, and the battle was too chaotic now for a messenger to reach me. I could only presume he was dead, but I forced the thought from my mind. We would all join him in death soon enough if we could not turn the tide.

A Marsi legionary, who looked identical to our own men, save the darker color of their tunics, thrust his sword in my direction. The jab was precise and trained. He'd fought under the Roman Eagle before.

In a different life, he and I might have shed blood together. We might have stood in formation and protected each other with our lives. Perhaps we would have stayed in communication after the campaign and gathered for the breaking of bread and the sharing of wine, the swapping of old war stories.

But not in this life.

Our swords clanged as I parried his attack. He recoiled. I stabbed forward. He tried to feign, but the tip caught him in the triceps.

He grimaced. Snarled to show his teeth.

The Marsi warrior drove his shield into my own, and I faltered. It was bound tightly to the nub of my left arm but was not as stable as that of a two-armed warrior. Crouched as I was, he stabbed down at me.

I lifted the off-kilter shield just in time to save my life. I lunged with what little strength remained in my limbs, driving the blade through his leg, just above the knee.

He continued stabbing down at me, as if he felt none of the pain. But then his leg shifted and split. He collapsed.

I would have ended his suffering if I could, but more warriors stepped forward to take his place. Their onslaught was relentless.

"Reform, reform!" I bellowed again in my moment of reprieve. A few men attempted to heed my call, but a shield wall only works if all work in unison.

Vultures were circling above. I hadn't seen so many since the aftermath of Arausio. All the carrion birds of Italy seemed to have gathered here for the feast of the century. I'd seen how they leave a battlefield.

A burley Marsi legionary met my eyes from a distance, and I could tell immediately he would come for me. He pushed through a few of his men in my direction.

I steadied myself.

He stabbed. I crouched behind my shield. The

blade split through the wood just above my elbow. I thanked the gods I didn't lose more of my arm, but there was no more time for prayer.

The rebel attempted to pull out his sword, but it was wedged deep. Failing that, he grabbed the shield with both hands and ripped it away from me.

I fell into the mud on top of the still writhing man I'd just injured.

I spun onto my back as the large Marsi warrior brought the shield down. It might have shattered my throat had I not thrown my shoulder up at the last moment. Pain reverberated throughout my entire body, and for a moment, I could not breathe. He brought the shield down again, striking the same spot. I shot bile from my body with a violent cough. I could not move or reach for my sword.

He raised the shield again, but this time a legionary's blade shoved into his armpit. The Marsi warrior roared like a lion and turned to the assailant, but several other blades pierced him.

I rolled to my feet, still coughing, and struggling to breathe.

"For the love of the gods, reform!" I shouted with the last of the air in my lungs. But as I stood, I looked out over the Marsi and saw cavalry crashing down on their ranks. Thousands of legionaries, some with the white tunics of Sulla's Fist, and others with the scarlet of Sertorius's men, flooded in behind them.

Silo gave no official order for retreat, but his men fled regardless. It was too late now, though. The Marsi were surrounded.

I found my sword in the dirt and lifted it into the air. "*Instate hostibus!*" I shouted.

They complied and pursued the enemy. We would cut down more rebels before the day was done, but it was over for us.

The battle was won.

SCROLL XXX

Quintus Sertorius—The Nones of Sextilis, 664 Ab Urbe Condita

A legionary before me was sobbing and rocking a lifeless comrade in his arms. Another roared as he stabbed a dead enemy over and over again.

Most of them were shouting. Some offered insults to the fleeing rebels. Others cried out for friends they could not find. The wounded cried out for aid, for their mothers, or for death.

I shouted, "*Sinite milites exsultare!*"

And they did. The legionaries rejoiced.

A few decided to act preemptively and begin searching the bodies of the dead for anything of worth—from ornate daggers to gold teeth. Those with renewed energy set off for the baggage camps to fetch wine.

It would have been unbefitting of a quaestor to go about cutting the signet rings off the fingers of dead rebels, but the spoils of war held little interest for me anyway.

I cared only about finding my son. Whether or not he wanted to see me, whether he would be as relieved to see me breathing as I him. I needed to find him.

A different chaos ensued, as any semblance of formations and military bearing ebbed away. The ranks of the various Roman armies interspersed and celebrated together. As I began my search, a few men nearby huddled to craft the lyrics for a new marching song, already exaggerating our exploits.

"Gavius!" I shouted. "Gavius!"

"Yes?" a legionary picking through the leather pouch on the ground replied.

"Uh . . . a different Gavius," I said. He continued his pilfering.

Fortuna has a way of interfering in moments of search like this. I could not find my son, but I found his commander.

In any other circumstance, the sight of Sulla would have sent me in the other direction. But I knew my son would be close by.

Besides, he and Gaius Marius had already spotted me.

"If it isn't the hero of the hour!" Sulla said with outstretched arms. The milky flesh of his face was dripping with blood, but somehow his white tunic still appeared unmarred.

Marius grunted and crossed his arms.

"Hail," I said. "You've won a great victory today." I saluted both of them. "I am looking for my son."

Sulla ignored my salute and threw an arm around my shoulder. He seemed to enjoy the look of jealous and distaste in Marius's eye as he watched us. "You have a knack for saving the day, don't you?" He smiled; his white teeth particularly stark against the scarlet droplets on his cheeks.

"I'm afraid I can take no credit today, legate."

Marius hmphed. "Going to thank the gods, are you?"

"I'll save my praise for Aulus Insteius. The eastern flank would have crumbled entirely if not for his bravery."

Marius plopped down on a mound of dead rebels. "I'll see he's paid thirty thousand sesterces and given a civic crown."

"I'll double it," Sulla said. "If it wasn't for your timely arrival, my own front might have collapsed. And without my own fortuitous assault, I fear our dear Marius may have succumbed to rebel steel."

Marius shook his head. "We were outnumbered two to one, and still taking ground. My legions would have been victorious regardless."

Sulla's grin widened as the beads of sweat mixed with drops of blood and fell from his chin. "Tell the newsreaders in Rome what you like. Leave only truth to those who experienced it."

I was determined to end this line of conversation as soon as possible. It wasn't leading me closer to Gavius, and it was bound to end up in another war of *dignitas* I wanted no part of.

"My son . . . can you point me to him?"

Sulla's smile faded. My heart sank. His mouth opened, and it appeared as if he were preparing to deliver a very difficult message.

"Do you not trust me?"

"Excuse me?" I braced myself.

The smile did not return to his lips, but humor glimmered in his eyes. "I told you I'd keep him safe," he said. "And I am a man of my word."

He pointed across the battlefield.

There were so many legionaries ambling about in similar armor, in tunics of white and scarlet, that I could not see him at first.

"Lying down." Sulla squared my shoulders with where he was pointing. "But very much alive."

"He's hurt." The seized breath escaped my lungs.

Gavius was there, lying against a rebel *aquilifer*'s corpse, a *medicus* working on his leg.

"He earned his scars today. Just as we did many years ago." Sulla lifted his chin, as proud as if Gavius were his own son. "But he will live. Notice that he's the only man on the field receiving care? I designated my personal *medicus* to tend to him."

I finally tore my gaze away from my wincing son and looked at Sulla. I did not know whether to embrace or strike him.

He plucked my boy away from me, stole him. He'd formed a wedge between us; I knew that the moment I saw him in the fortress. But he'd kept him alive. And that mattered more to me.

"Thank you," I said. And I meant it.

"I did not do it for you," Sulla said. "He's a fine young warrior. And I'll continue raising him into the kind of man you'll be proud of."

I wasn't listening, and it wasn't until later I fully perceived this insult. My attention was again on Gavius.

Both commanders turned from me now. Even over the cheering legionaries, I heard a chorus of curses growing nearer.

Poppaedius Silo, commander of the Marsi and consul of the rebel army, was being dragged toward us.

"Remove your hands from me!" He flailed against their restraints. "I am a consul of the Italic League, and I demand to be treated with the proper respect! I am a prisoner of war, not some whore slave for you to do with—"

One of the legionaries whipped him over the head with the butt of his gladius, and the rebel commander fell silent until he was on his knees at the feet of Marius and Sulla.

"Silo! How good it is of you to join us!" Sulla said.

The dazed rebel was still blinking his eyes awake as the legionaries bound his hands behind him with strips of leather.

"I ask . . . no, I demand . . ."

Marius's booming voice swallowed up his pleas. "You'll demand nothing." He reached forward and clutched Silo's face like he were a small child. He leaned over and made eye contact with his captive. "The game is over. You have lost. There are no more tricks. No more escapes."

Silo attempted to spit on the former consul, but the bloody saliva just dribbled out over his chin.

Sulla clapped his hands gingerly and raised them to the heavens. "Venus, praise you! I am so relieved you've survived the day, Silo. You will be the perfect ornament for a triumph through Rome's streets upon our final victory."

Marius released the captive and turned back to Sulla, the same vehemence in his eyes as before.

"I demand a fair trial." Silo leaned his head back and tried to catch his breath. "Let me defend my cause before the Roman people, and let justice rule the day."

Sulla's careless laughter rang out over the rancorous battlefield. "What I have planned for you is delicate compared to what the mob would do with you. They would make beads from your eyes and use your entrails as garlands. Truly, consul, I am doing you a favor."

Silo swallowed. Perhaps it was the thought of the people's justice that frightened him, or the glimmer in Sulla's eye. "Sulla, I commanded the auxiliary attachment at Vercellae. I command you—"

"This man is my prisoner," Marius said.

"What's that now?" Sulla tilted his ear toward the old commander, as if he hadn't heard him properly.

"He is my prisoner. I brought over twenty-five thousand men to this battlefield. I commanded the center. How many men did you bring? Five thousand?"

"Men, we have won a great victory today," I said. "Let us not argue over trivial matters while our fallen still await their honors."

"Ten thousand, but that's hardly the point," Sulla said. "Look at the tunics they're wearing." He gestured to the two men holding Silo.

Both were white as doves.

Marius said, "He *crucified* my commander, Sulla! *Dignitas* demands retribution. From me."

And Sulla smiled. "My men captured him. He is my prisoner."

To my surprise, Marius crossed his arms and stepped away. "Bring me wine," he ordered to anyone listening.

Now Sulla knelt by the captive. "You will be taken back to Rome, Silo. But not for trial," he said. "A noose will be wrapped around your neck, and you'll be fixed to a wagon filled with the plunder we'll take from your cities. Naked, you'll be scourged. The crowds will spit on you and throw anything at you they can find. Nothing too harmful, mind you, as no one would want to end the entertainment prematurely. You'll carry on until the bitter end, when I will give my signal, and the carnifex will choke the life out of you." Sulla licked his bloody lips. "The light will fade from your eyes to the sound of Rome's rapturous applause.

Silo fell silent now. He did not cry, but blinked rapidly. His cracked lips bobbed as he searched for words, but none came.

Sulla stood and accepted an amphora of wine a slave was extending to Marius.

The latter was already unsheathing his sword. In one swift motion, he thrust the sword through Silo's belly.

The rebel commander gasped, bloodshot eyes wide. He fell forward on the blade to the hilt.

Sulla's careless gait evaporated. The veins bulged in his neck and his face turned blue. "Who, in the name of Dis gave you the right to make such judgment?" he roared.

Marius shouted back, just as loud. "He served Rome once! Not some foreigner to be displayed as a trinket for your vanity. He deserved a swift death."

"He deserved? He DESERVED?" Sulla sputtered. "I anxiously await what the people of Rome will think he deserved!"

I'd heard enough. They continued shouting insults and veiled threats at each other, over their cheering and disinterested men, as I turned my back on them.

I hurried to Gavius.

"They say the women of Rome love scars," I said once I reached him. "That one will win you any maiden you desire in Rome."

336 | SULLA'S FIST

His eyes opened at the sound of my voice. He'd been biting on a wooden peg as the *medicus* worked on him, and he spit it out now. A wet rag was on his forehead, but he quickly ripped it off.

"Arrea told me Roman women love men of the Sertorii," he said, with more composure than I expected. "I doubt I'd have much trouble regardless."

A smile stretched his face. It was remarkable how that smile, one so grown, so strong a young man, could remind me of his little giggle when he was little more than a toddler.

I sat down beside him, leaning up against the same corpse.

"How do you feel?"

"Like a sacrificial cow drained of all its blood."

I laughed. "I meant about the battle," I said. "About all of this."

Any humor faded away as I gazed across the battlefield. No amount of drink and song could lighten the sight of so many dead young men.

"I try not to 'feel' too much." He nodded to the *medicus* for him to depart. "Isn't that what the Sertorii men believe? That reason should come before emotion and sensation?"

"Your grandfather taught us to never abandon reason in the pursuit of feelings but to feel nothing in the face of such . . ." I gestured out to the battlefield, but did not continue the thought. "It is permissible to feel some things, my son."

He swallowed then and began to blink. I wondered if he was light-headed.

"Perhaps you should ask me how I feel in a few days then," he said. "Now, I feel nothing but pain." He extended his arm, where a bandage was wound tightly. "I took a slinger's rock just like you."

He pursed his lips to stifle a smile, but even after these years I knew my son well enough to know when he was proud.

"Little bastards hurt, don't they?" I patted his unwounded leg.

"It's remarkable to be honest. So small, yet it felt like a boulder weighing down my arm."

I turned to find the *medicus* now working on a nearby horse.

"This your steed?" I pointed back with my thumb.

"He is. I told the *medicus* to work on him first, but he said Sulla's orders superseded mine."

He was a Sertorius.

I rocked to my feet. The stallion was stamping, threatening to kick the poor *medicus* if he moved any closer.

"Go on, lad," I said.

"Yes, sir." The grateful *medicus* hurried off, no doubt to work on the wounded for the rest of the evening while the others celebrated.

"Shh . . . shh, boy," I said. When he allowed me, I placed my hand above his nose. "Thank you from protecting my son," I said. The broken spear wedged in his flank wasn't deep. It was a serious wound, but just like us, he would feel most of the pain much later.

"I thought that spear might have killed him." Gavius struggled to stand. "But he seems to be better off than either of us."

I ran my fingers between the horse's ears and placed my head against his neck. "They're much stronger than us. You'd be surprised what they can endure."

Gavius's eyes glazed over when I said those words.

I didn't have to be his father to know the horrors going through his mind. The small number of Sulla's cavalry who'd survived the day told me everything I needed to know.

I said, "If you think he's up for it, why don't we ride away from the battlefield for a little while?"

Gavius seemed to perk up for a moment, but then his gaze shifted toward Sulla, who continued to argue with Marius.

He shook his head. "No . . . No, there is too much to do."

It was like looking at a younger version of myself.

I said, "There's a soft spring just north. Untouched by the

battle today. We can rest for a few moments and quench our thirst."

He lingered, eyes darting between Sulla and myself.

I prayed then, as heartily as I had during the battle.

"For a little while," he said.

I turned back to my son's steed. "What do you say, old boy? Strong enough to carry the both of us?"

He snorted and flicked his head as if to say he'd be fine going anywhere not covered with bodies.

I helped Gavius on first, as he ground his teeth to keep from screaming at the pain. I pulled myself up behind him.

And the two of us rode off to the north, leaving the celebrating legionaries, the butchered dead, and both Marius and Sulla behind us.

SCROLL XXXI

Every bounce of the horse sent a lightning bolt of pain up my leg. My eyes rolled back in my head as we rode, but I refused to ask for pity. I would not appear weak before my father. I wouldn't appear weak before any man, so long as I could help it.

Thankfully, Sertorius eased the horse to a gentle trot once we'd escaped the battlefield. We rode longer than I expected, and part of me wondered if he meant to carry on and not look back.

I didn't know if I wanted him to do so, but I did not stop him.

It wasn't long before he slowed my horse to a stop. "Here is a pleasant spot," he said. Despite his armor and the bruises and cuts that lined his limbs, he swept gracefully from the steed's back.

He offered his hand in assistance, but I bit my tongue and swayed my leg over the other way. Pain reverberated as if I was being wounded a second time, but other than a brief grunt, I didn't make the extent of my pain known. But he was a perceptive man. And he'd experienced this before.

We could barely hear the chorus of drunken songs back on the battlefield now. The gentle trickling of the spring, so meager in its way, overtook it.

He knelt by the water and scooped up a few handfuls to wash the blood from his face. I watched carefully, intrigued and amazed by this man who'd lived more in my mind than in my reality.

My father looked up, spring water dripping from his chin. "It's quite cool. Runs from the bottom of the Fucine Lake if I had to guess, or the sun would warm it."

I tried to kneel beside him, but it was impossible. Perhaps it was the stitching and the bandages, but my leg refused to bend. I swept my legs underneath me and plopped down on my arse beside him.

My chainmail, breastplate, and injuries prevented me from reaching the spring. He scooped a handful of water and let it trickle over my head.

The sun was still blazing in the west, and the heat still unbearable. My sweaty tunic clung to me like a wet blanket, and the breeze cooled it. The water sent shivers down my spine. It made me feel like a child again.

He was comfortable enough to sit in silence for a few moments. He dumped the wineskin at his hip and filled it with fresh, cool water and offered it to me.

I guzzled it like the first time I'd tried wine. My belly cooled.

The breeze picked up, carrying the faded cheers

of the infantrymen in the distance, but it was pleasant enough that it didn't matter.

Beside me, yellow narcissus flowers danced in the wind.

"Arrea and I used to take a carriage to the countryside in the spring to pick these." I ran my still-bloody fingers over the delicate petals. "She said her people used them for healing. The Greeks, too, she said. We'd pick ten every time we went out and—"

"Sacrificed one at the family altar?" he said with a knowing grin.

Surprised, I said, "Exactly. Nine for us, to plant the seeds and seedlings in our peristylum, and one for the gods . . . so they might heal and protect you while you were gone."

He dipped his hands in the spring to wash away the blood. "Gavius, I need you to know that all those years I was gone . . . all those days I served in Greece on a campaign that never seemed to end . . . I never stopped thinking about you."

I turned my attention away from him and back to the flowers. The pain in my leg and my arm numbed. All the energy within me was spent now on holding back the quiver of my lips.

"You were in my thoughts every night when I laid down," my father said. "What are Arrea and Gavius doing? Are they thinking of me? Do they miss me, as I miss them? What kind of man is he growing up to become?"

"Then why did you not come see me upon your return?" I asked.

He'd plucked a narcissus flower and rubbed the stem between his thumbs. "If I could forsake any responsibility to the Republic for the rest of my life,

I would. I would bury my gladius where we sit and never draw it again. I would retire my senator's toga in favor of a farmer's tunic and never . . ."

The words seemed to catch in his throat.

He uncharacteristically raised his eyepatch and rubbed underneath.

He continued. "When I departed for Greece, I thought I might be gone for a year. Perhaps two, nothing more. Eight years in a conquered province? Unheard of . . ."

He seemed to be speaking to himself now as much as to me.

"And all that time, somehow, I thought—foolishly thought—that when I returned home, you'd still be the same little boy. The same wild, sensitive, adventurous, curious boy I'd left."

He snatched the eyepatch from his head, and for the first time I saw the scarred tissue underneath. It did not frighten me, as I thought it might when I was a child. It warmed me. Was I seeing him for the first time?

"When I returned to find that you were already gone, it hurt worse than the slinger's rock ever could. I realized then how much I'd missed, how quickly time had moved while I was away.

"Helping you practice your Greek vocabulary before an inspection from your tutor. Encouraging you to finish your dinner even when it didn't delight your palate. Tucking you into bed at night and putting out the candles with a few words about how much you meant to me."

I reluctantly placed a hand on his shoulder.

"I realized I missed everything," he said. "I realized I know nothing of being a father except the love I hold in my heart for you. And sometimes, I suppose, that is not enough."

My head spun, from his words or from the blood loss, as I said, "I never expected—"

"But things can change. My term of office will end soon." He inhaled deep and exhaled deeper. "I've been thinking of it. We can buy a farm. In Nursia, perhaps, to be closer to your grandmother. Or we could move out to Baiae or Naples, somewhere by the coast. Something peaceful and away from bloodshed and wars. We can raise horses or turnips—your great-grandfather used to do that—whatever it is, it does not matter. We can be together. Start over, like Janus."

Visions danced before my already hazy eyes. In them, we laughed as we trained a particularly colorful colt. Told stories of our time apart until we both understood. Arrea would shake her head and make a clever quip, but with the glimmer of a mother's love in her eye.

"Father . . ." I took his hands in my own. "I have sworn a vow. And I will uphold it."

I cursed myself for those words once they were spoken. Everything within me cried out to accept. Sulla would understand. Wouldn't he? He'd shown me nothing but love and compassion since the day we'd met. Of course he would support my decision to leave the war effort. War season was almost over, and most of his officers would leave soon.

"I must stay on with my men until the war is over. Perhaps when the final battle is won, we will reunite then."

I recommitted despite myself, but there was no wavering in my voice. How could I honor my

344 | SULLA'S FIST

father if not by living as he did? By sacrifice, by
honor, by devotion.

He cleared his throat again, and then something
like a laugh escaped him. "That is not what I
wanted to hear," he said. "But I am so proud of
you, Gavius."

After my father's transparency, I did not mind
to cry or appear weak, but there were no tears to
shed now. I would honor him by going against his
wishes. By continuing the fight, as he always had.
Perhaps I would desire the same things one day—a
farm, family, peace. I desired them now, but not
more than I desired to live up to my father's legacy.
Both of them.

"One day, father, we will have our peace."

He nodded with a keen understanding. I could
not tell whether he approved or not, but I knew he
was proud of me, regardless. Perhaps that's all I
desired.

"I should get back," I said. "Sulla will wonder
where I am. Are you ready?"

He pulled the leather eyepatch back over his
eye. "I think I'll stay here awhile."

If I'd known he would say that I might have
enjoyed the silence a little longer. But it was too
late now.

"I understand," I said. "I will see you soon,
Father."

I extended my hand. He accepted it, all the
composure and strength a man could want
returned to him in an instant.

When he did nothing else to dissuade me, I
struggled to my feet and then climbed back atop
my horse.

SCROLL XXXI | 345

The sun had now set in the west, and I was glad
he could not see the tears in my eyes.

"Goodbye, Father."

"Goodbye, my son," he said.

SCROLL XXXII

Quintus Sertorius—The Nones of Sextilis, 664 Ab Urbe Condita

I picked at a few more narcissus flowers. Arrea might have scolded me for plucking them before they were ready to seed, but they brought me great comfort. They reminded me of a time before I left for Greece.

I needed to return to the battlefield. By now, the pyres would be ready and the burning of our fallen would commence soon. I did not mind missing the plundering, drinking, and celebrating that comes after a battle, but I refused to be absent for the sendoff of men who fought for me.

Fighting a war with myself, I struggled to my feet against the weight of my armor and the soreness in my limbs.

The pale, rising moon fought the waning sun for supremacy. I gave one last look to the river, where the light of this confrontation rippled.

"I thought I might find you here," a raspy voice spoke from behind me.

I turned to find a carriage, with a single hooded rider at its helm.

Even in the growing darkness, I could see that dirt and blood covered the man.

"And how did you anticipate my movements so well?" I asked.

The man crept down from his wagon. "You're Quintus Sertorius. While the men drink, pillage, and whore, you are certain to be found just outside the battlefield contemplating. Contemplating war, life, friendship . . ."

I stepped forward. Despite the parched rasp of the speaker, I knew the voice. I knew who this man was. But I needed to see.

"All this time contemplating, and I'm still not sure I've found any answers," I said.

He removed his cloak. The moonlight illuminated just enough of the man's features that I could recognize my childhood friend.

"If I could help you find them, I would," Spurius said.

We stood several paces away from each other, but it did not seem far enough.

From the moment he fled, from the moment I read the letter he'd left me, I'd wanted to ask him so many questions. There was much I wanted to say. To yell, to curse. I could think of nothing now.

It was difficult for me to see him as a traitor. He looked the same as my dear friend Spurius ever had, although perhaps more haggard than usual.

"Do you mind if I drink?" He gestured toward the water.

"Did you fight in the battle today, Spurius?" I said. I needed to know. If the blood on his face was Roman, I would have no choice but to kill him.

He knelt and craned his head to slurp up the spring's waters. "No. No, I stayed in the camp. I told them I wouldn't spill Roman blood, and they didn't force me." Dirty water dripped from his lips.

But he had spilled Roman blood. Perhaps not directly, but he had much to answer for.

How could he do this to his own countrymen? His brothers in arms? What was I supposed to tell Aulus? How could he betray all of us?

I asked myself these things, but found no answers and no words to say.

"I am sorry things ended like this, Quintus." The dried mud or blood dripped from his face.

"How else might it have ended, *amice*?"

He splashed water over his head one last time and stood.

"No one was supposed to be hurt . . . you least of all."

The words stung worse than if he'd ever spoke them. "I should kill you where you stand, and you know I'd be right to do it."

"You and Aulus were never supposed to be there when we went to get the grain. The legionaries were supposed to be captured. Held until the end of the war, at which time the rebels would release them. That was the deal I made."

I brandished my sword, the dried blood of fallen foes still clinging to the edges.

He did not make a move to defend himself.

"You would be right to kill me," he said.

Brief and hazy memories of childhood—of bathing in the river together and chasing one another with wooden swords— swam into my mind.

"I could try to dissuade you, but I'd have to speak falsely to do so," he said. "And for all the many mistakes I've made, I'd like to die an honest man."

"Spurius, speak to me honest then! Tell me, what happened! Why, why did you betray Rome?" I said. "Why did you betray your brother, me, and all the men who served with us?"

"You know, I always thought I was a wise man. I always thought myself to be a rung above Lucius. Certainly above Aulus. Perhaps not smarter than you, but I trusted my judgment." He hung his head. "And now I realize how foolish I was."

"Answer me!"

"I thought I could help. None of us wanted this war, yourself included. I thought if I disrupted the war effort long enough . . . I thought, eventually, the senate would give the tribes citizenship, and we could all be done with this bloody thing."

Finally, he turned to me. His teary eyes shimmered in the pale moonlight. He was not a man seeking forgiveness or redemption. Spurius simply wanted me to understand.

"So, to end a war prematurely, you caused the deaths of hundreds of men who stood up to fight for Rome, just like you and I?"

My words tasted bitter to him. He rubbed his eyes with muddy thumbs. "I was not involved from the start . . ." He considered elaborating, but declined. "When I saw an opportunity, I took it. Aulus wanted to, I think, but he wasn't smart enough . . . well, perhaps he was too smart. He hated the war with the Italians more than any of us, but he loved you too much to even question it."

"Your actions almost led to our deaths. My death. Aulus's death."

Spurius nodded. "I'm glad he is not here. I don't believe I could face him."

I tightened the grip around my gladius. "You're a traitor, whether I like it or not. I cannot let you live or I am a traitor as well," I said.

"Do what you must."

"I don't know if I can do it," I said.

I thought of his mother and father, and how they would haunt me if I killed their son. How would they not weep for the day of my birth?

My chest tightened. My friend, my oldest friend. He'd betrayed me. He'd betrayed all of Rome. But in his own way he thought he was doing the right thing.

He stood and prepared himself. "Before you do this, you should know I have three gifts waiting for you in my carriage."

"There is nothing that can change what I must do."

He shrugged. "I'm not sure about that. But that is not my purpose. I am ready for your judgment," he said. "If I should die, I would like it to be at the hands of a just man who loves our Republic. If I am to live, then at least I might spare myself some of the shame, for a good man believed me worthy of life."

The memories of burning grain, poisoned men, and the charred bodies of my men flooded my mind. I didn't know how much Spurius was personally responsible for, but it didn't matter.

"Raise your sword," I said.

"I don't want to fight you, Quintus."

"I will not kill you unarmed. Now die with honor and raise your sword."

With a sigh that echoed the remorse deep in his heart, he wrapped his fingers around the worn wooden handle of his gladius. The rasping sound of the blade against its scabbard resonated through the quiet countryside. The fading sunlight glinted on the tarnished steel.

He took a deep breath and composed himself. He knew it was time to contend with the fate he had brought upon himself.

As if propelled by the weight of his own remorse, Spurius launched himself forward. His swift assault contrasted jarringly against the tranquil hum of the spring, our swords clashing with a shower of cold sparks.

I deflected the stab and offered a riposte of my own. Despite his lack of desire to fight, his instincts won over and he blocked the attack in time.

There were weaknesses in his stance, and I knew him well enough to exploit them. Yet each opportunity came with an ache in my chest, a dreadful reluctance.

The image of the burned boy in the *valetudinarium* was the one thing that kept me fighting.

He lifted his blade overhead and brought it down with the same strength and precision I'd seen fighting beside him in

Greece. I stepped to the right and swiped the blade away with my own.

He prepared to lunge again, but I kicked his knee.

Spurius grunted and fell back.

I stabbed toward him as he recoiled. Just as the tip of my blade reached his armor, he brought his own down to save himself.

He slashed again, and I narrowly escaped it by jumping back.

What would Aulus say if he saw this now? He would never forgive me.

He pursued me now, extending his blade directly at my stomach. I deflected it to the side, the force of the ricochet causing him to stumble.

I was a soldier of the Republic first and a friend second. I swore an oath.

Duty compelling me now, I brought my blade down swiftly and it connected, tearing through the soft tissue of his exposed arm.

He collapsed, sword falling away from him, into the emerald grass.

I stood over him.

"Look after my brother. Tell Aulus I love him," he said, his words coming out in a fury as he expected the blow that would take his life.

I raised my sword and closed my eye. Exhaling in preparation, I asked the gods to forgive me.

"Quintus, no!" I heard a voice.

My eye shot open. I turned to the sound of my wife's voice, to find her climbing out of Spurius's carriage. Her hands were bound, but she appeared otherwise unharmed.

"What is the meaning of this?" I shouted, more perplexed than I'd ever been.

I turned my gaze to Spurius now, who'd made it to his knees. There was a flash of relief in his eyes, an unburdening of guilt.

"Marsi scouts captured them. They killed the guards. I told

them who she was, and they spared her poor treatment. Silo planned to use her to turn you against Rome," he said. "But when they departed for battle today, I decided I couldn't allow that to happen. The blood on my face is not Roman, *amice*. I slew the guards and freed her from captivity."

I no longer listened. My gladius fell to the Italian soil as I ran to my wife.

"Don't do it, Quintus!" she shouted before falling into my arms. She whispered then, "Or I know you'll never return to me."

I kissed her cheeks and ran my fingers through her hair. My heart beat swifter now than even during the battle.

"Are you hurt? Did they hurt you?" I hastened to remove the binds from her hands.

"I only left those on because she attempted to flee," Spurius said behind me.

Pollux burst from the carriage and ran to us. He jumped on our legs with an abundance of licks before turning his attention to Spurius. Tail wagging, he raced to my childhood friend with affection, totally unaware or unconcerned about the battle we just fought.

"No, no, I'm unhurt," Arrea said.

"Arrea, I am so sorry." I pulled her as close into my bloody arms as I could manage.

"We are safe now. We are together."

I turned to Spurius again. "You saved my wife," I whispered.

"This is not a bribe. I did this because it was the right thing to do. Because it's what you would have done for me," he said. "But I know this changes nothing. Do what you must."

Arrea squeezed my hand.

"Leave," I said.

He shook his head. "Quintus, you—"

"You must leave," I said. "Eventually, others will find out about what you have done, and they will kill you for it."

At length, Spurius nodded. "I will go east," he said. "We made friends in Greece. I will dwell there."

I pulled him to his feet and forced him to meet my gaze. "No. No! You do not understand," I said. "Wherever the Republic stretches its talons, you cannot remain. They will find you, and they will kill you. And perhaps I will be crucified alongside you."

He frowned. "I will not let that happen. . . . This was not your doing, Sertorius. I . . . I . . ."

"It does not matter."

He struggled to swallow. "Tell me where I must go."

"To the land of the Lusitani," I said.

The lands of the Lusitani were notoriously savage, but it was free of Roman occupation. By the look in Spurius's eye, this was even more a curse than if I'd buried my gladius in his stomach.

"The Lusitani?"

"There is a man named Vallicus who is a respected member of their tribe. He told me once I could count on him if ever I needed anything. Speak no more, and he will ask no questions. Simply say my name."

Realization set on him then, exile being harder to imagine than death. "Wh . . . what about my wife?"

I took up my wife's hand again. "I will send your family after you. They will meet you in Corduba as soon as the winter snows have melted."

His breath was short and erratic now. "Can . . . can I embrace you before I leave?"

I threw my arms around his shoulders. "Thank you," I whispered.

As quickly as I'd embraced him, I pushed him away. "Go. Go! Get far away from here."

Spurius hurried to untether his horse and departed with only a sad look over his shoulder.

Pollux whined at his departure but quickly turned his attention back toward us.

"Come here, boy," I said. I gave him scratches behind the ear before returning to my wife.

I took her hands in my own and ran my fingers over them to find any signs of harm. I found none.

"I don't know which god to thank," I said. "I . . . I . . ."

"How about Juno?" she said.

That was a strange goddess to choose, and one I'd never heard Arrea reference before. I looked at her inquisitively.

There was a smile in her eyes that reflected a joy completely untouched by whatever hardships she'd endured in rebel captivity.

"Juno is your goddess of fertility, is she not?"

I released her hands and watched as they instinctively moved to rest on her slightly rounded stomach.

"Arrea," I whispered.

"I'm pregnant, Quintus," she said.

She led my hands to the soft mound of her belly. It was barely perceivable beneath her tunic, but full and alive against my bloody palms.

My hand rested there protectively, a silent vow to our unborn child. Arrea searched my face, her eyes filled with timid hope, and awaited my reaction.

My heart, so recently torn with the terror of war and the sorrow of betrayal, fluttered now with the anticipation of new life. Of hope. Of a new future.

GLOSSARY

GENERAL

Ab Urbe Condita—Roman phrase and dating system "from the founding of the city." The Ancient Romans believed Rome was founded in 753 BC, and therefore this year is AUC 1. As such, 107–106 BC would correspond to 647–648 AUC.

Acropolis—The ancient citadel of Athens.

Agnomen—A form of nickname given to men for traits or accomplishments unique to them. Many conquering generals received agnomen to designate the nation they had conquered, such as Africanus, Macedonicus, and Numidicus.

Amicus (f. Amica)—Latin for "friend." The vocative form (when addressing someone) would be amice.

Arausio—the location of a battle in which Rome suffered a great loss. Numbers were reported as high as ninety thousand Roman casualties. Sertorius and Lucius Hirtuleius barely escaped with their lives, and Sertorius's brother Titus died upon the battlefield.

Ave—Latin for "hail" or "hello."

Balatrones—"jesters," an insult.

Boni—Literally "good men." They were a political party prevalent in the Late Roman Republic. They desired to restrict the power of the popular assembly and the tribune of the plebs while extending the power of the Senate. The title "Optimates" was more common at the time, but these aristocrats often referred to themselves favorably as the boni. They were natural enemies of the populares.

Buccina (pl. Buccinae)—A C-shaped Roman military trumpet.

Cac—Latin for "shit."

Caldarium—hot baths.

Carcer—a small prison, the only one in Rome. It typically held war captives awaiting execution or held those deemed as threats by those in political power.

Carnifex—Latin for "executioner."

Carthage—an ancient city that struggled against Rome for supremacy of the Mediterranean Sea until it was completely destroyed in 146 BC.

Carthago delenda est—"Carthage must be destroyed," a saying made famous by Cato the Censor.

Centuriate Assembly—one of the three Roman assemblies. It met on the Field of Mars and elected the Consuls and Praetors. It could also pass laws and acted as a court of appeals in certain capital cases. It was based initially on 198 centuries, and was structured in a way that favored the rich over the poor, and the aged over the young.

Century—Roman tactical unit made of eighty to one hundred men.

Cimbri—a tribe of northern invaders with uncertain origins that fought Rome for over a decade. Sertorius began his career by fighting them.

Client—A man who pledged himself to a patron (*see also* **patron**) in return for protection or favors.

Cocina—Latin for "kitchen."

Cognomen—the third personal name given to an ancient Roman, typically passed down from father to son. Examples are Caepio, Caesar, and Cicero.

Cohort—Roman tactical unit made of six centuries (*see also* **century**), or 480–600 men. The introduction of the cohort as the standard tactical unit of the legion is attributed to Marius's reforms.

Collegium (pl. Collegia)—Any association or body of men with something in common. Some functioned as guilds or social clubs, others were criminal in nature.

Comitiatus (pl. Comitia)—a public assembly that made decisions, held elections, and passed legislation or judicial verdicts.

Conium Maculatum—hemlock, used as a poison.

Contiones (pl. Contio)—a public assembly that did not handle official matters. Discussions could be held on almost anything, and debates were a regular cause for a contiones to be called, but they did not pass legislation or pass down verdicts.

Contubernalis (pl. Contubernales)—A military cadet assigned to the commander specifically. They were generally considered officers but held little authority.

Contubernium—The smallest unit in the Roman legion. It was led by the decanus (*see also* **decanus under Ranks and Positions**).

Cum Ordine Seque—lit. "follow in good order."

Denarius (pl. Denarii)—standard Roman coin introduced during the Second Punic War.

Dignitas—a word that represents a Roman man's reputation and his entitlement to respect. Dignitas correlated with personal achievements and honor.

Dominus (f. Domina)—Latin for "master." A term most often used by slaves when interacting with their owner, but it could also be used to convey reverence or submission by others. The vocative form would be domine.

Domus—the type of home owned by the upper class and the wealthy in Ancient Rome.

Ede Faecum—lit., "eat shit."

Elysium—concept of the afterlife, oftentimes known as the Elysium Fields or Elysium Plains.

Equestrian—Sometimes considered the lesser of the two aristocratic classes (*see also* **patrician**) and other times considered the higher of the two lower-class citizens (*see also* **plebeian**). Those in the equestrian order had to maintain a certain amount of wealth or property to remain in the class.

Es mundus excrementi—lit. "you are a pile of shit."

Faex—Latin for "shit."

Falernian wine—The most renowned and sought-after wine in Rome at this time. The grapes were harvested from the foothills of Vesuvius.

Filii Remi—lit. "Sons of Remus," a name used by Roman citizens who opposed Roman rule during the Social War.

Filius Canis—lit. "Son of a bitch."

Garum—fish sauced beloved by the Romans.

Gerrae—"Nonsense!" An exclamation.

Gladius (pl. Gladii)—The standard short-sword used in the Roman legion.

Gracchi—Tiberius and Gaius Gracchus were brothers who held the rank of tribune of the plebs at various times throughout the second century BC. They were political revolutionaries whose attempts at reforms eventually led to their murder (or in one case, forced suicide). Tiberius and Gaius were still fresh in the minds of Romans in Sertorius's day. The boni feared that another politician might rise in their image, and the populares were searching for Gracchi to rally around.

Ides—the 15th day of "full months" and the 13th day of hollow ones, one day earlier than the middle of each month.

Impluvium—A cistern or tank in the atrium of the domus that collects rainwater from a hole in the ceiling above.

Instate Hostibus—lit. "Chase the enemy!"

Insula (pl. Insulae)—Apartment complexes. They varied in size and accommodations but generally became less desirable the higher up the insula one went.

Jupiter's Stone—A stone on which oaths were sworn.

Kalends—The first day of the Ancient Roman month.

Latrina—Latin for "bathroom."

Latrunculi—lit. "Game of Brigands," a popular board game of sorts played by the Romans. It shares similarities with games like chess or checkers.

Lorica Hamata—chainmail armor worn by Roman legionaries

Lorica Musculata—anatomical cuirass (breastplate) worn by Romans made to fit the wearer's male human physique.

Mos Maiorum—lit. "the way of the ancestors," this is the unwritten code of social norms used by the Romans.

Murum Aries Attigit—lit. "the ram has touched the wall." This expression was used to indicate that it is time to strike, or that it is too late to turn back.

Nomen—the hereditary or family name of the Romans. Examples are Sertorius, Julius (as in Julius Caesar), or Cornelius (as in Lucius Cornelius Sulla).

Nones—the 7th day of "full months" and 5th day of hollow ones, 8 days—9 by Roman reckoning—before the Ides in every month.

October Horse—A festival that took place on October 15th. An animal was sacrificed to Mars, which designated the end of the agricultural and military campaigning season.

Optimates—*see* **boni.**

Oscan—a language spoken by several Italian tribes.

Passum—a raisin based wine, originally developed in ancient Carthage.

Pasteli—honey cakes with sesame seeds, a beloved Greek pastry.

Paterfamilias—the male head of the family or household.

Patrician—a social class made up of Rome's oldest families.

Patron—A person who offers protection and favors to his clients (*see also* **clients**), in favor of services of varying degrees.

Peristylum—An open courtyard containing a garden within the Roman domus.

Pilum (pl. Pila)—The throwing javelin used by the Roman legion. Gaius Marius changed the design of the pilum in his reforms. Each legionary carried two and typically launched them at the enemy to begin a conflict.

Plebeian—Lower-born Roman citizens, commoners. Plebeians were born into their social class, so the term designated both wealth and ancestry. They typically had fewer assets and less land than equestrians, but more than the proletariat. Some, like the Metelli, were able to ascend to nobility and wealth despite their plebeian roots. These were known as "noble plebeians" and were not restricted from any power in the Roman political system.

Popular assembly—A legislative assembly that allowed plebeians to elect magistrates, try judicial cases, and pass laws.

Posca—vinegar wine, typically consumed by the lower class and considered to be of poor quality.

Praenomen—the first name given to Roman males, generally eight days after their birth. Examples are Gaius, Quintus, and Lucius.

Proletariat—one of the lowest social and economic classes, comprised of the poor and landless.

Res Publica—"Republic," the sacred word that encompassed everything Rome was at the time. More than just a political system, res publica represented Rome's authority and power. The Republic was founded in 509 BC, when Lucius Brutus and his fellow patriots overthrew the kings.

Roma Invicta—lit. "unconquered Rome," an inspirational motto used by the Romans.

Salve—Latin for "hail," or "hello."

Salvete—a casual, familiar greeting.

Sancrosanctitas—a level of religious protection offered to certain political figures and religious officials.

Saturnalia—A festival held on December 17 in honor the Roman deity Saturn.

Scutum (pl. Scuta)—Standard shield issued to Roman legionaries.

Servus (pl. Servi)—Slave or servant.

Sesterces—an ancient Roman coin, roughly $.50 in today's value.

Sibylline Books—a collection of oracular texts the Romans considered to be prophetic.

Sinite Milites Exsultare—lit. "Allow soldiers to rejoice."

Stola (pl. Stolae)—the traditional garment of Roman women, similar to the toga worn by men.

Taberna (pl. Tabernae)—Could be translated as "tavern," but tabernae served several different functions in Ancient Rome. They served as hostels for travelers, occasionally operated as brothels, and offered a place for people to congregate and enjoy food and wine.

Tablinum—A form of study or office for the head of a household. This is where he would generally greet his clients at his morning levy.

Tata—Latin term for "father," closer to the modern "daddy."

Tecombre—The military order to break from the testudo formation and revert to their previous formation.

Tesserae—a common game of dice. Rolling three sixes was called a "Venus" and was considered the highest score one could achieve.

Testudo—In military terms, the "tortoise" formation. The command was used to provide additional protection by linking scuta together.

Teutones—a tribe of northern invaders with uncertain origins that fought Rome for over a decade. Along with the Cimbri, they nearly defeated Rome. Sertorius began his career by fighting these tribes.

Toga virilis—Lit. "toga of manhood." It was a plain white toga worn by adult male citizens who were not magistrates. The donning of the toga virilis represented the coming of age of a young Roman male.

Torna Mina—lit. "Turn and charge!"

Tribe—Political grouping of Roman citizens. By Sertorius's time, there were thirty-six tribes, thirty-two of which were rural, four of which were urban. This term is also used to describe the various Italian tribes, some of which were Roman citizens, others were allied with Rome but not citizens, and others still were hostile toward Rome.

Triclinium—The dining room, which often had three couches set up in the shape of a U.

Triumph—A parade and festival given to celebrate a victorious general and his accomplishments. He must first be hailed as imperator by his legions and then petition the Senate to grant him the Triumph.

Vale—Latin for "farewell," or "be well."

Valetudinarium (pl. Valetudinaria)—a hospital, typically present in Roman military camps.

Via (pl. Viae)—Latin for "Road," typically a major path large enough to travel on horseback or by carriage.

Zeno—The founder of Stoic philosophy. Sertorius was a devoted reader of Zeno's works.

DEITIES

Apollo—Roman god adopted from Greek mythology. Twin brother of Diana. He has been connected with archery, music and dance, and the sun.

Asclepius—The Greek god of medicine. There was a temple to Asclepius overlooking the Tiber River, and this is where Rabirius and many other wounded veterans congregated.

Bacchus—The Roman god of wine, orchards, and fruit. Sometimes connected with madness, ecstasy, and fertility. His Greek equivalent is Dionysus.

Bellona—The Roman goddess of war and the consort of Mars (*see also* **Mars**). She was also a favored patron goddess of the Roman legion.

Bona Dea—the "Good Goddess," she was connected with chastity and fertility among married women. The term was occasionally used as an exclamation.

Castor—Along with Pollux, twin half-brothers in both Greek and Roman mythology. Sometimes both are referred to as mortal, other times they are both considered divine. Most often, one is considered to be born mortal and the other divine, with the latter asking Jupiter to make them both divine so they could stay together forever. They were eventually transformed into the constellation Gemini (meaning "twins"). Their temple in Rome's forum was extremely important and sometimes facilitated meetings of the senate and elections.

Cybele—*see* **Magna Mater**

Diana—The Roman goddess of hunters, the forest, and the moon. Twin sister of Apollo. Quintus Sertorius gives her credit for saving him in a previous battle, and therefore he considers her his patron goddess. Her Greek equivalents are Artemis and Hecate.

Dis Pater—The Roman god of death. He was often associated with fertility, wealth, and prosperity. His name was often shortened to Dis. He was nearly synonymous with the Roman god Pluto or the Greek god Hades.

Fortuna—Roman goddess considered to be the personification of luck, chance, and fate. Lucius Cornelius Sulla believes he is beloved by Fortuna.

Gaia—Greek Goddess considered to be the personification of the earth.

Hermes—The Greek god of messengers, travelers, orators, and occasionally thieves. His Roman equivalent would be Mercury.

Janus—the Roman god of beginnings, gates, duality. He is depicted with two faces, one looking back and the other forward. The month of January was named after him, which represented an opportunity to reflect on the previous year and look forward to the next.

Jupiter—The Roman king of the gods. He was the god of the sky and thunder. All political and military activity was sanctioned by Jupiter. He was often referred to as Jupiter Capitolinus for his role in leading the Roman state, or Jupiter Optimus Maximus (lit. "the best and greatest"). His "black stone" was something to be sworn on.

Magna Mater—"Great Mother," she was adopted by the Romans in the late third century BC from the Anatolians. She was connected with and sometimes assimilated with aspects of Gaia and Ceres.

Mars—The Roman god of war. He was the favored patron of many legionaries and commanders. Unlike his Greek equivalent, Ares, he was respected and considered a "pater" of all Romans.

Mercury—*see* **Hermes**

Pluto—the Roman god of the underworld and the afterlife. His Greek equivalent was Hades, but Pluto often represented a more positive concept of the god.

Pollux—*see* **Castor**

Proserpina—the Roman goddess of the underworld. Her Greek equivalent was Persephone. She was connected with female and agricultural fertility, as well as the springtime.

Saturn—God of the Roman Capitol, time, wealth, and agriculture. He was the father of many Roman gods, including Jupiter. His Greek equivalent was Cronus. His temple in Rome's forum at the base of the Capitoline Hill was extremely important throughout Roman history.

Somnus—Roman god who was the personification of sleep. His Greek counterpart would be Hypnos.

Tiberinus—the god of the Tiber river.

Venus—The Roman goddess of love, beauty, desire, sex, and fertility. Her Greek equivalent was Aphrodite.

Vulcan—The Roman god of fire, metalworking, and the forge. He was often depicted with a blacksmith's hammer and a lame leg due to a childhood injury. He was considered to be the ugliest of the gods but was at times a consort of **Venus**, the goddess of beauty.

Zephyrus—Greek god of the West Wind. He was associated with flowers, springtime, favorable winds, and speed. His Roman equivalent was Favonius.

BUILDINGS, ROADS, AND LANDMARKS

Appian Way (Via Appia)—the oldest and most important of Rome's roads, linking Rome with farther areas of Italy.

Aqua Marcia—the most important of Rome's aqueducts at this time. Built in 144–140 BC.

Argiletum—a route leading to the Roman forum.

Basilica Aemilia—located at the juncture of the Via Sacra and the Argiletum, this was one of the most celebrated buildings in Rome.

Basilica Porcia—the first named basilica in Rome, built by Cato the Censor in 184 BC, it was the home of the ten tribunes of the plebs.

Basilica Sempronia—built in 170 BC by the father of Tiberius and Gaius Gracchus. It was a place often used for commerce.

Circus Maximus—a massive public stadium that hosted chariot races and other forms of entertainment. It's speculated that the stadium could have held as many as 150,000 spectators.

Cloaca Maxima—the massive sewer system beneath Rome.

Comitium—a meeting area outside of the Curia Hostilia. The rostrum stood at its helm.

Curia Hostilia—The Senate House. The Curia was built in the seventh century BC and held most of the senatorial meetings throughout the Republic, even in Sertorius's day.

Forum—The teeming heart of Ancient Rome. There were many different forums, in various cities, but most commonly the Forum refers to the center of the city itself, where most political, public, and religious dealings took place.

Field of Mars—"Campus martius" in Latin. This was where armies trained and waited to deploy or to enter the city limits for a Triumph.

Fucine Lake—known as Fucinus Lacus to the Romans, this was a large lake in central Italy.

Liris River—one of the primary rivers of central Italy.

Mare Nostrum—the Roman name for the Mediterranean Sea. This means "our sea" in Latin.

Ostia—Rome's port city, it lay at the mouth of the river Tiber.

Pillar of Hercules—a phrase used to describe the promontories that flank the Strait of Gibraltar, which connects Spain to Africa.

Porta Triumphalis—the triumphal gate. Triumphing armies would ceremoniously enter here.

Regia—a building just off the Via Sacra, the Regia was originally the main headquarters for the kings of Rome. By the late Republic, the Regia was used as the residence for the Pontifex Maximus, the highest religious official in Rome.

River Reno—a river in northern Italy, near Mutina.

Rostrum (pl. Rostra)—A speaking platform in the Forum made of the ships of conquered foes.

Senaculum—a meeting area for senators outside of the senate house, where they would gather before a meeting began.

Servian wall—the defensive barrier around the city of Rome, constructed in the 4th century BC.

Subura—a rough neighborhood near the Viminal and Quirinal hills. It was known for violence and thievery, as well as for the fires that spread because of the close proximity of its insulae.

Tarpeian Rock—a place where executions were held. Criminals of the highest degree and political threats were thrown from this cliff to their inevitable deaths.

Temple of Asclepius—located on the Tiber Island, it was a temple of healing. The sick and ailing made pilgrimages here in hope of healing.

Temple of Bellona—dedicated to the consort of Mars and goddess of war, this was a temple often used for meetings of the Senate when they needed to host foreign emissaries or meet with returning generals awaiting a triumph. It lay outside the city limits but close to the Servian wall.

Temple of Castor and Pollux—oftentimes referred to simply as "Temple of Castor," it remained at the entrance of the Forum by the Via Sacra. It was often used for meetings of the senate, as it was actually larger than the Curia. Speeches were often given from the temple steps as well.

Temple of Concordia (Concord)—a temple devoted to peace and reunification in the Roman Forum. It often held meetings of the senate.

Temple of Jupiter Capitolinus (Optimus Maximus)—a temple devoted to Rome's patron God, which resided on the Capitoline hill. It was sometimes referred to as the "Capitol."

Temple of Saturn—a temple of deep religious significance that lay at the foot of the Capitoline hill in the Roman Forum. Sacrifices were often held here following a triumph, if the generals didn't surpass it to sacrifice at the aforementioned Temple of Jupiter.

Tiber River—a body of water that connected to the Tyrrhenian Sea and flowed along the western border of Rome. The victims of political assassinations were unceremoniously dumped here rather than receive proper burial.

Tullianum—a prison for captives awaiting death. (*See* **Carcer under General Glossary**.)

Via Appia—*see* **Appian Way**.

Via Cassia—the northern road from Rome, this road passed through Etruria and was one of the main routes for travelers heading north.

Via Latina—"Latin road," led from Rome southeast.

Via Sacra—the main road within in the city of Rome, leading from the Capitoline hill through the forum, with all of the major religious and political buildings on either side.

Via Salaria—"Salt Road" led northeast from Rome. This was the path Sertorius would have taken to and from his home in Nursia.

Via Triumphalis—the "triumphal way" leading from the Field of Mars to the Capitoline hill. Roman generals awarded a triumph would take this road during their triumphal ceremony.

RANKS AND POSITIONS

Aedile—Magistrates who were tasked with maintaining and improving the city's infrastructure. There were four, elected annually: two plebeian aediles and two curule aediles.

Aquilifer—the eagle bearer of each Roman legion.

Augur—A priest and official who interpreted the will of the gods by studying the flight of birds.

Auxiliary—Legionaries without citizenship. At this time, most auxiliaries were of Italian origin but later encompassed many different cultures.

Centurion—An officer in the Roman legion. By the time Marius's reforms were ushered in, there were six in every cohort, one for every century. They typically led eighty to one hundred men. The most senior centurion in the legion was the "primus pilus," or first-spear centurion.

Consul—The highest magistrate in the Roman Republic. Two were elected annually to a one-year term. The required age for entry was forty, although exceptions were occasionally (and hesitantly) made.

Decanus (pl. Decani)—"Chief of ten," he was in a position of authority over his contubernium, a group of eight to ten men who shared his tent.

Evocati—An honorary term given to soldiers who served out their terms and volunteered to serve again. Evocati were generally spared a large portion of common military duties.

Flamen Dialis—Priest of Jupiter Optimus Maximus.

Hastati—Common front line soldiers in the Roman legion. As a result of the Marian Reforms, by Sertorius's time, the term *hastati* was being phased out and would soon be obsolete.

Imperator—A Roman commander with imperium (*see also* **imperium**). Typically, the commander would have to be given imperium by his men.

Immunes—those who were exempt from physical labor within the Roman legion.

Legatus (pl. Legati)—The senior-most officer in the Roman legion. A legatus generally was in command of one legion and answered only to the general. The vocative form would be legate.

Legion—the largest military unit of the Roman military. A legion was comprised of roughly 4,800 men at the time of Sertorius.

Legionary (pl. Legionarii)—soldiers which made up the Roman legion.

Medici Optimi—the senior most medicus.

Medicus (pl. Medici)—The field doctor for injured legionaries.

Military Tribune—officer of the Roman legions. They were, in theory, elected by the popular assembly, and there were six assigned to every legion. By late second century BC, however, it was not uncommon to see military tribunes appointed directly by the commander.

Optio (pl. Optiones)—second in command of a legionary century, they served directly under a centurion and were generally considered next in line if the centurion was to fall.

Pontifex Maximus—The highest priest in the College of Pontiffs. By Sertorius's time, the position had been highly politicized.

Pontiff—A priest and member of the College of Pontiffs.

Praetor—The second-most senior magistrate in the Roman Republic. There were typically six elected annually, but some have speculated that there were eight elected annually by this time.

Prefect—A high-ranking military official in the Roman legion.

Princeps Senatus—"Father of the Senate," or the first among fellow senators. It was an informal position but came with immense respect and prestige.

Proconsul—A Roman magistrate who had previously been a consul. Often, when a consul was in the midst of a military campaign at the end of his term, the Senate would appoint him as proconsul for the remainder of the war.

Publicani—Those responsible for collective public revenue. They made their fortunes through this process. By Sertorius's time, the Senate and censors carefully scrutinized their activities, making it difficult for them to amass the wealth they intended.

Quaestor—An elected public official and the junior-most member of the political course of offices. They served various purposes but often supervised the state treasury and performed audits. Quaestors were also used in the military and managed the finances of the legions on campaign.

Rex Sacrorum—A senatorial priesthood, the "king of the sacred." Unlike the Pontifex Maximus, the rex sacrorum was barred from military and political life. In theory, he held the religious responsibility that was once reserved for the kings, while the consuls performed the military and political functions.

Tribune of Plebs—Elected magistrates who were designated to represent the interests of the people. Sometimes called the Plebeian Tribune or People's Tribune.

Tribunus Laticlavius—lit. "the broad-stripped tribune" the senior of the six tribunes assigned to each legion.

CITIES AND NATIONS

Acerrae—A Roman colony in Campania. Acerrae would serve as a base of operations for the Romans throughout the war. Samnite general Papius Mutilus besieged the city early in the war.

Aesernia—An important Roman colony in Samnite territory, it remained loyal to Rome despite being surrounded by rebels. It was quickly besieged by Samnite armies, and those within were faced with starvation and disease.

Alba Fucensis—sometimes called Alba Fucens and othertimes referred to simply as Alba, this city was located near the Fucine Lake and Marsi territory. The city remained loyal to Rome but was swiftly attacked by the rebels.

Asculum—The city situated in Picenum was the first to rebel against Rome. They rounded up and butchered all Roman citizens, which sparked the Social War. This city was a target for both sides throughout the duration of the war.

Capua—the primary city of the Campania region and therefore an important stronghold for Rome during the war. The city was specifically known for its gladiator spectacles.

Cisalpine Gaul—The portion of Gaul on the Italian side of the Alps. Sometimes referred to as "Nearer Gaul." It was conquered in the third century BC. Although it comprised much of what is today northern Italy, it continued to be administered as its own province.

Corduba—A city in Hispania, it was originally conquered by the Romans in 206 BC. A Roman colony was established there roughly fifty years later.

Corfinium—A city situated within the tribal territory of the Paeligni (and close to the Marsi), it was chosen as the new "capital" for the Italic League when they rebelled against Rome. It's military positioning was the cause of this distinction. It was renamed **Italica** at the onset of the war.

Firmum—An important city within Picenum. It was sometimes called "Firmum by the sea" as it was a coastal city. Several battles took place near Firmum during the Social War.

Genua—The capital city of Roman Liguria. It was originally destroyed by the Carthaginians during the Second Punic War but was rebuilt and received municipal rights from the Romans following the destruction of Carthage.

Herculaneum—a city in Campania, near Pompeii. It was either taken quickly by the rebels or joined willingly after the onset of the war.

Italic League—The name for the fledgling nation of Italian tribes who were united against Rome. Their aims were likely on achieving the citizenship, at least originally, but after the onset of the war, the Italic League likely sought to destroy Rome and replace her entirely.

Italica—*see* **Corfinium**

Lusitani—The Lusitanians were a collection of tribes native to Hispania that fought many wars against Rome. Although the most notable Lusitanian general, Viriathus, was betrayed and assassinated in the mid-second century BC, the Lusitani continued to oppose Rome.

Mutina—A city in northern Italy, which was made a Roman colony in 183 BC. It served as a citadel throughout several wars, as its high walls were difficult to penetrate.

Numidia—An ancient kingdom comprising much of northern Africa. Gaius Marius and Lucius Cornelius Sulla both earned a great deal of prestige for their parts in defeating the Numidian king Jugurtha. The notorious cavalry of Numidia thereafter served Rome in battle.

Nursia—Sertorius's home, located in the Apennine Mountains and within the Sabine tribes. It was famous for turnips and little else until Sertorius came along.

Pompeii—A city located in Campania, Pompeii joined the rebellion soon after the Social War began. Pompeii had a large port that was very important during the war.

Salernum—A city located in Campania, Salernum fell to the Samnite armies under the command of Papius Mutilus soon after the onset of the Social War.

Stabiae—A city located in Campania, Stabiae was quickly captured by the Samnite armies under the command of Papius Mutilus soon after the onset of the Social War. Like Pompeii, it was a port city and therefore of strategic value to both the Romans and the Italic League throughout the war.

For updates on to receive Vincent's spinoff series "The Marius Scrolls" for FREE! Just scan the QR code below.

ACKNOWLEDGMENTS

First off, I want to thank Larry, Jim, and Steve for mentoring me and helping me develop my craft as an author. At times the process of learning from each of you felt like I was an apprentice to skilled craftsmen. While I still have much to learn, the time, dedication, and care each of you gave me has put me on a path to being a craftsman myself. I promise to honor your hard work by treating each book I write with the same level of care and dedication that you each displayed.

I also want to thank my wonderful editors. I've worked with some phenomenal wordsmiths throughout my career, and you all are at the top of the list. Any remaining errors in this book are my fault alone, but you all are responsible for making this book as clean and polished as it is. Steven and Susan, thank you.

Writing a book like this requires an enormous amount of resources. I have an entire shelf of old books I used during the research process, and each one contributed something that this story would be lacking without them. That being said, I want to specifically mention the work of Philip Matyszak. He is one of the few modern historians to really analyze Quintus Sertorius, which has been invaluable to me. His book *Cataclysm 90 BC* was a constant companion of mine throughout the writing of this book. *Sulla's Fist* would not have been possible without his extensive research and his wonderfully accessible prose. Thank you, Philip.

I want to thank my beautiful bride, Ashley, to whom this book is dedicated. Words cannot describe how much you mean to me and how important you are to everything I accomplish. Your understanding and patience with me as I've worked to compile this manuscript, your unwavering support and belief in me, your interest in my work and your feedback along the way . . . I rely on that more than I can ever express. You keep me sane, you make me laugh, you make sure I don't take myself too seriously. You help me calibrate and remember our family is the most important thing in this world, and to never get lost in my pursuits. When I started this book, we were dating. As I write this, we're now married. I am so honored and joyful that I'll never have to write a book without this wedding band on my finger and you as my wife. I love you.

And finally, I want to thank *you*. This crazy journey I began six years ago would not have been possible without all of those who are as interested in experiencing the past as I am. I must offer a special thanks to my "Legion" (newsletter subscribers). You are the foundation of everything I'm building, and without you I cannot continue doing what I'm doing. For your unwavering support and interest in my books, I genuinely thank you from the bottom of my heart.

As always, amici mei . . .

Keep Fighting,
Vincent B. Davis II
August 28, 2023

ABOUT THE AUTHOR

Vincent B. Davis II writes historical fiction books to keep the past alive through the power of storytelling. He is also an entrepreneur, speaker, and veteran who is a proud graduate of East Tennessee State University and was honorably discharged from the US Army in 2022. Armed with a pen and an entrepreneurial spirit, Vincent quit his day job and decided it was as good a time as any to follow his dream. He went on to publish nine historical fiction novels, four of which have now become Amazon International Best Sellers.

Vincent is also a devoted and depressed Carolina Panthers fan and a proud pet parent to his rescue pups, Buddy and Jenny. Join Vincent in celebrating the past through the pages of his books. His newsletter, The Legion, is more than just another author email list. It's a community of readers who enjoy free additional content to enhance their reading experience—HD Maps, family trees, Latin glossaries, free eBooks, and more. You can join the community and snag your freebies at vincentbdavisi i.com.

Made in the USA
Columbia, SC
04 July 2024

38100913R00240